THE CRUELEST MERCY

NATALIE MAE

RAZORBILL

RAZORBILL

An imprint of Penguin Random House LLC
New York

First published in the United States of America by Razorbill,
an imprint of Penguin Random House LLC, 2021

Visit us online at penguinrandomhouse.com.

Library of Congress Cataloging-in-Publication Data is available.

ISBN 9781984835246

Manufactured in Canada

1 3 5 7 9 10 8 6 4 2

Design by Theresa Evangelista
Text set in Perrywood MT Std

For Lori G.

Thank you for always being there.

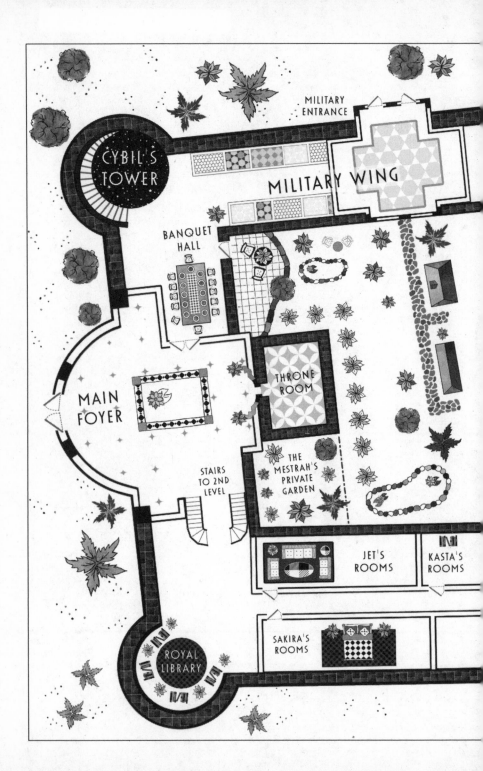

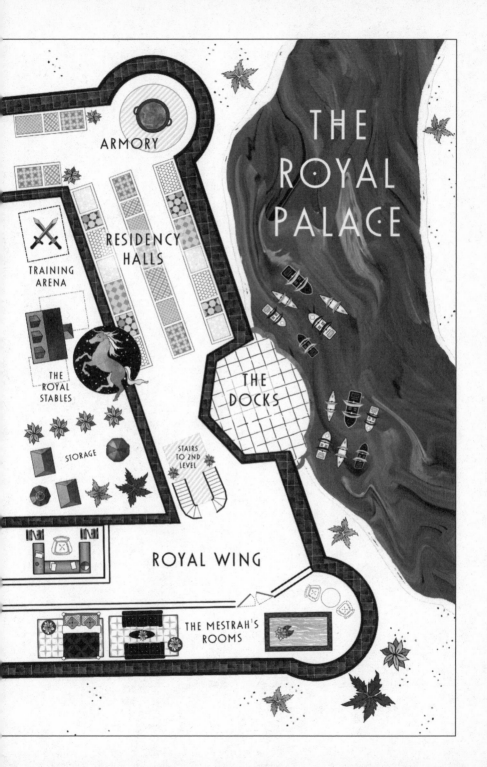

LIKE so many things in the palace, the map is deceptively beautiful.

Jet smooths the creamy parchment on the desk, its golden border glimmering as he weights the corners with stones, a piece of artwork with gilded details and jewel-studded houses that turn my stomach. This is not how my hometown looked the last time I saw it. Memories spin as I trace the little buildings, remembering the horror we returned to at the end of the Crossing, with smoke billowing from Mora's home and my father's stable abandoned on the hill. Here's where I almost jumped into crocodile-infested waters. Here are the roofs of the cratered estates I ran past with Marcus, Melia, and Jet on my heels, until I found a soldier who knew where the evacuees had gone. Here's the leveled bakery where I fell to my knees in relief, after learning my family had made it safely to the next town over.

All of these lines should be jagged, smeared.

"There were three bombs," Jet says, the sunlight dappling his arm where it shines through the palace windows and into his room. "Sixty dead. Mostly in the market, and here by the estates. We think Wyrim targeted your hometown because it's close enough to the major cities to make a statement, but too small to have thorough security. But you have my word that our best soldiers are on this. We haven't been able to link the attack to Wyrim's queen yet, but we will." His fingers curl around the hilt of the sword at his hip. "They will pay for this."

The edge in his voice pricks up my neck. I can't remember,

after the moon we've spent apart, if it was there before. It sounds more like the *other* prince I knew, and that's the most I'm going to think about it. That one haunts me enough without starting to see him in other people, too.

I'm not sure I want the answer to this next question, but I have to ask. "Are you going to declare war?"

His brow pinches, the question setting lines in his face. He looks so much older than he did on the day we said goodbye, like we've spent years apart, and I wonder what else he's learned in this time that's aged him. A fine blue tunic drapes his swordsman's figure; a crown of silver leaves circles his close-cropped hair. At a distance he's still the joking boy from the banquet who helped me with the food, ivory scabbard and all, but close up, I find myself searching for him. He's nervous today, though I guess that's probably natural since his coronation is in an hour.

I'll admit I've been anxious for today, too. But also excited, like settling back into the saddle of a horse who once took my breath away on a glorious sunset ride and then threw me over a cliff. Such are my complex feelings for this luxurious place that turned me into a human sacrifice. But even though I've sworn off adventure for the rest of my life, the glass boat Jet sent to fetch me and my family this morning to be his honored guests was still a very welcome sight. It's been a grueling moon, between relocating to the nearby city of Kystlin with most of our neighbors while repairs start on Atera, and helping the Kystlin Whisperers alongside my father, as they now have another town's worth of refugee pets and livestock to care for. Mora and Hen have found work, too, and while I haven't minded the long days, since they distract me from thinking about certain dead princes, we've all been looking forward to the day we can return home.

Back to our average, boring, wonderfully normal lives.

"War," Jet repeats sadly, working his hand over his jaw. "No, I don't think we're there yet. I'm hopeful other tactics will discourage them. Embargos, reminders of our military strength over theirs without taking lives. There are ways to make them sorry without killing people."

This, at least, sounds more like the merciful boy I saw as a king, and I exhale. Jet has a plan, and I chide myself for even thinking he could sound like Kasta, because of course he'll find a way to do this with the least amount of pain possible—he doesn't want a war. He has no point to prove here beyond wanting to protect his people.

"Good," I say.

"Now, in that same vein . . ." He rolls the map, and freezes. "Not in this same vein. I don't know why I said that. This vein is terrible, this is terrorism, and what I want to ask you isn't—do you want something to drink?"

I lean against the desk. "It's really strange seeing you this nervous."

"Nervous?" He laughs, as only someone half panicking can. "This isn't nervous. I've been in war rooms with Orkena's deadliest soldiers telling me to start wars, and *this* does not make me nervous. I was raised to face giants." He points at me like I'm about to disagree. "I am the Steel of Orkena—"

"Jet! What do you want to ask me?"

He closes his fist in front of his mouth, grimacing. "I . . . have a present for you? Follow me."

I would point out this is yet another change in subject, but he's already striding through the door and I have no choice but to follow. And I really do mean no choice, because being in Jet's "room," it turns out, is vastly more complicated than being in any other normal bedroom, as it comprises multiple suites and hallways and secret passages and false doors, and I'm concerned I will get very lost in here without him. And so I gladly leave behind the study's maps and disconcerting thoughts of bombs, duck through the hidden door of a greenhouse fluttering with jewel-winged butterflies, cross a room that houses an actual pool, and step back into the original space we entered at the start of this tour—the main bedroom.

Again, I'm using that term loosely. No bedroom I've ever been in has been made entirely of silver-veined Icestone to ward off the day's heat or had a ceiling several stories high, especially one with domed cities carved into it and backlit by enchanted fire. Likewise it seems decidedly more ballroom-like to have seven windows the size of carriages along one wall and a balcony that could host a large dinner party. That also overlooks the inner palace gardens. With spindly trees strung with light potions that look like stars.

"It's not a ballroom," Jet says loudly, because that's what I told him it reminded me of the first time we walked through it. "I told you, think 'warrior's den.' 'Swordsman's lair.' There are sixty weapons on the wall over there."

"I'm really sure I didn't say anything out loud this time."

"I can feel you judging it."

I smirk. Now things are starting to feel easier, more like we were at the end of the Crossing, and I acknowledge that maybe things have only seemed stilted today because I've been nervous to see him, too. It's been an entire moon. During which I've alternated between wondering what it would be like to actually kiss him, and worrying that I only started feeling for him because I was in a high-stress situation and thus found the idea of anyone who didn't want to kill me attractive. I'm still not sure where I've landed on it. But remembering this ease, this safety, is a good start.

Jet leads me to a recessed section of the floor—which, I might add, would be perfect for dancing if the couches were cleared—and turns around with a grin. "Close your eyes."

This is the kind of statement that years of friendship with Hen have taught me not to trust, but if Jet and I are going to move anything past awkward, trust is probably a critical thing to begin with. Also, I like presents, and I'm hoping it's chocolate. I close my eyes.

Sandaled feet slap the floor. Something wooden slides over tile, and then there's no sound at all, to the level that I can't even hear the birds outside—Jet must be using his Soundbending to keep quiet. This piques my curiosity to unbearable levels, but just as I'm cracking an eye open, he moves in front of me.

"All right," he says. "You can open them."

The first thing I see is his warm eyes and that cheeky smile he wears so well—and then I take in the spotted, wriggling bundle of fur in his hands.

"Oh. My. *Gods*." I reach for the feather-soft, purring animal. "You got me a *kitten*?"

"I believe she was item number four on your list of things I owe you for your near-death experience." His smile quirks. "Do you like her?"

"Do I!" The kitten gazes up at me with bright green eyes, little pearlescent universes that send all other thoughts scattering from my mind. Thumb-sized spots cover her golden fur from head to tail. It should be stated that I've already been affected by the sheer size of everything in the palace, for calling her a "kitten" is like calling Jet's suite a bedroom. She *is* young, but she's also the size of a large house cat. "I love her! Is she a leopard?"

"Yes, and actually she's a cub, but I thought you might forgive me the technicalities. She'll be a loyal companion, and a fierce protector when she's grown."

"Thank you. Really." I rub behind the cub's ears, my heart swelling. "I'm going to call you Jade. Do you think you're a Jade?"

She chirps and nuzzles me, my magic translating her sweet, childlike words in my head. *Jade*, she agrees. *You, mine!*

Jet claps a stack of crates. "Also from your list of demands: salves for your stable. Three crates to start, and if you need more, just write. The bottom crate is four weeks' worth of chocolate, with my apologies for being late, since I believe you specified 'weekly shipments.' Rest assured the others will come on time."

"Oh my gods, Jet—"

"Item five: a job for Hen." He lifts a scroll from the crate. "It turns out the Royal Materialist is looking for help, and she's been following your friend's work for some time. This is an offer of employ to assist her here in the palace."

I can't make my mouth work. I gape between the kitten and the tower of crates, which is easily half a year's worth of supplies, and back at Jet.

"Last but not least." He holds up a silver key with a delicate white rune carved into its top. "After the coronation today, come with me to the stables. This will glow when you're outside the stall of your new horse."

"I have a horse?" I squeak, then yelp when sharp teeth bite into my arm.

Ouch, Jade thinks. *Squeeze!*

"Sorry." I set her down, and she tears off across the room. "Wow. I just . . . I don't even know what to say."

"If you think of anything else, by all means, tell me. I wouldn't be here at all without you."

Heat builds behind my eyes, and I shake my head in bewilderment. "It's definitely enough. But you do realize I was joking about that list?" I press a hand to my head, laughing. "I made it while we were soaked in blood, and had both nearly *died* . . . You didn't have to come through on it."

"I felt like I owed you." He steps closer, and my pulse ticks up. "Also, I tend to buy presents when I miss someone, and I . . ." He fidgets with one of his silver bracelets, and I swear I feel a flash of nerves, as strongly as I would from Jade. "Well, that brings me to my next point. I was wondering if . . . that is, if you want to, and you definitely don't have to, but I thought maybe you'd be interested, or maybe you'd want to go home, but in case you didn't—"

My own nerves build, and I almost shake him. "Jet, *what*?"

He inhales and reaches into his tunic pocket, and panic jolts through me as I realize this is starting to look a lot like a courtship proposal. By which two people would make a relationship official, and very public. Except, as I reflected just a moment ago, what Jet and I have is barely a ship. This is a friendship; this is two people who survived something horrible and thought it might be nice to kiss this person sometime and see what happens, except I know the royals like to move ridiculously fast—

He pulls his hand from his pocket. But where I dreaded there might be a couples' necklace, instead a wide silver armband shines in his palm. "Will you be my advisor?"

"Oh, thank the gods," I say, relieved that maybe we're on the same page after all. Jet looks slightly concerned by my reaction, and I clear my throat. "I mean, yes. Maybe? What would I need to do, exactly . . . and why is there jewelry?"

Jet snorts. "What did you think I was going to ask you?"

"Nothing! Absolutely nothing, I just like to make things awkward— What were you about to say I'd do?"

Jet snickers, likely putting together exactly what my assumption was, and holds up the band. "There's jewelry because this is what all advisors wear to display their station. It'll give you access to nearly anyplace I can go in the palace. There's a symbol here, see?" He shows me a golden lantern stamped into one side. "You'd be on a team, helping me make decisions about things like taxes and laws and how they would affect people."

I blink. "You're going to put me in charge of laws?"

He gives me a look. "Don't discount what you can do. You're my best eyes and ears for how to help the working classes. I've also asked Melia and Marcus, who've agreed to stay, bless them, and I'll likely pull in a top scientist, and one of my father's advisors, too. Your help would be invaluable in so many ways." His smile turns clever, and he nudges my arm. "I also rather like having you around, you know, in general. Melia tries, but no one can throw out demeaning compliments quite like you."

I nod. "You do make it easy sometimes."

"Is that a yes?"

I pluck the armband from his hand, weighing my potential responsibilities in my palm. This would mean decidedly not returning to a normal life, with the problems with Wyrim just beginning and all the pressures this job would entail. Already Jet has had to make decisions that have no happy outcome, like choosing his life over his brother's. There would be a *lot* to learn—about politics and the court, trade and taxes, and I know there would be days I'd long for simpler times at the stable. Not that all my work is easy there, either, but at least my decisions don't determine the fate of *kingdoms*.

But it wouldn't all be stress. I could see Jet and Marcus and Melia whenever I liked. I would never again worry about what would happen to me after my magic fades, when I'd otherwise be assigned to various jobs around the country, separated from my family, until I served Orkena my full sixty summers. And instead of wishing laws like that would change . . . I could be the one behind the changes. I could help other Whisperers in a way that would actually matter.

Which feels like the perfect ending for my story . . . and maybe the beginning of something greater.

I turn the wide band, feeling oddly shy. "Can my father live here?"

"Absolutely. And Hen and her mother, too, if they want. Why do you think I made sure Hen's job was here?"

Ever the strategist, in all the best ways. "Then yes. Definitely."

His eyes shine bright as bronze. "Yes?"

"Someone's got to keep you in check." I clasp on the armband and tap it with a finger. "I'm also going to need a list of all the places this can get me into."

He pulls a small scroll and a miniature quill from his pocket. "I'll work on that."

I snicker. "You don't have to do it *right now*. Aren't you supposed to be meeting the priests soon?"

"There's only a hundred or so places to list. And it's not like I haven't been late to palace meetings before."

I freeze in adjusting the armband. "Wait, you're being serious? And what do you mean 'been late before'? When are you supposed to meet the priests?"

Jet glances at the water clock on a golden end table. "Ten minutes ago?"

I grab his wrist. "Are you trying to give me a heart attack? Do you know who gets blamed for these things in the stories? *The new advisor!* We are leaving, right now. I'm not being dragged behind a horse or hung from my toes or whatever it is you people do to disappointing servants."

He chuckles. "Those punishments are archaic, and you are most definitely *not* a servant—"

A knock sounds on the door. "*Dōmmel*," a man says. "May we come in?"

Jet grins and pulls gently from my grasp. "Ah. See? If you wait long enough, the priests come to you." He looks to the doors. "Enter."

And it's like a terrible flashback to one of the worst moments of my life: in walks the grumpy priest who deemed Kasta's knife mark on my wrist divine, followed by his haughty young apprentice, who still looks like a paler, meaner version of him. Except this time, instead of glaring down her nose at me, her gaze drops to my chest. Where her eyes widen in recognition at the vivid red scar the sacrificial knife left over my heart. And I again begin to question my life decisions. It seemed like such a good idea this morning, when Hen and I were getting ready, to choose a *jole* with a particularly low neckline—in this case, one cut almost to my navel—as I know the nobility will ask about the knife's scar whether they can see it or not, and I'm determined to show them it belongs to me and not the boy who made it. That's still my plan, but I'll admit the staring is getting awkward.

The apprentice drops to one knee . . . and raises her fingertips to her forehead, like she would for a Mestrah.

"*Gudina,*" she says, the light gleaming off her blonde hair. "It's an honor to be in your presence."

Gudina: Holy One. I glance uneasily at Jet, and at the grumpy priest, who—impossibly—is not regarding me with even a hint of a sneer. Well, maybe there's a little bit of a grimace. But he looks like he's trying very hard not to, which is still an improvement.

"Living Sacrifice." The priest dips his head. "My honor as well."

His apprentice rises, keeping her eyes on the floor. It's only after the priest has turned to Jet that I realize they addressed me before addressing the crown prince. Which Jet warned me this morning might happen, at least until he's crowned, because that's how the priests scrambled to explain my survival at the end of the Crossing: as divine intervention. Apparently they've even gone so far as to claim the girl I was actually *did* die on the end of the sacrificial knife, and that a goddess returned in my place.

Hiding my identity as the Living Sacrifice was easy enough in Kystlin, where I was just one more nameless refugee. But tonight that ends.

"Perhaps you missed our summons, *dōmmel*." The priest gives Jet a look like he knows that isn't the case. "But it's time to get dressed, and then the Mestrah would like to go over a few final ceremonial details. *Gudina*, are you sure you wouldn't like to watch from the royal dais?"

I almost laugh. "Gods, no." I may be here to make this scar mine, but the last thing I want is to be studied like a piece of art for the better part of an hour. I realize too late this is a very uncourtly way to respond, and hastily correct myself. "I mean, no. Thank you."

Jet pockets the scroll and quill. "Has the Materialist finished her alterations on my tunic?"

"Ah." The priest rubs his bald head. "I forgot about the hole. Alise, will you check on that immediately?"

"Of course, *adel*." She bows and takes her leave.

"There was a hole in your coronation tunic?" I ask. No wonder Jet wants the Royal Materialist to hire Hen.

"A purposeful one, though for an outdated reason." Jet taps the top of his chest. "In a normal contest, the sacrificial knife would have created a mark here on the winning heir. A circle of Numet that proves they completed the sacrifice. Galena referenced old paintings for her coronation design, where the tunics used to open at the center to show it off. We reminded her there wasn't a sacrifice. No mark." Jet smiles. "Thank the gods."

"Oh." Dread prickles my arms, and I touch the wide necklace around my throat. "Right."

"I need to ask her about the banquet tunic, too," Jet says, this time to the priest as they start for the door. "But I suppose we could always draw a mark if needed, for the purposes of tradition . . . Zahru, are you coming?"

They turn in the doorway. I haven't moved. That dread climbs my throat now, thick as smoke.

"Yes!" I pipe. "I just . . . need to check my face."

"All right. We'll be right outside."

I dart past the bed, suddenly grateful the room is so much more than a room. A washing basin waits inside a lavish en suite, and I catch my balance on its cold marble edge, panic shoving against my skull.

I steel myself and look up at the gilded mirror.

"It's not, it's not, it's not," I mutter, raising shaking hands to the bronze necklace. Hen and I chose this piece not only because its gemmed flowers add color to the plain gold of my dress, but also because I still have a nasty bruise on my chest from the sacrificial knife, and this is the best way to cover it. So maybe it's a little strange, now that I think about it, that this particular bruise never faded to green or yellow with the rest of my bruises, and that it's closer to the base of my throat than to the knife's scar. Or that Hen and I had just been joking about how it seemed to be taking on a shape, and we were going to start charging people to see it, like someone might for a slice of cheese that looks like Sabil's face. Coincidence. No one in the world can possibly be this unlucky.

I lift the heavy gemstones, and my breath catches.

The deep scarlet of the swirling circle of Numet smiles back at me.

"Oh, no," I whisper.

II

LIKE any rational person, I decide this is a problem I can ignore.

I conclude the mark is irrelevant, as firstly, I am not a princess, and secondly, I did not perform a sacrifice, and thirdly . . . I don't want to know what it means. A bombshell like this would be much better brought up in casual conversation, like in a few moons' time when Jet and I are meeting over some critical civil affair and I could slip in, between the presentation of the issue and my possible solutions, that I have this annoying, persistent bruise on my chest and isn't it funny how it kind of looks like the mark the winner of the Crossing is supposed to receive? We'll laugh, and more importantly, Jet will remember he's already crowned, and there's no need to look into it further.

I'm just freaking myself out. It's not a gods' mark, it's a stubborn bruise. It will go away.

It *will*.

I've convinced myself of this so thoroughly that by the time I join Jet and my family under the soaring stone-and-glass ceiling of the royal hallway, I'm smiling. I may be overdoing it slightly, because Jet is looking rather worried as he leaves to do whatever it is he has to do before he becomes a god, but he doesn't ask any questions, so I'm declaring that a victory.

Except that the second he's gone, Hen whirls on me with the intensity of a giant hawk. "All right. Spill."

Her fingers clutch my shoulders like talons. She's really very intimidating in full makeup, with gold dust flashing along her beige skin and tiny metal skulls wrapping sections of her black hair. Kohl lines her eyes in edges so sharp they look fine enough to cut.

This is the terror mice feel before they're eaten.

"Spill?" I laugh, a little too forcibly. "Spill what?"

"This is not the smile of someone who just bedded a prince." This makes me choke, and I glance at Fara, but he's mercifully far away enough to not be paying attention. "Your hair is too perfect for that, anyway. This is a panicked smile. An 'I just saw a dead person' smile."

"Ah, no," I say, thinking fast. "This is the smile of someone who just became an advisor to the crown!"

This I say loud enough to draw my father's attention, and he and Mora turn our way, their fine clothes shimmering in a slice of overhead sun. Orange for my *fara*, a compliment to his deeply tanned skin, and pink for Mora, to add a pretty blush to her beige complexion. Gold even lines their eyes—Mora's doing, no doubt—and my father especially looks many years younger than I'm used to.

I happily bound over to him, away from Hen's still-suspicious glare, and throw my arms around his stomach.

"An advisor?" Fara asks, sounding appropriately impressed.

I beam. "Yes! We're moving to the palace, and Hen can work under the Royal Materialist if she wants, and you're invited, too, Mora!"

"Really?" Mora clasps her hands. "This is wonderful! Oh, we should get you alone with that boy more often." Fara cuts her a glare, but she waves it away, along with him, to hug me.

16

"Congratulations, *kar-a*. And don't be a prude, Aron. Unless you'd like me to start in on the stories I know about you and her mother."

"Please, no," I whimper.

"We were older," Fara grumbles.

"By a year." Mora smirks and arranges loose waves of my brown hair over my shoulders. "Now, if he starts in on you about partners, you just let me know. We still want you to be safe—"

I groan. "Mora—"

"You don't think I see how low this neckline is?"

I jab a finger into my scar. "It's for this! I'm showing people I'm not ashamed of it. Like an empowering, taking-ownership-type thing."

She gives me a look.

"I'm serious! And we really don't need to have this talk. There's still a lot Jet and I have to figure out."

"Which is all the more reason to remind you . . ." She slowly straightens my dress, arranging my cape over my shoulders. ". . . that some things have lifelong consequences."

God of death, take me now. I make desperate eyes at Hen, who claps loudly, causing the guards along the walls to grab for their staffs.

"There's no time for this!" Hen's voice echoes down the marble corridor. "Her Holiness has decreed there will be no more Talks of Embarrassment or unsolicited partner advice. Also, she'd like to reach the chocolates before the rest of the riffraff. Come, sacred family."

She holds her arm out, and I quickly take it, ignoring Mora's snickers as we head for the foyer where the rest of the guests will be gathering. But whatever momentary relief I felt at this rescue dies the second Hen pulls me closer.

"Don't think I've let you off the hook yet," she whispers. "I know there's something else you're not telling us."

"I think you're being overly suspicious."

"I think you've forgotten who you're dealing with." Her brown eyes narrow. "No one has secrets from me. When the queen has secrets, I have people who bring them to me."

"Yes. I've often worried when you might be arrested for that."

"Just think about whether you'd like me to find this out on my own, or whether you'd like to tell me." She pats my arm in the worrying way I've seen Mora do before she slips itching powder into a troublesome customer's order of potions. "It's up to you."

A compelling argument, but I hold my tongue. I love Hen, and I don't normally keep secrets from her, but this is a case where I absolutely must. It was hard enough feeling her sobbing body against mine when we reunited in Kystlin, after she'd feared that she'd lost me forever and that it was her fault for sneaking me into the palace in the first place. So telling her now that the bruise on my chest actually is a strange, divine symbol, and that I might not be in the clear yet, is not an option. Also, we're in a public hallway, and I won't risk word of this getting back to the priests. For all I know, if someone has the knife's mark and isn't an heir, it means they really were supposed to die.

Hard pass. I will take this to my grave, and I'd like to see Hen try to pry it out of me before then. Which is really a much bolder thought than I'm willing to share with her, so I just point ahead of us and change the subject. "Wow, is that really how many people will be watching?"

We've reached the end of the corridor, where the milky alabaster floor yields to wide, theatrical stairs that overlook a towering foyer. We step past the Silencing wards that shield the royal wing from the commotion of the main hall, and a hundred conversations hit us in a gale. What has to be the entirety of Orkena's elite mill below in a rainbow of *joles* and fine dark tunics, their heads adorned with extravagant, leafy crowns and metal circlets, many glinting with little charms: tiny rattlesnakes and golden jackals, glittering swords and miniature wings.

"Actually, this isn't that many," Hen says. "A few hundred, maybe? The throne room fits two thousand. I'm pretty sure ten times that have been invited to listen outside."

"Good *gods*," I wheeze as the leopard-masked soldiers guarding the stairs step aside. "Isn't the ceremony starting soon? Why aren't they moving into the coronation room?"

Hen looks over, a strange smile in her lips. "Because they're waiting to see you."

The entire three-story foyer goes quiet. No one announces us, but apparently standing at the top of the royal stairs is as good as shouting. Eyes take me in like I'm a trophy, gloved hands cover whispers, and the confidence I'd felt in making the knife's scar my own fizzles. *They're going to ask you what happened*, Hen warned me on the boat ride here. *They're going to ask what it was like.*

Let them, I said, but under the pressure of so much attention my vision blurs, and a flash of blue eyes, of a trembling knife, of white-hot pain cuts under my skin. Anxiety climbs my neck, fever-hot. I force it back. Hen and I practiced how I'd tell my story, anticipating every uncomfortable question and needling comment, until I could answer each with a smile. I exhale and assure myself this will only last a few hours. I'll satisfy everyone's curiosity, enjoy the celebration, steal off mysteriously into the night like proper nobles do, then begin an utterly wonderful, possibly anonymous new life as a Mestrah's advisor.

Behind us, Fara squeezes my shoulder, and I glance back with an appreciative smile.

We start down the stairs. Jet said the guards would be watching in case anyone causes us trouble, but I can't help but notice this is a lot of people to watch at once. Voices spin up with each of our steps. At the bottom of the stairs, Orkena's elite part like water; a man in green intensely holding my gaze as we move forward, a woman in blue dipping her head and muttering prayers. The panic in my skin shifts to discomfort. Clearly there are different opinions here regarding whether I'm an actual goddess, since a trio of older girls simply glances over as we pass. But too many others watch me like jackals, daring me to prove what I am.

We're halfway to the open doors of the throne room. Just as I'm hoping my reputation as the Living Sacrifice means no one will dare speak to me at all, a tall woman in a bright yellow *jole* steps in our path.

"*Gudina.*" She bows low, fingertips held to her pale forehead, and tears brim in her eyes when she rises. "A blessing for my house, if you would? My daughter has been very ill since the planting season."

In Hen's grip, I go rigid. Everyone in earshot turns toward us. All of them look devious now, their smiles coy, their eyes glinting. Will I dare blaspheme and bless her? Will I cruelly turn her away? It's made worse by the stressed, pleading lines in the woman's face. She's not one of the jackals. She's hurting, she's desperate, and I can practically see the fragile hope inside of her, a thread of glass my words will strengthen or shatter.

Static builds along my skin, and I feel strangely like I would in the stable with a hurt animal, the intensity of its emotions such that even from a distance I can feel its anxiety. But though I look in confusion at the woman's jeweled purse to see if she's carrying a pet, I'm very certain no animals are allowed at the coronation. Great. Now even my magic is going haywire from stress. I'm threading together an answer when Mora's hand drops to my shoulder, and the static vanishes in a snap.

Do you need me? she mouths.

I shake my head and slowly turn back to the woman. I have a feeling this is going to be a very long night.

"I-I'll pray for her," I manage. A safe, ambiguous response that anyone here could give, but the woman sobs like I've promised much more.

"Thank you, *adel*," she says, bowing again and again. "I will never forget your kindness. Long may you live!"

Her retreat opens the floodgates. Chatter erupts around us, and a man in a deep red tunic pushes forward, tiny gazelle heads dangling from his ivy crown.

"If it pleases you, *adel*, would you bless this charm? I have a very important event coming up, and I could use your luck—"

21

"Will you sign this dress for me?" calls a shorter woman, making me jump when she grabs my elbow. "I have a quill—"

"Unbelievable what the sheep will believe these days," grumbles a wrinkly old man. "She's a filthy *peasant* who bathed and put on a dress!"

"Hen," I say as someone pulls my cape. "I don't know if I can do this—"

"The Illustrious Zahru will take no requests now!" Hen shouts, stunning the group into silence. "Her Holiness is here to support our new Mestrah. If time allows, she may speak with a few of you after the ceremony, but until then, you will give her space. Heed this warning, or have your darkest secrets brought to light."

Disbelieving snickers ripple through the crowd. The two women closest to me shrug, and the noise rises again as they offer me their gods' charms.

"Will you blow on these?" the shorter one asks. "We want your luck, too!"

"Gods, *look* at that scar." Her friend jabs a finger into my chest, and I jerk back.

Hen slaps her hand away. "Lady Penna, does your friend know you want that luck because you're trying to steal her son's fiancée for *your* son?"

Horror ripples through Lady Penna's face, but not nearly as strongly as it does her friend's. The crowd titters again—this time not at me.

"That . . ." Lady Penna stammers, ". . . is absolutely not true—"

"You *snake*," her friend hisses. "That's why you two have been so helpful these past weeks?"

Hen's eyes narrow. "Don't act so innocent, Lady Mira. *You've* been jealous of Penna's looks for so long, you started slipping aging powder into her tea!"

The taller woman gasps. "*You're* the reason for my wrinkles? I've been paying a fortune to have them removed!"

"Good!" her friend snaps. "I should have put the entire jar in, you thieving wench!"

She cracks her hand across her friend's face, who screams and tackles her to the floor. Chains of crystals go flying, two guards *finally* appear to separate the women, and Hen, arms wide, glowers at the nobility collected around us.

"Would anyone else like to challenge the gods?" she says.

I bite back a laugh as the nearest people quickly shake their heads. Clearly they've never faced the full power of a small-town gossip before. They back away, eyes shifting between my petite friend and the disheveled women who have just regained their feet. When Hen gestures to the doors of the throne room, the people blocking it move.

"There we go." Hen beams as she takes my arm.

"Gods, I love you," I say. "Also, you're now officially my bodyguard."

"I'm so proud of you, Hen," Mora says, wiping a finger under her eyes.

Fara grunts. "And she only committed a small amount of sacrilege to do it."

"My dear Aron." Mora pats my father's arm. "It's like you don't even know us sometimes."

But with the crowd away I can breathe again, and I sigh in

relief as my father and Mora argue about the proper situations in which one might impersonate the gods. I can't say I'm looking forward to doing this over and over, but if that was the worst of it, I'll manage. Who knows, maybe by the end of the night I'll be so comfortable with the attention that I'll have half a performance planned and be reenacting my story from atop a table.

Admittedly, that exact scenario may also require wine. But I think I'm ready for this, either way.

And soon, despite my nerves, the throne room presses all of that away.

The last time I was here, it was at the mercy of a stone-eyed Mestrah and his ruthless son, but the ghost of Kasta's grip on my arm fades as I take in the splendor of the new decorations. The giant columns gleam a deep midnight blue, their scalloped sides wrapped with gossamer ribbons and gold-dusted lilies. Enormous tapestries, each depicting different gods presenting gifts to a woven Prince Jet, line the walls between blue-burning torches. The sprawling ceiling has been painted like the sky. It's black and splattered with stars at the entrance we walk beneath, and silver-tipped and glowing on the far side, as if the sun will soon rise.

A gathering crowd waits on either side of an aisle strewn with palm leaves, but before a new group of nobles can converge on us, a pair of guards strides over.

"*Gudina*," says the first, crossing one arm over her chest. "My apologies for the unruliness outside. We will stay much closer from here forward. If you'll come this way."

Torchlight flashes from her feathered armor as we follow. She takes us around the eastern spectators and into a rectangular space to the side of the thrones, where a plush scarlet rug marks the area as separate and cushions our feet. Six guards line its edges, and I've just started to realize we're in very selective company when Hen tugs my arm and points at a young man with light brown skin and a fine red tunic.

"That's the duke of Constanta," Hen says, not nearly quietly enough. "World-class Airweaver, suspiciously good at cards, and possibly illegitimate." She suddenly sobers. "Gorgeous, too. I'd planned on him being your rebound if things didn't work out with Jet, but he just got himself engaged to the Amian king."

"You're already plotting rebounds?" I say. "Jet and I are barely at the 'figuring it out' stage!"

"Shh, his mother is right there."

"Whose mother?"

"Jet's!"

My heart drops into my stomach. I follow Hen's gaze to a stout, striking woman with dark brown skin and bronze armor crossing her chest and back in an X. Tiny golden swords circle her short afro, and she rests her weight on a jaguar-headed cane. Her General's honors glint from strings of leather wrapping her bicep: Cybil's tiny metal helmet, for favor from the goddess of war; a collection of little silver wings, one for every kill; a balancing scale for wisdom.

It's strange to see her here and not on the dais when it's her son being crowned, though maybe that's normal, since she and the Mestrah haven't been romantically involved since Jet's birth. That was, apparently, the moment the queen realized her husband had been lying about not still being in love with his childhood friend, and thus things between him and the General quickly ended. It's actually a little heartbreaking, considering the Mestrah's marriage had been arranged by his mother—to his clear disapproval—though I think he and the queen do love each other now.

I make a mental note to introduce myself later and pull Hen closer. "We're standing with the General," I whisper. I mean, yes, I probably should be used to famous people by now, since first, I apparently am one, and second, I've been much closer than this to her son, but it turns out that a death-defying race across the desert makes me even more intimidated by the finery of the court. Also, I've been living this past moon in a barn.

"I know," Hen says, nudging me. "And *she's* standing with the Living Sacrifice."

I roll my eyes. "Please. I have enough issues already without you adding more."

"Girls." Mora puts her hands on our shoulders. "They're starting."

She nods toward a fair-skinned man in a red *tergus* at the base of the thrones, who's raising a silver-capped oxhorn to his lips. He takes a deep, full breath and blows.

The marble floor vibrates with its commanding hum. Conversations hush, and the last of the crowd bustles inside, packing the designated standing areas. Hen and I move to the edge of the aisle, an arm away from the Constantan duke and two from Jet's mother. Anticipation runs a slick finger down my back. This is what I braved a desert for. This is what I almost died for.

The horn bellows again, and eleven priests walk in.

The masks of gods cover their features: the feminine face of

Talqo, goddess of healing; the winged face of Rie, god of death; and on and on as the nine other priests follow, the last of them wearing a golden mask crowned by Numet's brilliant sun. Incense twists above the wooden bowls in their hands, and trains of gossamer fabric drag behind their robes, all identical shades of gray. Only their arms show any glimpse of distinction, their skin oiled shades of oak brown, silvery umber, pale peach.

Behind them march the three High Priests, all unmasked and tattooed. Again, there's my quasi-nemesis, the grumpy man who continues to burden me with life-altering news every time I see him, and beside him walks a woman with short purple hair and stars inked around the edges of her face. The last is a tall woman with a shaved head and kind eyes, and when she takes her place on the fourth stair, she looks over the room with a smile.

The Mestrah and the queen are next. Jet's father looks stoic and strong, the deep olive of his bare chest gleaming beneath a mantle of twisting antlers and a cape of flowing white silk. Strips of silver adorn his ceremonial kilt, and his scorpion-tined crown sits level on his brow. But my heart sinks as I notice that the sheen on his arms is sweat, not oil, and that he's leaning into his falcon-winged staff more for support than ceremony. The queen is quiet and tight-lipped beside him. She looks lovely with her skin powdered to a porcelain finish and her hair in a sleek copper bun, but she does not smile at her people. Her hands are curled and tense, and though her eyes are green, not Kasta's blue, a familiar shiver plucks at my arms when she turns their fire on the General.

Jet's mother pays her no heed. Not with a nod of challenge or a wince of fear, though a brief shadow of pity weakens her smile and reminds me what the queen truly lost. With the Mestrah's trackers still scouring the desert for Sakira, it's not just that her children will never sit on a throne. It's that neither of them even came home.

Anger flares through me at the thought, and I turn back to the entrance. The horn lifts and bellows a third time.

Jet steps into the doorway.

Pride surges through me as cheers erupt from the crowd. With his shoulders square and the torches bright on his face, Jet is a vision that shames even my memory of him from minutes ago. He's changed into the most elaborate tunic I've ever seen, the fabric a liquid blue that I suspect is literally woven from water, its edges gilded with silver prayers and Numet's lanterns. Gods' symbols glow white on his dark brown skin, and strings of leather twine around his shins. Only his shoulders and short hair are without adornment—the places where the Mestrah will transfer his antlered mantle and the scorpion crown.

If Jet's nervous about this, I can't tell. He walks steadily, nodding as the nobility shouts his name, and the sight of him after everything we've been through brings a prickling heat to my eyes.

He finds me in the crowd and grins.

The people bow as he moves, and I with them, until he stops at the base of the stairs. Behind him, four jaguar-masked guards spread into formation. A single slam of their spears quiets the last of the cheering. Smoke from the priests' bowls twists above the dais, and the Mestrah raises his arms, and as one, the entire assembly drops to one knee. The queen does, too, though her jaw is tight, and she doesn't bow her head.

But it's the first time I've ever seen the Mestrah smile.

"As Numet rides across the sky at day," he begins, looking only at Jet, "and retires to Paradise at night, so does the reign of Mestrah begin and end. It is this Numet herself, Divine First Queen, did so declare for her children: that only the most honorable, the most deserving, and the wisest of us would be marked to lead, not by order of birth, but by—"

He stops, the echo of his words chilling in the sudden quiet. The crowd shifts, exchanging glances, and just as I'm worrying the Mestrah's silence is the fault of his illness, I notice his gaze is no longer on Jet. It's fixed on the back of the room, near the now-closed doors.

Where someone is still standing.

Someone dressed in a white merchant's tunic instead of a fine *tergus*. Someone whose bronzed, muscled arms are sand-dusted and cut with shadow. Someone whose bicep is marked with a rigid, scythe-like scar . . . one of many wounds that should have bled him dry.

My own scar burns like a vicious new brand.

"Oh gods," I whisper.

Kasta.

III

I can't breathe.

Murmuring simmers around me like locusts' song, but the ringing in my head soon overtakes it. This can't be real. This is one of my nightmares, the kind that begin with Hen and Jet and everything that's wonderful in my life, and end with Kasta and his dagger. He cannot possibly be alive. I saw how badly he was bleeding in the caves. I saw Maia corner him, two deadly swords in her hands.

I heard him cry out when he died, a sound that still grates against my memory like steel against stone.

But I realize . . . I only *heard* his cry. I never saw Maia stab him. I just assumed—

"Zahru." Hen grabs my arm. "You said the stabby prince died."

The nobles stir, conversation bubbling. Kasta's name surfaces on the whispers, a harrowing buzz in my ears. When he steps forward, the quiet breaks like a river down a canyon.

Terror shoves through my body. I know there are guards here. I know Kasta is focused on his father, but my mind races with questions, each one making me dizzier than the last. How did he survive? Why is he here? Does he have the knife?

Can he still perform the sacrifice if he does?

Kasta's face is steel as he starts forward. I shrink between a kneeling Fara and Mora until my father's broad frame hides me and my eyes have no chance of meeting Kasta's. But the closer Kasta comes, the more I wonder if he's even thinking of me. He doesn't look away from his father even once, except when Jet and the guards rise.

The slow smile that pulls his lips sparks a warning through my blood. But Jet only stares in response, with the kind of shock I'm sure I mirror: that we're seeing a ghost.

"Zahru." Hen turns on her knee, her expression strangely somber. "Would you like to tell me about that secret now?"

"I swear, I didn't know he was alive," I say, though guilt swirls in my gut, because I'm realizing there are far more secrets than this—especially concerning Kasta and how I escaped him—that I still haven't told her.

Fara goes still. *"That's* the boy who sacrificed you?"

"Don't, Fara," I whisper, though I know my father is disciplined enough not to start anything at such an event. Fara only exhales and pulls me closer.

The queen, once still, muffles a sob and rises.

The Mestrah raises a hand to stop her. "Kasta," he says, and though he doesn't yell, his voice silences the crowd. His expression wars between confusion and anger. "This is not the time."

Not *Thank the gods you're alive* or *I prayed for this moment.* No move to embrace or welcome his son. Only the queen looks ready to break apart, her hands cupping her nose and mouth, tears smearing her makeup.

"Yes, it is," Kasta says, his hands curling. "For you are about to crown the wrong king."

Gasps from the crowd. Jet still hasn't moved. The guards start uncertainly toward Kasta, but the Mestrah shakes his head, and they halt.

"The wrong king is the one who stands before me now." Pity creases the Mestrah's brow. "I am sorry, my son. But without the blood of the sacrifice spilled—"

"It was spilled," Kasta snaps, and anger flares in my chest at the bluntness of those words. "And then spared. But not before the gods marked their victor."

He pulls down the collar of his tunic—and lightning flashes through my veins. On his chest, blood-red and prominent, is a swirling circle of Numet that looks terribly familiar. Hen turns to me, eyes wide, but I shake my head fiercely and mouth, *He's lying*. He has to be. Just like when he tricked the priests into believing I was the Crossing's sacrifice; just like when he tricked an *entire country* into believing he had magic he didn't.

Obviously that last part is not the greatest of Hen's concerns, as I imagine she's also noticed his mark looks dreadfully familiar. But I ignore her urgent poke to my knee. The Mestrah frowns and motions to the closest High Priest—the smiling woman—who dips her head and hurries to his side.

"Test him," the Mestrah says.

The audience begins to stand, and we stand with them, though everyone is far too enraptured to speak. The High Priest moves quietly before Kasta. She measures the mark with her fingertips, and I can tell it's the same size as mine. My blood buzzes in my head. This confirmation that my own mark is far more than I want it to be is overwhelming, but that's still not the biggest of my problems. My mark could mean death. *His* would mean Mestrah.

It's fake, I assure myself. He's orchestrated this, but it will fail. This is too important for it not to—

"Zahru!" Hen whispers, jerking her chin toward the back of the crowd.

I shake my head and move closer to Fara. I'm fine, for now, but I'm not moving. Kasta will see me if I move. Hen exhales and starts pantomiming, but I can't focus on her for what's happening on the dais. The High Priest has drawn a small jar from her belt. With her thumb, she applies a white paste to Kasta's chest. The priests standing behind her inhale as the mark flashes gold in response.

Then all of them bow low, fingers touching their foreheads.

The High Priest looks to the Mestrah in disbelief.

"No," I breathe, my chest squeezing.

"You told me there shouldn't be a mark," the Mestrah mutters. He glances at Jet, who stands with a hand pressed over his mouth.

"The sacrifice lived," the High Priest says. "We assumed her death was required."

The Mestrah sighs and dismisses her, his closed eyes turned to the ceiling as though trying to hear the gods. Or cursing them, maybe. When his gaze returns to the crowd, the ice in it is enough to render even the smallest murmurs silent.

I grip Fara's hand. *Say it's too late*, I think. Kasta can't possibly come back after everything he did, after what he did to *me*, and win. There's no justice in the world if he can. And gods, Jet *just* found peace with his new responsibilities. After all his fears and doubts during the Crossing, after believing himself not worthy of the decisions he'll have to make, he finally sees himself as his supporters do. He will be a fair king. He will be a *good* king, and surely the gods must see that.

They cannot possibly reward Kasta's ruthlessness.

33

They can*not*.

The Mestrah raises his hands. "The coronation will continue." The people lean forward, and I clasp my other hand in Mora's. "For my son Kasta, whom Numet has marked with her own hand."

"No," I choke out as Fara's fingers tighten. Mora covers her mouth in disbelief. The queen sobs in joy. Shouts of surprise and confusion echo from the walls, and the guards straighten when the crowd begins to shift, but the few nobles who protest are quickly urged to silence by their neighbors. It's no small thing for the Mestrah to declare someone divine. Jet casts a helpless glance first at his mother, then me, and I bite back tears as I hold his gaze. *We'll make this right*, I promise, hoping he can read the defiance in my eyes. Mestrah or not, I won't let Kasta get away with fooling the priests again.

"We will require a few minutes to prepare him," the Mestrah announces. "Hold your assembly." He gestures to the High Priests and to Kasta, but when Jet steps forward, the Mestrah raises a hand. "Join your mother," he says, glancing our way.

My chest pinches. Jet goes rigid. He's not only being dismissed, but he's also expected to drop quietly into the background on a day that was meant to be his. Jet opens his mouth to ask what I'm sure is the first of many questions, but the Mestrah has already turned away.

The royal party disappears through a scarlet curtain at the back of the room, and the crowd erupts.

"All right," Hen snaps, tugging me from the safety of Fara. "We are talking about this *right now*."

She yanks up the necklace to reveal my mark, and I snap it down again.

"No, we're not," I say. "Because for all I know, this just means he was supposed to kill me, and if I tell the priests, they're going to let him finish the job."

"Zahru?" my father asks.

"It's nothing, Fara." I cast a pleading look at Hen. "Just . . . give us a moment."

"Fine," Hen says. "But we're bringing an expert with us. Prince Jet!"

I start to protest—Jet already has enough to deal with right now—but I have to admit that knowing whether my gods' mark means I'm still supposed to die is rather critical information. I worry my thumb over my palm as he heads our way, though he moves in a daze, his eyes distant, his shoulders slumped.

"Bubble thing," Hen orders, when the three of us have gathered at the side of the scarlet carpet.

"Bubble thing?" Jet mutters, his eyes on the dais.

I touch his arm. "Jet, I'm really sorry about this, and I know a lot just happened. But can you put up your sound barrier? There's something I have to tell you."

"Oh." He shrugs. "Right. It's up now."

"Zahru has the same mark," Hen blurts.

"Gods, Hen," I say. "At least ease him into it."

Jet snaps awake. "You what?" His eyes drop to my necklace. "What do you mean, the same mark?"

"Look," I say, holding the necklace down. "First I want to say you *know* Kasta is faking this. I don't care what that paste is supposed

35

to prove; he's gotten around stuff like this before. Like when he cut my wrist to make me the sacrifice. Like when he faked being a *Deathbringer* for his whole life." I glance at the curtain where the royal party disappeared, static prickling through my blood. "We're going to figure this out. And after we expose him, you'll still be king."

"Zahru," Jet says. "Show me the mark."

I'm not sure he listened to anything I just said. But I slowly lift the necklace, half praying my mark really is just a bruise, half praying it will give me some crazy decisive power, like the ability to choose who rules.

"*Tyda*," Jet curses, but a wide smile breaks onto his face.

A pang of hope shoots through me. "This is good, right? A smile means good things? I won't be sacrificed again?"

"This is very good." Jet laughs, turning the necklace so he can see better. "How long have you had this?"

"A moon," Hen chimes.

"Zahru, this is a big deal." He looks at me like I'm made of gold. "Clearly we've never had a sacrifice survive before, so I can't say exactly what it means, but I know if the marks are present, the contest is definitely over. No chance of further sacrifice. But a very big chance that *this* is the real mark. The knife chose *you*, which is proof enough that Kasta's is fake. You can stop him, right here, before a crown ever touches his head."

I blink, certain I didn't hear him right. "I'm sorry, what?"

"*You* are marked to be Mestrah." Jet grips my shoulders. Like he's telling me I've won a trip around the world, or a new house, and not that I've possibly just inherited an entire kingdom and a war. "You can stop him."

My response is to stare. The rest of me is freezing up, maybe literally, gooseflesh spreading through my entire body as his words sink in. The mark does not mean death. It means that at the end of the Crossing, the gods reached out their hands and placed on my skin a symbol that's meant only for a person they deem worthy to rule.

My vision goes white. The world slips from my grasp like the edge of a cliff.

It's only Jet's and Hen's quick reflexes, and the appearance of a rather random stool, that keep me from experiencing the full glory of the throne room floor. I cling to them as they set me upright and try to remember how to breathe. This has to be a terrible joke. A punishment from the gods for the years I begged them to see the palace, to see the world, to see any place that wasn't my home. For evading death. For leaving Kasta knocked out in a tent in the middle of the desert.

They can't truly mean for me to be Mestrah. They can't mean for me to take the place that even Jet, with his entire lifetime of royal training, felt unqualified to accept.

"Very amusing, Valen," I whisper, a hysteric laugh bubbling up my throat. The god of fate must be loving this. "It's all right, I get it. I prayed way too much to be given an adventure, and it got annoying, but I've definitely learned my lesson and I've stopped. Can you pinch me so I wake up now?"

Hen does, hard.

"Ouch, *gods*—"

"You're not asleep," Hen says. "Remember what you were just saying about how we'd do anything to stop Kasta?"

"And get *Jet* back on the throne," I say, looking desperately between them. "You can't really think this is a good idea. When was the last time you saw me negotiate treaties? Or command soldiers? Or *rule an entire country*?"

"You'll have help," Jet says. "You can form your own circle of advisors for areas you're not familiar with. And you know I'll be there every step of the way, if you want me to be."

He sounds far too calm for someone who's just lost the throne. I imagine right now he's just relieved there's a way to stop Kasta, but I have to wonder if he'll be this happy after the rest of it settles in.

"No, it has to mean something else." I wipe my palms on my *jole*. "It's another of Kasta's tricks. He's the one who pulled me into this, and this . . . this is just more of it."

"More of it?" Hen says. "As in, he snuck into our room in Kystlin, into a barn where no one else knew we were staying, and put that mark there while you were sleeping?"

"Obviously not, but—" But I feel my excuses unraveling. Even if Kasta and I had been staying in the same room this last moon, there is no turn of events in which he would mark me with a Mestrah's symbol.

My mark is real.

Dizziness threatens to overtake me again, and I lower my head into my hands.

"The gods can't mean it." The words pinch my lungs. "It's a mistake."

Jet brushes a strand of hair behind my ear, his fingers soft on my jaw. He lets me breathe a moment longer before his hand drops away. "I know this is terrifying."

My reflection shines in his eyes, small and disbelieving, but I know he's not just saying that to be comforting. He knows this fear firsthand.

"Do you remember what you said to me when I was afraid to rule?" he asks.

I groan. "That's not even fair. You were raised for this. You're *supposed* to be Mestrah."

"That you believed in me. That you knew I would succeed because you could see me even as I couldn't see myself."

Tears blur my vision. I look toward the exit doors, toward freedom, and I know that if I asked him, Jet would let me go. The question is on the tip of my tongue. The coronation was supposed to be the *end* of my story, the ride-off-into-the-sunset, the finale—

"You said Kasta would be cruel," Hen says, quieter. "That he might want good things, but he'd hurt people to get them."

The scar on my chest burns, and I close my eyes. "Yes."

"Wouldn't you agree that literally anyone else would be a better ruler than him?"

This is not exactly the most supportive declaration, but she has a point, even if my mind is already working out the many ways this could go horribly wrong. My primary concern being that if we can't convince the Mestrah that Kasta's mark is fake, there's a very real possibility this results in yet another competition for the throne, for which Kasta has already proven how far he'll go to win. But just as I'm opening my mouth to present this worry, I realize—it doesn't matter.

Because something else is twisting through my thoughts, sleek as a serpent.

And when I look up, when I meet Jet's eyes, it's not justice I'm thinking of. It's not that this is the right thing to do, which it *is*, or that Kasta might be a disastrous king and I have a civic duty to stop him. It's that this is how I can reclaim the power Kasta stole from me when he first marked my wrist. This is how I'll make him regret, every day from here forward, the choice he made in the caves.

This is how I can get even.

"All right," I say. "What do I need to do?"

IV

I was wrong, a moon ago, when I thought walking down the stairs as the Crossing's sacrifice was the most nerve-wracking thing I'd ever do.

No—watching the Mestrah and the priests emerge from the back room with my worst enemy, who now looks untouchable in a white tunic embroidered with gold, while the people drop to their knees and a horn bellows the restart of the coronation: this is far worse. Not to mention that if Jet is wrong about my mark, this little stunt will likely land me in prison. And if we're right . . .

My gaze shifts to Kasta, who has stopped where Jet once stood and turned to face the thrones. If we're right, I might find myself wishing I'd been taken to prison.

In the travelers' tales, this would go down with flair: I would denounce Kasta in extravagant fashion, and the people would lift me on their shoulders and carry me to the front of the room, where I'd bow just in time to have the Mestrah set a crown on my head, and rise to greet my new country. Cheering would erupt, evil would be vanquished, parties would ensue. Instead, even though I'm standing, quite visibly, in the exact spot Kasta entered from at the back of the aisle, literally no one glances over due to how absorbed they are with the front of the room. I suppose I can't blame them. In a typical tale, the surprise-I'm-not-dead prince returning to claim his throne would, indeed, be the biggest shock of the story.

Oh, good people of Orkena, you don't even know what you've

gotten yourselves into. You're part of *my* story now, and I apologize for all that's about to entail.

The Mestrah raises his arms and launches into the same introduction he made for Jet. *He* sees me, judging by his quick glare, but of course he doesn't stop the ceremony, because that would make this easy. I steel myself and start forward, a hundred beetles in my throat. I'm a third of the way to the dais before the crowd finally stirs, and even then, the Mestrah preaches on like nothing is wrong. Instead, as he accepts a bowl of incense from a priest, he nods to the guards behind Kasta.

Who turn around with their hands on their swords.

It's now or never.

"Mestrah," I say, stopping. "Kasta isn't the only one with that mark."

The crowd gasps as I unclasp my necklace and drop it to the floor. The queen's smile vanishes. The Mestrah closes his eyes like he wishes he could make *me* disappear as easily, but I hold my ground, even when Kasta looks sharply over his shoulder. I refuse to look at him. But I feel his gaze on me all the same—burning across my face, tracing the spiral beneath my throat; sliding down to the scar he left on me.

"Would anyone else like to lay claim to the throne?" the Mestrah snaps, challenging the crowd with a look. A few of them snicker, but no one dares speak. The Mestrah turns to the smiling—well, now unsmiling—High Priest once more.

"Test her," he says, and to the guards: "If anyone else comes forward, remove them immediately."

This will be worth it, I remind myself as whispers sift through the crowd anew. I straighten and push forward, my pulse a drum in my ears. The High Priest meets me at the base of the stairs. At Kasta's side. Where I focus fervently on the glitter of her striking orange eyes, and not on the prince beside me. She lifts the jar she used before and smears the white paste over my mark.

The symbol turns frigid on my skin, and where the paste crosses it, it burns gold.

It's real. Whatever spell Kasta used to make his fake mark react, I needed nothing to achieve the same. The feeling that I'm in over my head, that I'll come to regret this, claws up my throat. But I swallow it back. First I have to stop Kasta; then I can think about what this actually means.

The priest's hands drop, and she offers a slow nod to the Mestrah.

"Apos's blood," the Mestrah growls. He pulls a tired hand down his cheeks and looks to the crowd. "The coronation is postponed. You are all dismissed."

The people shout in confused excitement. My family clasps hands, looking both anxious and hopeful, and Jet ducks around a guard, smiling as he joins my side.

"That was perfect." He raises a protective arm around me as his gaze meets the fire in Kasta's. "Welcome back."

"Both of you. And Jet," the Mestrah barks, descending the stairs. "The war room. Now."

In retrospect, I might have agreed to this too easily.

You honestly thought it would be fine? I imagine people asking, when I tell them it took all of five minutes for me to decide the best course of action was not to run away and be safe, but to challenge for the throne a boy who has already proven that he'll kill for it. *Well, no,* I would answer. *I really was just out for revenge.* And the people would nod and share grim looks, probably over my mangled body as a priest read my last rites, because that's one very real way this could end.

What am I doing?

Jet touches my elbow, and I cling to the echo of his words: he believes I can do this, as strongly as I knew he could.

Blue-burning torches light the narrow corridor we walk, the brown marble of the space making it cave-like and cold. With four guards before us and four behind, the space feels especially cramped. The Mestrah and Kasta lead the way, torchlight rippling over the Mestrah's cape and the pearlescent white of Kasta's tunic. But though I try to focus anywhere else, my eyes keep slipping to the scar on Kasta's arm. His last words, his *apology,* keep grating in my ears. The pain of dying splinters in my bones, as does the failure I felt in that moment, when he decided to trade my life for *magic.*

Lightning flashes through my blood, and I exhale through my nose. At least this time I know what Kasta's fully capable of. This time, I won't be foolish enough to believe this can end peacefully.

The Mestrah stops before an arched doorway bordered in glowing runes.

"See that no one disturbs us," he says without turning. "And send for the Speaker."

Two of the guards bow and depart. The rest file to both sides of the doorway as the Mestrah steps through, and I follow with a painful flicker of hope, remembering the kind way the Speaker last spoke to me. If it's their advice the Mestrah is counting on, I know they'll be fair. They'll know my mark is real and Kasta's is not.

The runes etched into the threshold turn red beneath our feet. Blue fire races inside a tray that runs the perimeter of the room, triggered by the Mestrah's entrance, and overhead a massive brazier ignites with a *whoosh*, its shadow eclipsing the center of the long wooden table that takes up most of the space. At least fifteen chairs surround it, all made of a dark, polished wood. At the far end glistens a grand chair of frosted glass. Numet's swirling circle adorns its backrest in scythes of gold, and when the Mestrah sits, the symbol haloes his head.

His glare tracks me like a lion's. "Sit."

Kasta takes his place at the Mestrah's right. I'm tempted to take the chair directly in front of me, which is as far from them as I can physically be, but if there really is going to be a contest for the throne, I won't give Kasta the satisfaction of thinking I'm afraid of him. I move past shining paintings of soldiers wielding fire and ice to the Mestrah's other side.

The chair scrapes the floor as I pull it out.

And I can avoid it no longer. I remind myself that yes, maybe Kasta tried to sacrifice me, but he also *failed* to, and I meet his cold, guarded eyes as I settle in.

But where I expected the same challenge in response—he looks away.

"Now," the Mestrah says, rolling his fingers into his temples. "I want to know the truth of what happened in the caves."

Jet takes the chair to my side. "Fara, I left nothing out of what I told you—"

"Not from you," the Mestrah says.

He turns to Kasta, but the prince's eyes are on my gods' mark. When Kasta realizes I've noticed, his attention shifts to the empty room.

"This is the welcome you have for me?" he says, his smile sad.

"This is the welcome I have," the Mestrah growls, "after I've offered half my treasury to the public for the return of your body, and you fail to write me, even once, to say the accounts of your death are false."

Kasta grunts. "Perhaps I knew it would make no difference. Perhaps I knew you wouldn't believe me unless you saw the mark yourself."

As if his return as *dōmmel*, not as a son, is the only thing that matters.

"We will talk of this later." The Mestrah leans forward on the table. "Right now, every diplomat in that room is sending word to their leaders that Orkena's court is a circus act. We must assure them everything is under control. So I'll ask again. *What happened* in the caves?"

Kasta finally looks at me, those sapphire eyes I've seen in so many nightmares. My fists tighten as my memory paints the caves and the altar around us.

"I offered her to the gods," he says, and I can't stop a bitter laugh, because I know firsthand he wasn't thinking of the gods at all during that moment. "But when I drew the knife out, the Shifter interfered and forced me aside. Jet's Healer was able to spare Zahru's life." He searches my face, as if looking for the same lie I'm seeking. "I thought the Shifter would kill me. She dragged me into the desert and said she'd leave me to fate, as I—" He bites down on the words, but I know what he almost said. *As he did to his sister.* A muscle twitches in the Mestrah's jaw, and fury stretches again in my chest. "She left me there," Kasta finishes.

So Maia couldn't bring herself to kill him after all. That must have been the cry I heard at the end, when I assumed he'd died—but it was the pain of her moving him with his injuries. My heart twinges thinking of my friend, hoping she's enjoying her new freedom.

"But you were bleeding heavily from our fight," Jet says. "You would have needed immediate healing to survive."

"You would know." Kasta thumbs a scar on his chin. "I thought that, too: that you would be the death of me. I tore my cloak to stem the bleeding, but I still lost consciousness. When I woke . . ." He opens his hands. "I was wearing Numet's mark, and my wounds had closed."

"That's a fine fish tale," Jet snaps. "You always did like to use the gods for—"

"Jet," the Mestrah says.

"This entire situation is preposterous! Where has he been for a moon, especially if he woke up healed the next day? Why didn't our priests foresee his return? I'll tell you why. Because he's been hiding out there, nursing his wounds back to health to fit this story, while also researching the exact dimensions of Numet's mark and how to trick marking paste. The gods would *never* choose him—"

"You are no longer *dōmmel!*" the Mestrah snaps, though regret

47

flashes across his face as he says it. "And it is beyond you to understand the gods' will. Do not speak to me of it again."

Jet goes still, hurt shining in his eyes, and he drops into his chair, seething. I touch his arm, meaning to reassure him this is temporary, but a spark of anger jolts my finger and I snatch my hand away, panicking that the emotion is my own and that he'll feel it. But Jet doesn't look over.

Kasta crosses his arms, his lips tugging at the edges. Enjoying their father's disapproval being switched.

"Even so," the Mestrah says, "it does not matter *how* Kasta returned to us. His mark is true, and he will be Mestrah. My concern is how *you* have the same mark."

All three of them turn, and the pressure I felt in the crowd tightens around me once more. But this is my chance to end this. To prove Kasta's lying, to clap him in chains; to never think of him again.

I touch the mark, worrying my thumb over the spiral. "I've had it for a moon. There was a lot of bruising after Melia healed me"—I shoot a glare at Kasta—"and when it started to fade, this spot just never did."

The Mestrah nods. "And the knife's gift? Do you have its magic?"

My breath catches. *Do* I have it? The knife's magic, the ability to Influence people's minds, is the most powerful there is. That doesn't seem like something I could have and just not know about, but I think back on these last weeks, trying to remember if there was ever a time I felt I got my way too easily. Certainly no one has had trouble telling me no in regards to certain care for their pets. Hen and her *mora* have been just as stubborn as ever, but then, I haven't really been around *people* so much as animals—

Until today.

Until *today*.

I drop my hand, remembering the surge of nerves from Jet before he asked if I'd be his advisor; the woman in yellow's prickling desperation. Jet's anger just a moment ago . . . that I mistook for my own. Little sparks of feeling that I'm only noticing now, because in the stable, they would have blended in with the animals'. It doesn't seem like that could be Influence, but it must be *something*.

"I think something's interfering with my Whisperer abilities," I say. "Almost like . . . like I'm starting to feel *humans'* emotions, not just animals'."

The Mestrah's brow rises, and Kasta uncrosses his arms.

"Come here, Zahru," the Mestrah says.

I rise, slowly, not sure this is a good thing, but my desire to stop Kasta is greater than my worry for what the Mestrah will ask. Up close, the king is both beautiful and intimidating, his black hair long and wavy and strung along his cheeks with glass eyeballs that turn as one to watch me. His own eyes are stern and otherworldly, the deep blue of a desert storm.

He lifts his hands to either side of my face. "Growing sensitive to emotions is a fledgling indicator of a mental magic. If you have the knife's power, I will not be able to Read your mind, just as you will not be able to Influence mine. Mental magics do not work on persons of similar talent. Shall I put this to the test?"

The question alone is a test. To see if I will back down, if I will confess to faking my mark before he scrapes the truth out of my memory himself.

I breathe out and focus on his shoulders. "You may."

His fingertips touch my temples, fever-hot. I brace myself, not sure what it will feel like if I don't have the magic, overwhelmed by the possibility that I do. Of course it's at this point that I remember Jet's story about the Mestrah making a prisoner's eyes bleed by searching his memories, which is seriously the worst timing of any thought I've had in my life.

A moment passes. Two. The Mestrah's eyes open wide. "I cannot. You have the gift. You'll need training to hone your true ability, but it's there."

Stunned silence follows. I should be cheering at this confirmation, this definite proof that Kasta is lying, but it only hits me that much harder, what it means that my mark is real. That the gods trust me with *this*, too. It's humbling and terrifying, and I'm definitely not sure it's a wise decision on their part, and that's the most I can think about it right now, because otherwise I'm going to pass out.

It's Jet who speaks first, his voice quiet and strange. "Then you see, she's the one the gods marked. Kasta's must be false."

"It's not false," Kasta snaps, though he sounds shaken. "A High Priest confirmed it. It's the same as Zahru's."

"And the power?" the Mestrah asks. The pressure in the room shifts to Kasta. "Do you have it, too?"

Kasta hesitates, and even with my fingers still shaking, I'm able to summon a flame of triumph. This is it. We've finally cornered him, and now the Mestrah will be able to Read not only what Kasta did to me, but also where he left Sakira and what he's been doing this whole moon—when Kasta rises.

"I do," he says.

I share an exasperated glance with Jet. It's just been acknowledged that I have a *god's power*, and Kasta is still undeterred. Is there anything he hasn't prepared for? Except—I twist my fingers into my *jole*. Except he's grown up with a Reader for a father. *Rie*. Of course he knows how to get around this, too.

But I'm praying this is when he messes up.

The Mestrah raises his fingers to Kasta's temples, and I hold my breath.

Seconds pass like hours. I have been standing there a thousand years when the Mestrah's hands slowly drop to his sides.

"I cannot," he says. "Both of you possess it."

"No," I growl. "He's thought of this already. He knew exactly how you'd test him!"

The Mestrah sinks into his glass chair. "This is not something you can fake."

"But they can't both be real," Jet says. "There is one Mestrah. Fara, you have to know something's wrong."

Kasta jerks his head at me. "What's wrong is even considering that her mark could mean she's meant to rule. She's not royal. The power of the Mestrahs would die at her rise."

I laugh in disbelief. "And power *is* everything, isn't it?" How quickly he's forgotten when he had no power at all—and an idea hits me. "You know, *that's* what we should check. Test his Deathbringer magic again. Or will you claim the gods conveniently got rid of that, too?"

"Enough," the Mestrah says, his brows rising as he looks between Kasta and me. But Kasta remains infuriatingly calm in light of my accusation. *Try it*, his eyes challenge me. *Insist on a test, and see how I will humiliate you.* I could scream.

The Mestrah, who clearly believes my accusation no more than a petty insult, continues on. "I agree it's strange for two to be marked. But I'm also inclined to believe the meaning is closer to what Kasta theorizes, that he is meant to rule, and Zahru is meant for a position of honor, perhaps as a priest."

"*Mestrah.*" I know I shouldn't disagree with a god, but this is getting ridiculous. "It's strange because it's a *trick*. This is exactly how Kasta made me the sacrifice in the Crossing. Your priests believed him then, and it was a mistake—"

"Zahru." An icy edge slips into the Mestrah's voice. "My priests have already decided on that matter, and found your claim to be baseless. *I* have already acknowledged your purpose in this, as one meant to live and not to die. Now I declare Kasta's mark and his power to be true. Do you dare argue otherwise?"

I shrink back into my seat. Of course I don't dare argue otherwise. Not until I find further evidence, anyway.

The Mestrah grunts in finality. "At any rate, I am not asking you three what this means. For that, I will rely on the gods."

His gaze shifts to the door, where the Speaker leans against the arching frame, the curve of a smile on their face. They're dressed today in a shimmering tunic that shifts from red to purple in the flickering light, and a silken, square hat that sits atop their bald scalp. Thick, curling lines of gold paint their eyes. They incline their head at the Mestrah's notice, though I note they don't move their fingertips to their forehead as is custom.

"Mestrah," they say, violet eyes glittering in amusement. "I can't say, in my two thousand years, that I've ever seen a coronation quite like *that* before."

"Sit," the Mestrah says. "And explain this to me."

He opens his hands to Kasta and me, and the Speaker obeys, taking the seat beside Kasta. Their knowing eyes rove over Kasta's guarded face, then settle on me with refreshing warmth. After the volatile crowd and this tense conversation, the Speaker's calmness is as welcome as a silky bath.

"I don't want to say 'I told you so,'" they say in their pleasing tenor. "But I told you so."

Heat rises to my face remembering our last meeting, when they insisted I had power beyond what I was born with. Even now I know they don't mean my new magic.

"I'm not entirely sure what happened, Mestrah," they continue. "No sacrifice in the history of the Crossing has ever survived. But I do know much about the cost of magic. And I would surmise, by what I've heard of our young people's journeys, that the marks exist because *two* sacrifices were made in that cave. One of blood"—they nod to Kasta—"and one of self. The critical detail being that Zahru was not just a passive vessel in the ceremony, but offered her life willingly."

A stone hits the bottom of my stomach. No. *No.* The Speaker was supposed to say there could only be one true mark. That Kasta

53

is lying. They were supposed to say marking two was impossible, and I look to Jet for any hint that something's off, that there's still a loophole, but only his fear prickles through me when our eyes meet.

He has no argument for this.

And realization breaks over me like ice.

The paste flashing gold on Kasta's chest. His miraculous healing. The Mestrah stepping back in disbelief, confirming Kasta has the knife's power. They aren't tricks, and I have no way to stop him. Kasta has confidently met every challenge because *his gods' mark is real.*

The gods chose him for this.

They chose him.

"And what do the gods mean by it?" the Mestrah asks.

"I think it's quite clear," the Speaker says. "These marks are only ever given to Mestrahs. Thus conveying the gods' desire that they are *both* meant to rule."

V

"BOTH?" I choke out, as Kasta shoves up from his seat. Jet drops his face into his hands, a jolting confirmation that he believes this, and the advisor's band pinches my arm. I'm meant to rule. I'm meant to be *Mestrah*, and now I'll certainly get my chance to make a difference for those like me, except it won't be at Jet's side, it will be at Kasta's, whose mark is true, who is destined to rule despite everything he did, and who's already proven he'll trade anything again, including me, for power in an instant—

An even worse thought strikes me.

"Both," I manage. "As in *marriage*?"

"But she's a peasant," the Mestrah says, raising a hand for my silence, and for Kasta to sit. "She knows nothing of politics or war. Her position would be ceremonial at best, and disastrous if she had to make decisions in Kasta's absence. Surely the gods mean something else by it. A priest's position. Or an advisor's."

The Speaker folds their hands. "Since the world began, the gods have never made a mark they did not intend. They trust her. And so must you. But I did not say she would be his consort." The Speaker glances at me, a look of reassurance. "Marriage is not what the marks intend, unless both parties wish it. The marks intend two Mestrahs. Two perfectly equal rulers. Anything they wish to put into law, both will need to agree on."

I look in panicked relief at Jet, though his smile is brief and pained. This still doesn't solve the problem of having to rule beside my worst enemy, but at least this gets rid of the awkward expectation for heirs.

Kasta grits his teeth. "But there have never been two Mestrahs. It will be impossible to get anything done."

"Anything terrible, yes," I mutter.

Kasta shoots a glare at me before turning to his father. "*Valeed*, you are the final say on anything the gods ask. It doesn't matter if ruling is what they intend. If I am to protect this country, I cannot be tied to this. Make her an advisor."

"Kasta." The Mestrah's tone sharpens, though I feel his aggravation is more for the entire situation than his son's words. "It is a Mestrah's duty to explore the reasons the gods have asked for this, not to blindly reject it. If I challenge their decision to mark her, then I must challenge the mark on you as well."

Jet, who I'd started to worry had frozen into silence, drops a heavy hand on the table. "And should you not?" He shakes his head. "Why are we even questioning Zahru's eligibility when *he* was the one who abandoned his own sister to starve to death in the desert? Or maybe you've forgotten Sakira's First, Alette, never came home either, or that Kasta tried to kill me, and nearly *did* kill Zahru—"

The Mestrah raises a hand in warning. "Jet—"

"You can't possibly mean to allow this—this *murderer* to rule! If that was how he acted without power, how do you think he'll act with it?" Kasta opens his mouth, but Jet cuts him off. "When I came home from the Crossing, you commended me for standing up for what I believed in. You said this was a new age for Orkena, one built on mercy and not ambition. You said it was how you knew I was *ready*."

His voice cracks, and I want to reach for him, but this part feels like my fault, and I stay still. It was Marcus, Melia, and me who assured Jet that his caution, his gentleness, was exactly what made him fit to lead, when he would have preferred not to stay in Orkena at all. I gave him this dream. I gave him this heartbreak.

Regret weakens the Mestrah's frown. "I know. And I am sorry, my son. But as you're learning, sometimes even I am wrong. The gods see beyond single moments in time. If they found Kasta's methods unforgivable, and yours preferred, you would already be Mestrah. But they stopped your ceremony today. They've made clear their plans for you are elsewhere."

"So it means nothing." Jet's eyes glisten. "What I did."

The Mestrah doesn't answer, and my heart twists at his implied agreement. This is so backward. In the stories the selfless prince is always rewarded, and the selfish one locked away. I shift in my seat, the unfairness of it burning through my chest.

"It didn't mean nothing to me," I whisper angrily.

Jet glances my way. But he doesn't smile.

The Speaker straighens a bird skull ring on their finger. "If I may, Mestrah. It seems Prince Jet has a point: there is cause for doubt on both sides, and the situation is certainly unusual. Why not verify with the gods that this is their will? Perhaps Zahru could take the harvest season to adjust to the court, and in the meantime, you could judge Prince Kasta's methods in contrast to your expectations. If all goes well, you can feel confident in crowning both."

The Mestrah taps his thumb on his glass throne. "Delay their coronation, you mean? A trial period for each?"

Kasta has gone very still. "What do you mean, *for each*?"

"It would be fairest," the Speaker says, ignoring Kasta. "And that way both must cooperate, versus making one strive to prove herself while the other feels his place is secure."

Hope flushes my veins, Kasta's panicked gaze shifts to his father, and Jet finally gives me the smallest of smiles. If the Mestrah agrees to this, we may not have stopped Kasta outright, but we'll at least have made *something* harder on him. And if we're lucky, he'll mess up on his own and lose the crown all the same. Which also means I run the same risk, but I'm finding that far less terrifying than going back out there right now and watching a crown drop on Kasta's head.

Oh gods, please agree to this.

The Mestrah thumbs a diamond in his braided beard, and Kasta slowly shakes his head.

"You can't really be considering this," he says, pain shifting through his voice. "Your precious Jet throws out accusations like he didn't nearly kill *me*, like Zahru didn't leave me to the same fate as Sakira! I have walked through *fire* for this. I've had to prove myself a thousand times more than any king—"

The Mestrah nods. "Then it will be easy to do it once more."

Kasta gapes, and a flash of vengeance pushes through me as he shoves back in his chair.

"I agree, Speaker," the king continues. "There is no harm in verifying, and we have a little time yet to spare. So it shall be." He sits forward, even as Kasta looks ready to explode. "Kasta, Zahru, I hereby declare you both *dōmmel*, with your coronation to take place in a moon's time. During this I will observe how you work together, and how you address the problems I give you. You will both learn to use your new magic. Zahru, you will begin classes appropriate to your station and ability. And while I realize there is *much* you two need to work through"—he glances between us, and Kasta relaxes with a bitter laugh—"your focus should be on proving why your partnership is best for Orkena. I'll take anything less as a sign this is not meant to be. So be warned now that if either of you hinders the other, or proves unwilling to yield for the sake of this country, I will demote that person to advisor on the coronation day."

Kasta scrubs his hands down his face. "This isn't happening."

The Speaker straightens their tunic. "Glad to have been of service, Mestrah. But I wonder if you might give Zahru just a bit more time? A moon isn't much, considering everything she'll need to learn."

The Mestrah sighs. "I cannot delay it longer. The High Priests have foreseen . . ." He stops, and I recognize the wall that builds over his face, given how often I've seen Kasta do it. "Change is coming. There must be a new ruler by then."

The Speaker shrugs, but I smile in appreciation for them trying.

"And with that, we are definitely finished." The Mestrah pinches the bridge of his nose. "I'm tired, my elixir is wearing off, and the entire continent is waiting for my statement. Eris?"

One of the guards enters the room and presses his fingertips to his forehead.

"Summon a scribe and my advisors. Jet, take Zahru and have the servants set up a room for her in the royal wing. Speaker, thank you for your wisdom. And Kasta . . ." The Mestrah considers his eldest son, his mouth thinning. Sakira's abandonment; Kasta's silence. I have a feeling Kasta is about to learn exactly how the king feels on both matters. "Wait for me in Sabil's temple."

◇

Jet and I walk side by side in the marbled hall, though our minds are a thousand worlds apart.

The pressure of what he's lost, of Kasta's victory, of what this means for *me* presses around me like deep water. I'm meant to be queen. I'm meant to be *Mestrah*. Orkena's problems are now mine—everyone's problems are now mine—and I won't be getting my revenge on Kasta, because I will be expected to cooperate, I will be expected to *rule*, and as much as I want to feel shocked, overwhelmed, humbled that I even get the chance to prove myself worthy of this . . . all I see are two people before the thrones.

Kasta and me.

Together, lifelong rulers of Orkena.

I've passed a mosaic of firestone gems and nearly bumped into a protruding torch before I notice Jet is no longer beside me. He's stopped a few paces back, and a stone turns in my throat as I take him in. The gods' symbols on his arms have smeared; wrinkles mar his royal tunic. One hand presses against his brow, and I see him again before the Mestrah, saying that nothing he did mattered.

I lean back against the wall. "I'm so sorry."

He presses quick fingers between his eyes and forces a smile. "You are definitely the last person who needs to apologize. This isn't your fault. I'm much angrier that my father could even *consider* Kasta ruling, after what he's done. And that I—" His jaw works. "It doesn't matter. The 'gods' have gotten their way; far be it from my father to make up his own mind. Are you all right?"

I shake my head. "It *does* matter. You should be the one with the mark. You're perfect for this, you deserve to be king . . ." I grit my teeth. "You did everything right. I hope you know that."

Jet sighs and pushes off the wall. "I just thought I had it figured out, you know? I'd already drafted treaties to strengthen our alliances, put in a proposal for world games to build bonds between our kingdoms . . . I was going to make it a law that the Crossing could never happen again. I went from not having any ideas about how I'd rule to envisioning years of it. And now I'm going to have to watch *him* do it instead."

"And me," I offer unhelpfully, my stomach twisting. "Sorry. I don't think that makes it better."

"Like I said, you don't need to apologize." But he thinks about that, torchlight glancing off the gold lining his eyes. "Though it does make it a little better, knowing you can veto whatever ruthless plans he has in mind."

"Oh, trust me. There will be so much vetoing. There will be vetoing of vetoing."

"I'm fairly certain that would just undo your veto."

"Then I'll re-veto. He won't be getting away with anything." We round a corner, back into the main foyer where the walls open around us, high and white—and a new worry itches under my skin. "Of course, he can veto my ideas as well. So I probably *shouldn't* veto everything. Otherwise it'll just be a veto spiral and literally nothing will get done." I freeze. "Which is exactly what he said in there." I grip Jet's arm. "Gods, did I just agree with him? Am I going to be agreeing with him on murdering people by the end of the week?"

Jet's eyes narrow. "Can we circle back to when I asked whether you were all right?"

"What?" I smile, widely. "Why wouldn't I be? I'm great. Never been better." I let go of him and smooth his sleeve. "I'm going to live in a palace, and see you every day, and have chocolate for every meal, and maybe never ever leave my room."

"Ah. That's a no, then."

"So maybe I'm a little worried about seeing Kasta all the time. And trying to learn how to use a god's power, and being responsible for stopping a war—"

"Zahru—"

"And I'll admit, I'm definitely nervous about memorizing years' worth of schoolwork on top of all this, which reminds me"—I clap—"I should probably learn how to read! But it'll be fine, right? I've got four entire *weeks* to master what Kasta's learned over seventeen *years*. It'll be fine. I'm fine. This is fine!"

Jet grabs my hands, which have been wildly gesturing, and presses them together in his.

"Yes," he says. "You will be fine. Because you do have *some* time, and you have help. You don't have to learn everything tomorrow."

I puff my bangs out of my eyes. "You're right, I'm overthinking this. Kasta will probably kill me again before that happens."

"He will *not*," Jet snaps, dropping my hands. "First of all, because I will break him in half if he tries, and second, because even his gods' mark won't protect him from the charges that result from a royal assassination. He'd be executed. I don't think that's a risk even he's willing to take."

I let out a shaky breath.

"Truly," he says. "We'll get through this. You are one of the most determined, adaptable people I've ever met. You've been through much more than any one person should. But you stood up to Kasta without hesitation. You accepted this drastic change of plans with an incredible amount of grace."

My laugh is hysterical.

He shakes his head. "Give yourself more credit. If that had been me—before I met you, anyway—I'd already be at the stables, grabbing that horse I gave you to take me as far away from here as possible." He sets his hands on my shoulders. "You can do this."

His fingers are soft, reassuring, and I close my eyes, trying to collect myself. I'm still terrified. There are still a thousand things I need to do in far too little time, but for a moment I let myself sink into the peace I feel just being with Jet, and accept that this is part of my future, too. And I make myself stop focusing on the things I'm afraid of, and remember how I got here in the first place.

I am the girl who made Kasta yield without a sword. I should have died, but I'm still alive. I was born to serve, but now I'll rule.

I raise each truth around me like armor. As overwhelming as all of this is, if the Speaker says the gods chose me for this, if the Mestrah himself is willing to give me a chance . . . then I must give myself a chance, too. I can still change who triumphs at the end of this story. I can still prove that the sacrifices Jet made, that *I* made, matter.

I look into Jet's eyes and nod.

I will prove I'm not a mistake.

It goes without saying that the first thing I do as *dōmmel* is ask Jet to be one of my advisors. Which goes about as awkwardly as when he asked, not only because it's such a strange reversal of our exchange this morning, but also because I try to give him the armband back. At which point I'm gently reminded that his bicep is much bigger than mine, and he'll need to have another one made. But he says yes, of course, and I feel accomplished that in my first five minutes as crown princess, I've managed to do something other than screaming.

Jet excuses himself to find the servants who will prepare my quarters, and I meet my family at the top of the stairs to the royal wing.

Fara, Mora, and Hen are understandably not certain how to greet me, because it's not every day that your loved-one-turned-human-sacrifice goes on to emerge from someone else's coronation with a hijacked crown and a seemingly immortal nemesis. Mora is emotional, wiping her eyes and hugging me every few minutes; Hen is ecstatic and already plotting how I might conquer the rest of the world; Fara is much more somber, alternating between worry for the responsibilities I'll be taking on and who I'll be ruling with, and outright awe.

"My daughter," he says, his hands light on my arms. "Mestrah of Orkena."

Mora sniffles, wiping tears from her cheeks. "This is huge. No one from the working class has even been allowed to *marry* into the royal family, let alone rule."

"You are the hope for all of us." Fara smiles, and though a sliver of nerves runs through me at the weight of that, I straighten. For that's exactly what I plan to be. I will change things for people like us, who were told that we were born to work, that our worth is based on something out of our control.

I will change the entire system.

"Yes, Fara," I say.

I ask Hen if she'll join my advisor team, but while I expect her to cheer at being offered a job where other people's business is literally a part of her duties, she actually grows very serious. Before snatching my old advisor's band right out of my hands and saying she'll find me again after she's "taken care of a few things." I take that to mean she's accepted, and I choose not to ask what she means by the end of that sentence, as I do not want to think about nor be responsible for whatever crimes arise from it.

By the time Jet returns, I've cornered a servant and relayed to him my desire for permanent rooms for my family, a job in the royal stables for Fara, a job amongst the palace potionmakers for Mora, and cake for myself. It's admittedly at this point that I figure out this person is a Gardener and has no ability to make any of this happen, but bless him, he agrees to pass on my message to someone who can.

Jet watches him go, and bows with an arm over his chest to Fara and Mora. "We're already working on your permanent rooms, actually, which should be ready shortly." He gestures to the elderly woman next to him. "If you would accompany Ryka in the meantime, she'd be happy to assist you with any matters you may need to take care of in Kystlin."

My father mimics his pose. "Thank you, *aera*. We indeed have a few things we'll need to discuss." Fara claps a hand on my shoulder and looks between us with a heavy sigh. "I wish you were the brother she was ruling beside."

Jet flashes a weak smile, and I bid Fara and Mora goodbye with kisses to their cheeks. Mora holds me for double the time, reminding me in a whisper that she has potions that can make certain princes quite miserable if I need them, and then I am alone again with Jet.

Who rubs the back of his neck with a grimace. "Your room is ready, too."

This is not exactly the most excited way of conveying this, and I have the sudden, irrational fear that maybe I've been assigned a broom closet. "Gods, is it that awful?"

Jet chews his cheek. "I'm going to let you decide that."

VI

BY "let you decide that," Jet means "Yes, definitely, it's the worst," because the next thing out of his mouth is that the Mestrah sent an additional order along after we'd left the war room: that my room should be the one right next to Kasta's.

I stop before we've even moved ten steps.

"No," I say.

"I know," Jet says. "I was vocal about it as well. But my father thinks that the more you see each other, the more likely you are to cooperate or some nonsense, and he won't hear any objections."

"Can't I have my room set up in a different wing? Maybe in another city?"

Jet sighs. "I wish. We may be able to change the Mestrah's mind, in time. But we'll have to make do for now."

"This just seems like a terrible idea," I grumble, starting after him.

"I did ensure you'll have guards around the clock. And I've personally seen to it that there is no access between the rooms. If Kasta wants an audience with you, he'll have to get permission and come through the main doors like everyone else."

"You really think he's going to *ask*?"

"He's going to have to, if he wants your cooperation at any point." Jet nods to the guards outside his own room and gestures to the black, sword-engraved doors. "Here we are."

I look from him to the doors, certain this is some kind of test. "Jet. This is *your* room."

He rubs a faded spell on his forearm. "I'm aware. This is the other reason I was so vocal about the decision."

I begin forming the start of several sentences, in which I waver between asking if we've already been paired in some kind of arranged marriage, or if all advisors live with their Mestrah, which seems odd, and possibly I should have decided on one of those instead of what actually comes out of my mouth. "We're going to be sleeping together?"

The guards choke back laughs, and Jet considers this with a pained, albeit not entirely opposed, blink of his eyes. "No," he says, clearly caught off-guard by the turn this has taken. "What I mean is, I don't live here anymore. You've been given my room, since I was informed it no longer makes sense for me, as an advisor, to stay in the royal wing."

I blanch. "Are you kidding? Where are you going to stay?"

"I've moved to the officers' suites near my mother. And before you say anything more, it's fine, and you don't need to worry about it."

"Don't tell me it's fine. Nothing about this is fine for you. You just lost the crown, and now you've lost your room?"

Jet shifts, tapping the door with nervous fingers. "It's just walls and furniture. Consider it an unofficial item on your list, and part of my never-ending apology. Maybe we could go in?"

I'm feeling increasingly uneasy about all of this, but of course I nod, and Jet pushes open the doors in relief. My throat clenches as I take in the new decorations. Gone are the sixty weapons along the west wall, replaced by a harp and a circle of thin-legged couches.

Gold satin drapes the giant four-poster bed instead of blue, and crystal-topped tables for dining gleam outside on the balcony, where practice swords and reading chairs once sat. Gossamer curtains shimmer like fireflies before the windows, an airy gold instead of silver.

I think of the dusty feed room I grew up in, the cot I slept on last night across from Hen. But it's a little hard to appreciate that all this finery is mine when it feels like I've stolen it.

Jet watches me, the hint of a real smile in his eyes. "Now it's a proper ballroom."

I step in farther, past a couch with lion's paws for feet, running my hand over its polished wooden back. Wishing I knew what to say. Wishing I knew how to fix this for him. I'm just starting to turn when a fuzzy head pops out from around the archway to the pool room, and Jade streaks over in a blur of spots.

Human! she squeaks in her sweet voice. *Play! Toy?*

"You're here, too!" I scoop her up, though my heart still twists. "Now it's perfect."

Jade, like most kittens, is not impressed with this or any displays of affection, and wiggles incessantly. *No love. Play! Play!*

"All right, all right," I grumble, setting her down. I scoop a feathered cat toy from the floor and throw it to the other side of the room. Jade tears after it, as fast as an arrow.

Jet watches her go, the afternoon light deepening his coronation tunic to a river blue.

I trace the cactuses carved into the back of the couch. "What can I do to help?"

Jet sighs, and drops into a chair with oxhorns crossing its backrest. "Be an absolute pain in Kasta's side from now until the day he dies?"

I nod. "I can do that."

Jet chuckles and scrubs his hands down his face. "Gods, what an absolute mess."

I drop my hand from the couch and sink onto one of its feather-stuffed cushions. Across the room, Jade throws the feathered toy in the air, catches it, and shreds it in a matter of seconds. "Would it make you feel better to imagine Kasta messing up this moon, losing the crown, and having to move into a tiny room, too?"

Jet scoffs. "Yes."

"I mean, it could happen." I raise a shoulder—and a shiver runs through me as a new idea takes hold. I thought the Mestrah had taken away my chance at making Kasta sorry . . . but now I'm wondering if he handed it right to me. "Maybe we could help it happen."

Jet raises his head. "What do you mean?"

"Well, Kasta still has to cooperate with me to prove we can work together, or he could get demoted, too. I could push him toward that. Make ridiculous, peaceful suggestions that I know he'd never agree to, and tell the Mestrah he's being difficult."

Jet taps the arm of his chair. "I don't know. That could also come off as *you* being difficult, and we don't want it to backfire." But I can tell by the spark in his eye that he likes this idea. "Though we might be able to get him on something else. If we can find plans he's drawn to inflame the war, for example. Some kind of proof he's dangerous as a ruler, or unstable."

A promising angle, since we're talking about the boy who once told me the last thing Orkena needed was mercy.

"All right," I say, settling against the couch. "So maybe we start with why it took so long for Kasta to come back, and see if there's anything to that? Do you think he was meeting with foreign leaders?"

Jet leans down to pick up the shredded toy Jade has dropped at his feet. "No, it would make no sense for him to do that without guards or without officially being named *dōmmel*. I'm still trying to figure out how he even survived so long on his own, especially considering his condition at the end of the race." He bounces the toy on his knee, and Jade crouches, eyes wide. "The sacrificial knife has no power to heal. Of course, Kasta can claim whatever he wants, since he's alive, but . . ." He chucks the toy and looks to me. "You knew Maia better. Do you think she would have taken him to a Healer? Maybe he bargained her freedom for his life?"

"She already had freedom," I say, my heart twinging in hopes that's still true. "We destroyed her binding collar as soon as we left Kasta. The army can't control her anymore."

"She wouldn't have been free for long if she'd really killed a prince. The Wraithguard has been looking for her, and they would have hunted her until they found her. They'll relax their efforts now that Kasta has returned." He shrugs. "It would have been a good bargaining chip."

I frown, wondering if it could be that simple. It still seems like it took a long time for Kasta to come home. And Maia had been so angry with him, doubly so after he'd sacrificed me. Would she really have just let him go? If freedom was all she wanted, she could have run after I was healed and left him there.

"Maybe," I hedge. Across the room, Jade springs over the toy and sideways onto the bed, and for a moment I picture a different leopard in her place: Maia with her glittering fur and sleek muscles, half a smile on her feline lips.

"But why not just *tell* us that?" Jet muses. "Why this elaborate story about being abandoned in the desert?"

I don't answer. An uncomfortable feeling is working up my neck, and the longer I watch Jade, the stronger it grows.

"There's no law against bargaining with Shifters," Jet mutters. "But if he was recovering in a village, it should have only taken a week or two at most to come home . . ."

Jade bites into a pillow and looks wildly toward us, spotted tail thrashing. A tent and a pale light potion converge on my vision: Kasta's downcast face, his confessing to having hunted a Shifter years before. His lingering anger at Maia, the girl who got in his way.

And there she was again at the end of the Crossing, standing between him and his magic.

"Jet," I whisper. I don't want to say what I'm thinking. Because that will make it real, and for so many reasons, I don't want it to be real. "How does the Shifter curse pass from one person to another?"

Jet freezes, and in his face is a horrible kind of confirmation, so that even before he answers, I'm starting to shake.

"*Rie*," he says. "I'm such an idiot. Of course. When the curse passes to a new host, *it heals them*, once and completely, to ensure the curse lives on."

"She could have left him in the caves," I say, grasping for any other explanation, for a way that this is wrong. "Maybe she did. Maybe someone else found him, and there was another way out . . ." There wasn't. I was trapped in those caves, I know there wasn't, but I can't stop. "Because it makes no sense why she'd take him somewhere else unless she wanted him dead, right? If she left him, the Crossing Healers would have helped him." My nails dig into my arms. "But they didn't. But he's not dead."

Jet says nothing, and my vision blurs. Because I'm realizing that I've just talked myself in a circle.

"And if you had magic for the first time . . ." Realization creeps up my neck like cold water. "You would need time to learn how to master it, right? You wouldn't want to return to the palace too soon. Especially if getting caught using that magic would put you in chains."

I close my eyes. Something dark and sinewy stirs in my chest, a feeling more suffocating than anger.

"Tell me there's no way I'm right," I whisper as Jet's weight sinks the cushion beside me. "Tell me she's still alive."

Jet's hand is warm on my back. "I'm sorry. I know she meant something to you."

"It's not fair," I growl, shoving to my feet. "Maia was finally *free*. She was going to start over—" I see her shy smile when she called me her friend; I see her in leopard form, snarling as she leapt between me and Sakira. "She shouldn't have come back for me."

"Don't you dare blame yourself for this," Jet says, standing in turn. "If she's gone, there's only one person at fault."

"Damn him." I pace to the other side of the couch, fury flashing through my ribs. "That's how he survived the desert, too. Maia had a falcon pelt. He wouldn't even have needed to trap one. Gods, *Maia*." I pull my hair. "Please tell me this is something we can use. This is the highest form of sacrilege, right? More than illegal? Eternal damnation? Against everything a crown prince is supposed to stand for?"

Jet nods. "Most adamantly so. Gods, I—" He shakes his head, bewildered. "There really isn't anything he won't do now, is there? If he could kill her."

"So we take this to the Mestrah." My blood is lightning. "Tell him our theory, and Kasta loses far more than the crown."

"Yes . . . and no." Jet starts for the study, beckoning me to follow. "It won't be as easy as that. His gods' mark is still real, and trust me, from my years of rivalry with Kasta, an accusation isn't going to be enough. The Mestrah knows how much you loathe him, and we can't risk our claim being dismissed as slander. We need to do this carefully, and we need to find proof even my father can't overlook."

I follow him into the study. This room hasn't changed as dramatically as the bedroom, but it still looks more barren than before. The same amber-brown maps cover the walls, and the same red slab desk sits at one end with its four wooden gods holding up the surface. But the quills and sword sculptures that once circled the top have gone, replaced by a collection of metal measuring tools and blank scrolls.

Jet fingers through a row of jewel-colored tomes set into the wall and selects a blue one with a spine as wide as my hand. "We need something indisputable that we can bring to my father," he says, flipping through the handwritten pages. "Something Kasta can't deny or attribute to the gods. Can you think of anything from your time with Maia?"

I remember Maia's inhuman strength, and that she could run for hours without tiring. Neither of which we can force Kasta to prove before an audience. Obviously changing into an animal is the biggest one—also impossible to prove without Kasta's cooperation. And then my blood sparks, remembering how I got to know Maia at all.

"I could hear her thoughts," I say. "Even if she wasn't in animal form. We could talk to the palace Whisperers and have them confirm they can hear his thoughts, too, and that should definitely be enough to convict him!"

Jet slams the book. "Well, that was easy. I forgot who I was talking to." He snickers—and goes still. "Except . . . wait. You can hear his thoughts?"

I chew my cheek, recognizing the immediate problem with this. "Ah—no. Actually, that's really weird, now that I think about it."

Jet reopens the tome with a sigh. "Actually, that makes sense. He has Influence now, remember? So you can't use any kind of mental magic against him."

My blood jerks. Fara has never referred to our magic as anything but a basic magic. "Whisperer magic is a mental magic?"

Jet shrugs. "One that happens between humans and animals, yes."

"And yet when it's only between humans, it's considered one of the most powerful abilities in the world."

"I'm just realizing that."

I blink. "I've been living my life in a feed room, Jet."

A trace of my favorite smile pulls his lips. "And what are you going to do about that, *dōmmel*?"

Heat pricks my neck. The world that I began weaving in my mind with Fara, one where these similarities between us and the elite powers are all brought to light, stitches tighter in my mind. "I'm going to fix it."

I expect Jet to beam at this, but oddly his smile flickers, and something anxious brushes my skin.

"Good," he says.

He pages through the text to the center. I watch him a moment, contemplating whether to ask what's wrong, but even though I didn't mean to use my new magic, I'm not sure he'd appreciate my knowing what he's feeling when he's clearly not ready to share. And so I set my mind back to the task at hand. To Maia, and what made her unique. The way she moved is hardly evidence, and while her vivid yellow eyes were compelling, that must have been how she was born, because I didn't notice a difference in Kasta's at all. Maybe when she slept, or what she ate—

Oh *gods*, what she ate.

"I'm pretty sure his eating someone else could not be passed off as divine," I say.

Jet gags. "Ugh. I forgot about that. No, that's definitely not natural in any sense." He taps the book. "That's hard to prove, though . . . he can still eat regular food, it just won't nourish him. But we could watch if he sneaks out at strange hours to hunt. It's a start." He turns the page, where a skeletal drawing of a Shifter changing into a jackal sends scorpions down my spine. "Here we are. Shifter signs: loss of appetite, irritability, insomnia . . ."

His finger trails over the ink, but the longer he stays quiet, the more anxious I become. Because the entire point of Shifters, of course, is that they're able to hide in plain sight. They're just themselves, until they're not, and Kasta has already proven he's very good at hiding what he is.

"'Laws,'" Jet reads. "'A Shifter shall be inducted into the army, for they should not be killed' . . . 'removal of the tongue' . . . oh."

Something heavy threads this new silence, and I peer at the page. "What does it say?"

"I've just been reminded of one very bad thing, and introduced to one that's even worse." His brown eyes meet mine. "You remember why we cut out Shifters' tongues?"

A memory of Maia opening her mouth flashes over my vision, and I shudder. "Because they can mimic voices?"

"Right. Which means don't speak to *anyone* about important matters if you can't see them. Even me or Hen . . . especially me or Hen."

"All right." I shudder at the idea of following Jet's voice down a dark hallway, only to find Kasta waiting at the end.

"The second one is very bad. I don't actually want to tell you."

I close my eyes. "What is it?"

Jet points to a block of writing outlined in red. "This law says that all Shifters must be persecuted, even if they're royalty, except that a Mestrah may take on the curse themselves without penalty, per the gods' guidance."

My stomach twists. "So if we don't prove Kasta is a Shifter before he's crowned . . . we can't stop him?"

"Right, because we won't be able to prove *when* he made the change. He could claim he went hunting after the coronation, as directed by the gods."

I press my fingers between my eyes. I was really certain things couldn't get worse than discovering Kasta is now literally a monster, but here we are. Now, on top of my schooling and the war and the Mestrah's tests and learning an entirely new type of magic, I have one moon to reveal Kasta as a Shifter before he becomes one of the deadliest powers in the world. And I become trapped permanently beside him, wondering when he'll turn me into his next meal.

The world tilts, and I grip the table. "And we need indisputable proof?"

Jet starts in with reassurances, that we'll find something, that Kasta is bound to mess up, but I've stopped listening. On the page opposite the laws, a sketch of Shifter armor gleams, runic symbols glowing on its beetle shell surface. Beside it dangles the binding collar that commands the Shifter, a copy of the necklace Kasta wore to keep Maia under control during the Crossing.

I run my finger over the square runes. "What about this?"

Jet looks over. "What about it?"

"Could we make one for him? We could literally make him Shift in front of the Mestrah."

The concern on Jet's face is not the reaction I was expecting. "It's highly illegal to create a controlling necklace without proof. This technology will work on anyone, Shifter or not. If we go this far, and we're wrong, there will be very serious consequences. Of which losing your crown would be the least."

He's watching me like this should bother me, too. But the part of me that might once have cared, that would have been horrified at the suggestion, feels distant and numb. "So we test it before we bring him to your father. Make him Shift for us first. But you *know* it's going to work, and I don't see how we can risk doing anything else. He can't be Mestrah. He'll shove us further into this war, and he'll sacrifice whatever and whoever he needs to to win. We don't have time to wait for him to mess up."

Jet exhales through his nose. "And if he's not a Shifter?"

A vicious kind of heat slithers through me. I can't believe I'm about to say this, but in Kasta's case, it feels justified. "Then I use the necklace to make him renounce his claim to the throne, and he moves somewhere far away. No one ever finds out what we did, and he's gone."

Jet looks between me and the drawing, his gaze dropping once to the scar on my chest. A thousand unreadable thoughts flash across his face, and again comes that breath of anxiousness, like static zipping over my arms.

He's not smiling when he says, "All right."

VII

I want to visit the palace Runemasters right away, because that's where Jet says the process for creating a necklace starts. But Jet wants to consult Marcus before we do something this serious, which reminds me I still need to ask Marcus and Melia if they'll be my advisors. The excitement of seeing them again is almost enough to brighten my mood. When we last parted, they'd just helped me locate Fara and Mora in Kystlin, but saying goodbye felt like leaving one family for another.

Except the moment Jet and I start down the columned hallway to find them, three people converge on us. The first is the Royal Materialist, Hen's new employer and the woman who gave me her lotus boots what feels like a million years ago before the Crossing. She doesn't recognize me, but before I can mention that we've already met, she's taken measurements of my waist, neck, arms, and legs, and promised she'll be back by morning with a new wardrobe. The second person is a young handmaiden who says I'm to come with her to tour the palace and meet the tutors, priests, and other staff I'll be seeing often, and the last is a steely eyed advisor, who has come for Jet—the Mestrah needs him. Jet and I share an exasperated glance, he promises he'll be back with Melia and Marcus as soon as he can, and we go our separate ways.

The tour, and meeting the staff, takes the rest of the day.

By the time I return to my suite, my feet ache, a hundred new names and faces cram my head, and I hold a scroll of my upcoming schedule—which I reminded the handmaiden I can't read—that I'm afraid to open, because it looks thick enough to unroll over half my considerably long room. The way the day has been going, I'm not even surprised when Jet arrives minutes later with the news that Marcus and Melia have also been called away to new duties, and that we have to wait until tomorrow to see them.

Jet collapses onto the golden couch, an arm draped over his eyes. "And the meeting with my father was useless. He only halfway apologized for how things are now, before asking if I'd train the entire army to use swords. You know, in case Wyrim's technology advances so much that *all* our magic becomes useless." He sighs. "I love him, but sometimes it really is like talking to a tome. All knowledge and logic, no heart."

"I'm sorry," I say, perching on a nearby stool. My mind still spins over a hundred things outside of this room.

Jet drops his arm to peer at me. "How was your day?"

In answer, I hand him one end of the schedule and roll the rest down his body like a blanket. Past his waist, past his knees, over his sandals. He watches the far end drop sadly over the arm of the couch, where it unfurls another meter.

"That . . . is a lot," he says.

I nod solemnly. "I don't even know what it says."

Jet sits up, makes space for me on the couch, and begins to read.

To my relief, I discover the schedule covers two weeks and is only half filled with classes and duties. The other half shows maps of everything in the palace, and thus tomorrow's packed agenda only draws quiet tears to my eyes and does not result in the full-out weeping I was expecting.

As to handling Kasta, we can't move forward without Marcus, so Jet and I reluctantly say goodnight. After he shows me how to free the hidden dagger from the bedside table, just in case.

And then I am alone in this giant, house-sized room.

It's odd to think this will be the first time I've ever slept alone. Fara and I shared a room in Atera, separated by bags of grain, and if I wasn't there, I was at Hen's, buried in pillows on her floor. Even during the Crossing, I was always fixed to someone's side. I'm realizing now just how comforting it was to have someone else there, even if asleep. The quiet presses over me like a weight, like the silence of a tomb.

No wonder the royals are always canoodling in places they shouldn't, when this is the alternative.

But I'm proving that I belong here, that I can rule as well as Kasta, and that definitely starts with being able to sleep alone in a luxurious suite. I check the golden lock on the balcony doors— twice—and ensure the guards are still outside my room, and lastly try to convince Jade to sleep beside me, but she literally tells me she's too busy and darts off into one of my seven side rooms.

It's fine, I assure myself, as I lie on my back in the dark. I have a dagger, the room is secured, Kasta isn't going to sneak in and eat me. I don't need to think about every travelers' story I've ever heard in which people are left alone and then possessed by ghosts or hauled away into burning portals. I focus on the little carved cities in the ceiling instead, above which tiny inlaid stars now sparkle.

I'm just starting to doze when a corner of the mattress sinks.

I snap awake, ready for war. But it's only Jade, spots like drops of ink on her golden sides, her face shadowed by the canopy. I sigh in relief and beckon her closer, glad that she might finally lie down with me. She starts over, and I lay back on the pillows, trying to calm my racing pulse.

She climbs onto my stomach, claws biting through my nightgown.

"Jade," I cough. "You're already too heavy for—"

She sits, her head tilting unnaturally quickly. Her thoughts are empty.

Her eyes are Kasta's vivid blue.

"Oh my gods," I breathe. *How did he get past the protection wards?* I lunge for the hidden dagger, but Kasta Shifts like a storm, his weight pinning me in place, his unruly hair curling like briars. His shoulders block out the windows and I grip the bedframe and twist free, hit my knees on the floor and sprint for the doors—Kasta streaks past me like a shadow. I slam into his chest. He catches my neck with one hand, his other digging into my arm.

I squirm and shove against him, but it's like fighting a wall.

"I heard you have plans for me," he whispers, his lips brushing my cheek. I growl and try to kick him, but something's wrong; I can't move my legs. "What a coincidence. I have plans for you, too."

My blood lurches as he kisses my neck, his teeth grazing the soft place beneath my jaw—then his mouth opens wide, and he tears into my throat.

◆

My scream ricochets from the ceiling.

The guards burst in, metal-feathered armor flashing, one holding aloft a knife of ice and the other a crackling ball of lightning. I kick free of the sheets and jerk against the headboard, gripping my neck where I swear I still feel the needle-fine pressure of teeth.

But the skin is whole. Early dawn glows at the edges of the curtains and over the tops of the furniture, silver and new.

I was asleep.

"*Dōmmel?*" asks the guard with the ice, his gaze darting to the corners of the room.

"Sorry." I drop my hand, still trembling. "It was just a nightmare. I'm all right."

They hesitate, the Stormshrike absorbing the lightning she made back into her hands. One last glance around the room and they touch their fingertips to their foreheads, back out, and close the doors.

From under the nearby couch, Jade pokes her head out.

Loud? she thinks. *Quiet now?*

I let out a shaky breath, hating that even though I know she can't be Kasta since I can hear her thoughts, a jolt still runs through me at seeing her. I rub the nerves out of my arms, and beckon her over.

"Yes," I say. "Quiet now. I'm sorry."

She trots over, tail high, watching me like she doesn't quite trust me not to scream again. But finally she leans into my hand. My palm tingles, remembering how she looked when she changed.

Because nightmare or not, this is yet another possibility Jet and I need to be wary of. Unlike in my dream, the wards in my room should actually alert the guards even if Kasta tries to enter as an animal, but the rest of the palace is not so protected. Not that I think Kasta would risk attacking me in any form with so many soldiers around, but he wouldn't need to to be dangerous. He could just be there, listening. A bird, a mouse . . . a cat.

The perfect eavesdropper. And I wouldn't even notice, unless I happened to see an animal there and started thinking about how odd it was that its thoughts were silent—

My hand stills on Jade's back, and I look down.

The perfect eavesdropper. But that works both ways. Because as a Whisperer, I can tell which animals aren't animals. And Kasta isn't the only one who can use them as spies.

I smile and lift Jade onto the bed. "Hey. Can you do something for me?"

I'm feeling so good about this plan with Jade that I actually drift back to sleep. Jade is now in charge of watching Kasta's balcony, and especially the birds in the garden, which she's very excited about. She'll tell me if any animals behave strangely, or if the birds suddenly scatter, indicating something unnatural is nearby. But most importantly, she'll tell me if Kasta leaves. I can't imagine he wants to be caught eating someone in the palace. The balcony is the easiest place he could slip out without the guards knowing he's gone, and then I could follow. And as long as Jade stays within the warded boundaries of my balcony—which I stressed she must—she'll be safe from Kasta impersonating her to become my nightmare.

She understood enough about the word *Shifter* to take that seriously, even so young.

I wake again to a knock at the door. Not much time has passed, I don't think—dawn glows brighter at the edges of the curtains, but the light is just turning golden. I sit up, still groggy, and very certain nothing on my schedule was supposed to happen until eight marks. But it occurs to me it could be breakfast, and I will never keep breakfast waiting. I pull a silken dressing robe off the back of a velvet chair and wrap it around me.

"Come in," I say.

Jet steps inside, looking refreshed and more himself in a tunic of royal blue—and startles when he sees me. "Wow, rough night?"

I touch my hair, which does indeed feel as though it's aspiring to become a sculpture. "Not one of my best," I admit.

"Sorry." He shuts the door. "That just kind of came out of me—how are you doing this morning?"

I slump into the armchair. "I mean, until we've stopped Kasta, the answer is probably always going to be *completely stressed.*" I tip my head against the backrest. "You don't have breakfast, do you?"

"Ah." Jet winces. "No. But I have good news!"

I sit up. "Good news?"

"And . . . also bad news. Which one would you like to hear first?"

Of course there's bad news. Hen is always warning me the royals can't go a day without something blowing up, but I really hoped that was an exaggeration. "Good news, please."

Jet turns a bronze statue of Klog, the falcon companion of the goddess of war, to face him on the dresser. "The good news is that my father is clearly taking your position seriously, because he's summoned both of us to an impromptu meeting with all ten of his advisors."

Nerves flash through me. "That's the *good* news? That I get to speak in front of ten advisors and the king without any warning?"

"It's a show of faith. The Mestrah wouldn't invite you at all if he intended you to become an advisor."

I exhale, acknowledging this is true, even if I still don't like it. "And . . . the bad news?"

"The bad news is that he'll also be assigning you and Kasta your first test."

I sigh, shaking my fingers through my tangled hair. "Great. One more thing to add to the schedule."

"I know. I'm sorry."

"When is the meeting?"

Jet gives me the same pained look as when I asked what time he was supposed to meet the priests for the coronation.

I drop my hands. "It's right now, isn't it."

"It's right now."

Without even a break for breakfast. I don't understand these people. This will be changing when I'm Mestrah, because I am just petty enough to make that kind of thing into a law. No meetings before food. I shove up from the chair, momentarily derailed from what is supposed to be a dramatic show of my displeasure because I need to get dressed, but I initially can't remember where the closet is. Finally I remember it's past the miniature glass boat displays and behind the harp, which a ridiculous set of directions for something now that I think about it, and I march irritably over and burst through the jade curtain—and my blood shifts.

This is the first time I've been in here since the Royal Materialist laid a sleeping gown and robe for me on the bed last night. How foolish of me to have assumed it would simply be a bigger version of a normal closet, with a few extra shelves and a chest.

This is a market square without vendors. Redwood shelves tower to the considerable ceiling, stacked with gowns of every fabric, color, and adornment—more clothes than I could wear in a lifetime. A crystal table in the middle displays jeweled beetles and necklaces of stamped coins, crowns of fresh lilies and tiny gods' charms, and mirrors cover the far wall, reflecting my shocked expression and making it difficult to see where the room ends. A brass bell gleams near the door, its delicate ringer shaped like a gazelle's horned head.

"Is everything all right?" Jet asks, because that's how long I've been standing here.

"Sure," I say, moving inside. The choices make me dizzy, but a shelf layered with golden *joles* seems as good a place to start as any, and I finger through silk threaded with crystals and satin that shifts like liquid under my fingers. One with red river reeds embroidered along its edges catches my eye, and I pull it free, shake it out—its creases vanish the moment it unfurls—and it falls into two pieces, one of which is either a belt or a cape.

"If it's any comfort," Jet calls, "I might be able to help with your test. Me and your advisors, I mean. We may be able to research something while you're with your tutors, for example."

"Thanks." I decide the bigger of the two pieces is the dress, wrap it carefully around me, and pull the second piece around my waist. The whole ensemble seems unusual when I consider it in the mirror, but honestly, most royal outfits look this way to me. The thin fabric warms against my skin like wool.

I emerge from the closet, still fussing with a knot at my shoulder.

"Oh," Jet says.

He does not say this with reverence or in the way you might want someone you are interested in saying this, like, *Oh, that looks very good on you.* This is the *oh* of someone on the brink of questioning his life choices.

"What?" I say.

Jet chuckles and pushes up from the couch. "That is sun silk, and unless you're planning to pass out from heatstroke before the meeting ends, you may want a different dress. Also, that's definitely not a belt."

I lift the side of the not-belt. "This is *supposed* to get warmer? Why is this even an option?"

"Here. Can I help you pick something out, so you don't get attacked by the cactus spire?"

I freeze. "There are things in here that *attack*?"

He correctly interprets my horror as a *yes, please, gods, help me,* and I wait graciously for him to enter the closet before I follow with far more skepticism. I've seen Hen work with plenty of unusual fabrics, but none of them ever turned on her. Imminent danger must come at a price only royalty can afford.

Jet browses the shelves and points out a folded gown of buttery emerald, its neckline embroidered with pearlescent spines. "For the record, that is cactus spire. It won't actually jump at you, but it likes to attach itself to its wearer in a very literal sense. Bonus points if you wear the spine bracelets and crown, which often need to be medically removed at the end of the day."

I give the stack of green *joles* a wide berth. "Again, at the risk of stating the obvious: *Why is this an option?*"

"Well, when you want to intimidate other countries, the right fabric inspires all kinds of fear as to the level of pain you can personally endure. It's all chest puffing, really. Here." He pulls free a square of shining silver. "Try star satin. It's woven with the cool of night, and has yet to try and strangle someone like the snakeskins."

I note the green-and-yellow snakeskins are also something to avoid before accepting this new *jole*, though my heart pinches in taking it. As if I didn't have enough to learn already, here's something so silly and simple the Mestrah didn't even think of putting it on my schedule, and yet I could have come out impaled by cactus spines if Jet hadn't warned me.

The feeling that it's too much, that I can't possibly do everything being asked of me, fills my throat like smoke. I swallow it back and force myself to focus on right now, one step at a time. The gown spills down from my fingers. In the light of the torches it shifts from white to black, like the sands on a starry night.

"I'll be right outside." Jet tips his head to the bell with the gazelle ringer. "We can also call the Royal Materialist, if you want help dressing."

"No, let me try again."

He slips out, and I pull the sun silk carefully off, feeling awkward with him being so close, feeling stranger that I don't know where we stand now. Do people still like people who assured them they belonged on a throne, then, however indirectly, took it from them, as well as their room and their closet? I know he's most upset with

Kasta, but when that's settled, it will just be me with his crown. Me reminding him from now until the end of time of what he almost was.

I slide the star satin on, knotting it at my hip, at my shoulders. The cape doesn't feel like it sits right, but hopefully Jet knows how to fix it. "All right," I say. "Better?"

Jet slips back in through the curtain—and this time, there is no judgmental *oh*.

"Much," he says, his gaze flickering down the gown. "But this one goes over one shoulder, not two. Can I fix it?"

I nod, turning as he undoes one of the knots, his fingers like feathers on my skin. In the mirrors, I look years older than the last time I stood in a royal gown, with handmaidens painting the sacrifice's symbols on my arms. Jet fixes the portion that makes the cape, where tiny glass beads form constellations: the leopard symbol of Tyda, goddess of patience; the antlers of her wife Talqo, goddess of healing. Wings for Rie, god of death. A housecat for Rachella, goddess of love. A scorpion, a rattlesnake, a balancing scale: Oka, Valen, Sabil. Aquila's scientific tools and Apos's chaotic swords.

Numet's spiraling sun shines on my chest like blood.

Jet secures the knot at my shoulder with a pin shaped like a water crane and hesitates, his fingers warm on my collarbone.

I finally look across at him. "Are you sure you're all right with . . . all of this?"

A flash of anger sparks through my skin, and I pull back without thinking. Jet looks at his hands, then helplessly at me. "Sorry, did I hurt you?"

I pull my arms around my elbows. "No, it's . . . my new magic. I can feel strong emotions now, especially through touch." I wince. "You're not all right with this, are you?"

He presses a hand over his forehead, and sighs. "Gods, I . . . sorry. It's not you. It's my father, and Kasta. It's a lot of change at once, especially since my father's been after me for *years* to rule . . ." His hands drop. "I'll adjust. But please believe it's not you I'm angry with. Never you."

His smile is encouraging, real, but he keeps his distance while I brush the knots from my hair.

And when he hands me a little tray of white glass lilies to put in the curls, he's careful not to touch me.

VIII

BY the time we enter the royal hallway, I decide I'm over-worrying with Jet. He needs time to process what's happened as much as I do, and it's unrealistic to expect things to go back to normal so fast, whatever normal is, when there's so much else to worry about. He still walks comfortably next to me; he still smiles if I look over. Just because he doesn't want to touch me anymore doesn't mean he's regretting helping me or contemplating running away again.

I trusted him during the Crossing, and he came through. He'll come through.

Also, I have approximately twelve hundred other things to worry about at the moment, so I have to hope that's true. I set my sights ahead, to the war room, where the Mestrah and his advisors do indeed wait inside . . . along with half the palace.

This might be a slight exaggeration; there are probably forty people total. But this is twenty-nine more than I was expecting, and I stop outside the rune-inlaid doorway. "I'm sorry, did you say there would be eleven people?"

Jet surveys the packed room, biting his lip. "That's what I was told. But now is probably a good time to admit that my father's plans can change on a whim."

And so they have. The brazier's circular shadow twitches over the long table, illuminating the faces of army officials in their metal-feathered armor, priests in their white tunics, and the Mestrah's ten advisors in their deep purple robes and golden capes, representative of the ten primary deities who serve Numet. It's of some comfort, at least, to realize I already met most of these people thanks to yesterday's tour. The General—Jet's mother—leans on her cane near the front of the room, and when she sees us, she nods, reminding me of the warm way she greeted me yesterday. I'd been afraid she might blame me as much as Kasta for taking Jet's crown. But all she did was clasp my arm, her fingers firm. *Thank you for bringing my son home.*

I return her nod.

Less comforting are the dozen messengers armed with listening scrolls who cluster at the edges of the room. My handmaiden warned me about messengers. Anything they write down, anything I do or say, will henceforth appear immediately on announcement boards all over Orkena. Anything I say. Immediately all over Orkena. The pace of their quills doubles when I walk in, and I'm thinking: *This is it for me. This is the last moment anyone in the kingdom wonders if I will be a well-spoken or sophisticated queen.*

"Jet," I whisper as we excuse our way through a trio of the Mestrah's advisors. "Exactly how many people live in Orkena?"

Jet gives me a look, as if this is a random question. "I think it was ten million at last census. Why?"

I muffle a laugh and try very hard not to give the messengers a reaction they'll feel compelled to write about. "No reason," I wheeze.

The soldiers make space as we approach the head of the table, where the Mestrah sits on his glass throne, looking much worse than yesterday. His scorpion-tined crown weighs heavier on his head; the circles beneath his eyes are more pronounced despite the makeup meant to brighten his face. Yet somehow he still looks apart from the nobility around him, more vivid and real; divine.

Only one other figure cuts the same contrast against the milling elite. My blood flashes as Kasta glances our way from the Mestrah's right, his eyes a spark of blue bordered in kohl. Numet's mark gleams on his olive skin through an opening in his tunic, and his favored crown of Valen's rattlesnakes twists through his hair, though I doubt the god of fate would approve.

The nightmare sings at the edges of my vision. Maybe fear would be a more normal reaction, considering Kasta was already dangerous before he held both Influence and the Shifters' curse in his grip. But I imagine the knife again in his hand, this time as he stands over Maia, and what stirs in my chest is not flighty or light.

"Zahru," the Mestrah says, his voice gruff. "Kasta. Please, sit."

The room goes quiet. Though I doubt I radiate the same unearthly grace as our king, the crowd's eyes gravitate to me—the one who is new, the one who doesn't belong. I press forward, and when I approach the chair I sat in yesterday, Jet tugs my cape.

"I can't sit with you today," he whispers. "But I'll be close by."

He slips into the crowd. The high-backed chair scrapes when a servant pulls it out, and I slowly sink into it, aware of the many faces turned toward me. But I literally almost died to be here. I look back, and it's their turn to look away.

All except for Kasta, who watches me with a quill twirling between his fingers, as if waiting to write down my faults himself.

The Mestrah raises his arms, and all but the messengers sit.

"Council," the Mestrah says. "I have gathered you today not only to consult with our new *dōmmel* Zahru, with whom most of you are now acquainted, but also to announce a promising new development in our research of the Wyri metal. You, and the people of Orkena, are no doubt growing anxious over our silence in regards to Wyrim. And while it's true that we've yet to link the attack to their queen, I would assure you this does not mean we're sitting idle."

He beckons to an advisor on the other side of Kasta, a woman with curling silver hair and light brown skin. She moves to the front with a long roll of parchment and unfurls it with the help of Jet's mother. It's a picture, painted by a skilled hand, of a male lion overlooking a lake. But unlike most lions, this one has thin white stripes lining its back, as if it were half tiger.

"Odelig?" whispers one of the messengers.

The Mestrah nods. "Our research continues on the magic-neutralizing metal Wyrim has developed, which we are now calling *forsvine*. And Odelig, the Immortal Lion, may be the key." He gestures to the painting. "Since we know charms must be adjusted from their human versions to be effective on animals, my advisors and I are exploring the possibility that animal magic may not be affected by *forsvine*. The problem we've run into is testing. As we know, only a handful of animals possessing magic are ever alive at once, and right now we're only aware of three of them: Naif, the Waterweaving whale who lives near the Wyri islands; Odelig; and Ashra, the Firespinning horse that bandits stole from my stables last moon."

I'm very glad the Mestrah isn't looking at me when he says this. There is no universe in which I would have been able to keep a straight face, or not admitted in front of a room of messengers that actually the thieves were Sakira and her team, which incidentally included me. Not that I was told ahead of time what we were doing or felt in any way that it was a good idea.

"As my soldiers have yet to locate Ashra, and hunting the whale would stir a great deal of political distress, we have decided to pursue Odelig as our test subject. We'll continue working on spells that might overpower *forsvine* entirely, but until then, we're hoping his bones may provide critical protection to our soldiers."

A hollow opens in my ribs as I realize his intention. Odelig is certainly infamous, especially among non-Orkenians, who avoid the eastern edge of the forest between Pe and Orkena for this very reason. Arrows and swords can't hurt him, but while magic can, he's been able to outsmart every hunter who has come for him so far. If our soldiers wore his bones as charms, and *forsvine* couldn't neutralize his magic, it would mean blades and crossbows couldn't hurt our soldiers, either. Making them essentially immortal against the Wyri.

But that's the very crux of the problem. In order to use an animal's magic, that animal has to be killed. In Odelig's case, he's large enough that a small army's worth of charms could be carved from his bones. I know there are many human lives at stake. I know it shouldn't even be comparable. But since being named the Crossing's sacrifice, I have stronger feelings about one life being traded for the benefit of many, especially when the Mestrah isn't even sure Odelig's magic will work.

"Zahru," the Mestrah says. I clench my seat, panicking that he's read my mind—until I remember he can no longer do that. "Your experience as a Whisperer is especially suited to speak on this. What would you advise of this theory?"

The quill stills in Kasta's hand. Anyone who wasn't already looking at me certainly is now, but as shocked as I am that the Mestrah just considered my Whispering useful in this situation, a stone turns in my stomach, because I can already feel it.

This is the moment I make myself infamous across every informational board in Orkena.

"I think it's awful," I blurt. Quills scratch in glee, and all I can really do at this point is keep talking. "I mean, even if we *do* find that his magic works against *forsvine*, the solution is temporary. There's physically not enough of him to outfit everyone. By the time you make as many charms as you can, you might have found another solution, and you would have killed a legendary animal in vain."

Kasta grunts. "Orkena's animals are made to serve just as we are. Odelig is especially dangerous, and so he's been left alone. Now the gods are calling him to a purpose. Surely you don't believe the life of a lion outweighs the lives of our people."

My blood boils. I am very, very tempted to make a comment about how his last sacrifice turned out, but we're in a room of messengers, so I control myself. "We don't even know if we can *find* him," I growl. "It could take moons, and by then—"

"It could be the turning point of a war." The quill spins again in Kasta's fingers. "The threat of a solution alone might be enough to end things. This is no time for Whisperers' sentiments, *dōmmel*."

There's a mocking edge to the word, and around the table sound murmurs of agreement. He's already turning them against me, making me seem foolish and naive.

Gods, I could strangle him.

The Mestrah raises his hand for silence. "You are wise to consider the cost, Zahru," he says, and surprise flashes through me again at his support. "But we cannot operate under the assumption that the Metalsmiths will be able to counter *forsvine* in time. As Kasta said, the gods have given us this possibility, and we would be negligent to ignore it." He leans forward, resting tiredly on the table. "But you needn't worry about it taking too long to find him. Magical animals are drawn to royalty, which is why I've decided that, as your first task together, you and Kasta will hunt Odelig and bring him here."

"What?" I say. Approving chatter rises around the room, and I shoot a panicked look at Jet. *This* is the first test. And it's definitely not something Jet or anyone else can help me with. The Mestrah is sending me back into the desert, with the person who clearly has no issue with sacrificing me to succeed, on a trip that will take days—all time I could be studying or putting together what we need to stop Kasta—with the intention of bringing death to an animal. *Death*, when I have dedicated my entire life to saving and healing.

Kasta drops the quill. "Will you need him alive?"

"No," the Mestrah says. "Do what you need to subdue him, but I'll expect that when you return, both of you agreed on it."

"Mestrah," I say desperately. "With all respect, couldn't Kasta go alone? That's a long time to go without my studies, and I don't know how to track—"

"Your studies can continue on the journey. Kasta will teach you to track."

"But—" I scramble for anything else. I know this might make me appear weak, but I have no choice. I can't go on this trip. I can't help Kasta kill this lion. "What about the bombing? Those mercenaries are still out there, and the Wyri—"

"Will see they have not shaken us in the least." The Mestrah's voice, though gruff, strengthens in volume. "We will not cower in the capital, waiting for their next move. You will soon be Mestrah, and *you* are what they should fear. If they're foolish enough to intercept you, we will remind them of it."

The nobles clap and voice their approval, and I can only look around the table, irritation clawing up my spine. It's always about a show of power in the capital: who is faster, stronger, more reckless. Another thing I plan to change once I'm Mestrah. And *Rie*, the one time I thought I could count on Kasta to argue with his father, to insist I don't go and mess up the hunt with my *Whisperers' sentiments*, and he raised no objections at all. He catches my eye as he sits back, his gaze as calculating as ever.

And a new thought slivers through the back of my mind.

Because I can think of a very good reason a Shifter wouldn't oppose being out with me in a forest, where people often get separated, and lost, and torn inexplicably apart by wild animals.

The Mestrah rises. "The expedition sets off tomorrow. You are dismissed."

IX

IT'S a testament to my current state of mind that I feel like I'm too busy to even worry whether Kasta might assassinate me on this trip. I don't have time to think about assassination. I have ten more classes to take today, a new lion problem, and I still need to ask Marcus about the whole controlling necklace situation, which reminds me I *still* haven't asked him and Melia to be my advisors.

I'm going to keep a dagger on me, and assume that Kasta may attack at any moment, and that's seriously the most thought I can give to that.

Jet and I have just reached my room when a woman in green approaches with a smile and a scroll.

I jerk to a stop. "If you tell me there's something else I need to do right now, I'm going to start screaming."

The woman pales. "I beg your forgiveness, *gudina*. I am only here to pack your things for the hunt tomorrow? I can come back . . ."

"Oh." I wince. "I'm so sorry, yes. That would be wonderful. Thank you."

She bows, touching her fingertips to her forehead, and the guards open my doors to admit her. Jet turns to me, his thumbs through two of the quarter moons that make up his silver belt. "You need a break."

"I do *not* need a break. I can handle this." I push into my room after the woman. "Kasta doesn't need a break. He's probably got everything planned for the trip already."

"He's also used to this kind of pressure, and he doesn't have classes."

"I said I'm fine!" I do not say this at all like a person who is fine, and I slowly relax my fists. "I can get used to this, too. Could you get Marcus and Melia for me? I only have an hour now until my first tutor arrives."

"Yes," Jet says, with the agreeability of someone who does not want to be lit on fire for saying otherwise. "Do you want me to get Hen, too?"

I suppose it would make sense to get the entire team together. I start to agree—and rethink it. Hen is amazing at many things, but she's also impulsive, and definitely doesn't consult with me on most of what she does. The thought of her taking Kasta's case into her own hands, and his catching her, sends a jolt of panic through me. "Maybe . . . not this time," I say.

Jet raises a brow. "All right. I'll be right back."

He spins on his heel, and I have time to feel guilty for snapping at him before I turn and collapse face-first on the couch. This is fine, I can do this, I'll figure out what to do about the lion, Marcus will make the necklace. These are the optimistic thoughts running through my head when Jade bounces over, a torn, glittering tassel in her mouth, and deposits the frazzled golden threads by my face. *Play!*

I sigh and sit up. "What did you tear this from?"

Her spotted tail twitches, and she looks at the bed. Where every single one of the dozen expensive, jewel-toned pillows is shredded in a still-drifting cloud of feathers.

"Oh."

And of course this is the moment the woman in green emerges from the closet with a stack of pressed *joles* in her arms.

"Would these please you for the journey, *gudina*?" she asks, as two feathers land atop the bundle.

"Um . . ." It's really very distracting to speak to someone who seems immune to the absurdity of this. I hide the tassel behind my back, and Jade charges off again into her pillow graveyard. "Are any of those cactus spire?"

The woman shakes her head. "I would not waste such finery on a hunt. Though I assure you, these more basic gowns will still set you apart."

Or maybe this woman is just used to absurdity, considering she's been asked to pack these when part of our journey will be spent scraping through tree branches. "I just don't want anything to attack me. And I feel compelled to clarify here that I'm talking about the dresses, not wild animals."

She wrinkles her nose. Like *I'm* the one being odd. "Of course, *gudina*. These are just your public dresses, anyway, for riding past the towns. I have your finest tunics packed for the hunt."

"Wait, there's *more*?" She's holding at least eight outfits. "How long is the Mestrah planning for us to be gone?"

"Well, it will take six days at the least." She beckons for me to follow her back into the closet. "Two for travel there, at least two for the hunt, and two more to return."

I think about this, acknowledging eight dresses probably isn't too many—until we walk through the curtain, and I take in the packed redwood traveling chest. Which brims with garments and crowns. I can't decide if it's more ridiculous that she's packed this many things, or that the closet doesn't look any emptier.

"Oh, no," I say. "This is way too much. Is someone going to carry that into the wilderness?"

The woman places her bundle atop the open chest. "No, *gudina*. I'll pack a satchel for your hunting clothes. This will stay on the boat, giving you plenty of options."

I gape at her. "Because this is *not enough clothes* already?"

"Ah." Her smile flickers. "I know it seems like a lot from what you're used to. But this is a blessing! You, *dōmmel*, are a blessing. Let us spoil you."

But my stomach twists as I watch her shift through the fine gowns, her touch soft and reverent. Like someone used to admiring such finery, while knowing she'll never wear it herself. Her own dress is plain and green, a rough linen in comparison to the rarities in the chest. She's so used to hearing what she just said to me—that I have these nice things, that I *deserve* them, because I am a blessing—that she no longer recognizes how this implies that she is not.

And a new kind of anger stirs in my gut. "No. I don't deserve these any more than you or anyone else." The woman jerks her head up in surprise. "And this is way too many clothes. Whatever's in the trunk, that stays here; that's what I'm wearing for the next ten years. I just need seven changes of clothes for the trip. And three nightgowns."

The woman clenches a dress to her chest. "Th-three?"

"Oh, just wait." I gaze around the towering shelves. "I have plans for the rest of this, too."

By the time Jet returns with Marcus and Melia, fifteen servants are bustling in and out of my room, their arms overflowing with fabrics. One nearly runs Jet over as he tries to come in, and he leaps back. This is the kind of chaotic, nonsensical scene I would usually come across at Hen's house, and I have to admit I'm starting to understand why she does this. There's a definite sense of satisfaction watching the confusion settle over Jet's face.

"What . . . is happening?" he asks, dodging another servant.

"I have too many clothes," I say, and brighten as Marcus and Melia push their way in: towering Marcus in his black armor, his blond hair curling around his ears and his pale arms wrapped in military charms; and petite Melia in a gorgeous purple *jole*, her umber skin glittering with golden antelope symbols and her queenly braids crowned in leaves. "Marcus! Melia!"

"Zahru!" Melia says. I pull her in for a hug, and she squeezes me tight. "It's good to see you. And congratulations."

"Thank you. It's great to see you, too."

"Zahru," Marcus says, clasping my arm in greeting. "Glad to see you well. And back at toppling ancient traditions, as usual."

I let out a panicked laugh. "Just another day in the life. How have you both been?"

"Quite well," Melia says. "I've been away visiting family, but I'm glad to be back. I even took on a young apprentice."

"That's amazing," I say. "They're in very good hands."

Marcus nods. "And I've been promoted to captain . . . and gotten myself engaged."

"Marcus!" I laugh, pouncing on his arm when he flexes

it to show me the bracelet. It's a handsome piece, a deep red leather woven in intricate knots. "Congratulations on both! Your pitchfork-wielding grandmother finally got to you?"

He chuckles. "We'll just say the Crossing rearranged my priorities. The world changes too fast, but people . . . you keep the good ones close." He nudges me, and I smile shyly back. "And yes, Grandmother might have made one too many comments about wanting to be alive for the wedding. Of course, the second I told her Tomás and I were engaged, now she's going on about great-grandchildren."

I chuckle, though I can definitely commiserate, seeing as I know Mora will make many, many more comments in the coming weeks about the ways I could still make Jet a king. "I'm so thrilled for you both. And thank you for coming."

The last of my tunic-burdened servants exits and the door slams solemnly behind her.

Jet gestures to the empty closet. "Can we talk about the clothes now?"

"Oh, right," I say, tugging the three of them with me. "I decided I had a ridiculous amount of outfits. I don't need that many clothes. No one needs that many clothes. So I'm sending them to Kystlin."

They duck into the emptied closet, eyes wide. Only the *joles* and tunics that had originally been packed in the trunk remain, a slender line of shelves dwarfed by the room. It's still much more than what I had at home.

"Kystlin?" Marcus echoes, examining one of the two crowns left on the middle table. "The city housing the Aterian refugees?"

"They definitely need them more than I do. I talked to the Royal

Materialist, too. Any clothes she was planning to make for me, for the foreseeable future, will go to the poor districts across Orkena. And all of the weird stuff is going away. No cactus spire, no strangling snakeskins. Just fancy things. I'm sending messengers out to get counts of what's needed."

"Zahru." Jet turns back to me, smiling. "You're amazing. I would never even have thought about that."

I force a grin, choosing to believe this means he's impressed and not that I've just pointed out yet another divide between us. "Anyway, it's just clothes. Do you all want to sit down? I have . . . a lot to ask of you. First, if maybe you'd want to stay on as my advisors? No pressure, though. I know it's not the same."

Melia nods. "Of course. I would be happy to. We are still the same team, are we not?"

Marcus claps my shoulder. "Agreed. We're in this together, no matter who's making the final decisions." He grins. "We trust you. We know you'll do what's right."

This unexpected show of support makes heat climb my throat, and I blink back tears. "Well, that's great to hear. Because I have something slightly illegal to ask you about."

We sit on the couches, Jade immediately jumping into Melia's lap, and I fill them both in on the hunt and the tests the Mestrah intends for Kasta and me, and then onto Jet's and my theory about Kasta being a Shifter. Marcus frowns deeply the entire time. Melia does too, though on her it comes off more as thoughtful, even sophisticated, or maybe that's just because most people would look regal while stroking a small leopard's back.

There's a long pause after I mention I want to commission a

rune necklace without the appropriate proof that Kasta really is a Shifter.

"Well," Melia says, wincing as Jade launches from her legs after a fly. "For the lion, I would say you do everything in your power to bring Odelig back alive. That way you have more time to think about what you want to do. Are you allowed to bring any of us with you on the hunt?"

I shake my head. "I asked. The Mestrah isn't allowing advisors to come. He wants Kasta and me consulting each other."

"Mm." She brushes some of Jade's fur—and a wayward feather—from her skirt. "Even so, you should still have a team of Healers, and the Mestrah's Wraithguard always accompanies royal excursions. Between them, you should be able to safely subdue Odelig and keep him under until he can be better contained here."

I rub my palms along my legs. "That's good to know, thank you. And the rune necklace?"

Jet shifts in his chair, maybe noticing how quickly I changed subjects. But this is the critical piece. Without this, nothing else I'm doing will matter.

Marcus leans over his knees. "I know a Runemaster we can trust to keep quiet about this. An old schoolmate of mine. But, Zahru, he's not going to craft it without proof. I can likely convince him to make it without the priests' permission, but we need *something* tangible that could stand up in a court. We're talking very serious charges for being wrong. Whippings. Exile. If we're going to do this, we need to be sure."

"If we're caught," I grumble.

"What?"

"Nothing," I say, shoving up from the couch. "It's just . . . this is exactly what Kasta's counting on. We don't have time to wait around and hope he messes up. If we're going to stop him, we have to take this risk."

Marcus grunts. "I understand your frustration. But you have to remember, even though *we* know he's capable of this, we've seen him as no one else has. Here, everyone believes him a noble prince coming into his birthright. I want to reveal him as badly as you do. But we can only do this if we're sure."

Melia straightens one of her bracelets. "I can watch him during training. All Healers are on call at the arena right now, with so many soldiers on staff. Kasta is there for a few hours every day. If I notice anything strange, I will let you know."

Jet nods. "I'll work on getting access to his room, in case he's hiding something that could help us. My mother is connected with everyone who's ever touched palace security. I won't tell her why we need access, but for us, she'll do it without question."

"And I'll watch the Shifter caches," Marcus says. "We keep bodies of deceased criminals on hand to feed the army's Shifters. If Kasta steals from it, we'll know."

"Fine," I say, dropping back again on the couch. "I'll watch him on the hunt, see if I notice anything unusual. But what am I even looking for?"

"For our purposes," Marcus says, "if we're going to do this without putting one of us in danger, then our best form of evidence is animal pelts. A Shifter must have them to change forms, and it's illegal to keep pelts outside of the army's guarded stash, considering what they can be used for. Kasta has to have them somewhere if he hopes to sneak out and hunt for his meals. Bring me one from his effects, and my contact will start on the necklace immediately."

I sigh and press my fingers between my eyes. This is going both better and worse than I'd hoped. Better because Marcus didn't say no, and now I have something simple to look for. Worse because I'd really hoped he would just make the necklace and this would be done.

"All right," I say. "I'll add it to my list."

Marcus claps his knees. "Sorry, Zahru. I promise, though, our patience will pay off—"

Bird! Jade squeaks, dashing in from the balcony with the speed of a sandstorm. I pat my lap for her, but she knocks me against the couch with how hard she leaps, and shoves her head beneath my arm.

Her fear, raw and cold, sinks through my chest like stingers.

"Jade," I say, holding her with one hand and quickly checking for injuries with the other. "What's wrong? What happened?"

She's shaking. Her heart thumps against her chest. She darts a look at the balcony, but outside, only the garden trees move, their ruby leaves fluttering in the sun.

Bird, she thinks, pressing against me. *Quiet.*

My blood jumps. She's heard something. Or not heard something, in this case. This still, unnatural quiet is how the horses described being around Maia, too.

Kasta is outside.

"Where?" I whisper. "How long?"

Trees, Jade says. *Not long.*

Jet sits forward. "Zahru? What is it?"

The windows are shut to the heat, and the balcony doors are enchanted to close again after letting Jade through, so I'm not worried Kasta overheard anything . . . but if I react and shut the drapes, or panic in any way, that will definitely tip him off that I think something's wrong. I can't let him know I'm paranoid about animals.

Gods, we're going to have to be so careful.

I pet Jade's back, forcing myself to relax. "She just got spooked by a protective jay outside." I would tell them what I really suspect, but I don't want *them* panicking or turning to the windows, either. "It's nothing. But actually, my first tutor is due anytime now. I should probably get ready."

Melia stands, pushing her braids over her shoulders. "All right. We will see you again soon. Perhaps with evidence, after the hunt?"

I hold Jade close. "I hope so."

"We'll get there, Zahru," Marcus assures me, rising and clapping my shoulder. "Be patient. He won't get away with this."

They take their leave, Jet with the promise to be back this evening, if our schedules allow. I sit on the couch a while longer, Jade in my arms, but soon a rainbow catches her eye in the pool room, and she's off again, as if nothing happened.

When I think enough time has passed for Kasta to lose interest, I slip the dagger from the end table, wrap it in the folds of my sleeve, and make my way as casually as I can to the balcony doors. I should probably stay inside, not give him any reason to think I'm looking for him, that I know what he is. But I near the glass, and that same recklessness I felt when I first suggested the rune necklace threads through me, wire-tight.

I slide open the door.

The sun presses against my shoulders; the trees whisper and click. I brace myself for a rush of wings, for a fury of talons and beak, and my fingers twitch around the hidden hilt of the knife. But only an eerie silence curls around me.

There are no animals in the trees at all.

I make it through lessons in writing, politics, and magic theory before I test my new power as *dōmmel* and insist someone replace my gossamer drapes with heavy curtains. I anticipate a reason might be asked for, and have already told myself fervently that *I'm afraid a bird is spying on me* is not a sentence that can come out of my mouth, lest Kasta hears of it later. But no one asks why. Maybe I'm already gaining a reputation for strange requests. Servants are called, and my tutor drones on about the various magical developments that have led to modern Orkena while people tug and fold fabric and climb bronze ladders behind him.

My lessons don't stop until after dark. At which point my brain is mush, so naturally this is when a messenger arrives to remind me that I'm still expected to meet the Mestrah at daybreak for an Influence lesson before we leave for the hunt. I think I agree to this, and then possibly fall asleep on the couch, because when I open my eyes again, Jet is tucking a pillow under my head.

"Oh," I say. "Hi."

He smiles. "Hi. You don't need to get up. I'll let you rest." He blows on an oil lamp on the end table, and the flame flickers and goes blue, the torches along the walls following suit until they glow at lowest light. I snuggle under the sheet he brought me and drift off before I even hear him leave. And this time, I don't dream.

But my nemesis is quickly becoming the main doors. Because I swear I'm only asleep an hour before someone is knocking at them *again*.

I groan and sit up, pinching myself first to be sure I'm not back in a nightmare. But dawn glows at the edges of the heavy curtains, and the water clock on the dresser confirms an entire night has passed. It's the messenger for my Influence lesson. The knock comes again, and with an exhausted sigh, I pad to the doors. I don't even bother with a robe—I'm still in yesterday's gown.

It occurs to me, as my hand falls on the handle, that I could have just asked this person to come in. But I'm already here. So I pull the door open.

A slice of white tunic. Two burning blue eyes. This is all I see before I slam the door and drive the locking bolt back in place.

"Zahru," Kasta says, the word like the tip of a knife against my throat. I lean against the wood, my heart pounding. "Open the door."

"No," I snarl. "It's not time to leave yet, and you're not allowed to be here."

"I don't want to be here, either. But they're the Mestrah's orders. So get changed. We're supposed to walk together."

I brace for him to shove against the lock. For the golden bar to bend; for blood to seep over the threshold where he's struck down the guards. Neither happens. Someone clears her throat outside—one of my guards—meaning she's still alive, and well, and guarding. Kasta is waiting for me like a normal person, not an assassin.

A knot builds in my throat as I step slowly away. *We're supposed to walk together.* As in, to *our* Influence lesson, because of course we both have to learn, and it wouldn't make sense for the Mestrah to teach us separately. Not when he wants us to do everything

114

together, so that I can see Kasta every day, every hour, every second I'm not studying; as much as the king can make possible.

I grab my hair and shout my frustration at the ceiling.

I storm to the closet, my blood a hot current beneath my skin. I select the first silvery satin dress I can find, relieved to have a more manageable selection to pick from, and wrestle it on. I pause long enough in front of the looking glass to brush my hair over my shoulders and darken the kohl around my eyes, and from the crowns I select one with silver leaves and twisting bronze thorns. When I set the brutal piece atop my head, I hardly recognize myself. I look predatory and cold, a blade in the shape of a girl.

I grab the dagger from the bedside table and secure the sheath beside my ribs. Then I return to the doors and twist the locking bar free.

Even though I'm expecting him, the sight of Kasta still lances my heart, a sharp needle of dread and resentment. Silver skulls crown his black hair, and his gods' mark swirls above the draping neckline of his tunic. His gaze lingers a moment too long on my face. Then he's moving, jaw set, and I drift behind him, frustration stretching against my ribs. I know I shouldn't be able to hear his thoughts, but I still try, hoping I was just distracted before, hoping to hear even the smallest hum.

But his presence is the same as always. Deadly. Charged. And silent.

We go on this way through the entire royal wing, down the theatrical stairs, into the marbled foyer. This early in the morning, the grand room is empty of people, silence drifting between its potted trees and statues of gods. White and gold banners shift along the walls, glittering with Orkena's seal of Numet's swirling sun. But instead of turning for the war room, Kasta heads for the archway that leads to the gardens.

"Where are we going?" I say, feeling suddenly foolish I've even trusted him this far. Guards stand at every corner, but the rest of the palace is asleep, and the gardens are vast enough that if he led me deep into them, it would take a while for anyone to reach us. A couple of guards would be no problem for a Shifter.

"I told you," Kasta says. "To our Influence lesson."

"In the gardens?"

"In the Mestrah's private garden. Our power is to remain secret, for now. Only a select few will even know we have it."

"He's not telling our allies?" I don't know why this should surprise me. To me, it would only make sense to reveal something this enormous to kingdoms we want to trust us, but of course, this is politics, and everything is about secrets and control. "Isn't someone bound to figure it out by, I don't know, looking at *any past Crossing result*?"

"You lived," Kasta says. "They have no reason to believe the knife still worked."

He says this like it's a simple fact, like he wasn't the one with that knife. I stop at the threshold of the exit, where white marble yields to paving stones, and he does too, reluctantly looking back at me. I scrutinize his stony features against the dawn: the tightness of his lips, the guarded darkness in his eyes. I don't know what I'm searching for. Regret, maybe. Or any indication of the boy he could have been, the one who confided in me, the one as desperate as I was to prove he was worth something, even without magic.

Does he remember the promises he made in the caves, to be a good king?

Does he wish he'd dropped the knife and trusted me?

But instead it is me—reminding myself of what he is now and that he killed Maia to become it—who regrets ever wondering at all.

"Fine," I say. "But I want to go first, *alone*, and you can follow in a few minutes."

Kasta shrugs. "Fine."

The answer is so unexpected, so agreeable, that I nearly argue with him just because it feels like that's what we should be doing. But staying near him feels like drowning, and I grip the skirt of my *jole* and stride outside. Into the cool desert morning. I breathe it in, the tightness easing in my chest, and push the memories away with the sight of the manicured trees, the scent of cactus blossom and fresh lemon. From the tour with the handmaiden, I remember the Mestrah's garden is the first turn past a hedge trimmed in the shape of a warhorse, at the end of a path bordered by pomegranate trees. But even amid such beauty, I listen for the rustle of footsteps behind me. For the shifting of leaves, the beat of wings.

The sheath taps against my ribs.

I arrive at the Mestrah's garden, alone.

A black gate marks the entry, its iron bars bent in symbols for the gods. The massive windows of my room run above one entire side of it, where trellises of red and gold ivy cascade like feathers. Green hedges border the rest, within which a vast, emerald paradise sprawls, dotted with well-manicured trees, orange calla lilies, and tiny white flowers that dust the grass like powdered sugar. An Icestone path cuts through it like a ribbon, the chill from which I'm sure will feel divine in the heat of the afternoon, but right now feels frigid.

I start toward the circular platform at the center, rubbing warmth into my arms. A figure sits alone there in a white tunic on an alabaster bench.

The Mestrah is praying. He faces me, but with his eyes closed and his body hunched forward, he can't see me. The fingertips of his right hand touch his forehead, and it's humbling to see him like this before the gods, without a priest, making a submissive gesture he has never made to any living person. I hesitate, not wanting to intrude.

Then he coughs, breaking the picture. His ribs heave and blue songbirds scatter from the trees, and a serving boy rushes in with a chalice of tonic. Between coughs, the Mestrah forces some of the medicine into his mouth, and after a painfully long moment, he swallows and notices me.

He straightens and slowly gestures that I should come forward.

"Mestrah." I kneel and touch my fingers to my forehead. The Mestrah coughs again, though it's weaker.

"Rise," he says. I do, and he glances behind me. "Where is Kasta?"

"He's coming."

Disapproval flickers across the Mestrah's face. He knows I couldn't have known where to meet him without Kasta telling me.

"You did not walk together," he says.

"The last time we were alone, he drove a knife into my heart. Please forgive me for wanting to be cautious."

His brow rises. Sapphire eyes study me, uncomfortably familiar, and I avert my gaze. My entire future rests in this god's hands. I chide myself for my tongue and wait for his reproach.

His voice is quiet. "Do you worship the gods, Zahru?"

I glance up. "Yes."

"But you consider what Kasta did to be personal."

Darkness stirs in my chest. "He cut my wrist to make me the sacrifice. My death was not the gods' will." *And neither was Maia's.*

The Mestrah sighs. "Even if that were true, you are not dead. It was not a sacrifice he made you, but a queen."

"But that wasn't—"

"What he intended?" The Mestrah shakes his head. "Look at me, Zahru, when I am speaking. We are nearly equals."

In shock, I look up. He's already a much different god than the one I remember chastising Kasta before the Crossing, and I expected him to continue treating me as a peasant, at least until I start meeting his requirements. But he defended me at the meeting yesterday. And now he's telling me to look up.

"In a moon's time," he says, "you may well be running a country beside my son. You do not have to forgive him. But you *do* need to understand what he did. Orkena means more to him than any one person, any one life. And so it must be for you. You do not have to make your sacrifices in the same way. But they must be made, if Orkena is to survive."

The words are an eerie echo of what I once told Jet, and I set my jaw.

"Yes," he says, more to himself. "This hunt will be very telling."

Dismissal threads his tone, and my chest squeezes. Even if he's giving me a chance at this, I haven't impressed him yet in any measure. Not that I thought it would be easy, but I don't think I'm off to a good start.

The Mestrah's gaze shifts, and I tense at the hollow, heavy presence that follows.

"Kasta," the king says. "Join us."

Kasta does, stopping too close to me, and I edge away as he bows. The Mestrah frowns at this, too. But it was he himself who said I didn't have to forgive Kasta.

The king gestures that we should sit, and we do, taking separate benches from the four smaller ones that surround him.

"We will begin simply," the Mestrah says, "with a technique that you can practice while you're away. After you return, I will gauge the progress you've made on it. And next time, you will arrive together."

A warning glance at us both.

"You have felt by now the bud of your powers." He lifts the crystal glass of tonic from the serving boy's tray and takes a sip. "The ability to sense strong emotions is the first stage of any mental magic, as your mind opens to a new part of the world. For some magic, like my own ability to read minds, I must let those emotions in so I can locate the memories beneath them. But to use Influence, you must press *back* on what you feel. You will learn to take hold of different feelings as deftly as a musician forming a chord, and when you're ready . . ." His gaze slides to me. "You will learn to change them."

I don't know what I was expecting from magic that could affect people's hearts, but it was much more along the lines of being exceptionally charming and likable. It wasn't *this*.

"Change them?" I echo. "You mean, control them?"

"You understand, then, why it is a power that only gods should wield." He dabs his brow with a cloth. "I will only be able to guide you so far as what I've read of it, and what I understand of my own abilities as a mind reader. No one has wielded Influence in centuries. It will be up to the pair of you to determine how best to use it."

Kasta glances my way. "But if we can't use it on each other, how will we practice?"

"On volunteers." The Mestrah gestures to a pair of men in brown tunics. "Starting with servants. And as your powers advance, on people of greater magic."

The servants shuffle forward, and nerves prickle my arms. I'm definitely not ready to work on people yet. I've barely begun to understand what Influence even is, let alone what I'm expected to do with it, and the thought of *changing* them, of making them adore or obey me for no reason beyond my wanting them to, feels like the worst kind of manipulation. Much more like slave and master than subject and queen.

But then, I remind myself, isn't that where the title of Mestrah—Master—comes from?

The Mestrah sets his hands on his bare knees. "Today, we will work on simply finding and identifying emotions. Don't try to change anything yet. Just open your mind to the energy surrounding your volunteer, and amplify it until you can tell me what he's feeling."

I breathe out. This, at least, seems innocent enough, and sounds very much like how my father taught me to use my Whisperer's abilities—to listen first, and let the feelings come on their own. As the shorter of the two men stops before me, I tell myself this is the only part of Influence that I'll use outside of these sessions.

The man looks back at me with gray eyes, his shoulders square, his long black hair a sleek curtain down his back. I don't need any magic to know he's nervous. His gaze skips between my face and the symbol on my chest, and very quickly to anywhere else.

"*Jener*," the Mestrah says, addressing the servants. "Each of you was given a piece of parchment with an emotion. You may now open it. Recollect memories that evoke that emotion, and continue to do so until your *dōmmel* has correctly named what you're feeling."

My volunteer reaches into his tunic pocket and unrolls a small note. He inhales as if to steel himself, and I wonder if it's for the emotion he's supposed to feel or for being involved in this at all.

He looks across at me, and I hold my breath.

But whatever he's feeling, it isn't strong enough to reach me the way the desperation from the woman in yellow did. The chill of the Icestone path curls around my legs; finches chatter and argue in the trees. *Food?* they ask. *Mine! Give!* I try to tune them out, to focus on only the man, but the birds are too loud, and when I reach for the man's emotions, I only get bursts of the animals' joy and irritation. I wish there was a way to turn my Whispering *off*. But then I remember Jet pulling away from me in the closet, the spark of anger that had moved through his fingers. I reach for the man's arm.

"Zahru," the Mestrah snaps. "Did I say to touch him?"

I freeze. "I . . . it's easier for me to read emotions through touch. I've actually done this a couple of times. It's the same with Whispering."

"It will be critical that you use this power without doing so. If you've already felt human emotions through touch, then it teaches you nothing to do it again now. Read his emotions from there."

Wow, I mouth, snatching my hand back. I clasp my elbows and wait until the Mestrah turns his focus to Kasta.

"Good job, Zahru," I mutter, because if the Mestrah isn't going to say it, I feel like someone needs to. "How impressive that you've already mastered half of this little exercise, before we've even had a single lesson—"

"Zahru." The Mestrah leans on one knee. "I may be ill, but I can still hear."

I clear my throat and refocus. My volunteer shifts on his feet. I feel Kasta's eyes on me, but I don't look over.

But fine, if the Mestrah wants me to do this without touch, then I will. It can't be that different from Whispering. I just need to do what I did with Fara all those years ago, to unfocus from what I can see and hear, and sense the energy that lies beneath. Like learning to look past the reflection of the sky in the river, and see the fish and the seagrass. I look into the man's eyes. Past my reflection. And there, faint but present, is the nudge of something new, like the first day my Whisperer powers surfaced.

And I realize—I might actually be good at this.

"Joy," Kasta says.

My focus shatters. I gape at Kasta, who looks far too pleased by my reaction.

"Close," the Mestrah says, his brow high. "See if you can refine it further."

Apos. Kasta is absolutely not allowed to do better at this than me. *I* was the one raised to read emotions, even if no one appreciates that, and I know if I could just block out my Whisperer abilities, I could focus enough to get it. I resist the urge to reach for the man again and press the birds' chatter to the back of my mind. The man doesn't want to hold my gaze, but I need him to, and even though the Mestrah didn't tell us to do this, I think of how I communicate with the animals—how I can send my own emotions across to ease their mind. I try sending calmness now. That he should trust me, that we're safe, that he can let me in—

Something cracks in my mind, and the man looks into my eyes.

Anxiousness splinters through me. I gasp as syrup-thick sorrow flashes under my skin, then scalding anger, then icy fear. This last one lingers, frigid hands grappling up my spine, until my heart quickens and nightmares flood my vision: Hen, her body broken and bleeding; Jet with a sword through his heart; Atera on fire, the flames clawing the sky. And then the images bleed into an inky darkness, and a hollow hum grows in my ears—

I break the contact, shoving him out of my head. The garden snaps into view. The Mestrah and Kasta stare at me, as well as Kasta's volunteer, and I wrap my arms around myself, shivering.

"Fear," I say. "His emotion is fear."

Which is the point my volunteer's eyes roll into his head, and he collapses.

"Gods!" I yelp.

"Brek?" says his companion. He shoots a panicked look at the

Mestrah but doesn't dare move. Two Healers dash over from the wall and ease my volunteer onto his side. My stomach twists. This has never happened with the animals. Their emotions always stay on my skin, never in my head, and certainly never to the degree that I could affect them—

"Zahru." The Mestrah beckons me over.

I step around the man and the Healers, shaking. "I'm sorry. I didn't mean to, I—What happened?"

"Did you try to change something?"

Heat flushes my neck. Gods, is that what I did, sending calmness between us? Wanting the man to look up, to give up his feelings so Kasta wouldn't be faster?

I grip my elbows. "I—I don't know."

"Because if you did, without knowing how to control it, you can cause a spike in your subject's emotion that can overwhelm you and cause you to black out. Or, if you shove back on it as you instinctively did, you'll do the same to your unfortunate subject."

He opens his hand to the man on the ground. The man wakes under the Healer's touch, sitting slowly up, but when his fluttering gaze settles on me, it widens in dawning terror.

"Oh." My throat tightens. "Right."

"That will be enough for today," the Mestrah says. "*Jener*, you are dismissed. Kasta, how did you fare?"

"Better than that," Kasta says with a sharp look at me.

"Did you decipher his exact emotion?"

Kasta sighs. "I was close. Then hers started whimpering."

"Keep practicing, Zahru," the Mestrah says. "While you're away, focus only on reaching for emotion, not demanding it.

125

Once you're able to do this reliably, we'll work on control."

A chill wraps my spine as the Healers help my volunteer to his feet. They shuffle out in hurried steps, whispering and glancing over their shoulders, and suddenly I'm very grateful they won't be able to tell anyone what I did today. And how, on my first try at Influence, I went right for the most horrible part of my magic, like some power-hungry tyrant.

I turn on my heel, ignoring how the Mestrah stands with Kasta, an approving hand on his shoulder as they speak in low tones. For once, it's Kasta who listened to directions, whose volunteer adamantly did not need the help of a Healer to walk away. I expect him to gloat. To give me the same wicked smile he wore after the Mestrah chided Jet in the war room.

But I swear when he glances over, it's with a flickering echo of the volunteer's fear.

XI

I do not think about the Influence lesson on the way back to my room.

I do not think about having to practice it this week, or what explanation I'll give to the guards if I make someone else black out, since I'm not supposed to reveal I even have Influence. I do not think of my tutors, or Kasta, or the hunt I'm supposed to leave on within the hour.

Instead, I think of Hen, and how odd it is that I haven't seen her in two days.

Granted, I've been a little busy, but I thought she would have turned up by now. But just as I resolve to look for her, the Royal Materialist arrives with a list of cities requesting my clothes program, a servant asks my preferences for meals during the hunt, and two commanders who'd been out when I first toured the palace stop by to introduce themselves. They talk my ear off for a quarter of an hour, and by the time they leave, a handmaiden in purple is waiting to take me to the boats.

I would like it noted that I still haven't had breakfast.

"Do I at least get to say goodbye to my family?" I ask rather snappishly, as again—no breakfast.

"Of course, *dōmmel*," the girl says, bowing. "They're already at the docks."

So they are, and I have to admit this is a relief since the last time I asked this question, as the human sacrifice, I was told there was no time to see them. Fara, Mora, Jet, and—finally—Hen wait in a landing area near stacks of wooden weapons crates, the river sparkling behind them, and upon it, the palace's finest ships. Glass party boats, stoic warships, and gleaming merchants' vessels float between the white oak docks like prized horses in stalls, the hunting ship standing out among them with its dark sides and its gangplanks clustered with servants. It waits on the water like a wooden knife, with sharp black sails and metal railings.

Hen sees me coming and grabs Mora's arm. "All right, stop talking about death. She's here. Zahru!"

She hugs me warmly, which is my first warning that she's been up to something.

"Hey," I say. "I was just starting to worry about you. Where have you been?"

She beams, as if she was hoping this was the question I'd lead with. Warning bells are screeching through my head. "Oh, I had some things to wrap up at home. Also, it was surprisingly difficult to get your history tutor fired."

And there it is. "*Why* would you fire my history tutor?"

"Do you want the long story or the short one?"

Someone blows an oxhorn from the boat—the first call for boarding.

"The short one," I say.

"The short one is that *I'm* now your history tutor, and I'm coming with you on the hunt!"

I almost scream in joy. "What! Really?"

"Yes! See, the guards told me advisors weren't allowed to come, Mestrah's orders, blah blah. So I asked who *was* allowed, and realized history was something I really could teach you.

Especially if I borrowed your tutor's notes. And now I'm coming!"

Mora puts a hand on Hen's shoulder. "You destroyed the evidence, right?"

Hen rolls her eyes. "It was the first thing I did, Mora."

"Evidence?" I exchange a glance with my father. And with Jet, who looks similarly concerned.

Hen nods. "I couldn't find anything to blackmail him with. Seriously, it's like the man has followed the rules all of his very long life." She sighs. "Very boring. So I gave him a disease."

I grip her arms. "You *what*?"

"On paper," she clarifies. "I just wrote to the Healers that he was exposed to fleshrot on a recent vacation, and he needs to be quarantined a few weeks to make sure he doesn't have it. Then I burned the letter so no one looks into the fake Healer name I used."

We're starting to get into long story territory, and this is where I draw the line so I can maintain plausible deniability. "That's amazing. This is the best news I've heard all week—"

Fara clears his throat, and I let go of Hen.

"I mean," I say, in my best scolding tone, "you shouldn't have put a man into quarantine just to come on this trip!" I lower my voice to a whisper. "But I'm really glad you did."

"Oh, he got off easy." Hen brushes sand from the shoulder of her green *jole*. "You should have seen the dirt I pulled up on the hiring advisor to make sure I got this job."

Fara steps over. "All right, that's enough talk of . . . whatever this is. Zahru, how are you feeling about this?"

"I'm doing fine, actually," I say, not that I would admit to my father if I was anxious, lest he spend the entire time I'm gone worrying and not sleeping. "There's still a lot to do, and I'm nervous about making the right choices about the lion. But there will be a lot of people on the boat, and the Wraithguard . . . and especially with Hen along, I feel like I can do this."

I'm startled to find I actually believe this. Maybe it's because I now have a friend fluent in blackmail and petty crime at my beck and call, or maybe I'm just overly optimistic that I'll find something on Kasta. Or maybe I've gone over to the other side of stressed and I'll break down crying later tonight. But for now, with Hen at my side and a knife in my tunic, I feel oddly charged.

"Please be safe," Fara says, his strong arms tightening around me. "It's very hard watching you sail away again."

I squeeze him gently. "I'll be back again. Just like last time."

Mora draws me in next, pressing a wet kiss to my cheek. "Of course you will, kar-a. Especially with these."

Something heavy drops into my pocket, and I pull the fabric open to see three small glass potions.

Mora winks. "In case you want to make Prince Kasta's journey as enjoyable for him as he made your last one."

I frown at the small tarantula floating in the topmost bottle. "You realize that even as dōmmel, I'm still not allowed to kill people, right?"

Mora laughs, drawing my dark hair over my shoulders. "Oh, no, my dear. They'll only make him wish he was dead."

I hug her tight. "Gods, you scare me. But I love you so much."

"I love you, too. Do watch out for each other, won't you?"

"You know we will."

The oxhorn sounds again, and a soldier from the docks starts our way. I have a feeling I'm going to be escorted soon if I don't go on my own.

"Love you, Fara," I say, giving him one last hug.

"Love you too," he says.

"Zahru?" Jet asks. "A moment?"

I nod. "Of course."

We step off to the side of the oak walkway, into the shadow of the packing crates. Hen doesn't even try to hide that she's watching us—she just crosses her arms and waits at Mora's side, smiling and staring like we're an act in a play. But Jet was literally born with anti-Hen magic, and when the bubble of silence closes around us, Hen scowls.

"How are you really feeling about the hunt?" Jet asks.

I exhale, looking past his shoulder to the boat. "Honestly, I think I'm all right. I want to catch him. I want to find something."

Jet knows I'm not talking about Odelig, and for a moment, he's quiet. "You're not scared, are you."

It's not a question. It makes me smile, a little, that he would think I'm this fearless.

"I'm nervous," I admit. "I don't want to mess up and tip Kasta off. But scared?" I probably *should* be scared. People conspiring to sneak through a Shifter's personal effects should definitely be scared. But I think of Maia, of the scar over my heart, and shrug. "The only thing I'm scared of is not being able to stop him."

Something unreadable flashes across Jet's face. He glances at my pocket, where Mora's potions sit, and takes a breath. "I had trouble sleeping last night, thinking of you out there with him again, while I have to be here. Not that I was much help in the caves." He grunts. "But it sounds like I don't need to worry."

I don't understand the sadness in his voice. "You did fine in the caves. Kasta had the Illesa, and the protection bracelet, and he just got lucky, being able to knock you out. But no, I know what I'm dealing with now. You don't need to worry."

He looks over his shoulder, squinting at the river. "Good. Just . . . don't forget to be careful, all right?"

I smile. "Careful is my middle name."

He tips his head. "That is a blatant lie."

"It was almost my middle name. Before—"

"You snuck into a Crossing banquet? Or dove headlong into danger to help Melia and me? Or handed Kasta a sacrificial knife?"

This is hard to argue with, and I close my mouth.

Jet sighs. "Listen, it's just . . . I've been down this path before. I know what it feels like to want revenge. It cost me more than I would ever trade again." He crosses his arms. "Be careful."

I'm not sure he's only talking about gathering evidence, and my ribs tighten at the realization that, as much as I want to assure him bringing Kasta down won't change me, the first suggestion I made two days ago was to commission a highly illegal necklace.

I smile. "Don't worry. I'm still me."

A feeling prickles over my skin, but Jet pulls away before I can identify what it is. I join Hen's side, looking over my shoulder, where Mora and Fara watch me with worry, and Jet with something harder. But he manages a smile when I wave, and I thread my arm through Hen's and turn for the boat.

Kasta watches us come from the prow, the enchantments in the railing lighting under his hands like fire. His arms flex, the wind pulling the sharp tails of his cape. A curved, jagged sword glints from his hip.

I touch the potions through my pocket.

No, I may feel many things for this trip, but afraid is not one of them.

XII

MY first chance to spy on Kasta doesn't come until the second day.

After the royal city fades behind a wall of palm trees and heat, I'm immediately escorted to the captain's cabin—a little enclosed room with darkened windows that I would have found dismal if the wooden walls didn't look like they were lacquered by a rainbow—for my schooling lessons. I vow that at the first break I get, I'll case the boat and find Kasta's room, but these people are relentless. My tutors cycle in one after another, and the servants bring my lunch, and outside the cities slide away into orange plateaus and desert brush as we enter the uninhabited stretches of northwestern Orkena. I consider using the time meant for my history lesson with Hen to search the boat, but I don't want to tip her off that I'm after Kasta, so I just enjoy her company and declare that she is indeed far less boring than my prior tutor.

By the time I'm finished, Numet has lowered her lantern below the horizon, and the chefs are preparing dinner belowdecks. And though I do locate Kasta's room on the first sublevel of the boat— right next to mine, of course—I'm informed he's inside. He doesn't come out for dinner, because we are not serving human flesh. He does not come out all night. Rie raises his white lantern above the dunes, and exhaustion pulls at me, and finally I give in and go to sleep.

In the morning, the servants drop off my hunting satchel and ask me to add any personal effects I'll need for the hunt, and I freeze halfway into hiding Mora's potions in the bottom of the bag. They're going to ask this of Kasta, too. And what better place to hide whatever animal pelts he'll want in the wilderness than at the bottom of his personal sack?

"Where are you storing these bags?" I ask the servant who returns to collect it.

The boy bows. "There's a closet abovedecks. I can show you."

I smile. "Please do."

He leads me up the narrow stairs and into the sun, where, toward the back of the boat, a wide closet connects to an enclosed glass dining space. The door faces the river, out of view of everyone but a couple guards at the railing. My smile widens as the servant places my bag inside with a dozen others.

"Is Kasta's bag here yet?" I ask.

"Not yet," the servant says. "We will be sure to get it, though, *dōmmel.*"

Noted.

It's in this good mood that I start my lessons, with the plan that when Hen comes in, I'll ask for a break and go back to search the closet. That should be plenty of time for the servants to have added Kasta's bag. Then the trickiest part of it is simply keeping Hen's suspicions at bay, but I already have a plan for that, too, which is really the most impressive part of this whole ordeal.

"Hen," I whisper later that day, as she sets out little sketches of past Mestrahs like a game board on the desk. There's actually no reason to whisper, since we're alone and the captain's cabin is soundproof. But it feels more official this way.

"I'm in," Hen says, even though I haven't said anything else. "What do you need?"

135

I would ask how she already knows I'm up to no good, but if I'm honest, it would be more alarming to me if she didn't. "I need you to play lookout."

"I'm on it. Where and why?"

I hesitate. This is the part of the plan I don't like so much, because it involves lying. "I need to search through the hunting satchels. I don't want Kasta to see me."

"Easy."

She blinks expectantly, and I know I'm not going to get away with not saying why.

"I want to check his pack for poisons," I say. "And get rid of them. As well as anything else he might plan to use on me and not Odelig."

Then again, I'm thinking this is not so terrible a lie, because this actually *is* something I need to check for, too. I'm just leaving out another big part of it.

Her eyes narrow. "Oh, that's very good. That way if he plans to get stabby again, or something comes to eat him in the night—he's got nothing." She taps her lip with a finger. "All right, I know what I'm going to do."

"It needs to be subtle," I add. "Don't even go near him unless you have to. And maybe bribe someone else to do the distracting, so he doesn't suspect I'm involved? Or whatever it is you do."

Hen tsks like a disappointed mother. "Zahru. This is what I live for."

So it is. We leave the Mestrah sketches on the desk and emerge, squinting, into the heat of high afternoon. Beyond the iron railings, the banks have narrowed, the sand thinning to make way for thicker bushes and lusher grass. Shining merchant boats and weatherworn fishing ships zip by in droves. We're only a few hours from the forest that marks the border between us and Pe, and this is the fastest route for mountain traders and travelers to reach our desert cities.

We're nearing the back of the ship, and I've just pointed out the closet to Hen, when the deck tilts hard under our feet.

"Gods," I say, clinging to Hen as we scramble for balance. The brown sail of a fishing boat flies past far too close, and overhead on the captain's stand, a soldier leans on the railing.

"Hey!" he shouts at the boat. "Watch your speed!"

He grumbles about civilian sailors, and even though what I'm about to do is in no way a crime—not entirely—I'm grateful the guards' attention has shifted to the river.

"No Kasta in sight," Hen says, her black hair fanning as she turns back to me. "I'm going to make sure it stays that way. You won't see me, but unless you hear a scream, assume you're fine to keep looking."

I find this both comforting and extremely disturbing. "You do mean your own scream, right?"

Hen shrugs. "Possibly."

I'm afraid to ask a follow-up question. Hen takes this as her cue and heads back the way we came, past the glass walls of the dining room and toward the prow, where another door leads down to the kitchen and bedrooms. I decide this is another perk of being *dōmmel*, since absolutely no one can question what I'm doing here except for Kasta—not to mention I have every reason to be here, since my pack is here as well. I'm possibly a little too excited to begin my life as a spy, because I throw open the door with a flourish.

Kasta's hunting satchel stands out among the others, the only one as large as mine and nearly identical, except the stitched lanterns and suns along its sides are white, not gold. With a glance over my shoulder, I flip it open.

Rolls of clothes greet me: the deep dyed greens and browns of forest tunics meant to blend with leaves; a cloak for cooler nights. Soft leather boots and a coil of white rope. I dig under the clothes and push aside a quill and capped tube of black ink. The listening scroll is blank, and I'm getting frustrated that this can't be all he's packed when I consider the servants are handling these bags. Kasta would know this, and he'd be careful.

Maybe there's a secret compartment.

I feel along the rough stitching at the bottom, pulling and prying. My nail catches under a rigid portion of one side, and I muffle a shriek of delight as I pull it upward and—

It's empty.

For a moment I can only stare. I flip the false bottom over; I check through again in case I missed the glint of a tooth or the edge of a feather. But there's nothing. My pack didn't have this extra piece, so he must have added it, confirming that he brought something to hide . . . and that I'm already too late in finding it. He must be keeping the pelts on his person.

This realization sends a jolt through me, remembering how I got critical items from him last time: my arms around his neck, his mouth parting mine. I shiver, shoving the memory aside, and touch the literal scar he left over my heart.

If he's carrying pelts, I will find them.

I growl and close the compartment, reorganize his effects, and shove the bag angrily next to mine.

Which is when I hear the scream—and the boat lists hard to the side, sending me to the floor.

"Brace!" the captain cries outside. "Guards—"

BOOM. An explosion rocks the boat, shattering the closet's round window and showering me with glass. I stare in disbelief at the slender lines of crimson beading across my arms.

What did Hen *do*?

Shouts fill the air; running feet stamp the deck. I push satchels off me and burst out of the closet—and run straight into the servant who took my bag this morning.

"*D-dōmmel*," he stammers, as we catch our balance on each other. His fear flashes through me before he quickly lets go. "I'm so sorry. I'm here for the bags."

This strikes me as not the most relevant info to impart. "What *was* that?"

"A cannonball." He blinks, and his eyes widen in horror. "We're under attack. The Wraiths think you're in the captain's cabin!"

My stomach drops. *We're under attack.* I can think of only one group in particular who would dare attack us, even though the Mestrah insisted it would be foolish to do so. This is not one of Hen's distractions.

Wyrim sent more mercenaries.

I shove past the man, into the sun. "Hen!"

"Get down!" the guards shout.

A flaming barrel arcs up over the deck. It seems to hang there above me, spinning in slow motion, before I dive to the side and it splits behind me in a long trail, showering silver powder across the boards. Flames engulf the deck. A Wraith emerges from the captain's cabin in his red armor and gleaming white tunic, but just as he finds me beneath the smoke, the fire roars into a wall.

Cutting me off from the rest of the boat.

"Hen," I whisper.

The deck shakes. Cables slam into the side of our boat as two fishing vessels, both clustered with mercenaries, latch on to us. Our attackers look like common bandits with their faces covered and their dark tunics, except they wear steel armor, and none of them wield magic the way Orkenian bandits would. The sail of one ship juts high over my head, where the prow ran right into us.

Cannons roll on their decks. In the crow's nest of the closest ship, a bandit shouts, and the crews start to leap over.

"It'll be fine," I mock. "Go off into the desert while a war is brewing! *What's the worst that could happen?*"

I shove to my feet, and a Wraith leaps the flames with another Wraith clinging to his side—the first must be an Airweaver. They land beside me in a *thud*. The Airweaver blasts two oncoming bandits back with a flick of his hands; his Stormshrike partner strings lightning between her fingers and fries a bandit with an ax.

"*Dōmmel,*" the Airweaver says, opening his arm. "Hold on to me. We'll fly—"

Another *BOOM* shatters the chaos, and the Wraiths dive on top of me as a cannonball streaks over our heads and smashes against the dining room's reinforced glass. Shrapnel spins past in silver winks. The Airweaver pulls me to my feet, but though he jerks as if lifting from the ground, we don't move. His gaze catches the Stormshrike's. Their masks hide the lower halves of their faces, but more alarming than the panic in their eyes is that I can't feel any of that emotion through the Airweaver's touch.

"*Forsvine.*" The Stormshrike turns her arm, where shrapnel glints like gruesome teeth. "We need to run. Now."

I fear some of it might have hit me too, until the Airweaver releases me, and my magic—and the hum of the guards' nerves—flushes back through me. But I still feel helpless as I look toward the prow, where Hen is somewhere on the other side of the fire. I remind myself I can't help her if I'm dead, and sprint with the guards for the back of the ship. More bandits follow. Two of them leap in our way; a man strikes at the Airweaver with a mace, and the guard yanks a saber from his belt, barely meeting him in time. The Stormshrike draws two three-pronged weapons and blocks another strike from the second bandit. I pull the dagger from inside my tunic, praying I don't have to use it.

Which is when I notice how clear the way is on the far side, the deck protected, for now, by its distance from the boats and the half-standing dining room. The fire won't be on that side. I can go after Hen.

I grip the dagger, and *run*. The Airweaver yells my name. A shadow moves over me, someone on the roof of the dining room, but I'm almost there, I don't stop—

Until this person, like a fist of the gods, smashes down onto the deck in front of me.

A bandit with arms the size of my legs and a thick wooden club rises to her full height like a massive rogue wave. Her long brown hair braids over her shoulder; scars pock her pale skin. My dagger suddenly looks like a butter knife.

She raises the club and swings.

I leap back, out of reach, stumbling to keep my balance. More bandits circle my guards. The woman raises the club again, and eagerness flashes over my skin, white-hot—hers, not mine. I gasp and reach after it, but it feels like groping through the dark, and I definitely can't focus. The emotion vanishes. The club swings; I yelp and plaster myself against the dining room glass.

The dagger goes skidding across the deck. I bounce on my heels. I think I can get to it before she can, and I dive, but she strikes like a snake, twisting her hand through the front of my tunic and lifting me in the air.

I pry at her fingers, and her eagerness sinks into my veins.

My magic sharpens like a looking glass.

She snickers. "I'm disappointed, little demon. They said you were dangerous." She raises the club. "But you'll still fetch us a pretty bit of gold, claws or not."

I take hold of her excitement like a lifeline. The emotion spikes, turning my stomach, blackening the sides of my vision, and I shove back on it, and the club comes down—and her eyes roll into her head. She drops me and crashes to the deck like a tree.

I land hard and scramble away, grasping for the dagger, holding it close to my chest.

Except I didn't need it.

I just stopped a woman four times my size from clobbering me, *with my mind.*

"Dōmmel!"

The Airweaver. He hauls me to my feet, the Stormshrike close behind and a dozen more bandits beyond.

"Wait," I say. "My friend—"

"Other Wraiths are in charge of the crew. Jump!"

He heaves me to the rail, and I have to follow. Wind whistles past my ears, and my feet break the river; cool water closes over my head. I twist and churn, surging for the surface, but I'm afraid I'll cut one of the Wraiths with the dagger, so I sheath it beneath my tunic and come up gasping. The Stormshrike tugs me forward. Arrows zip into the water around us. I dive when the Wraiths say to, staying low until my lungs burn for breath, and this is how we make it to shore, diving and swimming and praying.

When we finally crawl into the safety of the reeds, mud squishing beneath my fingers, I whip around, searching for Hen, and also certain I'll see at least ten bandits swimming after us with swords between their teeth.

But the bandits have scattered from the railing. They converge on a swordsman in white instead, who moves between them like a dancer, cutting through them like weeds. Two of them he barely touches, and they drop screaming and writhing to the deck. The rest bolt like sheep, flying over the railings, shoving each other to get out of Kasta's reach.

Alone, Kasta glances out at me, and flicks blood off his sword as he walks calmly to the other side of the ship.

"*Dōmmel*," mutters the Airweaver, tugging my sleeve. I shake myself and follow him through the reeds, until we emerge behind a low, red boulder the size of a shack. Another Wraith waits here, masked and slender, her brown fingers drumming her wrapped arms.

"Why are you crawling in the muck?" she asks.

The Airweaver sighs. *"Forsvine."* He lifts his arm to show her the embedded metal. "One of their cannonballs shattered near us."

"Rie." The new Wraith turns her amber eyes to the boats. "Please follow me, *dōmmel*. Prince Kasta wants a sample of the attackers' artillery, and then he will be along."

I look back at the smoking ship. "He's just going to board their boats and get it? Alone? Doesn't that seem overly risky?"

Not that I'm actually surprised. Between the poisons Kasta's clearly using again and his Shifter's reflexes, the mercenaries don't stand a chance. But maybe I can get the Wraiths to start finding his behavior suspicious, too.

The new Wraith lifts a shoulder. "Does he look like he's having trouble with it? And he has our best Dominator with him, anyway." As if this second person finalizes it. "Come. The others will be glad to see you."

My heart jerks. "Do you know if my friend Hen is all right?"

She nods. "For all the damage, we did not lose anyone. A few injuries that the Healers are tending to. But, *dōmmel*, I must inform you—we wrote to the Mestrah by listening scroll, and he has ordered a majority of the crew and your tutors to wait here for a new boat. He wants the rest of the expedition to go quickly. Only a few of us will be accompanying you and Kasta going forward."

I stop. "Wait. We're still *going*?" I cry, as behind me, an explosion splits one of the mercenary boats in half. "What about this seems like a good idea? I was almost just clobbered and held for ransom!"

"Yes. With the way things are changing, that is always a risk now. That's why *we* are here. But these mercenaries Wyrim hires are still unorganized and untrained. And now we will have possession of Wyrim's latest technology." Her gaze shifts to the burning ships. "Their *forsvine* is advancing faster than we thought. It's even more critical now that we finish our mission."

I pick at a rip in my tunic. "One of those 'unorganized' bandits was holding me up by the neck."

The Stormshrike pauses in plucking *forsvine* from her arm. "That *was* impressive, how you knocked her out. How did you get ahold of her club?"

I sigh, because of course I'm not allowed to tell them the actual reason. "Just a lucky break."

"See?" the new Wraith says. "We had everything under control. And here you are, unharmed."

This is both difficult to argue with while feeling immensely untrue. But I let it go. Thank the Mestrah—of all the unlikely people I thought I'd thank—for at least getting Kasta and me one Influence lesson before we left.

But my gut still twists as we step through dry desert brush to meet the others. I'm glad Hen is safe. I'm glad she won't have to go any farther on this reckless mission, where mercenary attacks are actually expected and sheer luck is considered *under control*. But whatever security I had in having her at my side, it's gone now.

And now I will be alone with the boy-monster who is almost single-handedly taking on two bandit crews.

I close my hand around the dagger under my tunic.

This is where the true test begins.

XIII

THE crew accompanying Kasta and me on the hunt is now nine: a Healer, a chef, five Wraiths, and two servants, including the boy I ran into in the storage room. Randomly, there are already horses when I arrive at the rendezvous point, because the Wraithguard seems to be able to conjure whatever they want out of thin air. In reality, I'm informed we have them on loan from a nearby ranch, which is not nearly as mysterious or impressive. I decide when I tell Jet about this later, they will be conjured horses. Possibly misty in nature, or made of soot. My story, my rules.

I think the increasing stress of my situation is making me snappy.

Kasta and the infamous Dominator, a Wraith whose name is Yashi, join us soon after splattered in blood and ash. From the certain way the Wraith spoke of him, I expected Yashi to be a mountain of a man, someone even more muscular than Marcus. But he's a boy probably a year my younger, slender and shorter than me, with sandy beige skin and sleek black hair that falls over one eye. His arms are toned, but not outrageously so. But then I have to remind myself it's his Dominator magic, not muscle, that makes him capable of lifting small houses.

Not that he's showing off any kind of impressive skill at the moment. He and Kasta are each carrying one of the bandits' heavy shrapnel cannonballs, but with the *forsvine* in them blocking Yashi's power, he's winded, and sweating, and cursing up a storm. The other Wraiths tease him, the Airweaver nudges him so he stumbles, and Yashi heaves the cannonball away, though it doesn't

146

go far. This elicits rampant laughter, until Yashi raises his arms, *forsvine*-free, and asks someone to try it again.

The laughter stops. Everyone steps back.

Yashi takes first pick of the horses after Kasta and me, but there's still snickering as we set out with the cannonballs loaded onto wooden slats behind one of the servants' geldings.

The too-familiar sight of passing desert and brush from horseback sends beetles down my spine. The heat is like the breath of a creature, slinking down the neck of my cooling cloak, thickening the air. I keep my hood low over my eyes. Brown oxen watch us from clumps of grass, and white cranes fly overhead on their way to the river, to which we move parallel, though well out of sight of the boats. The servants chat quietly. The Healer draws out a scroll to read.

And Kasta rides wordlessly beside me, the hilt of his sword still crusted in blood.

This is the uneasy arrangement I've forced on us, because I refuse to follow him, as if yielding to his charge. And so I keep my gray mare beside his, a carriage-width of distance away, and pretend he's Jet, or Melia, or any number of delightful people I would rather be on this journey with. It's made slightly easier that he's changed into forest colors of deep green and black, for I'm just now realizing I've never seen him in anything but white. But the kilometers pass. All the Wraiths except Yashi move to patrol out of view, and the silence shifts and thickens.

The trust I once put in Kasta, the trust he shattered, moves like broken glass through my veins.

I bite my tongue. I won't say anything, I won't cause a scene. I need to be thinking about my next move to find his animal pelts. I need to be thinking about Odelig. For a while, this works. I decide I'll use one of Mora's potions in Kasta's drink later—the note Mora left with them assured me the black vial is only a sleeping potion— so I can slip into his tent after he's out and search him. I decide I will definitely follow Melia's advice to insist on capturing Odelig alive. This is excellent progress. Except that Numet's lantern has barely moved overhead by the time I'm done.

And then there are only memories.

Kasta's hands low on my spine, his confession on my lips. *Give me some time,* he'd said. *I don't know what this is.* The certainty that I'd reached him. That I meant something to him, for risking my own freedom to save his life, for believing he was better—and then everything he did after, from abandoning Sakira to standing on that altar, the knife tip on my skin.

And then *Maia.*

And my care for not making a scene thins until it cracks.

"So," I say, my voice tight as a snare. "Is being *dōmmel* everything you dreamed of?"

A muscle twitches in Kasta's jaw. His gaze stays on the distant hills.

"Your father's attention," I press. "A god's power. You finally have everything you wanted. Worth killing me again, you'd say?"

He presses a breath through his teeth. "You know it wasn't that easy."

"Oh, wasn't it? You didn't seem that torn. You don't seem that sorry."

"That's because you can't even *imagine* what I—" He bites down on the words, but whatever calmness he's striving for, he can't quite smooth his face. "It was my life or yours. I couldn't trust you to help me. You and Jet would have turned on me the moment we returned to the palace, and you would have told them . . ."

His secret. My blood boils. "Because I'd proven to be so two-faced and merciless before that, yes?"

"You'd just poisoned me and left me to die in a tent. Would *you* have trusted you?"

"*If* you'll recall," I seethe, "I left because I asked if you were still planning to kill me, and the answer was not no."

"Do you know what it took for me to even say *maybe*?" He jerks on the reins, and his brown horse startles. "Do you know how long I lived in fear of—" He glances at the servants, and I know he almost said something about his father throwing him into the streets, making him join the magicless Forsaken. He lowers his voice. "By asking me to spare your life, you were asking me to risk my own. To throw away what was certain escape from a fate *worse* than death, for the slim possibility that mercy might work. And I—" He glares at the horizon, his brow pinched. "I was considering it."

A quiet falls between us. I watch him, unsettled, wishing he'd just say he's glad he did it. This other side of him is too confusing, a trickster moving a coin between his hands.

"I did what I had to to survive," he says, the cold returning to his words. "No different than you."

"*No different?*" I exclaim, laughing. "Let's see. You cut a symbol into my wrist and dragged me into an ancient contest, and I poisoned you to get away. Fine, on some twisted level, I guess that would make us even. Except *then*, I handed you a knife and begged you to side with me, and you *literally tried to kill me!*" An unexpected twist of despair drowns my anger, and my throat clenches. I won't cry. I won't let him see how much that failure haunts me, how much I believed he wouldn't do it.

I tighten my grip on the reins. "I trusted you with my life, Kasta. And you couldn't even trust me to keep my word."

He's quiet for a long while. I hate that even more, like my words are sinking in, like he's wondering if he made a mistake. My fingers shake; I press my hands into the gray mare's neck to hide it. It doesn't matter if he's sorry. It doesn't change what he did.

When Kasta speaks again, his tone is careful. "You would have betrayed your dear Jet, then? If I'd chosen you, you'd have done everything in your power to see me crowned?"

My gut twists. Kasta watches me a moment, and a slow, bitter smile pulls his lips. "I thought not."

I scrape a line of sand on my hand. "If you had trusted me," I say, each word like admitting a dark secret, "there would have been nothing I wouldn't have done to help you."

He closes his eyes. "Don't lie to me."

"It's not a lie," I say, aching. "Jet wanted a simpler life. He came back for the crown because of me . . . because of *you*. But if you had spared me, you would have proven yourself to be someone else. I can't say exactly what would have happened. But if I asked him to, I know Jet would have given you another chance."

Kasta's shoulders tense, but he says nothing more. The horses walk on, and I try to get ahold of myself, of the shame and disappointment threatening to rip me apart. This was so much easier to handle when I thought he was dead. Then, I could rationalize that he got what he deserved and move on. I don't know how to move on from *this*. From seeing him every day, from remembering, from agonizing over what he could have been, in another life.

I shake my nerves out, reminding myself it doesn't matter—and suddenly realize how silent it is, aside from the horses' steps. When I look over my shoulder, the servants startle and comment on the weather, and the Healer flips his reading scroll back up. Even Yashi quickly looks out into the desert. Great. By this time next week, half the country will know how much Orkena's future Mestrahs loathe each other.

We say nothing more the rest of the day.

But when Kasta glances at me now, the fire in his eyes is gone.

We reach the forest at dusk.

It's unfair how beautiful it is. I'm in the kind of mood right now where I want everything to be dismal and ugly just so I can be irritated about that, too, but the hills of western Orkena are rolling and *green*, as if the gods rushed to paint the desert and spent the rest of their time here. Color bursts from yellow and purple flowers within the grasses, and the hills roll like blanket folds, slight and round against the mountains jutting high behind them. Trees with white trunks stand solitary where the sand gives way to soil, growing thicker as they stretch to the horizon. Their leafy arms grow wider than they are tall, and the horses sigh in contentment when we move under their shade.

Rest, they think to each other. *Shade. Grass.*

Yashi moves his bay gelding between Kasta and me and tugs his mask down. "The scouts just wrote me," he says, his focus only on Kasta. "They've found evidence of Odelig near the Pe border. They think he's in the mountains."

"*Apos*," Kasta says. "We'll have to wait for him to come down. How far is the border?"

"Just an hour more. If we camp near it, your magic may lure him back over."

I loudly clear my throat. "Then that's what we'll do. Thank you for consulting us."

They both look over, Kasta with something unreadable, Yashi with a raised brow. But I see the pattern forming already. This is how it went with Gallus, too, my pompous Firespinning ex— anytime he had important company over, I went silent, which often took a great amount of willpower and a prayer, all because I was afraid of appearing out of place. It got to the point that one of his friends, who I saw weekly, asked three moons in what my name was. I do not want Wraiths, at the end of this trip, asking the Mestrah what my name is.

"*Dōmmella*," Yashi mumbles, using the plural of our titles. He presses quick fingers to his forehead and pulls his horse to the back of the group.

We set up camp an hour later, under a copse of trees tucked away in a hillside, just past a decrepit log cabin built in the Pe style, its floor strewn with cracked hickory diningware and the remnants of a dusty bearskin rug. A relic left over from before the Ending Drought, probably, when Orkena's borders last expanded. The

Wraiths again defer to Kasta, asking him where to put the tents and what he'd like for dinner, each of which I answer first, and with the sassy kind of look Mora would be proud of. At first this seems to make no difference, because the servants still raise Kasta's tent before mine and bring him water and a map without so much as looking at me. Yashi keeps going on about Kasta's impressive fighting skills, which is starting to press on my last nerve.

"A boulder of a man tackled him from behind," he says. "Had him in a headlock, but Kasta stood up and threw him overboard like he was nothing. And you know what it takes to impress *me, dōmmel* or not."

Kasta gives this a quiet smile, but while the Wraiths murmur their appreciation, I log this one in the back of my mind. Unusual strength, noted.

"I knocked out a woman four times my size while she held me by the neck," I say, not wanting to be left out.

This is greeted with uncomfortable, but impressed, silence.

The chef still makes Kasta's plate first. But they serve mine at nearly the same time.

Later, when the campfire burns high and the darkness shrinks the world to our hollow of trees, the Wraiths settle on logs with their waterskins, and I move in the shadows to my tent. I've already worked out a plan to drop the sleeping potion into Kasta's drink, which involves switching out his waterskin and telling a small white lie to one of the servants. All I need now is the potion.

I dig through my satchel, the light potion around my neck casting a liquidy silver glow on the fabric. The tents, too, are uneasy reminders of the Crossing, though not all in a bad way. This model reminds me of Jet's, with a low slope of a roof and a rainbow-striped sleeping mat. My heart tugs, imagining him stretched out on that mat, his chest rising gently in sleep. How he'd smile if I reached out to wake him, brushing his cheek with my thumb. How he might lift his hand to my face—until he saw the sleeping potion in my hand.

"Stop it," I whisper to imaginary Jet. "Kasta needs to sleep anyway."

My daydream vanishes. I lift the little black bottle from the bag, thumbing the wax seal. It doesn't mean anything that I'm resorting to drugs to search through my nemesis's personal effects. Compared to physically knocking him out, or using a potion that would make him ill, it's arguable that I'm even being *too* nice.

It doesn't mean I'm changing. I'm just . . . more resourceful.

I shake the little bottle, moving to tuck it into my cloak—and pause. Nothing sloshed when I did that. I raise the light potion beside it to see how full it is, and my stomach dives.

It's empty.

The seal flips off easily when I shove it. Only a single drop remains, falling sadly to the sand. I toss the bottle back into the bag and dig out the two other potions, but their seals are loose too, their contents dumped. I know these were full when we left.

Someone's been in *my* bag.

That these might have been used on me makes panic climb my throat—except that potions work within minutes, so I would have felt the effects by now. Whoever it was only emptied them.

And then put them back, so I'd know the bottles hadn't simply been lost.

I look over my shoulder, through the slit of the tent, where Kasta leans back on a log with his waterskin, his head tilted toward Yashi. Smiling, *laughing*, like he has no cares in the world.

His gaze flickers, firelit, to my tent.

My blood simmers.

This, I think, is how I'll learn about war.

XV

I sleep terribly.

Half the night I spend fuming that Kasta got ahead of me, and the other half I lie listening, my hand on the hilt of my dagger, jumping at every crackle of the enchanted campfire. The Wraiths assured me the tent is warded against animals, but I have trust issues. Unlikely things happen to me all the time. And I don't know if the protection spells would consider a Shifter an animal.

But if Kasta leaves his tent, I don't see it happen through the slit I've left open. And nothing comes to kill me.

Morning brings very little relief. I nurse a mug of melted chocolate before the fire, my cloak pulled around me for warmth, since the night's chill holds stronger here to the grass than the sand. But surviving the night was only the first step. If Kasta plans to get rid of me, his best chance to do it will be on this hunt. The Wraiths can't come with us for the start. Their lesser magic, strange as that is for me to say, will repel Odelig instead of attracting him, so they're not to come until we summon them on our listening scrolls. Meaning Kasta and I will be very alone.

At least today, in addition to my dagger, I'll have a hunting knife enchanted with lightning. For Odelig, of course. I nudge the hilt of it strapped around my thigh, and keep drinking.

Stay alive, take Odelig alive. The theme for the day is *live*.

Kasta emerges from his tent, his black hair mussed and curling at his ears, his hunting cloak dark and pressed. Stitched golden lanterns hem his tunic; a white rope hangs at his belt. Maybe it's my glare, or that he knows I can't ask about the potions he emptied without the Wraiths overhearing, but I swear the corners of his mouth twitch. Amused.

"Let's go." He starts for the horses, but I don't move.

"In a minute," I say.

I actually don't have a reason to wait. My drink is nearly gone, I'm dressed, there's nothing else to do. Except to remind him that I don't answer to him anymore.

It's my turn to smirk when I finally saunter to the horses, ignoring Kasta's glower, and swing into the saddle, my riding cloak spilling golden down my arm. The Wraiths give us a nod, I check that the listening scroll to summon them is clasped tight to my belt, and we start off.

Me and the Shifter, on our own in the woods.

The forest is loud. A dozen animal conversations buzz in my ears, from songbirds to squirrels to yellow snakes, all otherwise hidden in the branches and the tall grass. Though I imagine anyone from Pe would laugh to hear me call this a forest, since the trees don't grow nearly as thick here as they will in the mountains. Here, where the desert heat still bears down but the mountain streams trickle, the trees grow in sporadic clumps, long feathers of shade followed by wide stretches of grass. My gray mare sloshes through a tiny creek, lipping the pink flowers at its edge.

Treat, she thinks. *Good.*

We walk a kilometer, nearly two, our horses the distance of a house apart. I keep my hand near my hidden knife, but Kasta hardly looks at me. His attention flits to the trees, to the ground. Once in a while he stops, listening, and though I don't hear anything, he heads off in a slightly different direction. I don't think Shifters have any better sight or hearing than normal, but it's starting to feel like it.

After he does this the fourth time, I shift uneasily. "You're supposed to be teaching me."

To track, I mean. Kasta looks over from where he's stopped and shrugs. "You'd have to be closer."

I don't like this answer at all, especially because it makes sense, so long as he doesn't add *so I can kill you* to the end of it. I edge the mare nearer. Until we're two strides away, then one.

He regards this distance with narrowed eyes, then drops to the ground. "To find your target's prints, you can also track their prey." He pushes his fingers into the soft mud, beside which small hoofprints sink, two small lines near each other that must belong to an antelope. "These are fresh. If we follow them, we'll find where they feed. And eventually Odelig's own tracks." He slides his fingers over the earth, and taps a much larger, round-toed print. "Like this. We'll go on foot from here."

He moves on without waiting for a reply, and I curse under my breath as I dismount and tell the horses to wait for us, not wanting to tether them in case Odelig finds them before we find him. And there goes my fastest escape route. But even if I can't use Influence against Kasta, I still have the Wraith's scroll, and my knife. Let him try.

"Wait," he whispers. He pulls his hood down, a breeze catching the sleek ends of his hair. "Do you feel that?"

Gooseflesh rises on my arms as I look over the field, but the only thing I feel is an intense dislike of this entire situation.

When I don't answer, he starts off again. "We're close. Be ready."

I cross my arms. "You realize we haven't talked strategy yet."

"Yes, because there's only one strategy here that's going to work: I hunt him, and you stay out of my way."

"That wasn't your father's instruction. We're supposed to work together." I finally catch up to him, though I still leave distance between us.

"I already know you're not going to kill him," Kasta says. "What else is there to decide?"

"If we're going to kill him at all. It's a waste if his magic isn't immune to the metal. I want him captured alive."

"Odelig is not a housecat, Zahru. He'll be curious about our magic, and then he'll see us as food. I'm already limited to using a rope, because a crossbow won't work on him, and I'd rather make sure he's gone than give him an opening to make me a meal."

My blood flashes. "And that's always how it has to be, isn't it? Everything or nothing. Death or life."

"Death *and* life." Kasta shakes his head. "That's what you've never understood. Someone dies, but many more live because of it. It's a ruler's burden to decide who."

"Really? And when will you decide, again, that my life is worth the trade?"

Kasta stops. It's a moment before he looks at me, but when he does, I swear he grimaces. "Once was enough."

He starts off. I stand there, irritated, wondering if that means he felt it justified and he just doesn't need to again, because I can't fathom what else it could be.

"What does that mean?" I say.

No answer. I press a frustrated growl through my teeth. "Gods help me, Kasta, if you have any intention of this partnership actually working, you will answer that question."

I realize this is an ironic thing to say, since *I* have no intention of this ruling partnership working, but it stops him.

He turns, and his shoulders drop. "It means I could never do it again, so if that's what you're waiting for, you can stop."

He glances meaningfully at the place I've hidden the dagger under my cloak and moves on. I clench my fists, both hating how transparent he always makes me feel and confused by his answer. It wasn't an apology. But he could have ignored me and made clear that working with me was not his intention in the least.

I decide it doesn't matter. This is how he is, calm and thoughtful when things are going his way, when he believes he's safe. He wants me to realize how alone we are. That he knows where the knife is; that he could stage my death, with lion prints all around, and no one would be the wiser. But even if he doesn't want me dead right now, it doesn't mean that won't change. He was like this before, too, when he thought I was no threat to him. This is only the eye of a storm. A reminder of why I must be so careful in getting the pelts from him.

I follow in silence.

The leaves burn a deeper green as the sun rises, and butterflies, small and blue, flit around the crimson ties of my cooling cloak. I shove Kasta from my mind. I need to be focusing on Odelig, on how we can spare him, on how I can convince Kasta to consider it. I wish I knew more about the science behind magic. If I'd had more lessons, I'm sure there would be some clever formula I could convince Kasta with, some scientific theory. But he's done this *years* longer, and—

I snap my head up. Not only because of the idea that just came to me, but because of the actual tug in my gut.

Kasta jerks to a stop. "What? Do you feel something?"

Birds break from the nearest branches in a spray of red, and the meadow grows eerily silent. And I *do* feel something. An odd sense of familiarity, as if I've been here before, as if I've lived this moment a hundred times. Somewhere ahead of us, something is watching.

Kasta crouches and slides the rope from his arm.

"Wait," I whisper, dropping beside him. Gods, I hope this idea works. "If Odelig's magic really can help us, then fine, I'll agree the sacrifice is necessary. But you're a scientist. Don't you have ways to test the magical properties of things?"

"Of non-living things, yes," he mutters.

"And you're telling me that after years of study, you can't think of *one* solution to this that doesn't involve killing Odelig first?"

He shoots me a glare, and it's oddly reassuring to see a glimpse of his old defiance. "I told you. It's too dangerous to do this any other way."

"Too difficult, you mean." I shrug. "I understand. Killing him is the easiest way."

"It's not—" A branch snaps in the distance, and we both look up. The pull in my gut grows stronger.

"I will agree to this," Kasta hisses. "If you can make him yield without a fight, we'll do things your way. If he attacks, we do things mine."

He moves off at a crouch, and I don't think I imagine the strange silence of his footsteps or the unnatural ease with which he moves. But I can hardly focus on that for how stunned I am at what he just said. He's not going to *help* subdue Odelig peacefully, but he's going to let me try.

I would consider this as strange as him saying he has no plans to kill me, but then I remember the Mestrah's expectations extend to both of us. Kasta knows that if he doesn't listen to me, I'll tell his father, and he'll risk being demoted. Now I'll have to admit Kasta gave me a chance, however slim.

I bristle and follow, determined not to give him the opening. I will be there when he finds Odelig, and I'll know if he's acting in self-defense. *Please*, I beg the gods. *If you are still watching, please allow me this.*

We blend with the bushes; our dark trousers match the shadows, our green tunics the grass. We pass under branches and through bushes that come to our waists. Over a small stream, where the knot in my stomach tightens again. We turn west. The pull intensifies as we step through weeds as tall as my shoulders—

Into a boneyard.

Mercifully, Odelig is not here, but this still feels like a very bad place to be. Antelope rib cages, hog skulls, and a hundred leg bones and vertebrae litter the large clearing, half-sunk into the mud. The shredded remnants of a saddlebag trail over the decaying corpse of a camel, and near it, a pair of human skulls grin atop tattered tunics.

The tug in my core pulls backward.

"Back," Kasta says, his voice tight. "Move slowly."

I do, though each of my careful footsteps sounds like a crack. Back into the weeds we go. Away from the bones. Out into fresh air again, where we turn—

And come face-to-face with Odelig.

XV

THE lion is the size of a horse. His mane is a deep orange, and his pelt glistens like liquid gold, shot through with lightning-white stripes. More stripes line his face, rimming yellow eyes. His jaw could easily fit my entire head inside of it.

Paws the size of plates, and the claws hidden inside them, stand one leap away.

Kasta's hand moves to the rope.

"Easy," I whisper, though I'm not sure who I'm talking to.

Odelig growls, his ears flattening. My pulse quickens. I'd forgotten wild animals find it alarming to suddenly be able to understand a human, unlike domestic animals who've been raised around Whisperers. But Odelig only shifts his great gaze between us, his lip slowly dropping. I glance at Kasta, who stands stiff, and exhale as the lion's fear lightens with curiosity.

You speak? Odelig thinks. His voice is deep, and like Ashra, he sounds far older than he looks.

"I do," I say, the words thick in my throat.

His lip rises in a sneer as his gaze moves to Kasta. *You hunt.*

"No," I say, though this is half a lie. "We seek. We need your help."

A snort, like a laugh. Odelig's lips reveal canines the size of my finger. *Help?*

"Our king desires your magic," I admit, as Kasta's hand tightens on the rope. "But if you come with us peacefully, I think I can save your life. You'll be returned home as soon as possible, and treated as a god until then." I swallow. I don't want to admit this next part, but I can't risk him attacking without understanding what's at stake. "If you don't, they will kill you."

The lion growls. *Let them try.*

"I don't think this is working," Kasta murmurs.

"I know I ask a lot," I say, ignoring Kasta. "But you'd already be dead if it wasn't for me. Let me save you."

Save, the lion muses, his great claws flexing. *I am not one who needs saving.*

My blood chills. "Oh gods."

Foolish human, Odelig sneers. *I make no deal with prey.*

"Wait!" I cry as Kasta snaps the rope out to the side. "Please—"

Odelig springs—but not for me. I dive at the same time Kasta dodges the other way, the prince barely rolling free of Odelig's teeth. Kasta's on his feet in an instant. He whips the rope out, but Odelig shies, jumping out of reach before leaping on Kasta and slamming him to the ground. His mouth opens wide, but Kasta catches him by his massive mane and heaves him sideways—

I jump to my feet and *run*, away from the clearing, toward the trees.

"Zahru!" Kasta yells. "You can't run!"

But I'm not staying to be lion bait. The trees aren't far. I'm only twenty paces away, then ten, before heavy steps bound behind me. My blood jerks. I turn to see Odelig springing through the air, and I shriek and dive away, my shoulder jamming against rocks as I narrowly avoid his claws. My hidden dagger rips loose. I don't see where it goes. Odelig turns just as I yank the hunting knife free, the momentary spark of its Lightning enchantment making him recoil.

But he knows, as well as I, that if he can endure the initial jolt of the weapon, he'll be able to get to me. The blade will bend against him.

A flare of his impatience cuts through me and he circles, calculating when he'll jump. I don't dare look, but I imagine Kasta standing nearby, amused and waiting. He may not be out to kill me himself, but I definitely don't trust him to save me. His focus right now is Odelig. I can't imagine he'll care if I go down in the process.

Anger ignites in my ribs, and Odelig roars in response.

The lion leaps. I hardly think. I bring the knife up, and it bends against his jaw, a bolt of electricity surging from the metal through his face. He growls and leaps away, shaking his head before jogging around me again. One of these times I will miss, and there will be nothing between his teeth and my neck.

"Keep him distracted," Kasta says. "Let him jump. I'll snare him mid-leap."

"Right," I say. "And as soon as he's chewed my head off, you'll pull it tight."

"Believe it or not, I'm more interested right now in saving my soldiers than letting you die. And I meant what I said before."

Odelig snarls, darting low for my feet. I strike again with the knife. It jolts off his nose, and when a new rush of his frustration spills over me, I get an idea.

"I'm going to use Influence," I say as Odelig crouches. "Don't rope him, or he'll look away from me. I think I can knock him out if we maintain eye contact."

"You don't even know if it works on animals," Kasta says. "Your other plan already failed. Let me handle this."

"Don't throw it! I'm serious—"

Odelig leaps. His eagerness flashes over my skin, and I try to let it in as I did with the bandit—but before I can, a rope snaps into my vision. Odelig ducks and slams into my legs. The rope slicks over his back, and air bursts from my lungs as the lion's shoulder drives me into the ground. The knife flies from my fingers. Teeth snap for my neck, a flash of white daggers, but I'm touching him now and his surety presses into my palms—

I shove back in a panic, and Odelig yelps, but the connection between us snaps. He jumps off of me, yellow eyes widening—and bolts for the mountains.

"*Sabil*," Kasta growls. "I told you that wouldn't work!"

"And I told you not to rope him!"

He takes off after Odelig, and I cough and roll to my side, trying to catch my breath. Leaves crunch around my face. Soon Kasta and the lion disappear through the grass, no more than distant footfalls and quivering foliage.

I don't think the Mestrah is going to be pleased with how we handled this.

I groan and lie back in the grass, rubbing my aching ribs. I can't decide whether I hate it more that Kasta was right and I should have let him handle Odelig from the start, or that I never wanted to be out here in the first place. I might have ruined our chance at countering *forsvine*. For wanting to show mercy, I might have cost Orkena everything.

I don't know what's right anymore.

Wincing, I sit up, shaking leaves from my hair. I need to go after them. I need to call the Wraithguard. My hand hesitates over the listening scroll—if Odelig turns to fight Kasta, I could let fate play out. Maybe Odelig would win. But if he doesn't, or if Kasta never catches up to him . . . the Mestrah will not be impressed by my lack of action.

I grit my teeth and pull the scroll from my belt.

◆

With the Wraithguard's help, Kasta catches up to Odelig not far past the boneyard.

I never do find my dagger.

I let go of the Airweaver's pristine tunic after he brings me to a small clearing, my stomach turning at the sight of the lion's body. Yashi and the Stormshrike stand nearby, speaking to Kasta in low tones. The rope gleams white around Odelig's neck. His long back is to me, dusted in twigs and grass. One of Orkena's most legendary beasts, gone like a storm.

A strange mix of relief and sadness opens in my chest. I won't be the reason we failed anymore, but Odelig was still just an animal, a predator acting on instinct. We hardly left him a choice, telling him we needed either his cooperation or his life.

At least I did not have to kill him.

I move forward, rubbing my hands up my torn cloak, chilled despite the gathering heat. It's nearing midday, and with Odelig in hand, we should be back on a boat by dusk. I start for Kasta, not wanting to be left out of whatever decisions are being made . . . when the great lion's side rises, and falls.

I jerk to a stop.

"What?" I whisper. I rush to his side, not believing my eyes. But Odelig breathes again. The golden pelt shimmers over rising ribs, and falls once more. The rope hangs loose around his mane. His eyes are closed, almost peaceful.

"He's unconscious," Kasta says.

A hundred replies catch in my throat. I run my hand over Odelig's warm shoulder and down his side, and his skin twitches in reflex. There are no wounds on his body, no blood.

"I don't understand," I finally manage. "He attacked us. You said you'd kill him if he attacked us."

"I used the rope to catch him. The Wraiths tied him down, and the Healer was able to put him under."

My fingers shake in Odelig's fur. This is a dream. This isn't real.

"The Healer can extract a tooth," Kasta says. "We can test it against a sample of *forsvine* from the cannonballs. If his magic doesn't work, the Healer will return the tooth, and Odelig will go on as if nothing happened."

Tears blur my eyes. I run my fingers over the soft fur of Odelig's face and finally look at Kasta.

"Why?" is all I can say.

Kasta's blue gaze flickers to the ground.

"I made you a promise," he mutters before moving away.

So he did.

That he would remember, that he would claim to be making good on it, draws all the feeling from my fingers. The altar flashes before me; the knife. Kasta swearing on my life. That he would do better, that he'd be a good king. That he'd show others the mercy he couldn't show me.

The Healer kneels beside Odelig, his sure hands reinforcing a peaceful sleep over the lion as he extracts a tooth as long as my thumb. But it's Kasta I watch. Kasta who takes the tooth and pulls a palm-sized triangle of liquidy silver from his pocket. The top of the *forsvine* sample is punched through and corded with leather, and he offers me both of his hands, the tooth held in one and the *forsvine* in the other.

I made you a promise.

"Zahru," he prompts when I don't say anything.

I blink, watching him like he's a stranger. "How are we going to do this?"

"We know a piece of *forsvine* this size neutralizes human magic at a radius of three meters. If Odelig's power is immune, that means a person wearing his tooth should be able to stand within that radius and still be immortal against conventional weapons. We'll make sure his magic works on its own first, then test it against the *forsvine*." He lifts the hand with the metal. "Do you want to be the one with the crossbow"—he lifts the tooth—"or the magic?"

My stomach pulls. Maybe he isn't as changed as I thought. "You're going to shoot someone with a crossbow?"

"I'm taking whatever you're not."

I straighten. "I get to shoot *you* with a crossbow?"

Concern deepens his brow. "How else would we test it?"

I can think of many other ways, namely using one of the servants as a target, which I assumed would be his style. But as much as I want to delight in the prospect of repaying even a fraction of the pain he imparted to me, here's yet more disturbing evidence that something is different about him. Which I quickly remind myself doesn't matter, since he still killed Maia.

I reach for the metal, waiting for him to pull away, to give me the tooth instead. "Obviously that's the only way we can test it," I say.

He doesn't move. The *forsvine* slips between my fingers, as oily and cold as a fish—and my magic recoils. Emptiness drains through me, settling like grease in my heart, and it takes everything I have to push the cord over my neck and not throw it away. Yashi brings me a crossbow, and still Kasta holds the tooth, stepping beside a tree trunk just beyond three meters from me. Turning. Waiting.

I swing the crossbow up with all the experience of someone who has watched people use one without ever having used one myself.

"Yashi," Kasta says.

My smile is small. Here it is. He'll switch with the Wraith, he'll make an excuse. But Kasta just nods at me and my questionable form.

"To your shoulder, *dōmmel*," Yashi says, his wrapped fingers guiding the weapon into the right place. "Line up the sights where you want to shoot and pull the trigger. I would suggest aiming for a shoulder or an arm, just in case."

I breathe out, a shiver running through me as the sights flash over Kasta's neck, his heart. Still he doesn't call for someone to replace him. I don't understand. Even if his focus is on testing the tooth, he knows how much I loathe him now. How easy it would be for me to "miss" and strike something vital. How can he trust me like this?

I fit an arrow into the groove, agitation twitching through

my fingers. Yashi shows me how to notch it into place.

I fire without warning. The shot runs truer than I thought it would, reckless, and Kasta staggers as the arrow splinters apart over his stomach, scattering bloodless to the ground. He lets go of his unharmed torso with a gasp. With the Healer close, that shot wouldn't have killed him if the tooth hadn't worked, but it would have hurt far, far more than if I'd struck an arm. The company goes quiet, and Kasta exhales, his kohl-lined eyes narrowing when he looks up.

But he doesn't scold me. Doesn't call for a replacement. Just steps closer, inside three meters now, where the tooth might be rendered useless by the *forsvine*, and moves against a tree trunk. Knowing where I might aim again. Daring me to do it.

I notch the next arrow, my fingers shaking. Jet's warning about revenge slithers through my ears, and I make myself focus. Maybe that's why I ask this time.

"Ready?" I say.

Kasta squares himself and nods.

A chill prickles my arms. But I tighten my grip on the weapon, force my aim up, and fire.

"*Apos Rachella*," Kasta curses, twisting as the arrow sinks into his shoulder. The Healer is there in an instant, apologizing as he works his hand over the wound. Kasta sinks to the ground, and I'm torn between the conflicted satisfaction of seeing him in pain and the deeper realization of what just happened.

Odelig's magic did not work against the *forsvine*.

We still have nothing to protect us.

XVI

LATER that night, on a new boat sent by the Mestrah and surrounded by a fleet of guard ships, I stand on the deck, looking out at the starlit dunes. We moved quickly away from the Pe border after replacing Odelig's tooth and releasing him, and now we're at full speed to return to the capital. The Mestrah even closed this section of the river to the public so we wouldn't be hindered. For kilometers it has been little more than tufts of dark palm trees and stretches of silver sand.

I should be thinking of my next move to expose Kasta. I should be practicing my Influence, circling the deck and reading the guards' emotions. I should be tracing letters in my cabin, practicing my signature, doing what little I can to keep learning without my tutors. I should be worrying what it means that we still don't have an answer for *forsvine*.

Instead I'm thinking of Kasta before that tree, his gaze steady as I raised a weapon to his heart.

The door that leads belowdecks rolls open. I turn, and Kasta and I freeze—him with his hand still on the latch, me halfway to moving away. But a moment passes. Two. He doesn't go back in, and I don't leave.

"It's late," he says, staying where he is.

Not that he's dressed for it. He shed his forest garb as soon as we returned to the boat, and the gold symbols trimming his white tunic glitter in the boat's torches—attire fit for being seen in public, not for sleeping. I pull the plush edges of my robe tighter around me.

"Yes," I agree. "Are you going somewhere?"

I keep my voice light, though the question is loaded. Now is the perfect time for a Shifter to sneak off and find a meal before morning.

"Just for some air," he hedges. His gaze flickers to the dunes and back to me. "I've been studying the cannonballs."

A likely excuse for why he hasn't dressed for bed. I cross my arms, unconvinced. "And?"

"I don't have the right tools here to test them." Slowly, he moves for the rail, and though I consider for a moment that I no longer have my dagger . . . I don't move.

He stops beside me, an arm's length away, his gaze on the desert.

"Do you think you can counter *forsvine*?" I ask, realizing this is something I actually hope for.

He's quiet for a long while. "I don't know."

We stand in silence. Crickets chirp from the shore; water trickles against the boat.

"What happened with Odelig . . ." he says. "We can't do that again."

I pick at my nails. "You not listening, you mean?"

"*You* didn't listen, either." But there's no edge to the words, and he leans his arms on the rail. "I think we can agree this isn't an ideal situation for either of us. But for the sake of Orkena, I am willing to compromise." I feel him look over, though I keep my focus solidly on the shore. "You saved me from making a mistake today. I would have killed Odelig for nothing, and even though that was the Mestrah's order, I know he and the court would have found a way to berate me for it."

I snicker. "Are you saying . . . I was right?"

Kasta is quiet a moment longer. "I'm saying I think we could work well together, if we try."

I bristle against the admission, this continued agreeability that feels like a mask, a lie. It has to be. Because otherwise it means that despite what he believed of me before—that Jet and I tricked him on purpose, that I left him to die—he's willing to press past it. To move on. To *forgive* what he believes I did, even while I vengefully refuse to do the same.

Which is so backward and such a complete reversal of what he and I were during the Crossing, I almost laugh.

It has to be part of some grander plan. One to get in my head, to be kind so I'll suspect nothing, so I'll think that my sacrifice changed him and that he would never go on to kill Maia. He still searched through my bag, emptied out the potions.

So you couldn't use them against him, says a devilish little voice in my head. *Maybe he just didn't want to be poisoned again.*

It has to be an act.

"We'll see," I say.

The boat creaks. Stars wink between the shadowy branches of olive trees, and the torches of a small town slip closer, the sounds of muffled conversation speckling the night. Music drifts from a riverbank tavern, a lively horn and a drum, and people dance beneath strings of blue-white orbs, bronze goblets glinting in their hands. A young woman splashes in the water, soaking a couple who were, until that point, very wrapped up in each other. The pair splashes her back, starting a game of it, and the scene is so relaxed and comfortable and absolutely ordinary that I'm allowing myself a smile—when I feel it.

A tug in my gut, like the one I felt near Odelig.

I bolt upright.

"What?" Kasta says, his fingers touching the hilt of his sword.

"Odelig couldn't have followed us here," I say. "Could he?"

Kasta raises a brow. "No . . ."

"Then there's another legendary animal close by." I search the shoreline, not sure what I'm looking for. "Don't you feel it?"

Kasta stills, listening. But after a moment he shakes his head. "Whatever it is, we should keep going. We already know its magic can't help us against Wyrim."

"But doesn't it seem weird there's one here at all? The Mestrah said we only know of three of them right now." The whale, Odelig . . . *Ashra*. My heart trills. We've very far north of the Crossing, but it's been long enough. A Firespinning horse could have made her way here, whether on her own or with a new master.

I raise my hand at the nearest guard. "Stop the boat!"

"What are you doing?" Kasta says. "My father is expecting us by tomorrow afternoon. We don't have time for a detour."

"There's something here I think your father will want back." I grin. "We'll be fast. You can keep an eye on the time."

He scoffs. "You assume I'm going with you?"

"Why not?" I ask, my smile widening. "You have something better to do?"

This is, I'm thinking, one of my more ingenious traps. He can't answer that without explaining himself, and there's nothing else he could reasonably need to do in the middle of the night. I'm mentally tallying a point for me when he shrugs.

"Yes. I'm going to bed." He starts for the door.

"But—" He can't get away this easily. I need to watch him. I need to make sure he's not hunting while I'm out. "What if it's dangerous? What if I need help?"

He turns at the door, his lip curving. "You have the Wraiths. Unless there's a reason you'd prefer me, personally, beside you?"

His own loaded question. My stomach tightens. Now it's me who can't answer without sounding like . . .

Like something we aren't.

Point to him.

"No," I say through my teeth. "Goodnight."

A smile, and he slams the door. Just as I turn around, Yashi jogs over, still securing the buckles on his red armor, and I feel a little guilty that he was likely called out of bed for this. "Are we really stopping?"

"Yes," I say, sighing. "But will you do me a favor? Can you assign someone to watch Kasta and follow him if he leaves? I don't want another situation like the mercenary ambush." I shrug. "You know how he can be."

Yashi snickers. "Yesterday you two are ripping into each other; today you're assigning bodyguards. Must have been a good hunt."

He winks and moves off to handle my order. This is definitely how rumors start about canoodling royals, and I'm beginning to understand now how the travelers' stories get so skewed. Sure, one explanation for me assigning bodyguards and following

Kasta around could be lovesickness, but it could also be spying or stalking or mutiny, and I can't even correct the rumors, because that would reveal my Plot. So I just have to sit here while the rest of the world starts betting on when we'll go public.

I can't even care anymore.

The boat docks, a redwood gangplank drops directly into the muddy shore, and two of the Wraiths take invisible positions ahead of me, while a regular guard joins my side. The little town rests in the moonlight like a tray of fresh rolls. That feeling of being watched, of having been here before, heats my front like sunlight, and I follow, anticipation crawling under my skin as we pass patched storefronts and small houses formed from the desert's orange sand. The streets are tidy here, the glassless windows lit with oil lamps, and even though I have no idea where we are, I find myself relaxing as I move. There's something cozy about this place, small as it is.

The feeling pulls me west, toward the end of the street, where the stone-layered road turns to dirt and the houses end. A small stretch of brush-covered desert opens before me, parted by a narrow road that leads to a large estate and a stable. All the windows in the house glow with light. The stable sits quietly in the shadows of palm trees, its torches burning low and blue, and the strange tug sparks in my veins, growing eager.

There, it seems to say. *There.*

I step off the road into the sand, navigating moonlit bushes and black scorpions that dart under rocks. And about halfway to the stable, I realize it's absolutely bizarre of me not to approach the house first. The owner is clearly awake, judging by the lights and the music drifting from the wide windows. Laughter reaches me in bursts. They're having a party, and I'm sneaking around with guards in their yard.

But then I consider: this is the moment I've been waiting for all my life. The royals in the travelers' best stories never show up knocking at doors. They're either in disguise, or inexplicably fall through roofs, or sneak about on divine missions, like I'm doing right now. I always wondered how that happens, but this is it. I could go to the front door, as is socially responsible, but I'm already halfway to the barn and I don't feel like changing course, so I'm just going with it. And if anyone finds me, I'll just throw out my fancy *dōmmel* title, and they'll gasp, and soon stories of my brilliant mysteriousness will be circulating the entirety of Orkena.

I was born for this.

I consider the epic speech I'll give as I approach the barn. Like many of Orkena's stables, this one is topped in three bronze domes to draw the heat away from the stalls, though as the property of a richer person, its walls are made entirely of gray marble, not mudbrick. Likewise, it's surrounded in painted columns that form a shaded porch all the way around, and carvings of plateaus and wild horses cover the sliding door on its side, as fine as palace artwork.

The door stands ajar, a slit of darkness against the stone.

"*Dōmmel?*" asks my guard.

"I know," I say, sighing. "I didn't think about going to the house until a minute ago. We're just sticking with the barn, all right?"

I can't see her face, but I swear she gives me a *look*. Possibly this is

179

why the guards wear leopard masks, so when royals start going off on something ridiculous, they can't see their guards judging them.

She gestures to the door. "I was only going to say I should probably go in first."

"Oh." I snicker at myself. "Yes, go ahead."

She rolls open the door, frost steaming up her arms. Not that I expect to be attacked in a random barn, but it's still reassuring to have someone else go in first. Straw shifts, and I sense, more than see, something large lift its head.

Whisperer? comes a very old, very familiar voice.

My heart flips. In the dim light, I can just make out the outline of tulip-shaped ears and the glint of a golden halter.

I was right.

"Ashra!" I rush past the guard. Even in the night, the Firespinner is as striking as she was the first time I saw her: her blood-red sides shimmering like live coals, her eyes a symphony of sunset colors. She drops her head over the half wall of her stall, and I reach for her soft cheek. Granted, this reunion feels a little strange considering the last time I saw her, she'd just thrown Sakira off her back and set a hill on fire, but then, I have to admit those were extenuating circumstances.

"What are you doing here?" I say, awed. "You're so far north. Who found you?"

Found? The mare tilts her head. *No find me. I find them.*

"Who?"

A door on the far side rattles, and the mare turns her head. The guard forms a sword of ice, and anticipation bursts through me.

Here it comes. This is my moment of glory, when I'll finally get to *be* the mysterious princess in the barn.

The door flies open. A girl stumbles in, laughing, followed by three others.

"Don't hurt him yet," slurs a girl in the back, her straight black hair swinging over her shoulder. She catches her balance against the doorframe. "I've heard these stories. Thieves are always very attractive—"

The torches flare to life, activated by one of the girls, and I wince in the sudden brightness. Their laughter turns to silence. When I lower my hand, my breath catches.

The girl who first spoke wears a cloth headband, her hair a little longer than when I last saw it half-burned from our excursion to steal Ashra . . . her gorgeous features unmistakeable even in the dim light. But it's the girl in front I can't look away from. A girl with bronze armor crossing her pale stomach in an X, and short, dark hair, and striking, familiar blue eyes.

"*Dōmmel*," she says, her grin lopsided. Her companions— including *Alette*—immediately fall to one knee, their fingertips to their foreheads. The girl in front follows, slowly, and at my side, my guard inhales in surprise, her ice sword vanishing.

"Sakira," I say.

"I thought you were dead," I add, which is possibly not the most graceful thing to say to anyone, ever, but it's what I can manage at the time. Alette—the girl in the headband, and Sakira's First in the Crossing—shifts behind her. It's equally bizarre to see her whole and unharmed. Kasta never said outright what happened when he ambushed them, but I'd assumed, from the blood splattering him in the caves, that he'd killed her.

"Sakira?" says another of her companions, a curvy girl with silver-blonde hair. "The lost princess?"

"I think you're confused," Sakira says, and at first I think she means her friend, but her smile is for me. "Grief is such a terrible thing, you know. I heard our *dōmmel* and sweet Sakira were close, and our blessed crown princess has been wandering the countryside since, sobbing and calling out Sakira's name." Sakira looks to her girls, who frown and nod drunkenly. I squint, about to ask what in Numet's creation she's talking about, when she slips her finger, quickly, over her throat. "Would you excuse us for a moment, ladies?"

"Of course," says Alette, putting her arms around the other girls and swiftly turning them. "But don't forget we're starting a new game of crystals. That pretty duke won't play if you're not."

"Don't worry, I'll get him for you later," Sakira says, winking. "I'll only be a few minutes."

The girls tip their fingers once more to their foreheads—which jolts me a little when I realize I'm coming to find that normal—and burst into excited chatter as soon as they're out of sight. Before Sakira slams the door, I have time to think how strange it was that not even Alette questioned my being here. I suppose they were drunk, but do they really think I have nothing better to do than wander the desert? Is this a normal thing, for royals to pine for weeks over people who once held them hostage?

"*Dōmmel*," says my guard. "We should notify the Mestrah immediately."

I nod, still in disbelief. "Yes, of course. I should be fine to get back with just the Wraiths, if you want to go now."

My guard crosses an arm over her chest and takes her leave. Sakira's focus stays on me, her eyes flitting to the mark just visible beneath the clasp of my cloak.

"Well, Living Sacrifice," she says. "Look how things have changed."

"You know your parents have been desperately looking for you?" I say, since my first statement seemed to have no impact. "And I'm sure Alette's parents would be relieved to know she's alive, too—are you all right? How long have you two been here?"

But I can tell from the glow of her creamy skin and the coy light in her eyes that Sakira has been all right for some time. She shrugs and approaches Ashra, running her hand down the mare's sleek forehead.

"We've been here a couple of weeks," she says. "We'll write home, eventually. It's just nice to take time to regroup once in a while. Keep a low profile, ponder the meaning of life."

"But . . ." I look around the stable, at the dustless shelves holding neat piles of riding gloves, brushes, and buckets. "Kasta said he left you in the middle of the Barren."

Sakira's fingers curl, and she drops them from Ashra's nose. "Yes. Holding on to my unconscious best friend."

A chill settles over me as I think again of the blood that splattered Kasta's chest. "Gods, Sakira. What did he *do*?"

"Oh, you know, the usual. I wouldn't tell him where you were, so he dislocated each of my fingers until I did. Then he used his filthy Deathbringer magic to knock Alette out so she couldn't pray for his failure." She looks over, her red eyeshadow glinting. "At least I managed to cut him before he got my sword. But Alette was delirious for a week. Do you know how hard it is to move around the desert with dead weight and dislocated fingers?"

I close my eyes. "I'm so sorry."

"Not as sorry as I am for you." She pulls a sugar cube from a leather pouch near Ashra's door and offers it to the mare. "Though he must not think you're much of a threat, if you're still in one piece. For your sake, I hope that doesn't change."

An echo of the exact thought I had earlier. "But how did you . . . you walked here?"

"Part of the way. I knew which stars to follow, but after we ran out of water, I couldn't really focus on that anymore." She strokes the mare's cheek. "I thought I was hallucinating when Ashra came."

Me, Ashra thinks, nudging Sakira's shoulder.

"Ashra found you," I muse, marveling at the mare. "Alette could still pray?"

She laughs. "Oh, no. Alette barely knew who *I* was. So I prayed . . . I prayed more than I ever have in my life. You know the old legend about Rachella, who split her soul between eleven animals when she crossed into Paradise so her mortal children wouldn't have to be without her? Apparently some version of that is true. We needed help. I called on the goddess." She considers Ashra, her eyes glittering. "She answered."

A lump forms in my throat at this reminder of the gods

working in our lives, of the power behind the mark on my chest. "And now I'm here, after hunting another magical animal led me to you."

Sakira laughs. "Don't read too far into it. Some things are fate. This is coincidence."

"Pretty big coincidence," I grumble, thinking of the tiny town outside.

"Oh, I know it must be." She pushes away from the stall, her red skirt flaring. "I've been praying to never be found again."

I jerk my gaze back to her. "Never?"

"You see, I had an epiphany." Her smile widens, half-wild. "And you know what I realized? My father was right. This is where I belong, out of the way, hosting parties and doing whatever I like, and not worrying about who wants to kill me."

"But . . . you hated that people saw you that way!"

"And I hated that they might think I was soft. But after you, and that week in the desert . . ." She shoves away from the stall. "I'm done. I found the kind of life I want to live. Is there something you need, by the way? Or are you just here to steal from me? Which I'm rather impressed by, if it's the latter."

Her grin grows impish, and I shift, uncomfortable. How am I going to tell the Mestrah and the queen that I found their daughter, but she doesn't want to come home?

"No," I say. "I mean, I was here for Ashra, but I didn't actually know it was Ashra. Sakira . . ." A new idea hits me. Sakira claims this is coincidence, but I can't help but hope it's more. "If there was a way for you to get back at Kasta for all he's done, would you?"

She tilts her head. "I'm listening."

"I think . . ." I look over my shoulder, and though I know the guard should be well out of earshot, I keep my voice low. "I think he's a Shifter now. He was really hurt at the end of the Crossing. As in, wounds he couldn't have survived without a Healer. We left him in the caves with Maia. But somehow he came out unscathed."

Sakira, who went still when I said *Shifter*, nods once.

"I'm trying to make a case against him, but he's been really careful. You have a lot of friends at the capital, right? You could get some of them to watch him. Or . . . or you could mark him with Obedience when he's not looking! Get him to admit the truth, and he'll lose the throne!"

Sakira doesn't look nearly as excited about this as she should. She gives me that terrible, pitying smile, and sets her hands on my shoulders.

"You want me to leave my little haven, ride back to the palace as a loser, and risk my life by marking the brother who already left me to die, so you can have the throne to yourself?" She laughs. "Zahru, I'm liking you more and more. But when I'm on this end of things, the answer is absolutely *no*."

My stomach drops. "But—he's a *Shifter*! He's going to be Mestrah. If we don't do something—"

"None of this is my problem anymore," she says, sauntering to the door. "It was good to see you, mostly. Now if you'll excuse me, I have a party to get back to."

"Seriously? What happened to the girl who loved her country? Who would do anything to protect it?"

Sakira turns, tapping her cheek. "Speaking of protection, you might want to check on your guard. Alette's been using Forgetting spells on anyone who starts to recognize us, so by now your guard isn't so sure where she is anymore, and she definitely won't remember the little encounter we had here." She winks. "See that it stays that way. Because you know, if they drag us back to the palace after this, I'll make your life even more painful than it already is."

She casts me a feline smile and turns for the door. I stare after her in shock. I can't believe that the girl who never backed down from a challenge, who used her charm as both a weapon and a shield and strove to make our allies see us as friends and not gods, is now going to just hide away in a corner of the desert, partying herself into oblivion. I might not have appreciated being in her possession as a human sacrifice, but I know she was made for more than this.

"You're right," I say as she yanks open the barn door. "Sakira must be dead. The one I knew never gave up this easily."

She pauses, and for a moment I dare to believe she'll change her mind.

Then she steps into the night and slams the door.

XVII

I'M in a bad mood when I return to the boat, not only at losing Sakira's help, but also due to the guard I had to find wandering toward the dunes, who keeps asking me where someone named Gereth is. I do not know a Gereth, and I have no energy to make up a story for my guard about why she's out in the middle of this random town when she last remembers eating dinner on the boat. I tell her she must have had a bad reaction to the cucumber soup, hand her off to the Wraiths, and look for Yashi, who informs me with a cheeky grin that Kasta hasn't left his room at all.

And helpfully accompanies me to my cabin, I suppose to see if I intend to check on Kasta myself.

I do not.

Instead I spend a paranoid minute going through my gilded room, checking my things in case Kasta's been through them, triple-checking the lock on the door.

And when I finally collapse on my bed to sleep, it's with the feeling that the only progress I've made is backward.

"I am . . . pleased with this," the Mestrah says the next evening, looking surprised at his own choice of words. Having just returned, Kasta and I stand before him in the throne room at the base of the dais. The queen sits beside her husband, an elegant vision wrapped in layers of pink satin. She looks much happier than she did watching Jet walk down this aisle, but her green eyes are still guarded. I wonder if she thinks losing Sakira was worth gaining her son as Mestrah. I wonder how things might change, if I could tell her Sakira is alive.

"You considered her counsel?" the Mestrah asks Kasta, who nods. The king looks to me. "And you summoned aid for him, when you had a chance to let Odelig go free?"

I nod. The Mestrah sits back, both hands on his knees. Fresh Strength spells paint his arms, but even this small movement seems to wind him.

"Never in ten thousand years," he says, "would I have guessed this outcome. You approached this thoughtfully, met the goal I had set for you, and returned without having sacrificed more than you needed. But more than that, you worked together." His brow rises. "You did well, *dōmmella*. I am beginning to see why the gods have paired you."

We bow quickly and thank him, Kasta nearly choking on his words, but my heart hardens, rejecting that last statement. By unspoken agreement, Kasta and I neglected to mention the arguments that led up to capturing Odelig, and that both of us could have died if it weren't for quick reflexes and a lucky burst of Influence. It doesn't mean those arguments didn't happen, and it doesn't mean things will improve. We're not meant for this. And when I expose Kasta for what he is, the Mestrah will see that, too.

"Now," the Mestrah says, coughing once. A serving boy offers him his tonic, and the king takes a drink before continuing. "As you realized from the attack on your boat, Wyrim has no plans to wait idle while we sort things out. They continue to use mercenaries to avoid a full declaration of war, but we are very near to tracing the Atera attack to their queen. And when we do, and especially if we've still no answer to *forsvine* . . . we will need help.

"I have invited our strongest allies to the capital next week, from Greka, Nadessa, Amian, and Pe, for a celebratory banquet to honor your upcoming coronation and introduce you to their rulers. While this, to the public eye, will seem no more than a party, it will be up to you to impress the delegations. Our alliances with Pe and Amian, especially, are slipping. I will be counting on you—both of you—to show them not only that you are the strongest leaders to take Orkena's throne, but also that we are still a force to be reckoned with. You must prove to them that keeping alliances with us is far preferred to the uncertainty of siding with Wyrim."

I worry my fingers over the crane pin at my shoulder, looking away when the Mestrah turns to me. There's no way to tell, of course, if we'll be strong leaders or if we can stand against Wyrim, but the implication is clear. We must pretend, if we hope to win help for the war.

"Zahru," the king says.

I look up. "Mestrah."

"You need to realize that you, especially, will be under scrutiny. The rulers of these countries know your humble origins. I've delayed the party as long as I dared to give you time, but you'll need to prove not only Orkena's value, but your own."

I clench my teeth. Of course I will.

"You have one week," the Mestrah says, sinking tiredly into his throne. "I will see you tomorrow morning for another lesson."

◆

After a relieved reunion with Fara, Mora, and Hen, and a promise from each of them that they'll do whatever they can to help me prepare for the party, I return to my room, exhaustedly resolved that I need to formulate a new plan for finding Kasta's pelts. Really, I just want to sleep, or call on my friends to play cards and crystals, or just relax in the pool before the chaos of everything starts up again tomorrow, but we're officially one week down.

Only three left until the coronation. And I have nothing more than a Wraith's comment on Kasta's impressive strength to show for it.

Jade chases my cape as I pace, and I finally pick her up, stroking her spotted side while she recounts all the exciting birds she saw while I was gone. I remind her she'll need to start looking for quiet ones again, starting tonight. She nips my finger and springs off.

And someone knocks on the door.

"Oh my *gods*," I say, whirling toward them. "I've been back for five minutes!"

But this is my life now. So all I can do is storm theatrically over, fling the doors open—and nearly run into a tower of orange calla lilies.

"What on— Jet!"

His smiling face pokes around the bouquet, which is actually a potted plant. Seriously, he's holding a painted ceramic base.

"I thought you might need some cheering up, after being trapped with a tyrant for five days." He shifts one arm, under which a wrapped parcel crinkles. "I also have lemon cookies."

I swing the door open wide. "Yup, come in."

I realize this makes me sound like a person who will admit

anyone into my bedroom if they're carrying cookies, and I have to admit this is probably correct. At the least, I would always answer the door for the promise of baked goods. Maybe not if Kasta was the one holding them . . . maybe even if he was. If only he knew how easily food would win me over.

Except seeing Jet only reminds me that I know his sister is alive, and that he'd be very relieved to know that. And thus begins a new moral crisis.

"I'm glad you're here," I say as a tantalizing whiff of sage and leather follows Jet in. "I couldn't find anything on Kasta on the trip, so we need to talk about that, but also there's something else I should probably tell you—"

He turns, and I lose my train of thought. This is not just Jet showing up with flowers and cookies. This is Jet in a tunic nearly as fine as the one he had for his coronation, a fitted deep blue with silver gods' symbols sewn into the trim and silver armbands that draw the light to his muscles. He's also shorn sharp patterns into the sides of his hair, and his dark brown skin shines, fresh with that tantalizing oil.

I don't know what it means that my first thought is that I don't have time for this.

His smile turns devilish. "Maybe all that can wait?" He unwraps the parcel, tossing the string to Jade. "I thought, you've been working nonstop, you've just returned from a stressful hunt with my literally accursed brother . . . maybe you'd like to take a night off?"

He offers me a cookie, which is really the most unfair thing about this.

"Um . . ." I take it. "That really does sound amazing."

"Here's my plan for the night." He frames the starlit window with his hands. "A walk through the gardens. There's a pond with Firelily pads in the middle, so you can even burn something if you're feeling stressed. Then up past the kitchens for more snacks, then we pick up Hen, Melia, Marcus and his fiancé, and anyone else you want to invite, and have a pool party." He gestures to the archway on the west side, where I'd imagined all of us doing just that, not five minutes ago.

I look down at the cookie, thinking of the secret I need to tell him, of the help I could get with Kasta and the debut party if I don't.

"Oh . . . no, no, no," Jet says, lightly pushing my hand, and cookie, closer to my mouth. "Tears are not the reaction I was going for. It's all right; if you'd rather just talk strategy for this week, we can do that, too."

"No, it's fine," I say, blinking my eyes clear. "This was really thoughtful of you, and I really, really want to go, but I'm under a lot of stress right now, and I—"

I bite my lip. *I have something to tell you* is what I should say. It's not like I'm worried about what Sakira will do if I tell Jet, because I think I can swear him to secrecy and Sakira will eventually forgive me.

I'm worried about me. About the help I'll lose if he goes to her, instead of what Jet will gain.

What is *wrong* with me?

"All right." Jet lifts off my gold-feathered crown, which I hadn't realized until now had been digging into my scalp. "Just breathe for a minute. Easy in, easy out."

He rubs my arms, his hands warm and strong, his concern a soft comfort sinking through my shoulders. I breathe in with him—*one, two*—and breathe out—*three, four*. I'm fine, I have a lot to do, but I've survived a week. And I absolutely have to tell him this secret, because if our situations were reversed, and I thought Hen was dead and he found her alive, I know he'd have already told me.

"Your sister's alive," I say before I can change my mind.

For a beat, Jet's hands go still. Then joy sparks between us, and the most glorious, disbelieving grin brightens his face. "You're serious? They found her? Why didn't I know?"

"Well, because—"

"Zahru!" He spins me, lifting me off the ground and laughing, so full of light and happiness that I immediately ache for him when he lets go. "You're amazing. Is she recovering? Is that why no one else knows yet?"

"She's fine," I assure him. "And so is Alette, actually. Ashra found them and brought them to safety. They're doing really well." My smile slips. "But they're not here. They don't want to come home."

His grin falls. "What? Why?"

"They're hiding away in a town up north. Sakira changed her name. No one there knows who she is, and Alette's helping her keep it that way." I nibble on the cookie, though I don't really taste it. "She's different, and she told me I'd regret it if I spilled her secret. So please don't tell anyone else? But I thought you should know."

He's quiet a moment. "But my father . . . and Alette's mothers. And I may not care for the queen, but she's been lighting candles every night for Sakira. I can't tell them?"

"I—" There's no way I can deny grieving parents this knowledge. I may as well just accept now that Sakira is going to come for me in the night. "I mean . . . I guess?"

"No, no, that's all right; I'll pose that question to Sakira myself. I'm just grateful you told *me*." He exhales, running a hand over his short hair, and I hate the pang of regret I feel at the confirmation that he's going to visit her and not be here for me. "I need to get her a new listening scroll. And new spells, and ink for her brush. Where are they living? Do you think they'll need anything else? Food? A carriage?"

"I don't know," I say, dropping the rest of the cookie on an end table. "Sakira bought an estate. She looked pretty well-off."

"Definitely some gold, then, too. I know what she brought with her for the Crossing, and if she bought a house, she can't have much left." He's a bundle of energy, moving, strategizing. I can only take comfort in knowing that if it was me who needed help, he'd be just as ready.

He catches me looking and grimaces. "I'm sorry. If there's anything you need me for tonight, I'm happy to get the other advisors and discuss, but then I have to see her. I'll respect it if she wants to stay, but she often appears like she's doing better than she is. I need to make sure she's truly all right."

"I understand," I say, forcing a smile. "And you don't have to wait around. I can work with the rest of the team on next steps." I pause, remembering what we discussed as a team last time. "Did you happen to get access to Kasta's room?"

"Oh! Yes, I was just about to get to that." He pulls two strings of leather from his tunic pocket, each threaded with square stones.

"My mother tracked down the Enchanter who designed the protection wards for the royal suites, and he made us these. They'll mask your presence for a quarter of an hour, so be out before then, or the Wraithguard will be in to investigate. Marcus can recharge them if you need to go in more than once."

"All right," I say, accepting the necklaces. "This only makes me feel slightly panicked about how easily Kasta could make the same request."

"Not anymore." Jet smirks. "We paid the Enchanter a pretty sum of your gold to look for a job outside of the country."

I blink. "My gold?"

"Well, it's certainly not mine anymore. The Enchanter won't be back, anyway. He wants nothing to do with a feud between you and Kasta."

"Huh." Though it's more for the strange realization that I'm rich. I'm a person who has gold. It hasn't even occurred to me until now that I could buy things.

"Anyway." Jet arranges the flowers beside the couch. "You'll want to go between two and four marks in the afternoon. Kasta trains with the army then, and that's the only time I can guarantee he'll be out. And don't go alone. You notice there are two of those."

I scoff, though that's exactly what I was just thinking. "Why would I go alone?"

"Because you don't want to put anyone else in danger, and you'd like to set his room on fire?"

"I wouldn't set his room on fire. It's right next to mine." But a weird feeling starts through me at this, because I imagine myself doing just that, lifting a torch over Kasta's desk, his books. The *forsvine* samples, with all his careful notes and calculations.

Except I can't imagine lowering the flame.

Which is not right at all.

Jet points a finger in my face. "See? You're thinking about it. Don't. You'll get your chance for revenge, but only if we do this carefully."

I look down at the necklaces. "Right. Revenge."

"Write me if you need anything. I'll have my listening scroll." He strides for the door and pauses on the threshold, looking as out of reach as a star. "I'll be back before your debut party. Maybe we can try tonight's plans again then?"

"Sure," I say, leaning sadly against the dresser.

And he's gone.

I rub my hand along my brow, burying the resentment for Jet's absence and the stress of the upcoming party and Kasta's strange agreeability under the promise in my palm.

Tomorrow, at least, I will solve one of these.

I lift the rune necklaces and look out at Kasta's balcony.

XVIII

I don't wait for Kasta the next morning before going to the gardens for our Influence lesson, which earns me another side eye from the Mestrah when I arrive alone. At least this time I don't knock any servants unconscious. This time I stay far away from changing any minds and focus only on emotions, and my magic springs to my fingers like a horse under saddle, sharpened by the practice I got during the trip. It only takes me a few minutes to start naming feelings from a distance, and I get the time down to seconds toward the end of the lesson. The Mestrah is so pleased with this he actually smiles, but it's made even better by Kasta guessing wrong on his volunteers the entire hour. His Influence hasn't progressed at all. The Mestrah explains it may take moons to master, and that my progress is likely due to Influence's similarity to Whispering, and I hold my tongue about how difficult it must be for Shifters to learn two completely different magics at once.

I don't need the barb, anyway. I'm the one who gets an approving shoulder pat.

My schooling lessons do not go as well. My tutors, now with the debut party to prepare for, pack my brain with the names of foreign rulers, cities, current trade agreements, customs, laws, and various diplomatic strategies. By the time Hen arrives to teach history, my head is soup. I try to focus on the Mestrah portraits she lays out, on who conquered the northern tribes first and united them, but my mind keeps sliding to the rune necklaces in my pocket, my gaze to the curtained windows beyond which Kasta's balcony waits. It's nearing three marks. Now would be the perfect time to go.

And despite Jet's warnings, I'm not sure I see the point in taking someone with me. I could leave one rune necklace here, search alone, and if I don't find anything, return immediately with the second necklace—giving me twice the time before I have to get them recharged by Marcus.

And if Kasta happens to come in . . .

I find, oddly, that I'm less afraid of what he would do to me than of what he might do to my expendable friends.

I've just decided I'll ask Hen for a break when a scroll thwacks my knuckles.

"Ouch!" I say, snatching my hands off the desk. "What was that for?"

"For keeping another secret from me," Hen says, her eyes narrowing.

"What?" I laugh. "I don't know what you're talking about. I'm trying to study, here. Though I really do need a break soon. I don't even remember the name of the Mestrah you were just talking about."

Hen taps the scroll against her hand, dust motes sparkling around her raven hair like a hundred new suspicions. She rolls the blank parchment out on the desk. "Fine. I will grant you this break, but we end the lesson with a little writing practice."

She scrawls a word onto the parchment, then spins it around so I can read it. The ease of this is enough to spark my own suspicions, but I decide to just go with it.

"*L-i-a* . . ." I copy each letter and shoot her a glare when I get to the last one. "Wait. That spells *liar.*"

"Yes, it does, you liar of liars. You said you'd never keep a secret from me again!"

"I did *not*! I literally never said that. And trust me, Hen, this is one you're really better off not knowing."

She gives me the kind of grin I imagine Apos, the god of deceit, gives his victims before he devours them.

"Better. Off. Not. Knowing?" she says, her teaching quill bending perilously. "The last secret you thought I didn't need to know, you became a *crown princess*. You are telling me this secret. You owe me this secret, or so help me, Zahru, I will quit."

I snicker nervously. "You won't quit."

"Yes, I will, and you'll be left with that crabby lump of a tutor they first assigned to you. And"—she braces herself on the desk, hovering over me like a pixie-sized demon—"I will tell everyone you hate chocolate."

I gasp. "You wouldn't!"

"I *would*. I'll tell them you've developed a terrible allergy, and that no matter how hard you beg for it, they should never, under any circumstances, give it to you." Her eyes glint, and I stare back at her, incredulous. "So. What's it going to be?"

I shake my head in disbelief. "You are a terrifying, diabolical person."

"Not a secret."

"But, Hen, this time . . . this could put *you* in danger."

"Now you are *definitely* telling me."

"I'm serious. It's just better if you—"

"—worry about you at all hours of the day, wondering what I could be doing to help, while you continue to lock me out *for my protection?"* Her shoulders drop, and the hurt on her face is far worse than her anger. "Is that what you would want from me? If I was in trouble, you wouldn't want to know?"

"What? No! Of course I would, but—"

"You told Jet! I know you two haven't been canoodling. You're far too snappy for *that* to be going on. So why does he get to know? Because he can defend himself, and you don't think I can?"

I blanch. "Never!"

"Then what is it? Have you . . ." She shrinks back, a hand over her heart. "Have you replaced me?"

"I could never replace you! And I would have told you, except . . ." I hesitate. My Influence stirs against my ribs, nudging my hands like an eager dog. If I reach out, I know I'll find Hen's frustration, her hurt. The magic pulls at me, whispering that it can help, that it can make her decide she's happy about this and doesn't want to know more. I could go to Kasta's room in peace. Hen would never bring this up again.

I shudder and press back against it. I'm absolutely not changing anything in my friend's head, never mind that I still don't know how to do that without knocking someone out.

Which leaves me only with the truth. And the panicky realization that if I'm going to keep this friendship from my old life, I can't lock Hen out of my new one.

"All right!" I say, dropping my quill. "All right. I'll tell you, but you're going to want to fix it, and I need you to swear to the gods you won't do anything without talking to the team first."

Hen's eye twitches. "A. *Team.* Knows about this?"

". . . which we'll round back to another time! The point is—

you have to swear you won't wrangle in your contacts, or cash in favors, or even vaguely mention this to anyone in any context. Not even Mora can know about this."

Her eyes narrow to two oak-brown points as intense as Apos's flaming spears. She doesn't like having to make this promise, but she nods, and the pressure in my chest relaxes. For me, she'll do it.

"Good," I say, drawing the rune necklaces from my pocket. "Because it would actually be amazing to have your help."

As I knew she would, Hen takes in Kasta's now being both a Shifter and an almost-god with an extreme amount of grace. Also as I knew she would, she takes being able to sneak into his room to look for evidence with an extreme amount of excitement.

"I have a lot of experience with this" is the concerning statement she makes after I tell her our plans to gather evidence.

"You absolutely do not."

"With sneaking into places and finding things, I do. These give us a quarter of an hour?" She taps the rune necklace at her throat, which she put on even before I started talking. I nod. "Plenty of time. You came to the right girl."

I would remind her I didn't actually come to her, and that she threatened this out of me, but I'm finding I'm relieved she did. Now all my secrets are off my chest, and Hen and I can go back to what we were before, or at least as much as possible with me now in charge of an entire country.

I adjust my own rune necklace as we move out of the study.

"Remember, we need something indisputable. Animal pelts, preferably. But also anything out of the ordinary. Cryptic letters to people, bloodstains—"

"Bodies?" Hen pipes, too brightly.

I grimace. "Yes. Ew, but yes. But if we don't find anything, we'll have to go in again, so we can't mess anything up that he'd notice . . . Why am I telling you any of this?"

Hen turns in front of the glass balcony doors, smiling like a patient mother. "Go on. These are all good tips. It's encouraging to know you have all this on your mind already."

I sigh. "The only thing I haven't figured out is how to get *in*. He has guards outside his door around the clock, and Jet already made sure there's no way to get between the rooms."

Hen's still giving me that look. There's an amused edge to it now, like if I think a little harder about what I just said, I'll come to the answer.

"You've already figured out how to get in there, haven't you?" I ask.

Hen beams. "Yes."

"How? And why does this not make me feel better about keeping Kasta on his side of the wall?"

"Because he doesn't have me, or these runes. Which makes our job very simple." She throws open the balcony door and steps into the sun, and I'm readying myself for any number of questionable solutions, which I can only imagine involve drugging guards or sawing through Kasta's roof, when she points next door.

"You're right next to him," she says. "We'll jump over to his balcony."

"Oh," I say, entirely disappointed. "That's it? I thought you'd drill out a passage in the ceiling or something."

"Also a good idea," she says, looking impressed. "But too time-consuming. And it would require an Earthmover, whom you've forbidden me to speak to."

At least the *don't tell anyone* part of my instructions got through to her. I glance at the water clock on the dresser: three and a half marks. Only half a mark until Kasta returns. It's now or never.

"All right," I say. "Let's do this."

I follow her outside, the dry afternoon heat skimming my arms like teeth. Jade bounds out after us, swatting at dragonflies, and we pause at the marble rail, Kasta's windows waiting dark and quiet on the other side.

"Stay," I tell Jade, who responds by sitting grumpily on one of the glass party tables.

Anticipation shivers through me, and I pull myself onto the stone railing.

The top is wide enough to set a plate on, which makes it alarmingly easy to jump the distance. But a comforting pulse of heat on my neck reminds me that the rune necklace is working, and that Kasta has no way to get his own. Hen peers into the first window, then the second, and curses.

"*Rie*," she says. "What is it with you royals having the curtains closed all the time?"

This gives me a jolt, not only for being referred to as "you royals," but also for the realization that my paranoia is starting to look a lot like Kasta's. I glance back at my own drapes and shove the thought away. This isn't the same. This is temporary.

"He should be at training," I say, sidling over to the balcony door. A small slit remains between its curtains, and I peer inside, ready to jump away at the smallest motion. But only darkness waits within.

Nerves flash through me, and I grip the serpent-shaped handle. This is where it began.

It could also be where it ends.

I slide the door open just wide enough to squeeze through.

The damp blue light of the torches spills over me. Memories unspool in the shadows as I take in the room, from the surgical cleanliness to the thick blue curtains. There's the couch where Kasta cut the sacrifice's symbol into my wrist; there's the table he overturned after I struck him and got away. There's the window Jet broke through, before my mother's protection rune knocked Kasta cold.

I force myself to move. Hen slinks ahead of me, lifting a stack of papers from an ebony desk. One of many desks, I realize, as my eyes adjust to the light. In the same corner where my room has bookshelves and a reading chair, Kasta has four curved, polished tables arranged like a horseshoe. Glass instruments line the tops in neat displays, some connected by delicate tubing. A metal cylinder sits over a circle of burned wood. I don't remember any of this being here before.

"He rebuilt his laboratory," I say, that same strange feeling coming over me as when Jet joked about me burning this room. Kasta destroyed his first lab when he was a child, after he realized he'd never possess the magic he was so fascinated by. A palm-sized square of *forsvine* sits on a wooden stand, pieces of it cut off and missing. Another forms some kind of bracelet, the edges so soft that fingerprints mar its sides. In a nearby tube, more of the metal bubbles in liquid form over a low green flame.

He wasn't lying about studying it.

"Yes," Hen grumbles. "And he's one of those irritating people who puts everything away. Which means we need to be careful how we put things back. Start on those scrolls, and pay attention to how you get them out."

I slide a letter from the next desk, but my shoulders fall when I unroll it.

"I can't help with these," I say, despairing at Kasta's tight scrawl. "I don't even recognize a *the* in these first sentences."

Hen squints at it. "I'll go through them. You look for bodies."

How she delivers that line without cracking a smile or grimace, I don't know. The girl is savage.

"Thanks," I say. "That's exactly what I was hoping you'd say."

She's too busy with the letters to grace me with a response. I consider the rest of Kasta's room—the open doorway to his private pool, and doors to other rooms besides. But I'm not thinking of bodies. Kasta wouldn't be that careless. I'm thinking of pelts, and how they'd need to be someplace accessible, and also someplace no one could come across by accident.

The white curtain over the closet flutters, and I wonder.

I creep past the main doors, holding my breath as I picture the guards standing alert on the other side, but soon I'm through the curtain and staring at the shelves. Orange torchlight dances across a monotony of white. White tunics, white *tergus* kilts and capes and robes; the color favored by Mestrahs, as it's the hardest to keep clean. A crown of twisting rattlesnakes, Kasta's favorite, shines atop the head of a featureless stone bust on a pedestal. Strange that the model isn't in the likeness of one of our gods. As if Kasta is only wearing Valen's symbols to *mock* the god of fate, which makes an awful kind of sense when I consider how Kasta broke free of what Valen intended for him as Forsaken. Or maybe Kasta simply believes himself above the gods now altogether.

Focus. I gingerly lift stacks of soft linens and silks, grateful that at least among all this white there can't be cactus spire—except I realize halfway through that if I were Kasta, the last place I'd hide a pelt would be in a closet. That's expected. Predictable. Two things Kasta has never been. But just as I'm shoving back one of the piles in defeat—I hear it.

A soft crunch, like parchment.

I ease the stack free and set it aside. A scroll rolls on its edge at the back, and carefully I lift it, noting it was on the left side of the shelf.

"Hen," I whisper as loud as I dare. I poke my head around the curtain, and Hen replaces a book she was looking through and jogs over.

"You're surprisingly good at this," she says, closing the curtain. "I know who I'm calling on the next time I need something found."

"Absolutely not. I'm already halfway to a heart attack right now." I hand her the scroll. "What is this?"

"Hmm." She unfurls it, and my skin prickles, electric. This is it. We've done it. It will be an order for bodies, or pelts, or maybe a list of people who won't be missed by their families—people Kasta could make disappear without anyone noticing.

But Hen sighs and hands it back.

"It's nothing," she says. "It's an order to locate the Forsaken. The only weird thing is that he's dated it for the future."

"What?" I say, looking down. "No, it has to be something. He hid it. What does it say?"

Hen follows the words with her fingers. "'General Nadia, you will gather all the Forsaken who were sent out of the orphanages and build them lodging in Luksus. I want every living person found and treated as is fitting of a noble. You will provide them with new clothing, food, and belongings. If any should harm them or speak against you, lash and imprison them. I will deal with any unrest.'" She lowers her finger to a jagged signature. "'Mestrah Kasta.'"

I stare at the words in disbelief. Hen has no reason to make any of this up, but what she's saying doesn't make sense. Even if this isn't a copy of the law allowing Mestrahs to be Shifters, it should be something similarly terrible: a demand for prisoners' bodies, a declaration of war. Not an order to gather the people Orkena has cast aside and provide for them.

I made you a promise.

And this is another.

"But . . . that can't be all of it," I say, feeling numb. "He's signing it as Mestrah. Why? Why hide it and not send it now?"

Hen rolls the parchment. "Look, I don't want to defend the stabby prince any more than you do. But you realize how controversial an order this is? This wouldn't get past his father."

"No." I search the shelf for another scroll; I take out the stack of clothes next to it. "There's more to it. He's using this to distract from something. Or . . . or he wants to eat them!"

"By first treating them like nobles and building them homes?" Hen hands the scroll back to me. "I know you want to find something, Z. But this isn't it."

A door clicks. Hen and I freeze, dread lancing down my spine, and slowly, so slowly, I dare to look through the slit between the curtain and the wall. *Kasta*. His head is down, his hair stuck up with sweat. He studies a curling slip of parchment in his hand. I jerk out of view and grip Hen's sleeve. He's back early.

Follow, Hen mouths, tugging my elbow. With the deft silence born of panic, I slide the scroll and the folded garments back in place with little more than a whisper. Kasta's footsteps sound in the room, moving away. Hen pulls me to the rear of the closet, where the finest of Kasta's tunics hang. We cram into a corner behind a swath of floor-length capes—where I slice my heel against something sharp.

"*Tyda*," I breathe. Hen elbows me, and I bite the inside of my cheek. Hot blood trickles down my heel.

Kasta's room falls silent.

My heartbeat thuds in my ears as his footsteps resume, this time drawing closer. Hen grips my hand. Folds of white and red satin are all that separate us from view, and I close my eyes against the *screech* of the curtain jerking aside, the sudden shadow that darkens the room.

I would rather be found by the Wraithguard than him.

As if the gods accept this challenge, the runes on my necklace flash cold—a warning that their magic is nearly depleted—and I almost laugh.

More silence. I open my eyes, expecting the tunics to be flung aside, a hand to grab my throat. Nothing happens. It's quiet for so long that I'm wondering if he left, when grit crunches under a sandal. Clothes slide from a shelf. Footsteps move *away*, and the curtain jerks closed.

Hen taps her necklace, eyes wide, and counts down from ten on her fingers before gesturing for me to move. We slip from our hiding place. Kasta's steps fade, and I peek through the curtain in time to see him disappear into the pool room.

My heel aches. Hen slips forward, but I grab her arm and point to my foot. Blood streaks the tile. She grabs a folded *tergus*, rips a piece free with her Materialist's magic like it's clay, and I wrap the strip tight around the wound. We use the rest of the garment to wipe the floor, but just as I start for our hiding place, Hen grabs my hand—no. The runes pulse cold on our necks. We're out of time.

We pause at the curtain long enough to hear the splash of water, then sprint for the balcony doors, my blood rushing so hard I'm sure it'll soak through the bandage. We slip outside, close the latch without a sound, and leap to my railing, and it's not until we've slammed the door and shrieked our victory in the safety of my room that I realize we didn't actually achieve anything.

No pelts, no bodies.

Only more proof that Kasta is not the monster I want him to be.

XIX

HEN says she'll handle the bloodstained tunic, which I accept with an expert amount of nonchalance, and we call in Melia for my heel. I should be grateful the small cut is the worst that happened. But while Hen writes to Jet to tell him what we found—and to inform him she's now in charge of our coup—impatience stirs in my chest. This new version of Kasta can't be real. It has to be a game, a false light, as Maia put it, and I can't fall for it again. Even if he showed Odelig mercy. Even if he's already planning to help the Forsaken, without any prompting or pressure from me.

But despite what I *know* must have happened for him to survive, a splinter of doubt pushes into my mind.

Maybe he didn't.

Maybe Maia is still alive, and he's trying to make up for everything by doing good.

I squeeze my eyes shut against the thoughts. This is dangerous thinking, and the last time I hoped for him nearly cost me everything.

It won't last. I must stop him.

I won't let him fool me again.

The days start to pass like dripping water. Each the same, and gone far too soon.

Every morning I ask Jade if she's seen the quiet bird or anything else in the night that shouldn't be there. Every morning the same answer: *No*. I go to my Influence lessons, carefully timing it so I never have to walk with Kasta, especially now that I'm regularly sneaking into his room. My Influence strengthens. Soon I can not only identify emotion from a distance, but also amplify it by reinforcing the emotion with my own feelings, until my volunteers are overcome by joy or sadness or fear.

Each lesson I leave shaking. From the oily feeling of having manipulated someone; from the intoxicating satisfaction of being looked upon—me, a once-lowly Whisperer—with such fascination and respect.

Kasta still can't do more than occasionally name the right emotion. But though I always glance over his clothes for blood and his skin for scratches, all I ever notice is how tired he looks.

My tutors teach. Hen and I sneak into Kasta's rooms again, and the first day we find a mercifully smaller pool of blood than I feared I'd left behind in the closet, as well as the scorpion tunic pin that stabbed me. But we clean up the blood, and there is nothing else. Day after day, nothing. Melia reports on Kasta's unremarkable training sessions each night, and Marcus stops in to recharge the necklaces.

My anxiety grows. In desperation I recruit a pair of green-eyed rats—animals known for their penchant to steal and get into impossible places—to start searching Kasta's walls and ceiling. It's a lot of trust to place in wild animals, but I'm running out of time.

And every night I write to Jet. First with Hen, who helps me read that Jet's "negotiations" are going well, which I take to mean that Sakira has accepted his help, but she still doesn't want anyone to know she exists. *Here's how to write "I miss you,"* Hen shows me. *Here's how to write "Come home soon."*

But in bed, with parchment on my lap, I draft a different letter. One that's mostly symbols, because I don't know how to write the right words. One that Jet will never read.

I feel like I'm losing myself, I write. *I think something's wrong.*

The morning that Jet is due to come home—the sixth day since he left, and one day before the debut party—I stand before my mirror, powdering the dark circles under my eyes.

Another week down; another week without any evidence against Kasta.

A reckless impatience is taking hold of me, like a fever rising. I smear red pigment onto my lips, my fingers agitated, and think— this failure, this inability to find anything on Kasta when I *know* he killed Maia . . . this is how Kasta felt when his magic wasn't surfacing. This is how it was for him in the weeks before his eleventh birthday, when he knew he'd have to show some kind of magical aptitude or else be turned onto the streets with the rest of the Forsaken. This is what pushed him to study poisons and become someone else.

My mind drifts to the binding necklace. Do I really need to wait for proof? What if I did the same as him . . . and made the outcome I wanted?

I could have Hen track down pelts. I could have her *fabricate* them. She's used to working with feathers; she could make cotton look like fur. I'd only need a couple of them. And why would the

Runemaster or Marcus or Jet even think to doubt me, the honest good girl, especially once I prove what Kasta is?

My heart quickens with the want of it, with the promise that this could be over that easily. But I can already see Jet's frown, warning me against being hasty, and still comes that annoying, soft voice in the back of my head: *What if you're wrong?*

"I'm not wrong," I tell my reflection. "All these good things Kasta's doing are just an act, and it's only going to last until he's crowned. It's not real."

My reflection gives me a look, and with a jolt I remember Kasta accusing me of the same thing: that I was plotting against him with Jet, that my kindness was an act to deceive.

I growl and drop my brush. "Fine. I won't fake any evidence, but I'm going to find something on him, and then you're going to apologize for ever doubting me."

I realize talking to myself like this is possibly another sign that I am not all right. But I decide to give myself a pass. I've been studying and preparing for the debut party all week, no time to relax, with the overhanging knowledge that I could be partially responsible for a war depending on how I handle things tomorrow. And so I feel allowing myself a few mirror arguments is more than justified.

I straighten the golden ivy leaves on my head and leave for my Influence lesson.

As usual, I arrive early, and without Kasta.

The Mestrah sighs, long and low, when I sit on the curved white bench before him. For a moment he says nothing, the glass eyes shifting restlessly in his hair, a warm breeze slipping under the collar of my *jole*. I study my nails, listening to the calls of morning jays. *Sun*, they sing. *Food. Mine!*

The king drums his fingers on his bare knee. "You have not walked with Kasta once since the hunt."

A week ago, I might have studied his sandals and declined to answer. Now I meet the king's eyes. "No."

His fingers curl, noticing. "Why?"

"I don't trust him."

"You think he'll hurt you?"

"No."

His brow rises, the quickness of this answer startling me as much as him, and now I do have to look away.

"Then what is it?" the Mestrah asks.

Words tangle on my tongue. I'm confused; I'm running out of time. I don't want to talk to Kasta, to let him draw me in again, when I must stay focused on stopping him.

The Mestrah taps his knee. "I do not ask much. These are important opportunities you are missing to speak to Kasta when there is no business to speak of. I don't expect you to become friends, but you do need to be able to tolerate each other. It should be no ordeal to spend a few minutes at his side."

This is temporary, I want to say. *It doesn't matter.* "Yes, Mestrah."

"Zahru."

I'd looked away, toward the servants' entry in the wall of the garden. Impatient for the volunteers to emerge. "Yes?"

"I will not require it. But I am hoping, when you are ready, you will show me by honoring this."

I nod. *I* am hoping Kasta is in chains before then.

And then Kasta arrives, and it's a small miracle that I don't blurt something that would give away my entire plan.

All week he's looked exhausted, dark circles haunting his eyes, and his focus has been off, often not bothering with a crown or even eyeliner. But today bronze leaves twist through his hair, kohl borders his eyes in sharp, dark lines, and his olive skin glows. As if he got a week of sleep in a day.

Or, more likely, *like he ate someone and feels much better.*

He catches me staring, and I hastily look away.

But despite the nearby servants now whispering about how long I looked at him, relief settles over me like sunshine. Obviously appearing refreshed is hardly damning evidence on its own, but these are the little inconsistencies that stack up, that prove I'm not just going mad.

The Mestrah waves over today's volunteers.

A petite woman in a tan working slip moves before Kasta, but the man approaching me comes over with a smirk, and the burst of triumph I'd felt vanishes. He does not look like a palace servant. Lines age his russet skin, and embossed silver armors his *tergus* kilt. Tattooed lanterns cover his muscled chest, marking the lives he's delivered to Rie, the god of death, in the name of our country. He looks down at me with a square jaw and vivid yellow eyes.

An ex-commander. Behind him, three Healers pause at the wall—two more than we usually have on hand. Warning bells are sounding in my head even before the Mestrah speaks.

"Kasta," the Mestrah says. "Today you will again work on identifying emotion. Be patient with yourself. Focus only on looking beyond what she's showing you, and give yourself time with it before answering."

Kasta stiffens at this, as he does every day. I bite back a flare of satisfaction that I continue to be the one who excels at the magic he tried to trade my life for.

"Zahru." The Mestrah turns to me. "Your only direction today is to get this man to tell you his name. Which means you'll need to change his mind, since he has been promised far more in reward for *not* telling you than for giving it."

The soldier's grin widens with the confidence of a war veteran who could keep a secret under more torture than I could ever imagine, and the Healers whisper, making bets on whether I can do it. Kasta's not even making an attempt with his volunteer. He watches me, waiting.

All of them, waiting to see if I will change this man's mind. By force.

My Influence stirs in my chest, electric and ready. The man's certainty fills my head, as much a part of me as my own breath. In a blink, I could amplify his bravado and have him strutting around the yard, boasting of his war conquests. But the thought of taking this confidence away, of twisting it to something *I* want—

I should say no. I should say amplifying emotion is the furthest I ever want to go, that I'm not ready to change people, that I don't want to do this.

But the soldier jeers down at me with every expectation that that's exactly what I'll do. He assumes that if I try, I will fail. I'm only a Whisperer. I'm only a girl.

My fingernails dig into my palms, and I steel myself. It's just a name; it's just one man. I won't use this part of my power otherwise unless I absolutely have to, and I really *might* need it for emergencies, for when it could protect someone else. A sword is not a killing tool unless it's used for killing. I'm just learning how to hold it, how to swing.

Is that what you're telling yourself now? comes that small, savage voice in my head. Except now it sounds like Kasta, and though I know the thought is mine, I look over as if he'd spoken. He crosses his arms, his interest waning. He doesn't think I'll do it, either.

I relax my hands. "But what do I do? The last time I tried this, the man passed out."

The soldier's bravado flutters, for a satisfying second, in my grip. He glances at the trio of Healers. I really want to tell him we usually only have one.

The Mestrah strokes his braided beard, thinking. "Try again what you did the first day, letting his emotions in instead of keeping them at the surface. But this time, ease into it. Like cracking a door open instead of flinging it wide. Then hold it at that low level and send your will through."

Thinking of how that felt, that momentary flash of being out of control, sends gooseflesh down my arms. But so does the realization of how close I was to succeeding at this on my first day.

I meet the soldier's yellow eyes.

And I'm very grateful Fara is not here to see this.

The garden and the murmuring Healers fade away. The soldier's confidence hums between my fingers, slick and ethereal, but I picture absorbing it instead, letting it in. My heart quickens. My skin warms. His certainty climbs my throat and swirls my ribs, as intimate and terrifying as touch, but unlike the first volunteer's fear, this emotion is far more stable. It feeds my want to do this, my own surety that I can. New pictures flip through my head: our allies eagerly signing treaties; myself as Mestrah without Kasta. And this time when I push back, when I think about how I want the soldier to yield, the emotion shifts beneath my fingers like water.

The soldier's smile drops. The Healers go silent.

I shudder, hating how natural this feels. "Tell me your name."

The soldier opens his mouth—and shakes his head. "Not that easy, *dōmmel*. I've been promised a palace east of the river for keeping it to myself."

Or maybe it just feels natural because I'm doing it all wrong. I shake my arms out, dropping the connection between us, and the Mestrah settles back in his throne. Kasta chews the inside of his cheek, his expression ever warring between jealousy and frustration.

I try four more times, each time letting the man's confidence in a little more, but I'm terrified to go too far again, to knock him out like I did the first volunteer. The Mestrah tells me to let go of that fear. I try; I almost *do* knock the soldier out. The Healers lean against the wall, chatting, having entirely lost interest. Kasta names three correct emotions and fails on three more. My frustration grows. I know how to do this. I *need* to do it, so I can stop coming to these lessons.

I'm just starting to reach for the man's confidence for the tenth time when Kasta says, "You know, if you don't actually want him to tell you, he isn't going to."

The connection shatters, and I grit my teeth. "I'm sorry, would you like to come over here and show me how?"

I will now confirm I get very snappy under stress, though I'm not entirely proud of this last statement. Regardless of our history, I've just mocked someone who has never used magic before for having trouble using magic. Which is really not my style.

I have the Healers' attention again, though not for the reason I want.

Kasta sneers. "My apologies, *gudina*. But I'd remind you that just because I don't know how to use the magic doesn't mean I don't know how it works in theory. But fine, ignore me. You know best, of course."

Every one of those sentences is layered, a reminder of who we used to be: powerless, but not worthless. I shake my head and try to focus. The last thing I need is Kasta rattling me when there are already too many people watching, and the Mestrah with his expectations, never mind that I don't even want to be doing this—

I close my eyes. *I don't want to do this.* Damn Kasta for knowing that about me before I even recognized it myself. Of course the soldier isn't going to tell me his name if I'm secretly hoping it won't work. And now I either continue to fail and keep having to come to these classes, or I give Kasta the satisfaction of being right.

The Healers slip closer, and the soldier straightens when I turn, his confidence overflowing because of my failures. Certain I'll fail again. But I press my fingers between my eyes, not even looking at him, not needing to, because I've already practiced this part of it ten times. I just wasn't sending back the right message.

I let his confidence seep over me, thick as mud, and I imagine this being the last time I come to this garden, the last time I have to do this. But in order for that to happen, I need him to trust me. To remember he doesn't need a second house by the river. It's only a name.

"Let's try this again," I say. "Tell me your—"

"Alistar," he says. The Healers gasp and laugh, and the man's certainty vanishes from my grip. He turns to the Healers, confused. "What? She didn't do anything; I just feel sorry for her. My family and I just moved into a nice place, we don't need something new . . ."

He continues defending his answer as if it was his idea, as if I didn't use magic, and the Mestrah stands, clapping, looking between Kasta and me like we're made of gold. I expect Kasta to bask in this, but the prince only stares at his own volunteer, something like sadness softening his face. I try not to let it affect me as the Mestrah asks what the woman is feeling, and Kasta shakes his head. He doesn't know.

Good, I tell myself as the soldier insists again that I did nothing. *Kasta would be far too dangerous with this power, too.*

Except I can't stop watching him. Secret Shifter powers or not, Kasta still sacrificed everything to get the knife's magic—he sacrificed *me*—and yet, instead of being enraged that he can't use it . . . he's helping me.

The Mestrah drops a heavy hand to Kasta's shoulder. "Magic always was a challenge for you. Perhaps it's for the best."

I try not to care as Kasta watches his father leave.

XX

I throw myself into my morning classes.

If I'm focusing on foreign policies and the Pe minister's estranged cousins, I'm not thinking about the addictive aftertaste of changing the ex-commander's mind. If I'm crying over this brain-melting concept in mathematics called *variables*, my memory won't keep replaying the betrayed way Kasta looked at me after I snapped at him. And if I ask enough repetitive questions of my writing tutor, to the point that she starts pulling her hair and gesturing dramatically, I definitely have no time to wonder why, despite how I've treated him and when it could only serve to make him look weak, Kasta would help me to become even more powerful.

I ask my writing tutor again what a noun is, and her eye twitches.

Lunch comes and goes. I finally convince myself that the only thing to take away from this morning's lesson is that Kasta has recently eaten someone, and turn my mind to what's ahead. With the debut party tomorrow, the Mestrah has canceled all of my afternoon classes, leaving space instead for a meeting with Kasta to discuss our strategy for each kingdom and to decide what we'll say in our welcome speech. After which I plan to watch the rulers come in with their entourages, as all of them will arrive at the palace by the end of the day, and to meet up with Jet, who should be back by sunset. And finally I'll have his help again, and the steadiness of his presence.

But I still have a little over an hour before my meeting with Kasta, and that's precious time I plan to use. I call Jade over, who tells me again that she's seen nothing unusual outside as I stroke her spotted back. The rats I recruited haven't returned since I sent them over. I drum my fingers on a hidden compartment in my bedframe, where the rune necklaces lie inside a hollowed leather book of gods' stories—but if a week of searching Kasta's room hasn't turned up anything, I doubt a week more will. We need a new strategy.

I shove up from the bed and leave to find my friends.

I'm halfway to Hen's room when I suspect I'm being followed.

It starts with a strange gray jay who hops between olive branches outside, alighting conveniently on a tree beside whatever window I'm passing and always within clusters of other songbirds, so if I listen for thoughts, I can't tell its voice from the dozens beside it. Neither can I tell if it's silent. So I veer for the palace's inner hallways, out of view of any windows, and that's when the cat appears.

A small silver tabby winds through the legs of the kitchen servers, emerging just as I reach the end of the hall. Far enough away that I can't hear its thoughts or see the color of its eyes. But I turn a corner and reach the end of the corridor, and there it is again, a slip of silver between potted plants. I take another hallway, this one in the wrong direction from Hen's room, and eyes shine behind a statue.

It's both thrilling and terrifying to consider Kasta following me. On one hand, here is extremely solid proof that I'm right about him, but it also makes me wonder if there have been other times, when I haven't been so alert, that he's trailed me. I comfort myself that at least Jet and I had the foresight to ward all my advisors' rooms against sound so we can speak together without fear of being overheard—until I remember we only soundproofed them against *human* hearing, and I have no idea if animals can hear through the wards.

Regardless, I need to lose him.

I weave my way under vaulted ceilings, back the direction I came. Back to my room, where I close the door and sprint to my balcony, through the glass partition, over the railing, and dangle down, down as far as I can before I let go, the shock of the landing biting up my legs. The Mestrah's private garden is mercifully empty, but I don't charge for the exit. Kasta could easily run through his room and see me that way, so I slink back under the balcony, behind a hedge, where no one overhead can see, and where anyone jumping down would have a hard time finding me.

I've only been there a few seconds when Kasta's balcony door whispers open.

Footsteps on his landing. My blood pulses in my ears, and I hold my breath, exhilarated by the certainty now that he was the one following me. Of course, this victory will be short-lived if he finds me here, and I hold my breath, praying to Numet that he stays up.

The heat swells; moments tick by like days. But finally Kasta's footsteps move away, and the partition glides, and he's gone.

I breathe out, sliding down the wall. Triumph fizzles against my skin. For someone who shouldn't have anything to hide, Kasta certainly seems worried about what I'm doing. And I wonder again if he might be hiding more than just Shifting. If that was all, he'd only need to be careful about where he put his pelts and how he sneaks out for his meals. He shouldn't care at all what I'm doing in the meantime. But he's tracking me. Like he's afraid I might have found something else.

And now he's getting as desperate as I am to uncover what *I'm* planning.

It makes me smile.

I take the long way to Hen's. And this time, no animals follow.

Hen answers on the first knock.

"Zahru!" she says, her brown eyes widening.

"Hen!" I say. "You won't *believe* what just—" The words catch in my throat, not only because I'm remembering that I should wait until we're inside to spill this new information about Kasta, but also because I don't know how to process what I'm looking at. Hen is in a strange green dress, the collar ruffled and as high as her chin, the sleeves tight and ending in white gloves. The skirt hangs long enough to cover her toes. Her sleek hair piles atop her head in black curls, and she's cleared her face of makeup, save for a brush of emerald at her temples. I'm fairly certain this is the current Nadessan fashion, which still does not explain anything about this.

"Wow," I say. "You look . . . unusual?"

"Unusual jobs call for unusual measures." She grins, but before I can ask about this extremely concerning statement, she swings open the door. "Look who's here, everyone!"

"Zahru!" Melia calls, from where she stands before one of the large room's two windows, dressed in a similarly covering purple dress with black gloves. She fixes the high collar of Marcus's silver suit while he shifts uncomfortably, tugging at the outfit's stiff pants. "It's good to see you free. Do you have the afternoon off?"

"I . . . sort of," I say, caught completely off-guard both by their coordinated outfits and the concept that they've all been hanging out together. "I have a meeting in an hour. Hi, Marcus?"

"Zahru." He nods, a triangular hat sitting roguishly atop his blond curls. It's strange to see the full length of his legs. Orkenian *terguses* and tunics are always long enough to not warrant trousers.

All of this is alarming enough that I decide my news about Kasta can wait a moment. "What is happening here?"

Hen fixes a pearly button on her sleeve. "Marcus and Melia are just about to help me with something. Did you know the Nadessan emperor arrived this morning?"

I do not like this at all. "I've been studying, so no. Please tell me you're not planning to sneak onto their boat."

"Oh, you're getting very good at guessing," Hen says, looking impressed. "But you're not entirely correct. We're going to visit their Fortune bird."

I grab the side of the dresser. Nadessa's Fortune birds are only one step down from Orkena's own legendary animals, for the simple fact that their power dies with them, versus the magic living on in their bones, but also because it's only ever one type of magic, and one type of bird. They're extremely hard to find. And definitely not the kind of treasure Nadessa would bring ashore to share.

"You mean the emperor's prized pet?" I say. "Which is *on his boat*? How is this not sneaking onto it?" I open my hands at Melia and Marcus. "You two are going along with this?"

Melia adjusts a tiny purple top hat over her braids. "Hen is like the bad influence I always needed." Which accurately sums up most people's feelings for Hen, I think, but is shocking to hear from law-abiding Melia. "And I believe it's not sneaking, because she has permission. Though I have decided not to ask from where."

Marcus shrugs. "I was promised custard, and a bird answering any question I want. That was enough for me."

Hen nods. "I have all the details worked out. They'll never know we were there. You want to come, too?"

I gape between the three of them. "I think if a crown heir disguises herself and sneaks onto a foreign ship, that's called *espionage* and grounds to spark an international conflict! And none of you can leave yet, anyway. Kasta just tried to trail me here as a cat. He is *laughing* his way through this moon, and we need a new strategy for exposing him!"

Melia freezes. "You saw him Shift?"

"Well . . . no," I admit. "But this tabby started following me by the kitchens, no matter where I went, and then I ran back into my room and over the balcony and dropped down and then Kasta came outside to see—"

Marcus blanches. "You jumped off your balcony? How high is that?"

"I mean, maybe two stories." I shrug. "I'm fine. It's not my first time; I did it during the Choosing banquet with Jet. The point is"—I raise an important finger—"we're on the right track, and we need to be extra careful about looking for him anytime we have one of these meetings."

This is not met with the cheers and impressed claps on the back that I'm expecting. Instead, Melia taps her lips. "Was it a silver tabby?"

"Yes!" I say. "With four white socks. Has it followed you before, too?"

"That sounds like Etta," Hen says. "She's the kitchen cat. She follows anyone who smells like food."

My chest pulls. "He killed the kitchen cat?"

In answer, Hen smells my sleeve.

"What?" I ask.

"You smell like cupcakes," she says.

Understanding dawns on me as I look across the patient, pitying eyes of my advisors. "You . . . don't think it was him."

Melia shrugs. "It's probably good to be careful, just in case."

I pull back from them. "But then why did it follow me for so long? And after I went outside, it was *seconds* before Kasta came out—"

Marcus clears his throat. "Have you considered that maybe he was working, and saw someone jump over your railing, and went outside because he wasn't sure what he'd just watched?"

This makes me sound like a person who has come unhinged, and my stomach tightens. "But the cat was hiding! It wasn't just following me; it didn't want to be seen!"

Hen and Melia share a conspiratorial look.

"You're right," Melia says. "It's bad. Look at those bags under her eyes, too."

Hen tuts. "We've let this go on long enough. It's time for an intervention."

I huff, putting my hands up when she starts toward me. "I know what I saw! And I don't have time for an intervention. I still have half an alphabet to learn, allies to secure, and two weeks before a Shifter plunges us into a war and starts eating people!"

Marcus adjusts his white gloves. "We have a saying in Greka: if you keep firing the same pie, you'll end up with ashes. And no dessert. It's only an hour, *dōmmel*. Come do something fun, and later, *after* your debut, we can meet again to discuss Kasta."

I stare at him, betrayed. "You too? Does no one else care how serious this is?"

"Zahru." Melia offers me a golden Nadessan suit and white gloves. "Sometimes looking away from something for a while is the only way to see it fresh. Come with us and let this go for a bit. We'll have *haru* masks, the bird is on public display . . . We'll be in and out before you know it."

"And you can ask the bird any question you want." Hen drops one of the lavish *haru* masks, with iridescent feathers across its porcelain brow and red ribbons to tie it, atop the suit. Garnets line the eye sockets; the rest of the mask is molded to hide the nose and top half of the wearer's face, since unmarried Nadessans are expected to don these until their wedding day, to ensure they choose their soulmates based on personality. "If you want to be boring, you can even ask it about stopping Kasta."

From the gleam in her eyes, I know she's aware of the effect this will have on me. I can't even care about the burst of triumph I feel from her when I don't immediately answer. Because even though I'm no longer sure what just happened with the cat, if this fortune-telling bird can set my mind at ease, if I can go forward knowing I'll be able to stop Kasta, then I can stop worrying about every little thing like this.

I should possibly be more concerned about what it will mean if the Nadessans find me sneaking around on their boat, but then I consider that after this morning's Influence lesson, there's no way we can be caught. If anyone starts to get suspicious or thinks they recognize us, I have the power now to change it.

That's *emergency use?* comes Kasta's amused voice in my ears. I shove the thought away. I need this answer.

I clasp my hands around the suit. "All right. You win."

The emperor's boat waits on the river like a floating palace.

An Earthmover had to physically adjust the wooden docks to make space for it, and it glitters like a frosted cake on the water, three levels of railings and windows and gold that dwarfs the silver Orkenian warships beside it. Seamless porcelain forms its sides, an obvious commission of Orkenian craft, especially considering the gold threaded in curling vines along the upper tiers. Spells that cost more than Fara and I would once have made in a year hum along its sides, warding it from breakage and wear.

It's a great compliment to my tutors that my first thought is how I might use this in our negotiations. Those ship spells have to be constantly reapplied, and we're the only country that can supply them. Greka may have a handful of Enchanters, and magicians have been born on rare occasions to Amian families, but most foreign-born magicians move here to make their living, where they have the best access to tutors and other magic. Something I'll be sure to remind the Nadessans of if they want to keep traveling in such luxury.

Guards patrol the first level with spears and pressed black suits that look extremely uncomfortable for the high afternoon heat.

As I can personally attest, given how much I'm sweating in my own.

Hen hands me, Melia, and Marcus each a lacquered square of parchment. "We're part of the emperor's extended family. His third cousins, specifically, though no one's going to look too closely. Lots of people will be coming on and off the boat to visit the palace. Though you have to have one of these cards, or they do a full background check on you."

I turn the glossy square. "Where did you even get these cards?"

"I'm borrowing them." Her eyes glitter behind her crystal-studded mask.

I almost drop it. "You *picked these off allies* I'm trying to convince to trust us? Do I even dare ask where you got the clothes?"

"Don't be silly; I made the clothes. Relax, you're ruining our vibe."

I tug the ribbon on my own mask, making sure it's tight, grumbling about deviant Materialists.

Marcus nudges me, his porcelain brow glittering with silver dust. "This is what fun is like, remember? Let us handle the worrying. That's our job. You just worry about which type of custard you'll try first, and what you'll ask that Fortune bird."

He winks, and I breathe out my nerves as I join Hen's side. Melia and Marcus link arms behind us, and I look only forward, to the answer I'm going to get, to an hour where I can pretend

I'm just me again, out with my friends. And technically I'm still fulfilling part of my royal duties, getting this answer about Kasta.

The guard checking the cards must have a great deal of faith in these small, unassuming pieces of paper, because he waves us onto the boat with barely a glance.

I make it ten steps before I look over my shoulder. "That felt really easy. Wasn't that way too easy?"

Hen shrugs. "They're inside a guarded dock with people trying to impress them. Why would they have high security right now?"

I frown. "I just have concerns about being allies with people who don't even check paper cards."

"*Dōmmel.*" Melia pokes my shoulder. "No more of this ruling speak. Nadessa is one of our most sympathetic allies, anyway. Which is nothing to dismiss in this climate."

A fair point, as I remember there are kingdoms like Melia's own birth country, Amian, who have only recently begun to accept magicians as human beings, and with whom we had to forge a treaty a century ago so they'd stop executing their few magicborn and send them here instead. Which is only slightly more horrible than Orkena's own treatment of the Forsaken, who we may not kill, but who we still separate from their families and send off into the world with nothing.

Kasta's note flashes through my head, and for once I don't shove him away. This is another thing that will change when I'm Mestrah.

Melia points ahead. "Oh, wow. What is this made of?"

A grand indoor gallery opens before us, and we enter a wide, square tunnel, where the second and third floors of the ship cut away to a tall ceiling and a stunning view of the palm trees and white sand estates on the opposite shore. Everything glitters a smooth, iridescent white. The market stalls lining the paneled walls, the sharp chandeliers, the fine ice sculptures rising through the center of the gallery, each a different ocean creature native to Nadessa. Sparkling white flakes cascade constantly from the ceiling, and I inhale when we step out of the sun, our boots crunching into something cold and soft.

"It's snow," Marcus says, opening his hands to the falling flakes.

"It's *true*," I whisper as several of the glittering pieces melt on the back of my hand. For once, something the travelers told me wasn't an exaggeration. They claimed the Nadessan palaces were made of ice, and while this is not quite ice, if the emperor would pay for this level of magic just for his transport, I can only imagine what he's commissioned for his home.

It's everything I have not to take off my gloves and dig my fingers into the floor, to feel this rare substance all over my skin.

Melia grunts. "Well, that explains why they dress like this even while they're visiting. It's freezing in here."

"Tiny dolphins!" Hen says, tugging my sleeve. The nearest market stall holds shelves of clear goblets swimming with the blue and pink creatures, and I'm just starting for them when Marcus lightly smacks my arm.

"Dessert," he says.

This is an extremely effective way to get my attention. I follow his pointing finger to the sculptures in the aisle, where a handful of unmasked Nadessans mingle in their high collars and pearl-studded gloves, because the sculptures are not just pieces of art, but *tables*. A vast, sparkling clamshell yawns open, little pink and white delicacies set in the crushed snow around a bowl of red sauce; a dolphin pod curls around cauldrons of chilled soups; a giant octopus with golden suction cups holds up trays of chocolate and yellow pudding and little cakes topped with whipped cream.

"This is why we're friends, Marcus," I say, taking his arm. "What are those pink and white things?"

"Shrimp," he says. "It's kind of like a fish. And that golden, shining cup of perfection by the cakes is called *custard*. Tomás's mother makes a version of it that could convert you away from chocolate."

I snicker. "I'm going to need you to prove that sometime."

"Zahru." Hen grabs my arm and pulls me so I can see around the tables. "There's the bird."

This is the only thing that could draw me away from the promise of golden, shining cups of perfection. At the exact center of the room stands a snow pedestal topped in a silver cage, firestone gems lining the bars for heat, real sapphires embedded down its sides. Though the bird itself is admittedly disappointing. I really assumed a fortune-telling animal would look as mystical as our own legendary animals, maybe with flowing golden feathers or a rainbow plume, but the bird is . . . typical. A tiny songbird with black feathers and a white head. Nadessans form a short line before it, ushered close to the cage one at a time by a woman in a silver suit and a black mask. They ask a question, the bird flits its wings, and some of the people walk away with smiles, some with curses.

"It's so . . . plain," I say.

Hen itches her cheek beneath her mask. "Yes. The only difference between it and normal Nadessan songbirds is the marking on its head. Supposedly hundreds of them hide out near the ocean, but even the emperor hasn't managed to find more than one."

"Weird. And it really can tell the future? Like our priests?"

Hen nods. "In an extremely narrow sense. It doesn't always answer."

Marcus gestures to the sculptures. "Custard?"

I shake my head. "I want to ask my question first. I'll come back for the food."

Though his eyes stay cheery, Marcus's mouth thins, and he beckons Melia to come with him in a subtle way that, under other circumstances, I might have found suspicious. Maybe it *is* strange, the notion of my prioritizing other things above food. But not concerningly strange, right? Isn't it good that I'm starting to put my country before my stomach?

Hen and I get in line for the bird.

Melia and Marcus glance at me from the snow sculptures, little bowls of soup in their hands.

"Hen," I say, tugging the suit's uncomfortable collar. "I'm doing all right with everything, right? You'd tell me if I was taking something too far?"

She places her hands, very patiently, on my shoulders. "You're in the middle of an intervention."

"Oh, yes," I say, wincing.

"But you really are doing well, all things considered. Maybe just take a little more time off, when you can. Here, you'll need this. One ticket equals one question. They're very expensive, so I thought I should probably only get one for each of us."

She places a shining slip of silver paper into my hand. I decide I don't want to know if this came from the same place as the admission cards.

"Thanks," I say.

We wait in line, in which I can confirm our dear Nadessan allies feel quite safe here, since none of them really glance at us or seem overly worried about whether we belong. The temptation to reach out and see what they're feeling, to know we're safe, grates against my nerves, but I make myself contain it. The only time I cave is when we reach the woman in the silver suit, who takes my ticket.

"You have one minute with the bird," she says, marking the ticket with a quill whose clear ink turns gold against the paper. "And she must be able to answer your question with yes or no. Two wing flaps is a yes, and one is a no. If she doesn't answer, you can try another question."

"Thanks," I say, bracing for her to ask my name or some other Nadessan detail that will require my magic to smooth over. But her level of interest stays mercifully even, and I approach the bird with a stone in my throat.

Tired, the bird thinks. *Rest? Food. Bored.*

She flits to the upper tier of her cage when I approach, plucking at a string of honeyed seeds. A small number eight stands out in black on her forehead. It occurs to me that even though her strange magic isn't Orkenian, it must be similar to my own Whispering if she can understand humans.

And now for my question. For a moment I hesitate, considering that there are far more important things I could ask her about than Kasta: if Orkena will win the war; if I will secure our allies tomorrow. If my family will stay safe in all of this. But those are terrifying questions to get the answer *no* to, and so I decide on my original strategy. It's much better to have peace of mind about the immediate issue at hand, to know the gods are on my side at least in this.

I lower my voice to a whisper only the bird can hear. "Will we stop Kasta from becoming king?"

The bird pauses in eating. Her head tilts, perhaps knowing I don't belong here and neither does that question. Her wings don't move. The woman in the suit turns a timekeeping device on her wrist. I wait, and the bird keeps eating, and I sigh and acknowledge that this is probably for the best. At least I got some time away, and I can still enjoy the custard before I leave.

I'm just thinking of a different question to ask when the bird hops over on her stick, and her wings flit. Once.

No, she thinks. *You won't.*

XXI

FOR a moment, I can only stare at this bird and its evil, beady black eyes.

"Excuse me?" I snap.

The bird hops back over to her food, but though her wings don't move, she mocks me with every jump. *No, no, no. No!*

"That is *not* the right answer," I say. "Do you even have real magic? Do you just guess?"

The woman in silver crosses her arms. "Her answers are final. Please move on."

"No, this bird is a fraud." Behind the woman, Hen bounces on her toes, but I can't stop. "I have been through the literal *wringer* for this. There is *no way* he still wins—"

Marcus's hand closes on my arm. "Z," he whispers urgently. "Perhaps we could make a scene elsewhere?"

I almost pull away, but I have the attention of the entire gallery now, though from the pitying expression of the woman in silver and the amused titters of the crowd, this reaction is quite common. I unclench my fists and let Marcus steer me out of the snowy hall, into the sun, where he tucks a cup of custard into my hands and tells me to breathe. Hen and Melia follow, glancing over their shoulders, and the Nadessans go back to browsing the shops and sipping their glass dolphin drinks like the world didn't just tilt on its side.

A new kind of pressure builds in my chest, thick and choking. The bird can't be right. I can't be killing myself to do all this studying, to spy on Kasta, to have gone through everything I went through, to be told that nothing I'm doing will matter in the end.

"It said *no*," I growl when the four of us are alone at the railing. "I asked if we would stop Kasta from becoming king, and it said no!"

Melia rubs my back in soft circles. "Easy. I know this seems bad, but Fortune birds can be very tricky. They often find loopholes in questions. It doesn't mean Kasta will definitely become king . . . right, Marcus?" Though she's looking at him as if she, too, hopes this is the case.

He shifts uncomfortably. "Er—"

"How direct were you?" Hen asks, somehow having already obtained a plate of shrimp. "Did you ask it about Orkena specifically?"

I stare at the custard in my hands. "No. But what else would he be king of?"

Hen shrugs. "Maybe you marry him off in the future. Send him to terrorize some other country."

The thought of me doing this is so strange, I'm not even sure how to answer her. "Marry him off? Like I own him? So he can rule another country that could wage war on us?"

"Well, probably not," Melia concedes. "But it may not mean right now, either. Maybe you have no heirs, and in forty years he takes the throne."

I almost drop the custard. "I'm not going to have kids?"

Marcus gives Melia a look. "Or maybe *we* don't stop him, because technically that's what the High Priests do when they deliver his sentence as a Shifter. There's no use panicking about it when we still have time to act. It would have been nice to get a yes, but it doesn't mean much to get a no." He thumbs a pearl button on the cuff of his suit. "I'm so sorry. This was meant to be fun, but I think we've stressed you out more."

I sigh. "I think that's just what my life is now."

Melia drops her hand from my back. "Not always. For now, yes, but not always. We'll keep brainstorming, all right? Just focus on your debut, and we'll come to you in two days' time with new ideas on how to stop him. Can you let us do that for you?"

I wish they weren't wearing masks so I could fully see the way they're looking at me. But the concern in their eyes is enough, and if I'm honest, when *Hen* is the one running interventions, it's time to take a break.

"All right," I say. "Yes, that sounds good. But I think I've probably done enough damage here. I'm going to go."

They nod and go back inside to ask that infuriating bird their questions, and I take the long way back to Hen's room to change, rolling the custard cup between my palms.

Kasta as king. It's as terrifying to think of not stopping him as it is to think of him elsewhere, working against me.

I leave the untouched dessert on a serving tray by the kitchens.

Gods, I hope that bird is wrong.

By the time I'm heading to my meeting with Kasta, I've pushed the bird out of my mind. There are just too many unknowns to worry about it, as my team pointed out, and I can't let it affect my focus. The sacrificial mark was also supposed to mean something unavoidable, even if Kasta was the one who made it. But here I am, still alive.

I tighten the loops of bronze feathers that belt my *jole* and step onto the western wall of the palace.

Because the Mestrah is using the war room for other business, Kasta and I are to meet in Cybil's tower, which also happens to be the farthest structure from where the delegates enter the palace. Which, as vocal as the Mestrah knows I can be, is likely no coincidence. Ahead of me, the tributary tower to the goddess of war cuts the sky like a knife, Cybil herself rising from the alabaster foundation in a tunic of real satin. Polished, russet-brown stone matches the tone of her flawless skin, and real silver forms her armor, overlapping in jeweled pleats. Her arm drips gold-banded strips of leather where she raises her hand for Klog, her loyal falcon. The bird's enormous granite tail fans where he alights on her wrist, casting shadows over the narrow windows hidden in Cybil's sides.

I arrive within the goddess's head, back by the stairs.

The room domes high above me, and across the way, Cybil's enormous, oval eyes form windows to a swath of blue sky and orange sand. Gleaming redwood bookshelves curl around the space, overflowing with scrolls and bronze decorations: a standing compass, a sculpture of Numet's sun, and a statue of Klog himself, his talons gripping one of Valen's rattlesnakes. The goddess of war and the god of fate have a complicated history. Sometimes they're depicted as lovers, but more often they're at each other's throats.

Kasta looks up from where he leans over an enormous black table, eclipsed by the light of the windows.

My blood jerks. I can do this; we're just talking strategy, and this is actually something he can help me with. It's only an hour. Then I can escape his suffocating presence and watch Jet's boat come in, and clear my head before tomorrow.

"You're late," he says.

I shrug off my nerves and wander toward a row of jewel-toned tomes. "It's my first time here. No one warned me this tower was on the other side of the continent."

"You could have done your research and left earlier."

"Or I could have happily realized it would shorten the length of our meeting and not cared."

I look pointedly over, but he only grunts and rolls out a map on the table. "I forgot. You're very important now that you've learned to control people's minds."

My fingers stop centimeters from a book. "If you're referring to what I said to you earlier . . . I didn't mean it like that. I was frustrated, that's all." Which sounds very like an apology. My nails dig into my palms. "I'm only doing what I must to please your father so he doesn't make me your advisor. I won't be controlling people outside those lessons."

His smile is slow. "We'll see. At the rate you're taking to power, I don't see that happening."

My gut twists. "What's that supposed to mean?"

"It means you're fitting in here like you've always belonged." He anchors the corners of the map with stones, his face shadowed. "If you could change my father's mind to make *me* the advisor, would you?"

I don't like this line of questioning, or that this has somehow

242

turned into an interrogation when *I'm* supposed to be finding something on him. Especially when, without even thinking, the answer caught in my throat is *yes*.

I move toward the statue of Klog, relaxing my grip. "We're off-topic. We're supposed to be discussing our debut."

A knife of a smile. "Of course." He slides a pair of scrolls over from the side of the table. "The first order of business is the welcome speech. You'll deliver that."

I scoff. "And here I was under the impression we were supposed to decide things together. But, yes, definitely, let's have the girl who's never given a speech in her entire life deliver her first one in front of four countries. Nothing could go wrong with that."

He gives me a look. "You're the greater mystery. If I give the speech, you'll remain in the lesser position. They'll think you're a consort, not a Mestrah."

I sigh, trailing my finger over a crystal orb. "This is another of the Mestrah's orders, then."

"No," Kasta says. "It just makes sense."

He says it so matter-of-factly, I don't even know how to reply. He *wants* me to be seen in a position of equal power?

"After that," he continues, "we'll converse with each ruler separately and secure their loyalty. I'll do the talking then. They'll want to know specifics about trade advantages and the state of our defenses."

"I know about our trade agreements, too," I say, turning. "Shouldn't I help? Since you're so interested in showing that we're equals?"

"Sure. If you feel they're going cold on us, or if they ask about *forsvine*, you'll use your Influence to smooth things over and end the conversation."

My blood jumps. "I'm sorry, did I just imagine us talking, literally a minute ago, about how I'm never using that outside of our lessons?"

"You don't think you can?"

"I do, but—" I bite down on the words, on how quickly that answer came to me. And then I close my eyes, bitter realization pulling my smile. *This* is why he was helping me earlier. I should have known. "That isn't the point. We're trying to earn these rulers' trust. If they think I'm manipulating them . . ."

"I told you, no one knows we have Influence. And that's a good thing, because otherwise no one would agree to meet with us at all. You saw your volunteer. He was so certain it was his own idea to give his name, he actually defended you to the Healers." His lip twitches. "No one will ever know you've used it. It's what your power was made for."

For us—for *me*—to turn other people to our desires. I suddenly feel childish that I thought this party was anything else.

I lean back against the shelf. "It doesn't matter. That's not how I want to start things off with these rulers."

"Zahru." He unrolls the last scroll slowly, his fingers tense. "I yielded to your desires with Odelig—because you felt it was that important to appeal to me—and I feel it's just as critical to ask the same of you now. I can't use Influence like you can. So please, if you trust me in nothing else, will you at least trust me in this?"

Trust me. Please. The words burn across the faded mark on my wrist, the scar on my chest. Kasta with the knife; Kasta above

Odelig's sleeping form. Kasta telling me, during the Crossing, that he would do everything in his power to see Orkena thrive.

"I don't know," I hedge. His words are pulling at me again, like the moon at the tide. "I still barely understand what I'm doing."

"Fair enough. Just promise me that if it's the difference between securing an ally or losing them, you'll at least try."

This seems oddly reasonable, and I take a moment to consider whether this could be used for some nefarious agenda before I nod.

"All right," I say, pulling an anxious hand up my arm. "Is that all, then? I should probably get started on my speech."

"There's one more thing. Not something my father wanted us to go over, but a concern all the same."

"Oh. In that case, goodbye!" I say brightly, and head for the stairs.

"Zahru—"

"I'm sure you don't need me to figure it out. Just don't kill anyone tomorrow, and you'll be fine."

"I think there's going to be another attack," he says, and I stop with my hand on the stairs' marble railing. "Wyrim would be foolish not to strike again during the banquet. My father's being arrogant, hosting such a public event. We have no way yet to detect *forsvine* if someone sneaks it in, especially at the rate it's advancing."

I flex my hand on the rail. "I'm sure your father has considered the risks, especially after what happened to our hunting boat. You're being paranoid." As usual.

I don't think I imagine the glint in his eye. "Would it be without reason?"

There's a threat layered in his tone, and beetles crawl on my skin as I wonder if he knows I've been in his room. "You see a lot of things that aren't there," I say, my scar prickling.

"Maybe. But I know the best way for Wyrim to demonstrate their power in this war would be to kill a crown heir before we've even ascended."

I hesitate. "You think someone will try to kill us?"

"I think someone will try to kill *you*."

"Of course you do," I growl, shoving off the railing. "It only makes sense they'd go after the weaker heir—"

"Weaker?" He laughs. "You think, even without the world knowing about your Influence, that *that's* how they see you? You are the girl who survived death. Who convinced a king to let a commoner rule equal to his son. They are *terrified* of you. And it's in their best interests to kill you now, before you gain even more favor."

I bristle, rejecting that he could think of me as *stronger*. "I guess you would know. That's what you would do, right?"

"I *didn't have to do this*," he says, jabbing the table. "The Mestrah didn't ask me to brief you on security. *I* wanted to warn you. And to figure out what we'll do to ensure it doesn't happen." He flings a hand at the scrolls on the desk. "This is a map of the banquet room. Schematics of hidden weapons, assassination tools, common poisons. Last night was the first full night of sleep I've had in a week."

A thick silence fills the space, heavy enough to drown. I can't reply. Not only because of the possibility that *this* is why he's looked so run-down, but because I absolutely don't understand

246

him anymore. It would be so much easier for him to say nothing, to let fate play out, to let another country kill me. He wouldn't even have to get involved. It would be his father's negligence to blame if I died.

"Assume the worst of me," he says, leaning over his work. "But my priority has always been Orkena's survival. And it's become clear that *you* are instrumental to that."

My heart twists. These are lies. I need them to be, because I don't know what to do with them otherwise. Logically I know there's no other reason for him to warn me, especially if he thinks I've been poking around his room.

I am trying to ruin him.

He is trying to save me.

"You need me right now," I say, scrambling for a reason that makes sense. "Will you feel the same after you've mastered Influence, too?"

Kasta looks down at the scrolls. "That's not what makes you valuable."

"Then what does?"

The answer shouldn't matter. But I'm desperate to catch him in a lie, to prove he's out to destroy me as much as I am him.

Kasta inhales, then presses his next confession through his teeth. "You, Zahru. Your ideas. Your words. Your way with people."

My stomach drops. I have to lock the words out; I can't let him get into my head again. This is just like that moment after the Choosing, when he told me a Whisperer could be powerful and went on to cut a sacrificial symbol into my wrist. This is just like in the tent, before I asked if he was still planning to kill me.

I almost ask about Maia. But then he will know.

It's your Influence he needs, I think stubbornly. *Nothing more. Don't trust him. You can't trust him.*

But I cross to the table. I look down at the scrolls, these careful drawings that took days to draft. And I move to the other side.

Next to him.

"This is what I would do if I were them," Kasta says, his voice rough. "And this is how we will stop it."

XXII

DUSK is settling like blood across the dunes by the time we finish.

My mind swirls as I leave the tower. Half of it with quicksilver memories of weapons to watch out for, gifts I shouldn't accept, and actions to take if I'm poisoned or cornered by assassins. The other half with the quiet way Kasta explained each item, his shoulder centimeters from mine, his gaze focused. The silver in his eyes when he said the safest strategy was to stay near him all evening, so we could watch out for each other.

So he could *protect* me, if something went wrong.

Nobles stream by in excited groups as I head for my room. An older couple bows to me on their way to watch the Grekan monarchy come in on their sand skiffs; a group of boys my age, dressed in *tergus* kilts and ivy crowns and little else touch their fingers to their heads, on their way to party with the Pe attendants. Cactus blossoms hang from the orange tapestries, breathing a sugary lemon scent over the halls, and jewel-blue butterflies flit in my path. The Mestrah spared no expense to impress our guests. With a sigh I remember Jet's boat should have come in hours ago, and that I missed it, and that there's no way we'll be attempting any kind of redo of the night he left me, because I still have a speech to write.

But I do want to see him, even if just for a minute. I head for the officers' wing.

Except he's not in. Because he's at *yet another meeting* with the Mestrah and other key officers to discuss their roles and the process for the banquet tomorrow, and no one knows when it will be over.

And this is when I start to get especially irritated. I have spent *way* too long going over all the different ways people could kill me, I have adamantly not had enough sleep, and also, I have not had dinner.

I storm to my room and shove open the doors.

"I have *had it!*" I shout, my voice carrying in satisfying echoes. "When I'm Mestrah, we are working half days, we are serving cake at all meetings that talk about assassination, we're going to fight wars via dance competition, and so help me, if someone springs *one more meeting* on me or someone I want to see—"

"Brr?" says Jade, leaping off the end of my bed. *Zar? Need love?*

I frown as she trots over, her spotted tail twitching. Without even thinking, without remembering that I live alone now in this giant room, I just started off as I would have on any day back in Atera, bursting into the stable, Fara always there to listen, and Hen half the time, too. My heart pinches as the silence wraps around me. I could go find them, of course, if I felt like I had the time.

"Sorry for ranting at you," I whisper, heaving Jade up. She's rapidly passing large housecat status. Soon I won't be able to hold her.

I smile. "You just said my name, didn't you?"

Zar, she thinks, nuzzling my head. *Love.*

I sigh and carry her to the windows, sliding one of the thick curtains aside. Fireflies wink outside like wishes, and distant couples wander through the trees beyond the Mestrah's gated garden, many in foreign attire. The Pe with their mountain furs and high boots; the Amians in scant pastels, their limbs and necks covered more in jewelry than fabric. No crowns, meaning these are just the honored company that attends each monarch. Tomorrow, I'll meet their rulers.

And all of Orkena's future will be decided.

"Please, gods, guide my words," I mutter, squeezing Jade. No matter what strange game Kasta's playing, figuring it out will have to wait. If I can't prove to Orkena's allies that we're fine, his ascending the throne will be the least of my problems.

"One day," I promise Jade. "One day of peace with him, then I'm getting to the bottom of this."

As it happens, I *do* get to see Jet that night, but of course when he walks in, I've just torn up my seventh attempt at any kind of respectable welcome speech and screamed at the ceiling. It's not my best look. Jet enters very cautiously, his blue traveling tunic wrinkled, the black liner smudged around his eyes.

I stand up guiltily from the couch, hopeful that even though the door was slightly ajar when I yelled, maybe he didn't hear it.

He hesitates on the threshold. "I can come back."

I half laugh, half sob, and rub my hands down my face. "No, please come in. I'm just working on this speech . . . I need a break." I cross to a bronze tray that holds remnants of my dinner: an empty soup bowl, fish bones, chocolate flakes from the pudding I definitely ate first, and a little kettle of hibiscus tea. I pour some of the red liquid in a crystal cup and turn. "Tea?"

Jet's gaze shifts from the heavy curtains covering the windows to the empty tray. To the crumpled balls of paper littering the floor, one of which Jade chases beneath the lion-pawed couch.

"No," he says slowly. "Thank you."

The uneasy way he says that sends a cold droplet down my spine. My Influence flexes. I could check. I could bring what he's feeling to me in a blink and know if he's upset or just tired.

But reaching for something he's not sharing in words feels very different from waiting for a burst of strong emotion. Those I can't control. This I can.

I turn back to the tray and top off the cup. "How was Sakira?"

Jet's sandals scuff the floor; he reaches down to stroke Jade, who drops a parchment ball at his feet. "Stubborn as ever. And very unhappy with you. But I assured her her secret would go no further, and she extended her threat of making life here terrible for both of us if it does, so. At least you won't have to suffer alone if one of us spills."

My heart sinks. "You can't tell your father she's alive? Or Alette's parents?"

He throws the ball for Jade, who tears after it. "No, though I gave them a good guilt trip for it. Sakira will come around, I think. It was very strange to see her like that . . . like she just didn't care anymore. That week in the desert really rattled her."

What *Kasta* did to her rattled her, I remind myself. I hold to the words like a lifeline.

"Anyway," Jet says, "she was still happy to see me, and very happy to see the gold I brought. Thank you again for trusting me with that. Especially during such a stressful time."

I slide my thumb along my cup, grateful he can't read my emotions as clearly as I can read his. I can't help but wonder how much he might have helped if he'd been able to search Kasta's rooms with me. He could have sent Sakira money anonymously; he could have gone to see her only after we'd found something on Kasta. He could have secured her support and brought her back.

He told me he'd be here when I needed him.

"Of course," I say, smiling.

"Now then." He rubs his hands. "You said something about a speech? Anything I can help with?"

I sip my tea and gesture to the crumpled balls. "Well, I'm in charge of greeting the rulers tomorrow at the banquet, so I thought I'd start by giving my and Kasta's names, welcoming everyone, and then fainting before I spark international outrage."

He scoffs, as if that was a joke, and unfolds one of the speeches. "All right, let's take this step by step, then. What do you keep getting caught up on?"

"I don't know!" I say, dropping my cup on the tray. "Everything. I have no idea what I'm doing. My tutors keep telling me I have to be firm, that I can't show any uncertainty, that I have to pretend we're in the position of power and say we expect our allies' help . . ." I rub my forehead. "That's just not who I am. I can't stand up there and threaten people. Or lie and say I'm the strongest ruler Orkena has ever had. I don't know if I am. I mean, I'm *not*. And Kasta's worried about losing them because we don't have an answer to *forsvine*, and he wants me to just use Influence and be done with it . . . because I could now. I changed an ex-commander's mind today. I could."

Jet's hands go still on the speech he's holding. "And what do you want to do?"

My stomach flips. The confession waits on my tongue, sour as bile, my Influence stirring through my blood. It would be so easy to use it. To not care at all what I say in my speech and be as ruthless as everyone's expecting, and then use my magic to fix it. *Remember when I threatened you? That was just for show! You know we'd never really hurt you. Here, swear yourself to us in blood.*

I close my eyes. "I don't know." Those letters I wrote to Jet these past nights, the ones I won't ever show him, swirl through my memory. "What would you do?"

The second I ask, I fear I've made a mistake. His hand tightens on the speech. A flash of something like anger slices over my skin—his, strong enough to reach me. And I start to wonder if he left because he needed to get away from this . . . from me.

But his grip relaxes. The emotion vanishes quick enough that I wonder if I misread it, and when he picks up another crumpled ball, his voice is smooth.

"I would follow my gut," he says. "And if something didn't feel right, I wouldn't do it."

"I know, but . . . you know what comes out of my mouth when I'm stressed. If I'm honest with them, if I don't use Influence . . . I could lose them."

Jet shrugs. "I suppose that's always a risk. But I think you've forgotten that you've spoken to three almost-rulers before. At length. And you didn't need Influence to reach *them*."

He gives me a look, and I smile weakly, wishing I could take comfort in his kind reminder. "You do remember one of them is now my archnemesis."

"Yes, which I imagine he'll very soon come to regret, if he

doesn't already. But this party won't be as intense as the race, and I have no doubt whatsoever that you'll win tomorrow's rulers over. You have a good heart, Zahru. You'll know exactly what to say."

I'm not sure he'd believe that so thoroughly if he knew that I considered fabricating pelts earlier this week, or that I nearly used my magic on him just moments ago. But I cling to the words anyway. To the reminder that I *have* done this before, by finding the similarities between myself and strangers, and from there, building trust. Building a feeling of safety. A starting point that would be much easier to branch out from if I didn't just remember that Kasta said the world was terrified of me.

But I trace the mark on my chest, my fingers soft. Because that's what started this very conflict. Fear of the unknown, of Mestrahs using magic to conquer, to control. So much that even though these other rulers don't know I have Influence, they still worry I have *something* that can hurt them. Which, yes, they're correct about, but if I could somehow assure them we're on equal ground, that I would never use that power against them . . .

I think of the *forsvine* sample, and the radius of its reach.

And I look up. "I know what I'm going to do."

I am possibly more excited about my idea not because it's the right thing to do or because I'm sure it'll impress our allies, but because I know how much it will irk Kasta. And the thrill of proving his methods wrong yet again is just too much not to savor.

I stand very still the next morning as the Royal Materialist and her assistants fuss to dress me for the banquet. They wind under one another like dancers, tying the shimmering ends of a golden *jole* at my hip and shoulders, looping strips of gossamer fabric around my fingers and wrapping it in spirals up my bare arms. Two girls lower an interlocking sculpture of bronze feathers onto my shoulders, where talons at the back hold the corners of a wine-red cape. Another girl lines my eyes in curling kohl, enhancing each mark with dots of vivid red. Numet's spiraling sun gleams through a decorative split at the front of my bodice.

The Royal Materialist places a crown of gold-dipped feathers onto my head, pinning it into the waves of my hair.

And for the first time since this started, I look into the mirrors and see a queen.

My father cries when I emerge from the dressing room. Mora and Hen clap approvingly, admiring the tiny white lilies dotting my hair, but it's Fara who pulls me into his arms, his grip tight.

"You look just like your mother," he whispers.

When he steps back, it's me wiping my eyes.

Kasta is already in the throne room when I arrive, a deep red cape dripping down his back, and when he turns, my heart jerks. His blue eyes are oceans between twisting lines of kohl, his deep olive skin glistening with oil. A gleaming bronze mantle rests atop a pure white tunic, but instead of feathers, two rattlesnake heads are poised to strike on his shoulders. Their long bodies twine across his chest, circling Numet's dark symbol. More of the snakes crown his hair.

Valen's serpents. Cybil's feathers. I would be amused by the Royal Materialist's choices if I wasn't so flustered by the insinuation of how we make up after our fights.

"Zahru," the Mestrah says, his voice hoarse. Even with a dozen *trielle* spells glowing on his skin, he looks much worse than I've seen him. Sweat glistens on his bare chest, and only a plain, albeit luxurious, *tergus* wraps his waist—a normal sight for the court, but certainly not an outfit for receiving company.

"Are you ready?" he asks.

"Yes, Mestrah," I say, bowing.

"Good. I will not be going with you."

I look up.

"They are here for you," the Mestrah says. "That is why you both wear Mestrahs' mantles. Get each of the four rulers to commit in blood that they will assist us—the contracts require a drop of it, and you will remind them that if their loyalty wavers, we will know, and they will be considered sided with Wyrim. Work together. I do not expect—" He winces, bringing his fist to his heart, and swallows. "I do not expect to hear at the end of this that you got in one another's way."

A terrible cough rakes him, and the boy servant rushes closer, but the king can't stop long enough to grab the chalice he offers. The guards shift. The Mestrah coughs over and over, his back heaving, and a Healer runs in from the side, placing her hands quickly on his shoulders. Nothing happens at first. The king heaves, and the boy servant quickly exchanges the tray for a bucket sitting beside the throne. I cringe at the sound of the king being sick.

Finally it stops, the Mestrah trembles beneath the Healer's hands, and for a moment, a tense silence thickens the air. I glance at Kasta, but whether he's distressed to see his father this way, I can't tell from the stone of his face.

The Mestrah sits up, waving the Healer and the servant away. After a lifetime of being the greatest power in the world, I imagine he loathes this. Appearing dependent. Out of control. Blood glistens at the corners of his mouth.

When he speaks, his voice is little more than a whisper.

"The gods chose you for this," he says. "Prove they were right."

XXIII

WE leave in silence, Kasta with that same stiff, impassive expression, and me with static riding my veins, both for what I'm about to do and for the king's declining health. I knew the Mestrah's time was drawing to a close. But it's another thing to see it, even if he's not my favorite person given how harsh he's been with his children and the cutting things he can say. He's still the one who defended my position to his advisors. Who is giving me a fair shot to prove myself, even going so far as to put Kasta on trial *with* me.

But more chilling is the worry that he may not survive till our coronation. And if that happens, according to all my history lessons, the priests will crown Kasta and me right away.

The idea of the fake pelts grazes the back of my mind, a teeth-laced whisper.

But what I'll do about it will have to wait until tomorrow, after I have hopefully not ignited a war. I shift my thoughts to what's coming, going over again how I'll say it. The guards lead us past the high archway to the gardens. Down a hall paved with sunlight, into an open gallery filled with life-sized gods' statues and even larger indoor trees. Kasta stays quiet at my side. I can almost imagine he's a bodyguard and I'm alone, and this is one of many meetings I'm used to having.

I survived the Crossing. I can survive this.

We reach the massive doors to the banquet hall. A marble Rachella, goddess of love, smiles from where she sits on one of the banisters that borders them, and more overwhelming than the burst of conversation that hits us when the doors open is the sudden quiet that follows.

This is what it is to be royalty.

In the banquet room, at least a hundred people turn to us from beneath palm tree columns that drip strings of crystal, from seats around the rim of the jeweled crane fountain at the center of the room, from between a dozen high, fluted tables set with steaming platters of food. Crystal wine glasses glitter in ringed hands; crowns glisten on brows. They smile, and I remember these people have been doing this since birth. They smile, and it reminds me of jackals.

Despite my better judgment, I step closer to Kasta.

A thin, solemn-faced man bows to our side.

"His Royal Highness," he announces, "Deathbringer, Crossing Victor, and *dōmmel* of Orkena: Kasta, son of Isa. And Her Highness, Living Sacrifice, Whisperer, and *dōmmel* of Orkena: Zahru, daughter of Lia."

The royal entourages dip their heads, though the kings and queens only look on.

Kasta stiffens. "They bow for my father," he mutters.

A physical reminder of how power in our world is shifting. Murmurs bubble, and my nerves with them—it's time for my welcome speech. But it's one thing to practice in front of decorative pillows and another to actually stand before a hundred pairs of eyes. My Influence sparks and reaches; a panic reflex, not a command. Emotions press against my skin. Amusement, curiosity, doubt, and something hostile: an anger as sharp as a blade.

My breath hitches. My mouth goes dry. I need to let go, to

remember that eagerness I felt just this morning, but my silence only makes their doubt stronger, until it bites down and presses its fingers into my head and I'm not sure my plan will work at all—

A feather-light touch on my arm. The pressure vanishes. It's like holding *forsvine* all over again, except this time, instead of my magic ripping away, it simply . . . rests. Quiet, waiting.

I look down at Kasta's fingers. He snatches his hand back, but I can't tell if it's because he felt the same thing or because he only meant to shock me into paying attention.

Honored guests, he mouths, prompting me.

Helping me.

I tear my gaze from him and turn back to the room. The people are just people now, no suffocating doubts or hostilities.

Focus. I can do this, I belong here.

"Honored guests," I say, glancing at Kasta. "I know you've heard many things about me, from my life as a Whisperer, to my journey across the desert as the Crossing's sacrifice. You've also heard how I came into power, and no doubt that there's as much conflict within our palace walls as the war brewing outside of them."

Charged silence from the crowd. This is exactly what they want to hear, and this is how I'll rewrite those rumors as mine.

"But I want to assure you that when it comes to Orkena, Kasta and I are of the same mind. This country and its people were worth trading my life for. Together, there is nothing we wouldn't do to see it thrive."

I can feel Kasta watching me, and it brings a smirk to my lips. He won't like this next part nearly as much.

"That said, we want you, our friends and allies, to feel

261

comfortable and on equal ground during your stay here. When I was a Whisperer among this same company, I felt entirely out of place. Entirely inadequate. I had magic, but mine was the kind reserved for stables and servants. I can only imagine what it must be like to be among us with no magic at all."

Kasta shifts, and I realize I've accidentally hit on the reality of his life before this.

"Which is why both Kasta and I will be wearing *forsvine* tonight."

Kasta jerks his head at me, and shocked exclamations ripple through the gentry. I smile. Jet draws the crowd's attention to where he stands at the side of the room with two of the army's *forsvine* samples, holding the little bracelets high. Each one contains just enough metal to neutralize our own magic without affecting anyone else—Jet's idea, so we don't accidentally disarm any guards if we need them. To prove they work, Jet lifts the bracelets to an enchanted torch, and the fire snuffs out.

"I realize *forsvine* is a tool of our enemy," I continue, "but tonight, it's our reassurance to you that we plan to speak on equal ground. No tricks, no wondering if we've mastered some kind of secretive magic to use for our advantage. So please enjoy our hospitality, and do not fear that it's being used against you. We are the new Orkena. Welcome."

And *I* bow, my fingertips to my forehead. The room squawks in surprise and delight, grins breaking across faces, though Kasta doesn't echo my gesture. It doesn't matter. When I rise, I reach tentatively for the room's emotions, meaning to this time, and now they're warm with true approval. Doubt is still there in tight

262

strands, and so is that eerie anger, but we're closer than before.

So far, so good.

Kasta takes to this just about as well as I hoped he would. "Next time," he growls in my ear as we step off the raised platform, "I'm going to say we absolutely shouldn't use magic at all, so you'll actually do it. Are you happy now? You just threw out our best strategy!"

"I threw out a lazy strategy, and believe it or not, I didn't do it just to spite you. We can earn their trust without cheating, *and* there's no fallout if people ever find out I have Influence, because I can still prove we didn't use it to gain their help." I smile as Jet approaches with our bracelets. "Relax. I read the room, and they're already much happier with us."

Kasta works his jaw but says nothing. Jet stops before me, his warm eyes glistening, and fastens the first of the bracelets around my wrist.

"That was perfect," he says. "I've never been prouder of you."

"Thank you," I say, bracing myself against the cold flush of the metal. "I almost threw up."

"Don't tell me that. Go secure some kingdoms to our cause."

He drops my hand and turns rigidly to Kasta, who crosses his arms and dares him with a look to come closer. At which point I remember that the last time they were this close, they were literally trying to kill each other, and I hastily snatch the second bracelet.

"Thanks again," I tell Jet. "I'll see you later?"

He pulls his glare from Kasta and nods. "I'll be around. Possibly helping confused guests identify food, as is my specialty."

He winks and slips away, and despite my nerves, I snicker at this reference to my clueless self at the Crossing's banquet. But just as I'm starting to take comfort in this, that maybe it's just the stress of these weeks that's been pulling us apart, Kasta's keen gaze slides to me.

"Hmm," he says, offering me his wrist.

I shoot him a glare. "Whatever you're thinking, stop. Can you put this on yourself?"

"No." Not that he even tries. "I'm just wondering if I was wrong about something."

"The safe assumption there is *yes*." My first attempt at fastening the bracelet fails, possibly because I'm trying not to touch him. And then I realize that in the effort to provide a snappy reply, I have no idea what I've actually answered. "Wait, what are you talking about?"

His wrist twitches under my fingers. "I think I believe you."

"What?"

"In the Crossing. You said you weren't his. I believe you now."

My fingers still on the bracelet. I don't like this conversation, and I don't like what it seems to be saying about something I'm not even sure about myself. "I wasn't his, but I could be at some point, and we are absolutely not talking about this."

He pulls his wrist away before I've finished—and ties the bracelet in two deft twists. "If you insist. Either way, I think he's mad at you for something."

My blood chills. "What? How would you even get that from"—I gesture to where Jet just was—"that?"

He shrugs. "No touch to your arm, no kiss." He smiles. "And he put your bracelet on the same way you just did to me."

Like he was trying not to touch me. I remember the way Jet looked at me in the closet when I accidentally read his anger, and my gut twists. Is *that* what's going on? Is he worried I'll read something from him without meaning to, or is he just wary of Influence in general? Except when I glance over to find him, Jet's chatting with a group of high-collared Nadessans, and when I catch his eye, he smiles and raises his drink. Like nothing's wrong.

I grit my teeth. "You're just bitter I threw out your idea. And probably jealous."

I don't know why I just said that last part. I really should not have said that last part.

"Jealous?" Kasta snickers, and grabs two glasses of sparkling juice when a servant moves past. "By all means, please, *gods*, turn your charms on him. I'd love to see him destroyed."

Considering I'm still planning to trap Kasta in eternal Shifter servitude, I am very ready to respond to this with *You have no idea,* except that will oddly prove him right, and also, he hands me one of the drinks. "I . . . Why did you get me a drink like we're having a civilized conversation?"

He leans closer. "Because even when we're arguing in public, we can't look like we're arguing in public." He toasts me. "Something I learned well from my parents. Are you ready for Amian?"

Well, I was before *this* entire conversation, and I would also like to avoid all future references to being like his parents, but I force myself to shove it aside; I won't think about this until later, if I even find it worth coming back to. What Kasta thinks of Jet and me doesn't matter in the least. I turn to the couple standing beneath the nearest palm tree column: the brown-haired Konge of Amian and his attractive fiancé, the same boy Hen had marked for me as my backup plan, both in cream-hued tunics as airy as gossamer, their arms bangled. Tall, horned necklaces climb their throats. The Konge himself is young, maybe only five years our elder, with fair skin and green eyes and oversized features that don't fit his boyish face. A great smile, though—at least until he sees us looking, and then it vanishes.

I rest the tip of the glass against my lips, wondering if we look like the jackals now. "It's the Pe who don't have any magical blood, right? Not even rarely, like the Enchanters born to Greka?"

Kasta nods. "Right. The same for Nadessa. Amian has a rare few from all specialties, but—"

"Their elders consider magicians to be demons. Yes, that I remember." I take a sip. "But the Konge is open-minded?"

"He's unsure, which means he's swayable." Kasta finishes his drink, and a servant slips over in a second to collect it. "Not that you need to worry about any of this, if you plan on following any part of our strategy from yesterday."

I shift the weight of the mantle on my shoulders and smile. "Oh, right. You do all the talking now."

His eyes narrow like he doesn't trust that answer in the least, which he shouldn't. But he has no time to get in anything else. I've already started forward, and the Konge has turned to us, and all Kasta can do is follow.

"Konge," Kasta says, with a warning glance at me. "How are you finding your stay?"

"Questionable," the Konge answers, and I snort on a sip of juice before I can stop myself. This earns me a disapproving glare from

Kasta, but the barest smile from the king. "You boast of placing us on equal ground," he says, though his eyes are light on me. "And yet each of your decorations is a reminder that we are not?"

He gestures to the room, where red wine bursts like blood from the crane fountain in the center, and enchanted weapons spin beneath glass cases, their blades burning or crackling with lightning, and soldiers fill the enormous paintings along the walls, devastating faceless armies with bursts of wind and walls of sand.

"Wow. These really were poor choices," I agree, studying the portrait of a soldier setting fire to a foreign general. "I wasn't asked about the decorations, but I will be next time."

Kasta gives me a look. "They are only to remind you of what we have to offer. I heard Wyrim approached you with a lot of bold promises, including Orkenian runes at half the current export tax. You realize to do that, they'd have to conquer all of Orkena and force our Runemasters to produce for them?"

"I do," the Konge says, letting his answer sink in. "They're also promising us half of northern Orkena. They've split your country into fifths, a generous slice for each ally. Can you do better than that?"

I stare, shocked at his bluntness, but Kasta doesn't even blink.

"For a worthy ally, yes," he says. "When we flatten Wyrim, their island kingdoms will be far more valuable than a section of northern desert. And I can promise that whoever does not commit to us tonight will also have land available. You'll get a choice."

A promise and a threat. The royal specialty. The Konge's lips thin, but not in fear.

"And how will you flatten them, prince?" he asks, quieter. "I heard your expedition in the west didn't go as planned. Odelig still lives, and your boat was destroyed. In fact, I haven't heard you have an answer for *forsvine* at all."

"Wyrim is a small annoyance, and temporarily lucky." Kasta's voice is the edge of glass. "We outnumber them, and our newest development is promising. You'll understand if we don't wish to share specifics."

The Konge taps the side of his chalice. "Indeed. If I had nothing, I wouldn't want to share specifics, either."

"Call it nothing at your own peril. Even if that were true, our magic still works outside the short radius of that metal. *Forsvine* can't stop an attack launched from a distance. Or a storm . . . or a wildfire."

Now a flicker of fear darkens the Konge's face. If Kasta had meant his threats for what might happen to Wyrim, a flood or a hurricane would have been more appropriate. This threat is for Amian.

"But we know it won't come to that," I say quickly, because this seems to be heading south, "because I've heard you're most worried about the dwindling supply of Sapphirous trees on the western side of Amian. Beautiful, jewel-toned wood. I'd love to commission a dining set for my family. But they only grow there, yes?"

The Konge's eyes slide to me, and I'd like to think the irritated look on Kasta's face is for how queenly and educated I sound, and not because I've just derailed his strategy with the subject of trees.

"Their numbers have been dwindling, yes," the Konge says, carefully.

"It's also your most valuable export. What if we sent Gardeners to cultivate the plants and help repopulate them?"

The Konge looks to his fiancé, who covers his mouth, but just as I'm thinking I've gotten through to them on a brilliant, non-threatening level, the Konge bursts out laughing.

"You want to save the trees?" he says, between gasps of laughter. "Oh, Prince Kasta, and here I thought you were the pretty one and she was the brains." He gives me a pitying look. "Dear heart, hasn't your fiancé taught you anything about supply and demand? The less the supply, the greater the demand. Advertising our 'concern' for the trees only drives their price higher."

I gape at him, both for the flippant way he rejected me—and for what he just said. "My . . . fiancé?"

"Oh." The Konge glances at my and Kasta's wrists, which are vehemently free of any engagement charms. "My mistake. Though I must admit you had us fooled, the way you look together. You'd be a charming couple."

"This psychopath stabbed me with a knife," I say before I can think better of it.

"After *you* poisoned me and left me to die!" Kasta presses a breath through his teeth. "I'm not going over this again. And by the way, this would be a critical time to come through on our original strategy."

I tip my glass, flashing the wrist with the *forsvine* bracelet. "I can't. And even if I could, I promised I wouldn't."

"Yes, except for the promise you made to *me* last night."

The Konge grunts. "Ah, so you're just not engaged *yet*."

"We're not engaged ever," I snap, pressing my fingers between my eyes. I'm cursing that I even spoke up. I should have let Kasta handle this. I thought I could work with what I'd learned from my lessons, but I'm realizing now that's only half the strategy. The rulers themselves are the other half, of which I'm lacking Kasta's lifetime of knowledge. The Konge clearly can't be won over with niceties, as Kasta knew, and whatever inclination the king felt earlier to take our side is certainly weakened now.

And I am the reason.

Anxiousness trembles through me. I still want to do this my way, and be charming and pleasant and win the Konge over honestly, but I don't know what I'm doing, and I could mess up again. I could say something that would make him decide he's done with us entirely, and lose a fourth of our potential support in a snap. I can't let Orkena suffer for my clumsiness. I can't let my *family* suffer.

Gods help me.

I finish my drink, and a servant in a pale golden tunic collects my glass, and Kasta starts in on the Konge again, who has definitely cooled to us. I slip my hands behind my back, beneath my cape, where no one can see. Kasta reaches behind me, his tall frame shielding my side, his thumb tracing the bracelet. Already knowing what I have in mind, all too eager to help. And definitely not helping stop any assumptions that we are secretly together.

I am a terrible person. And I am letting him touch me.

"I'm sorry, prince," the Konge is saying. "There are clearly still issues to work out within your walls, and I worry what that will mean if it comes to war. I'm not ready to commit yet."

He tips his crowned head, ready to turn away, and my fingers shake as I roll the bracelet into Kasta's waiting hand. Kasta turns in to me, his lips at my ear. "I have to walk away for your magic to work again," he whispers. "Two bracelets have twice the strength. Fix your mess."

He leaves without another word, and my magic stirs in my chest, the Konge's amusement prickling along my arms like burrs. I leave my arms behind my back, despising everything about this.

"We're sorry, too," I say, reaching for that amusement and twisting it around my fingers. "There are definitely issues we're still working on at a personal level. But I assure you when it comes to the important things, we won't get in each other's way." I force a smile, even as the Konge's fiancé mutters something in his ear. "Are you sure I can't convince you? You said you were interested in a lower export tax on runes, and new land?"

A spark of desire from the king. Of my own manufacturing. I don't even have to make myself believe I want it to work this time, because this *must* work or Orkena will suffer.

The Konge turns back to me, twirling his glass of wine. "Go on."

"I'll let you set all the terms yourself," I say, feeling sick as the words sink into him, as I feel him yield. It will be *our* terms, of course, that will come out of his mouth. "But first, we need a promise in blood."

XIV

I secure Amian's alliance with only the smallest of puzzled looks from the Konge's fiancé, who I then charm with a twist of Influence until I've erased every last one of his reservations. I leave them with my fingers still shaking. Of course Kasta is so pleased by this that he actually beams when I join him, and tries to steer me toward the Nadessan monarchy without a pause, but I grab his arm and hold out my hand for the *forsvine* bracelet. He sighs and reluctantly slips it back to me, but his smile stays in place when we approach the emperor, his eyes sliding over me as they would a sword.

I shake my head tightly—*no*. I won't be doing that again. It was enough that I went back on my word like some underhanded tyrant even once. My arms will be staying in front of my body, and my words will be staying in my mouth.

And thus I determine to stay painfully quiet for the remaining conversations. Literally, it hurts not to speak when the emperor's daughter commends me for how well I clean up "considering where I came from," but I bite my tongue and let Kasta handle it. I'm sure I appear demure and quiet as a result, the truth of which is going to be shocking for these people if I ever see them again, but I don't care. There will be plenty of time to set the record straight after we have their loyalties. And Kasta is still having to win them over using what he knows, not using magic, and so we're still doing things my way, even if that's not how it appears.

It's almost enough to make me forgive myself for what I did to the Konge.

No one tries to give me any of the tainted gifts Kasta warned me about, but after we've secured allegiance from Greka and Nadessa, I beg for a break. Keeping silent in stressful situations, apparently, is just as draining for me as if I'd been talking the whole time, and the single "We're not engaged!" I shouted when the Grekan queen congratulated us was definitely not enough. My feet hurt, my head hurts, and I'm going to say something regrettable if I have to keep this up.

"Fine," Kasta says, but there's no bite to the word. He's still looking at me in that appraising, dangerous way. "Take a guard with you and get some air. The Pe minister will be the hardest to convince. Her sister married into the Wyrim nobility, and I've heard rumors they've already signed over their allegiance."

I groan. "Great. Something to look forward to."

"Zahru."

I look up at him, beyond exhausted.

"I'm not worried. I have you."

He leaves for the wine fountain, and I despise the flutter of heat those words stir in me. I don't care if he's happy with me. This brief peace between us will only last the day.

"Excuse me, *gudina*," comes a cheeky and very welcome voice from behind me. "I can't help but think you'd be happier at the side of someone far more charming."

"Jet!" I say, whirling—and stopping just short of hugging him, remembering what Kasta said. "Gods, I'm so happy to see you. I can't listen to any more veiled threats or how 'stacked' anyone's army is. Half these people think Kasta and I are engaged, the other half think we're related, and the Konge laughed at my tree idea!"

Jet shakes his head. "Then he's a very foolish man."

"Thanks, but he was actually right." I sigh, though my pulse ticks up. "If you have too many trees, no one wants them as much. Why didn't I think about that?"

Jet blinks, and I realize he's probably waiting for me to give him actual context for what I'm talking about, but I can only rub nervously at my bracelet. It's bad enough to acknowledge that no matter Kasta's methods, he's doing much better at this than me. I even capsized his plans last-minute and he adapted without a blink, not counting when I accidentally sabotaged us with the Konge. I could not have done this without him, and I realize it's *this*, moreso than what he said about Jet, that's truly bothering me.

"I need air," I say. "I need to have a conversation that's not about war, I need water, and I need at least six of those tiny chocolate cakes, because Kasta said we can't eat while we negotiate, and I've watched *way* too many of those trays go by."

Jet chuckles. "I can fix all of those. Come on."

He twines his fingers through mine, and vengeful defiance bursts through me, that Kasta is wrong, that Jet still trusts me. I'm tempted to raise our hands to the room both to prove this and to show how very not-engaged Kasta and I are, but the wonderful and terrifying thing about being *dōmmel* is that everyone is already watching. Brows rise beneath crowns, and the emperor's daughter pulls a hand to her mouth, swiveling with new interest toward Kasta. *Good luck!* I want to call to her. *He will literally eat you alive.*

And then I'm very happy to not have to think about any of that anymore, as Jet leads me through a servants' door and into the foyer.

Which is unexpectedly packed. The public celebration doesn't take place for another hour, giving us time to secure—or lose—the Pe before then, but this has clearly stopped no one from hoping the doors will open early. Hundreds of Orkena's elite glitter in their finest on the alabaster windowsills, on the white wood couches, in jewel-toned groups between statues and ruby-leafed trees. Most of them watch the main doors, but a few spot us at the servants' entrance, their lined eyes glistening as they rise from their seats. Getting some air might not be as simple as I thought. But just as I'm starting to worry this won't be relaxing in the least, Jet tugs open a hidden door between two massive paintings of glass ships, and into another room we go.

Or rather, into a closet, judging by the immediate darkness. But a green torch flares on, its pale light illuminating the space like Numet raising her lantern over the first glimpse of Paradise: over stone shelves packed with plates of slivered meats and fish, crystal bowls of soup, and glass-covered trays of tiny chocolate cakes— all the extra food for the banquet. Jet bows before them like a chocolate wizard, and Kasta's comments sift through my ears, and I don't know if it's that or this gathering panic inside me that if I've lost Jet, it means I've lost who I thought I was, too—but I kick the door closed, hook my fingers under his armor, and pull his face to mine.

"Mmph!" Jet grunts in surprise, but he smiles against my lips as we fall against the door and kisses me back. I wait for that fire to spark through my chest. For the comfort I've always felt with him to settle against me like a cloud, but he kisses me and there's nothing, nothing but my growing anxiety that something is off, that his arms are still rigid beneath my hands, that he's holding me a little away from him. I pull back, my head against the door, my heart thudding against my ribs.

"Sorry," I say, searching his eyes, because wearing the *forsvine*, I have no other way to read him. "Is this all right? I didn't actually mean to attack you—"

"No, no, it's . . . fine." But he pulls away. "It's just, maybe you could take that off?" He nods at my bracelet. "It keeps pulsing this cold, terrible feeling through me, and it's extremely distracting."

"Oh!" I exhale in relief, chiding myself for letting anything Kasta said get to me. Of course it's this. I roll the bracelet from my wrist, laughing. "Thank the gods. Yeah, this thing is terrible. Every time I put it back on it does that."

He pauses in straightening his tunic. " 'Put it back on'? Have you been taking it off?"

I freeze in sliding the bracelet onto the shelf. Oh gods. I wasn't sure when I was going to confess to Jet how we won over the Konge, but this was certainly not it.

"Um." I smile and reach behind me for the doorknob. "You know, this was very sweet to bring me in here, but we still need to convince the Pe, and I probably should get back out there—"

Jet reaches over me and slams the door. "Have you been using Influence? After you promised them you wouldn't?"

Now his closeness is suffocating. Even with the bracelet in my hand, I swear I feel his anger on my skin, white-hot curls of disappointment. Anger at *me*. My heart kicks in; lies tempt my tongue. *Of course not*, I could say. *The bracelet came loose; I only took it off to switch wrists.*

If I throw the bracelet away, I could make him believe it.

I press back on the temptation with a wince. "It was only once. I didn't want to, but we were going to lose the Konge—"

"Zahru!" He shoves off the door. "I can't believe this. After everything you told me yesterday about wanting to do things differently, and then one of the first things you do is go back on your word? What if the Konge finds out what you did? You'll definitely lose Amian then, *and* you could lose these other alliances once he tells them, and certainly no one will trust you after that—"

"He's not going to find out! My magic was made for this." I hate echoing Kasta's line, and I press on quickly. "And I only used it long enough to convince him to sign. He saw me wearing the bracelet the rest of the time, so even if they figure out later that I have Influence, he won't think anything of it."

He gapes at me. "Which is even worse! You lied to them, and now you've figured out how to have plausible deniability in case this comes up in the future? Do you know who you sound like?"

It feels like a slap. "Don't you dare compare me to him."

"Well, it needs to be said. You're crossing whatever lines necessary to get what you want—"

Something shifts in the shadows behind him. I have time to register a gray mask and the gleam of metal knuckles before I grip Jet's shoulders.

"Get down!" I yell.

SLAM. We drop just as a fist punches the door, and metal sings as Jet frees his sword, slicing at the person's ankles. They jump

277

lithely out of the way. I'm still trying to figure out how they even got in here when they grab a tray of cakes and fling it at us. Jet jerks his arm up, and cake splatters as the metal slings up and hits the door.

"I can't use my magic," he gasps. I fling my bracelet away, but I can't reach for Influence either. Our attacker must be wearing *forsvine*. I whirl and yank the door handle, spilling us into the foyer—

Into complete pandemonium. Mercenaries in gray tunics swarm the elite, some armed with throwing knives, some with double blades. Four Wraiths stand out among them in white and red, wielding swords and crossbows, protecting long streams of nobles as they flee. One of the regular guards forms a molten ball between his hands, but a mercenary steps closer and the magic fizzles out. A Wraith sprints over just in time to block a sword thrust to the guard's chest.

The person who attacked us jumps on Jet's back.

Jet stumbles, choking as their arm tightens around his throat, and I grab a bust of Aquila—with a muttered apology—and smash it over the person's head. Jet flips them, slamming them against the stone floor, and they go still.

Four more mercenaries surround us. I reach for my magic— and only a sickening cold answers.

They are *all* wearing *forsvine*.

"I don't suppose your magic can somehow overpower this?" Jet asks, his back bumping mine. The flames that usually coat his sword have vanished.

"No," I say, drawing my hidden dagger from my *jole*. If this happened, Kasta said, I'm to run for the Wraiths. Or for him. Engaging an enemy who could potentially turn my dagger back on me is a last resort, despite all the ways Kasta showed me how to use it.

The mercenaries jeer, drawing daggers to match mine. Even without Kasta's warnings, I would know what they're for.

I flex my grip on my knife. "Jet. This is not a kidnapping attempt."

The closest man dives. Jet spins, his sword slicing over me as I duck, and the man shrieks as the blade cuts into his chest. Blood slings across the floor. Someone grabs my ankle and pulls me off my feet, and Jet cries out as two more mercenaries leap, forcing him to defend himself. I kick the man who has me and drive the dagger into his shoulder—he curses and jumps back, but not before clamping something sharp around my ankle. Pain explodes up my leg. My muscles stiffen, and the man drags me around a corner, out of view of the hall, pulls the dagger from his arm and drives it toward my heart—

I gasp and roll away, my muscles screaming, and the dagger jams into an etching in the floor. The man grunts and heaves at it. I try to sit up, try to reach for whatever's on my ankle, but my muscles twitch, they won't listen, and the man abandons the stuck knife and jumps on me knee-first, knocking the air from my chest. His hands close around my throat.

Jet! I try to yell, but it comes out as a gurgle. My leg throbs. My memory cycles wildly through everything Kasta showed me for what it could be, settling on a paralyzing shackle, for which I need Kasta—and his antidotes.

I suddenly can't move.

I definitely can't breathe.

My body screams for air, but I can't even twitch. My blood goes heavy; my hands drop from the man's wrists. I'm not sure I could breathe even without him on me.

My vision darkens.

Just as the world turns cold, a sword plunges through the man's chest. His blood spills forward like flies, black and strange, blurry in my vision. Jet kicks him off of me and I choke, aching for air, but my muscles won't respond. Jet shakes my shoulders, but I can only look at him, gurgling and weak.

I think he tells me to breathe.

I can't. My head lolls, and I want to say *ankle*, but my jaw won't move. Jet sets me down, puts his mouth over mine, and tries to push air into my lungs. I cough, the air moving through my veins like sugar, but as soon as he pulls away, I'm choking again.

"Poison," someone says, the word warbling in the air. "Move."

Kasta's face replaces Jet's, furious and focused. My delirious heart jerks in relief. His hands slide down my arms; he feels my neck, and finally notices my feet. The anklet rips off. The pain there ebbs, but my body grows even heavier.

Star hazel, he says, though his lips don't move. Or maybe they do. I can't tell anymore. The arches blur overhead, and something pinches my neck, but the sensation feels distant, separate.

Then the feeling rushes back in like a punch.

I gasp and twist, grabbing my throat, and Kasta presses his lips over mine, forcing air into me. My body drinks it like a flood. He pushes another breath in, and the stinging in my chest ebbs.

Another, and my magic returns in a cold, numbing rush; euphoric after all the pain.

His lips linger, too long, on a fourth breath. My vision sharpens as I breathe on my own, with him centimeters away, his eyes burning, as ever, with my reflection. I fight against the gratefulness flickering through my chest. The comfort of having him close. The harrowing whisper in the back of my mind that saving me is much more than political strategy; that something has shifted between us again, as stealthily as a slow-rising tide.

His gaze drops to my lips, and for a moment I panic that he'll kiss me and it will not feel like nothing. Then a flash of tangled relief skims my skin—Jet's, I imagine, who must be close by—and Kasta grits his teeth and shoves away.

Jet replaces him in an instant. He helps me sit, his hand warm on my back, and I could cry in relief that the emotion pulsing through his fingers is only concern and nothing more. No eerie anger, no suffocating disappointment.

"We need to get you out of here immediately," he says. "We'll find Melia—"

"No." Kasta moves for the main hall. "She's the only one who can stop this. Zahru, come with me."

"Absolutely not." Jet helps me to my feet. "Maybe you're used to seeing her near death, but it scares the stars out of me. I'm getting her out of here before someone else tries to kill her."

"They're *killing our Wraiths*." Kasta jabs a finger at the foyer, his cape snapping. "You can use your Influence from here. On *all* of them. But you need to do it now, before another mercenary gets too close."

Jet pulls my arm around his neck, and I notice Marcus for the first time, his hazel eyes heavy with worry. He aims his crossbow around the corner, over a trail of gray-clad bodies that the three of them must have taken out getting to me. But I only make it two steps with Jet, the cries and clangs of the fight shadowing us, before I stop.

"No," I say. "I should try."

"You almost *died*," Jet says. "My mother will handle this. She's already barricaded the royal guests in the banquet hall and gotten as many of the nobility to safety as she could. You need to get to safety now, too."

"If I can stop it, I have to." I turn for Kasta, but my legs buckle. Jet catches me in an instant.

"Are you sure?" he asks.

My grip on him tightens. Someone screams in the other room, a scream that I know will be their last. "Will you help me?"

Jet closes his eyes, and his fear chills my fingers. But he nods.

We follow Kasta to the corner. A heartbreaking number of guards, mercenaries, and the Orkenian nobility lie bleeding and motionless on the floor, like bright jewels cracked open. At least three white-clad Wraiths lie amongst them. Five more Wraiths engage dozens of mercenaries outside the banquet hall doors. Jet said the royal delegates were barricaded inside, but if the Wraiths die, the assassins will find their way in.

Undoing everything we did today. Showing our allies we are helpless against *forsvine*, threatening them into changing their minds.

Proving, again, that violence is stronger than peace.

Rage boils low in my stomach. I reach for the emotions spiking from the opposite side of the room, but while it's easy enough to feel them, I've never tried focusing on more than one person at a time. This is like tracking a dozen flies. As soon as I've gripped someone's anger, someone else's fear or shock or pain replaces it. They're a rainstorm of emotion, and they slip through my fingers the same way.

"There's too many," I say, gasping. "I can't focus on any of them."

"You don't have to," Kasta says. "Do the entire room. Don't try to narrow it down to the mercenaries."

"But the Wraiths—"

"Will be fine. Do it now!"

The mercenaries have noticed us. Ten of them sprint our way, swords raised, daggers glinting, and I don't know what the radius of their *forsvine* is—it could be two meters; it could be twenty. Marcus raises his crossbow. One falls under an arrow. Two.

"I only have one arrow more," he says, fitting it into the notch.

Despair, pain, eagerness crash into me like a tide. Kasta and Jet draw their swords. Marcus fires his last arrow, and the excitement of the mercenaries, the bloodlust, reaches me in a tsunami—

I let it in. I let their savagery become mine, as scalding and heavy as a wildfire, until they are no longer separate people but one terrible force, an extension of my anger; until everything they send at me is mine. Darkness presses in on my vision. Heat bursts from my palms, from my face, and vaguely I'm aware of the black glow curling my fingers, as if I've taken their hatred and made it tangible. My chest rises. My toes skim the ground, the power of it lifting me.

I thrust my arms out and shove back.

Darkness bursts from me in a gale. It cuts the room like a thousand diving falcons, and the mercenaries running toward us lurch, eyes rolling as they go slack and slide on their stomachs like puppets cut from strings—

And behind them, the entire room follows.

Armor clatters. Swords drop. Bodies fall like a house of cards, and a bowl flips from a pedestal, singing across the floor before it finally hits the wall.

And then it's quiet.

Terribly, terribly quiet.

Kasta, Marcus, and Jet stand motionless at my sides, mercifully unaffected. But a tremble starts in the deepest parts of me as I take in what I've done. I stumble forward, collapsing before the nearest mercenary and wrenching her around, tears brimming in my eyes as I feel for a pulse.

When it comes, faint and steady beneath my fingers, I let out a sob.

They're not dead. Relief fills me as I look over the fallen shapes of our Wraiths, the eerie quiet crawling over my skin like scorpions. *They're not dead; this is fine. What I did was good.*

"Gods almighty," Jet whispers. I don't miss the pause, the hesitation in his steps, before he slowly kneels at my side. "Are you all right?"

Now he definitely doesn't touch me. I shiver and pull my arms in, afraid to touch him, either.

"Yes," I say, though it feels like a lie.

Kasta's footsteps sound behind us, heavy and sure.

"Very good, Zahru," he says. "*Very* good."

I don't register the walk to the Healer's temple. Or Melia's concerned face as she works over me, repairing the damage from the poison. Or the whispers in the halls as Kasta and I move for the throne room, Jet trailing us, a hundred new rumors peppering me like sand.

My secret is no longer a secret. I am no longer just a Whisperer from Atera.

I'm not sure what I am anymore at all.

Chaos greets us in the throne room.

The Mestrah slumps in his bronze chair, his brow glistening with sweat, and the queen sits beside him, her manicured fingers resting on his arm. All thirty of the army's top officials gather below them in full armor: commanders and captains and lieutenants and Jet's mother, her General's honors swinging from her biceps. Only the Wraiths are missing, having been sent off to be Healed or to mourn their fallen comrades.

"We should march on Wyrim now!" bellows a commander, his pale cheeks blotted with fury. "This was an outright assassination attempt. Not to mention the twenty they slaughtered trying to get into the banquet hall."

A lieutenant steps next to him, her red hair cut to her chin. "And we'll march on the Pe next. We know *someone* fed Wyrim our security protocols, and it's no coincidence the Pe minister excused her entire company for a break right before the attack. They can't have fled far. We'll kill the minister before she even returns home!"

"Agreed!" calls the commander. "This was an act of war!"

"That's exactly what the Wyri want," snaps Jet's mother. "We have no proof of any of this yet, and the Pe minister is well liked. Her murder would spark outrage, and the Wyri would use it as further evidence we abuse our power. We must be strategic."

"Company," the Mestrah grumbles, raising a half-hearted hand in our direction. "Your *dōmmella*."

The officers go silent, the rustle of their armor the only sound as they turn and drop to their knees. My ribs tighten. These are some of Orkena's brightest minds and most vicious fighters, most of whom could get away with a nod in the presence of royalty.

This is a gesture much deeper than a bow.

Beside me, Kasta smiles.

"Company dismissed," growls the Mestrah. "*Dōmmella* . . . Jet. Stay."

"Mestrah," the commander says, with an uneasy hand on his sword. "What about the assassins? What are your orders?"

The king sighs. "Burn their dead, and take the survivors to the prison. Arrange escorts for the other rulers and ensure they're delivered safely home. As for Wyrim and the Pe . . ." The Mestrah coughs, once. "Gather your ideas, and return to me in an hour."

The officers touch their foreheads and file out, casting appraising—and sometimes anxious—glances my way. I shudder, still not quite well even after Melia's healing, and press back against the pride their attention stirs in me. This is different from the pitying, reverent looks I received as the Living Sacrifice. They're not looking at me as they would a victim.

This is admiration.

This is *fear*.

The General pauses beside Jet on her way out, her hand light on his shoulder. I've never seen her look at him with anything but fondness. But her lips thin, her orange eyes narrowing with disappointment. She shifts that same gaze to me and continues out, her jaguar-headed cane clicking on the floor.

The Mestrah takes a small, painful sip of tonic from his chalice and slumps against the throne.

"The Pe have made their alliance with Wyrim clear," he says, his breath labored. "And news of the attack, and your near-death, Zahru, is already spreading throughout the continent. They're not even speaking of the impressive power you used to subdue the assassins. Do you know why?"

There's an icy edge to his voice that raises the hairs on my neck. This question is a trap. I knew this meeting would be tense considering what just happened, but I assumed we'd be focusing on the assassins.

I grip the sides of my *jole*. "No, Mestrah."

"Because all they can talk about is how easy it was to catch you unguarded! Why weren't you in the banquet hall, where I had Wraiths and commanders to watch over you? What were you *doing*, that a group of amateurs almost killed you without trying? You had better pray to the *gods* your answer is different from the one I've heard."

His gaze, fevered as it is, cuts to Jet. Heat bursts through my body. I do not have a better answer. I don't think I actually want to answer at all.

"Well?" he snaps, his anger thick as smoke. "What is your explanation?"

"Fara, it was my fault," Jet says, stepping beside me. "It was my idea to—"

"I was not speaking to you," the Mestrah says. "You are not *dōmmel*. It was not your responsibility to consider the risks."

Oh gods, *this* is why the brothers have so many father issues. No relief we're alive, no praise for Jet, who saved my life, or—as reluctantly as I want to acknowledge it—for Kasta, who assisted in that. No praise even for me, who stopped the attack completely. Instead, shame prickles down my arms, and I grimace.

"I needed a break," I start. "We only stepped out for a minute—"

"Into a pantry? Without notifying a guard or checking the servants' entry to the room?"

The servants' entry. I close my eyes. Of course there's a tunnel at the back, so the waiters can supply the room without moving through the halls. We're lucky only one assassin found their way in.

"I'm sorry," I say. "I wasn't thinking—"

"That much is very clear," the Mestrah growls. "But you are not a stable girl anymore, Zahru, free to tumble whomever you'd like at your leisure. You are a crown princess, and your country must always come first. Your *safety* must always come first. Your actions today not only risked your life, but could have resulted in a full-on invasion if the assassins had succeeded. You and Kasta are the only two powers right now standing between us and total collapse. Is that clear?"

I can only stare at him, shaking, both furious he would reduce me to a tumbling stable girl and terrified by what he's just admitted. That *he* is no longer the one the world fears.

It is up to me, and Kasta, to stop this war.

"I'm seriously considering demoting you to advisor. You would already be, if you were not also the one who stopped the attack." His scowl twists, as if I'm all the worse for having done so. "But your power has, for now, convinced the other rulers to keep the agreements you secured today. And I must reluctantly agree that your decision to wear *forsvine* was a monumental part of keeping their trust. So you will get one last chance. But one more careless mistake, and you'll be relegated to advisor—or less, depending on where Kasta sees fit to put you."

I clench my jaw. Beside me, I wait for a smile to ghost Kasta's lips, for his father focusing his disappointment on someone else again—and especially for the possibility of taking the throne without me. But he is stone.

"Do you understand?" the Mestrah asks.

"Yes, Mestrah," I say, bowing stiffly.

"You are dismissed. Kasta, come with me."

I turn on my heel, not even caring what the Mestrah could want Kasta for that wouldn't involve me, and burst out of the throne room doors. Jet jogs to keep up. My cape tugs behind me like an anchor, and I bite the inside of my cheek, but I won't cry, I won't let this get to me. Just because I made one mistake doesn't mean I'll be terrible at ruling, and I can't believe the king didn't say one good thing—*not one*—about how I handled it.

But my vision still blurs as we start up the stairs to the royal wing. I blink it clear, and Jet touches my arm. Softly . . . briefly.

"Hey," he says. "I'm sorry. I should have said more—"

"It's fine," I say, turning. "Your father wouldn't have let you. And it's not like he was wrong."

"But that was truly my fault. You haven't grown up in the court; you shouldn't have to be thinking about assassins when you're with me. Gods, you should have been safe." His voice cracks. "I'm sorry. From now on, I'll be much more mindful."

"I said it's fine." The words crackle like sparks, and I immediately regret their bite. But the reminder of why he was so distracted, of what we were arguing about, grates against my bones. Now I've even been yelled at by the Mestrah, the same as Kasta. "I don't want to talk about it. I think I just want to be alone for a while."

"Zahru, wait."

I'd taken a few steps without him, but I look over my shoulder, my heart clenching. There's already a new distance between us, like I'm looking at him through a fog.

"I'm sorry about what I said before," he says. "It just surprised me is all. I know you must have had a good reason to use Influence on the Konge. I know you wouldn't have if there'd been any other way."

A little of that fog fades, and I breathe out. "Thank you."

He waits for me to say more, but I don't know how to tell him how afraid I am that he was right earlier, or how terrifying it was that he so easily believed me capable of falling into Kasta's ways. And he slowly starts off in the other direction. Without me.

This is how it started with him and Kasta, too. A small split. A crack that kept growing until it was a chasm, but I grip my cape and remind myself that I'm nothing like that, that this is temporary. We're just stressed and running out of time. Neither of us is at our best right now.

I pull the crown off of my head and shake my fingers through my hair.

"Jet?"

He turns, and I feel instantly guilty for the way his eyes light up, hopeful I'll say something that fixes this. But I've already moved on. Back to my current obsession, to the only thing I know how to do.

"What's star hazel?" I ask.

His smile falls, but he shrugs. "A type of cactus. Their flowers harden into brown husks that look like stars, and sometimes the chefs use them in soups. Why?"

I make a face. "Why was Kasta talking about a soup flower when he was trying to save me?"

This is understandably a sentence that seems to come out of nowhere, and Jet's brow rises accordingly. "I don't remember him saying anything about star hazel. He said 'poison,' and then there was some rude shoving, and then he gave you the antidote." He thumbs the hilt of his sword. "Actually, I just remembered star hazel can be concentrated into an antidote."

A spark pushes through my veins. "But you didn't hear him say that. I know the name of the antidote he gave me, that you didn't hear him say."

"No. So how did you?"

I almost laugh, which would really top this day off with literally every emotion possible, and I sink back against the wall, my fingers trembling over my brow. Gods, I can't believe it finally happened. I can't believe Kasta *messed up*, and now I have the proof I've been so desperately seeking, proof that I'm not just paranoid, that I was right about him killing Maia from the start.

That I'm still me . . . and he is still him.

Sorrow spikes through me, unexpected and sharp. I've been waiting for this, *hoping* for this, but for some reason it suddenly hurts to know for sure.

I look down at Jet, my smile weak. "I know," I say, tapping my head, "because I heard him think it."

THIS is not quite the case-cracking evidence we need it to be, first for the simple reason that I was very delirious when all of this was happening, thus we have no way to prove to anyone else that Kasta *didn't* say it aloud and Jet just didn't hear. But also because it was clearly temporary. I haven't heard a single one of Kasta's thoughts since, despite spending time with him both at the Healer's temple and with the Mestrah.

But any lingering doubts I had about him are now gone. Kasta *must* be a Shifter if I heard him at all, meaning all his behavior up to this point has been exactly what I suspected: an act to win my trust, so that I don't think him capable of it. Even saving my life is just part of his strategy, to survive and ensure his own safety as Mestrah until he masters Influence himself.

He can't really have changed if the first thing he did, after making that promise to me in the caves, was murder his lifelong friend.

I task Jet with telling Hen, Marcus, and Melia what happened and warning them to be especially careful, and I spend the walk back to my room strategizing how I'll use this. Ignoring the ache in my chest. Focusing on what I can do so I don't have to acknowledge *why* this hurts. I'll get Kasta to drop his guard again; I'll ask where he might be hiding something in his room and get the answer through his thoughts. Clearly his Influence must protect him most of the time, which is why I can't hear him normally, so I just have to figure out what was different about earlier. The high stress of the situation, maybe. Or that he was touching me.

Which is the point when my nightmare surfaces behind my eyes, Kasta's lips like fire on my neck . . . his teeth sinking into my throat.

I will be trying high stress as a strategy first.

And so, before our Influence lesson the next morning, I wait for him.

The guards find this highly notable and don't even attempt not to stare while I lean against the paneling across from Kasta's doors, listening to the little fountain set in the floor, picking at my golden cape. No doubt all kinds of rumors have started about the method by which he saved me, and how it might affect things between us. And I start to wonder again about the travelers' stories. What if the princess in the stories was actually trying to destroy her rescuer? Everyone always assumes "happily ever after" is the end, but what if she only appeared happy so she didn't get eaten, and went on later to clap him in chains and dance outside his cell?

I am asking a lot more questions next time about what happens *after*.

Kasta's door clicks open. He steps out, adjusting the serpentine crown around his hair—and stops.

For a moment we stand there, me reminding myself that he's a liar, him looking around the hall for the reason I'm there. When he sees it's for him, he straightens. And moves past the guards, who are now discreetly reaching for their listening scrolls, to join my side.

We move, and he's as quiet as ever. Both in words and presence. I'll have to try this during our lesson, then. I'll tell the Mestrah to let *me* teach Kasta, and push him until he cracks.

We've just reached the top of the royal stairs when he glances over. I brace myself for a lecture on not following our plan; for a question I don't want. For him to ask what I thought I was proving with Jet.

"How are you feeling?" he asks instead.

My heart lurches, both at the shock of this question and the irritating softness in his face.

"You don't have to pretend you're worried," I say, quickening my pace. "You can get right to the part where you drag me over the coals for how I messed up."

It's a moment before he answers. "I wasn't going to. I've been on the other side of that too many times."

I want to shake him, to yell at him to stop pretending. I know who he really is. "What did the Mestrah want you for yesterday?"

His eyes narrow, and I chide myself for being so cold. I need to be careful. He can't suspect that anything's changed, especially since, if anything, I should be warming to him.

"To visit the prison," he says.

A hollow opens in my chest as we enter the empty foyer. The floors and furniture have already been restored, fresh gold and gems shining as if nothing happened here at all. Twenty of our own dead, almost including myself, each one of them pulling at me. It's even worse that Kasta won't say anything about it. I can't help but wonder how many of those people would still be alive if I'd listened and been at his side.

And I find that despite everything, I'm glad he was the one the Mestrah took to see the prisoners. They deserve him. "Did you make them talk?"

His brow quirks at the edge in my tone. Missing nothing. "Does it make you happy to know that we did?"

I relax the grip on my dress as we step into the cold morning air. "I'm not *happy* you tortured people, no. But I want the attacks to stop."

A grunt, like that answer was better than he expected. "I didn't have to do anything, anyway. The Mestrah pulled memories until he found a mercenary who'd overheard who hired them. We have our link to the Wyri queen, at last."

Which means we have grounds for a war. I stop at the corner of the path, a breeze pressing its icy lips to my neck. "What's the Mestrah going to do?"

"He's left that decision to me."

I push my hands up my arms. I'm certain I already know the answer to this, but I ask anyway. "What are *you* going to do?"

"I have an idea. I want to know what you think of it."

I almost laugh; he really is going all in to convince me he's changed. "You don't need to ask me, but you're going to anyway?"

The wind catches the edges of his hair. "It wouldn't make sense for me to do something you disagree with. You'll just work to undo it."

Now I do laugh. "Yes, I would. Except I already know that your idea is terrible."

He frowns. "You haven't even heard it yet."

"It's going to go something like this: *Kill them all!*"

"It is *not*."

"Then surprise me. What solution have you come up with that has nothing to do with killing anyone?"

Kasta scratches his forehead and sighs. "This is war, Zahru. They tried to kill *you*. No solution is going to get us out of this without someone dying."

"Right, except if they *had* actually killed me, since both of you seem to think death is the solution to this—would that really have inspired you to surrender right now?"

Darkness flashes in his eyes, and for an unsettling moment I get the sense that I've not only proved my point—that he'd be far from surrendering—but that he'd make them burn for it. But of course he can't say that without agreeing with me, and his face goes smooth. "I do think we should march on them, now. Before *forsvine* advances so much that we don't stand a chance. The faster we start this war, the sooner it can end, and with the fewest casualties."

"Yes. See, that's terrible."

"And you would suggest . . . what? Asking them to stop, please?"

"I would suggest finding out what they really want. No one can *want* to be at war."

"Don't be so naive. What Wyrim wants is to humiliate us and avenge their dead with ours. I'm asking what you'd do if you had to *fight*."

I bristle. Every fiber in me wants to disagree, to insist there's always a way around it, but I remember Jet talking about Wyrim during the Crossing . . . how angry they still were at the destruction his grandmother wrought on them to ensure Orkena survived the Ending Drought. This is not just Kasta wanting to prove his strength.

He's going to hate my answer, but I give it anyway. "I would ask Jet."

He glances at a pair of nobles who whisper as they pass. "I didn't ask what Jet would do. I asked what you would do."

"I don't know enough about this to make that kind of decision. I would ask Jet. And if you're being honest about valuing my opinion, you'll ask him, too."

A flicker of agitation crosses Kasta's face, but again, just as I expect him to snap at me or argue—he closes his eyes. And exhales.

"Fine," he says. "I'll talk to Jet."

"You will?" Now *this* is amusing. How far will he take this, just to appear agreeable? "It would probably be a good idea to consult with his mother, too. We will be keeping her on as General, won't we?"

He works his jaw. I know Kasta doesn't like the General, because his own mother, the queen, poisoned him against her years ago. Coughing sounds from deeper in the garden—the Mestrah, most likely—and Kasta continues down the path. "We'll see. There are younger candidates to consider."

"I think it makes more sense to keep her on. The soldiers are used to following her lead, and she has a lot of experience."

"I said I'd *think* about it—"

The Mestrah's coughing grows more urgent. It stops, suddenly, and a woman cries out.

"More Healers!" a man yells. "I need more Healers immediately!"

Kasta starts off at a run. Servants in tan tunics burst onto the path from the opposite direction, running past us with only the briefest touch of their fingers to their heads, and I jog after Kasta, gripping the iron gate as I swing into the Mestrah's garden.

The king sits on the bench, blood running between his fingers where he coughs into his hands. A single Healer stands behind him, gripping his shoulders. The coughs don't lessen. The Healer's brow creases, pained, as she begs more from her power, but the Mestrah chokes. Red splatters his white *tergus*. Another Healer bursts in, shouldering Kasta and me aside.

The king pitches forward. The new Healer eases him to his side and splays his fingers over the Mestrah's chest, and the king's coughs turn into gasps, into wet, wheezing sounds that can't possibly be drawing air. I dig my fingers into my arms, pleading with Rie to spare him. I still need two weeks to stop Kasta. I still need the king's *help*.

A silent moment passes. Two. The king goes limp, and the Healers exchange glances.

"The priests," one says, looking to a nearby guard. "Fetch the High Priests."

They turn the Mestrah onto his back. Kasta pushes through the circle of servants and Healers.

"*Valeed?*" He jerks his head at the first Healer. "Why aren't you doing anything?"

"We used a sleeping spell, *dōmmel*," the woman says. "It will force his body to relax and breathe, but . . ."

She catches the other Healer's eye, who gives a minute shake of his head.

"I'm sure he'll improve with rest," she finishes, smiling.

But even I can see from here that she doesn't mean it.

They take the Mestrah to his rooms.

In the private lounge outside the king's bedchamber, I sit with Jet on a velvet couch, the General on his other side and Kasta pacing before the windows. A thick wooden door bars us from any sound in the other room. The three High Priests are within, as well as the queen and all of the palace's top Healers, and for over an hour, no one has come out.

Outside, a storm builds over the roofs of the city.

I shift, eyeing Jet's hand, wondering if I should take it to comfort him, and end up pushing my fingers under my knees. Even that movement seems to echo in the gigantic suite. The main entry is as large as an inn, the recessed ceiling held up by columns laced with golden gods' symbols and lit by braziers cast to look like Sabil's balancing scales. A sparkling rectangular pool takes up half of the space, and glass makes up the entire far wall, so clear it looks as if I could step from the floor onto the treetops outside.

It's eerie to consider this could become my room within the week.

Jet's knee bounces. The General stares, unfocused, at the distant city.

"I should have stopped him," she says, barely above a whisper. Jet and I look over. "I knew the mercenary interrogations would be hard on him. The keener his mind gets, the weaker his body. I suggested . . . other methods. But of course your stubborn father

300

worried we wouldn't get what we needed." She looks down at where she holds Jet's hand and sniffs.

"This isn't your fault, Mora," Jet says, gently.

"I know it's not," she snaps, but she directs her anger at the door. "But thank you, *kar-a*."

She tilts her head against his for a moment, the familiar gesture of a mother who adores her son. My heart twists in sympathy. I feel intrusive here among the Mestrah's family, but Jet asked me to stay, and so I will.

From the other side of the room, Kasta watches them, his shoulders falling. His mother snapped at him to get out of the way.

He sees me looking and turns on his heel.

The door creaks. We all straighten as Melia swings it open, wiping her hands on the Healer's rag attached to her belt. Her face is drawn, her eyes wet when they fall on Jet. "If you would like to see him, you may. Though it should be one at a time."

Jet starts to rise, but Kasta is already striding across the room, and at a glare from him, Jet sits. Melia keeps her eyes on the floor. The door closes. I press my hands along my thighs and settle back against the couch. It's going to be a long day, and I dread how it might end.

But no sooner has Jet started to turn to me when the door opens and Kasta emerges, a glint of his old fire burning in his eyes.

"He wants *you*," he growls, that fire broiling into me. I stiffen, sure he means Jet, but when Jet nudges me, I jerk to my feet. My stomach twists as I move forward. This is a very strange time for the Mestrah to call me, especially before talking to the rest of his family. My skin prickles as I approach Kasta, who—for all the anger I see in his eyes—is still a deep void otherwise. I practically jog past him, and Melia lightly touches my back before closing the door.

Orange torchlight engulfs the room. Glass lines the outer wall here as well, but the servants have darkened it to a stormy gray, draping the royal city and the nearby river in a fog. A grand bed takes up a quarter of the space, its four posts carved in the likeness of the Mestrah's favored gods: Numet, the sky goddess and the Mestrah's blood ancestor; Tyda, goddess of patience; Sabil, god of magic; Rie, god of death. Five Healers and the High Priests hover around the king, as well as a *trielle* with his spell paintbrush. The queen sits beside the Mestrah's pillow in a pearl-white *jole*, her hand entwined with her husband's.

Under the golden covers, the king looks frail and human. The normally vibrant tan of his skin has paled to a sandy gray, and the makeup that would sharpen his eyes and cheekbones has been cleared, so that his features look off, shallow. His gaze, watery and fevered, shifts to me.

"Child of the gods," he croaks. "Come closer."

The title sends beetles up my neck. I approach, painfully aware of the queen's icy gaze, and stop a meter away.

"The rest of you," the Mestrah says. "Leave us."

"Are you sure?" the queen says, running her hand over his. "I would like the Healers to be near, just in case."

"These words are not for them." But despite the sharpness in his voice, he squeezes his wife's hand. "Please."

The queen exhales and kisses his glistening forehead. Her eyes harden when they meet mine, probably blaming me for what's happened, but she says nothing, and the company follows her out of the room. The door closes with a soft click.

The torches crackle. I am alone in the private quarters of a dying god.

"Mestrah," I say, feeling completely inadequate.

"Zahru." He winces against some unseen pain, and pushes higher on his pillows. "I must admit, when the Speaker first suggested you were meant to rule, I set my sights on disproving them. I could not imagine Orkena flourishing under the undisciplined, uneducated whims of a common Whisperer. I was sure you would fail at the tasks I set for you, and crack under the pressures of the court."

I flinch, the heat of the torches growing stifling.

"But then you began to surprise me. You began to *excel*, and to master the gods' magic as if you were born to it. And so I wanted to speak with you first, while I have my strength. Because if the gods are calling me home . . . I will not be revoking your status."

I snap my head up. I didn't expect it to mean anything, this show of faith, but a stone gathers in my throat. The king is not good with praise. This much I knew even before I spent these past weeks with him, and yet what he's saying—that he would entrust his kingdom to me—hits harder than any compliment could.

I'm blundering together a response when the Mestrah shakes his head.

"I know I was hard on you after the party. Because you frightened me. I had just begun to see you as a leader, as the perfect balance to Kasta's rashness, and then you went and did something rash yourself. And I almost lost you for it." He winces again, and swallows a cough. "I hope you understand my words were meant to get through to you the importance of your duties now. Mistakes are human. But you are a goddess. And Orkena will need you to remember it."

I brace myself on a low stool draped with red satin. *You are a goddess*. Remembering this, what it will truly mean to be crowned, almost brings me to my knees. "Yes, Mestrah."

He takes a shaky drink of tonic. "But I will be honest that this is as much a show of approval as one of strategy. Kasta has shown great improvement these past weeks with you, but I do not think he should be left to rule alone."

A strange numbness bites my fingers. I still don't intend for Kasta to rule, at all. "I would agree."

He raises a brow. "That is not to say I don't believe him capable. When things are going well, my son is the leader I always dreamed he would be. Cautious. Strategic. Informed. But things will not always go well. This war will not go well. And when it doesn't, I need someone in place who can temper him."

"I'll do my best."

He shifts in the sheets, watching me. I have the sudden eerie sensation that he can see more than what I'm telling him, and I force myself to hold his gaze.

"See that you do," he says slowly. "And that you do not become the same. This I entrust to you as my final wish." He coughs and brings a fist to his chest. "It has been my pleasure to know you, *gudina*. Use this new life well."

Guilt burns my veins, but I kneel, fingertips on my forehead. "I will, Mestrah."

He smiles as he lies back. "Stop bowing to me, Zahru. We are equals."

I nod and stand, gooseflesh prickling my arms, torn between the surreality of him speaking to me this way and the uneasiness of his warning to not become like Kasta. Because even now, I'm thinking less of his words and more of what I need to do. If the Mestrah dies, I will be out of time. I can't keep waiting for a lucky opening. Kasta will only continue this act until he's crowned, and then everything will change, and he'll hurt someone else— he may hurt *many* other someones—and I will always think back to this moment, when I knew what he was and didn't do everything I could to stop him. I owe Orkena—I owe *Maia*— much more than that.

Whatever I'm going to do, I have to do it tonight.

Which leaves me with only one option.

"Send Jet in," the Mestrah says, closing his eyes. "Nadia may come with him."

I turn, my nerves still buzzing, and pause before the closed door. The torches crackle and pop. I'm ashamed to say that I deliver this next line entirely to ensure Kasta doesn't know I'm up to something, and not to get him his rightful place in line.

"Mestrah?" I say.

"Speak."

"I think you should call Kasta in."

Surprise opens the king's eyes. He turns his head, squinting, and finally nods. Perhaps he thinks I'm softening to Kasta.

I don't know what it means that I hardly feel guilty about it.

When I open the door, Kasta is on the far side of the room, arms crossed and cape drawn around his chest like a shield. He doesn't even look over. He knows who the Mestrah will want next.

Jet catches my eye, but I shake my head.

"Kasta," I say.

Kasta's gaze jerks to me, then Jet, and it's a few moments before he moves. When he reaches the door, he pauses across from me in the frame. But he's not searching my face for a lie. He looks broken, like he wants to say something, like he wants to *thank* me, but this, at last, is too much for me, and I move away before he can.

The door clicks closed behind him.

Jet and the General lean against each other on the couch, and I kneel on the floor before them. And this time, I do take Jet's hands.

"How is he?" Jet asks, his voice thick.

I slowly shake my head. Jet's pain splinters between us, a bridge as bright as gold, and I glance at the General, who still stares at the windows. And I steel myself for what I'm about to do. Jet can't be involved in this next part of my plan. This is something I need to do on my own, and he should be here with his parents, not worrying about Kasta and proof.

He sniffs. "I'm going to tell him about Sakira. I think my father should know before he passes."

"You should." I brush my fingers over his knuckles. "Will you be all right for a while? There's something I need to take care of. I'll come back as soon as I can."

His focus clears. "Now?"

"You know what for." I touch Numet's mark on my chest.

Jet sits a little straighter, trying to shrug off his grief, and rubs his damp cheeks on his tunic. "I can come. Just let me talk to my father . . . I can meet you after that."

"No." His stubbornness bricks the connection between us, and I know if I leave it at this, he'll come find me anyway. Because that's what he does. Even when his father is dying and his heart is in shreds, even when things are shaky between us, he would still set it all aside to help me.

At least until he figured out what I intend to do.

"Stay," I say, twisting my fingers around his grief, untying the threads of his loyalty to me, one by one. "Your mother needs you. I can handle this."

He starts to argue. I watch his protest flare, and shift, and dull in his eyes. "All right," he says. "I'll be here."

"Thank you." I slip my hands from his, my chest pinching. "I'm sorry."

He doesn't even ask for what.

I close the Mestrah's door quietly behind me and start for Hen's room.

XVII

I do not think about what I just did as I walk the palace halls.

Not how easy it was. Not the way Jet's eyes dulled as my will overrode his. And especially not that the main reason I didn't want him to come—moreso than protecting him if I'm caught doing this—is that I'm afraid he'd stop me.

I knock on Hen's door.

She doesn't ask questions when I tell her what I need. I lie on her couch while she works, twisting my tunic between my fingers, bracing myself for the sound of horns that would mark the Mestrah's passing. They don't come. Within an hour Hen hands me a stack of five fake pelts, expertly tailored to look real: a falcon pelt of dyed crane feathers; a snakeskin of fish scales. A tawny velvet cat, a satin mouse, a silken blue bird like those that frequent the garden trees. Small animals useful for sneaking in and out of places.

It's a convincing stack. Kasta couldn't use these to change in reality, but a Runemaster won't know the difference.

Hen places the pelts in my hands and nods.

Marcus answers his door with a heavy frown.

"*Dōmmel*," he says. "How is the Mestrah?"

I tighten my grip on the sack I'm holding. The assumption that the suffering king is foremost on my mind pushes against my heart. "You can still call me Zahru, Marcus. And he's not well."

"Ah. I'm very sorry to hear. Do you think Jet wants company?"

"Maybe later. He and the General are with the Mestrah now."
Nerves flush through me, a rush of cold. Once I show the pelts to
Marcus, there's no going back.

"Is your Runemaster contact available?" I ask.

Marcus's hand drops from the doorframe. "Likely. Why?"

I hand him the sack. Marcus peers in—and inhales. He pulls the
drawstrings tight, glances around the hall at the distant guards,
and pushes the bag back into my arms.

"Give me a moment." He squeezes into his room.

The door floats closed, stopping just wide enough to show me
a slice of a redwood desk and part of a darkened window beyond.
The storm has moved in, wind snapping at the garden trees. A
low voice I don't recognize asks if Marcus is all right, but Marcus
answers too quietly for me to make out the words. His fiancé must
be in. In a moment Marcus reappears, a silver cape wrapped over
his broad shoulders and his hazel eyes haunted.

"I wrote my contact to meet us in the armory." He shuts the
door and ushers me down the hall. "Where did you find those?"

"In his room." I'm getting disturbingly quick at coming up
with lies.

"You searched his room while he's—" He cuts off. *While he's
with his dying father?* is how I imagine he meant to finish that,
which does nothing to make me feel like I'm still the hero. "Never
mind, I know you had to. And you found them not a day too late.
I just hope Conlee can work quickly if the Mestrah's time is truly
at a close."

How completely Marcus trusts me. He doesn't even find it

suspicious that right when I needed it most, critical evidence fell into my hands. But I promise myself I'll make up for this. Once this is settled and I've proven what Kasta is, I'll confess to everything. To Marcus and Jet, at least. The pelts, the plan, changing Jet's heart while he was worrying for his father. But right now I need to be a leader, and this, unfortunately, is exactly the kind of thing desperate leaders do in stories.

This is also the kind of things villains do, but I'm adamantly not dwelling on that right now.

By the time we reach the armory, I'm ready.

A massive, triangular door marks the entry, a bronze monstrosity stamped with Sabil's balancing scales to depict the balance between magic and its cost. Seeing it sends ice blooming up my spine. Not only because it's the same symbol that forms the hilt of the sacrificial knife, but also for the reminder that the Mestrah is dying in his thirty-eighth summer because of his magic. I imagine Influence won't be much kinder to me, depending on how much I have to use it.

I can't think about that right now.

A blast of heat hits us as we step in.

Having never been to an armory, I naturally assumed the inside might be a cave, or the opening of a small volcano, or filled with sweating, busy Metalsmiths who all have inexplicable accents, because that's what I've been told in stories. Of course the only thing inexplicable about the armory is that it's clean. The space stretches generously, as long as the width of Orkena's main river, with a domed bronze ceiling that reflects the room's many torches in a brassy sheen. At least fifty Metalsmiths and Runemasters hunch over rows of stone workbenches, shaping molten metal with their gloved fingers into swords and arrowheads, stringing runes on strips of leather. I suppose it could be cave-like, considering there are no windows, and maybe the pool-sized vat of molten metal at the center could be like a volcano. Though its sides are bricked and neat, and no actual flames spew from the surface.

Marcus leads me to the back, where a short, pale boy with a shock of red hair bends over a thumb-sized stone. More square stones stack in a pile to his right, a mix of onyx and garnet and marble. The Runemaster lifts the new rune, turning it once so the symbol on its face glows, and sets it in a pile to his left before noticing us.

"Hail, Conlee," Marcus says, clasping his arm. "Were you already working? I thought it was your day off."

"*Dōmmel.*" The Runemaster touches his fingers to his sweat-beaded forehead before turning to Marcus. "I know, but I can't afford to take it. We're working double shifts as it is. If I don't finish these tonight, it'll be that many more I have to do tomorrow."

For a moment I forget the pelts. The piles before the Runemaster reach his elbows, and hundreds of already finished runes hang on racks behind him. "You still have this many to go?"

"Prince Kasta's orders," he says wearily. "These will help the soldiers control their magic from greater distances, so their attacks can reach the Wyri before *forsvine* can disable them. The Metalsmiths have been working around the clock, too, casting swords and spears for emergencies. The entire army needs them."

Which is tens of thousands of soldiers. With a jolt, I wonder if *this* is the reason so little progress has been made on countering the Wyri metal.

"Is anyone studying *forsvine*?" I ask, baffled.

"No, *dōmmel*," the Runemaster says. "There's no time."

Marcus and I exchange a look, my skin prickling. Kasta told me he wanted to march on Wyrim soon and end the war before *forsvine* advanced too much, but that's no reason not to study the metal at all . . . unless he doesn't *want* us to have an easy solution. If I needed any convincing that Kasta intends to make the Wyri suffer and extend this fight as long as possible, I just got it.

I will be changing that soon, but I need to deal with *him* first.

"Marcus told you why we're here?" I ask.

The Runemaster nods. "We spoke about the possibility. Does this mean . . . ?"

His golden eyes dart to the sack, and I open the burlap folds.

"Gods' blood," he whispers. He glances at the crowded room and gestures to a door in the back. "Come with me."

He leads us into a narrow storage closet, its marble shelves stacked with bars of metal and rolls of uncut leather. The thick door closes. I hand him the bag, and while he lifts the snake and the mouse pelt, inspecting Hen's flawless handiwork, Marcus and I fill him in on Kasta's other inconsistencies. His miraculous healing at the end of the Crossing, his improved strength when our boat was attacked, me being able to hear his thoughts. When we finish, the Runemaster's face has gone as pale as milk.

"It's true, then," he says.

Marcus nods. "Do you think you could finish a binding necklace by tomorrow? If the Mestrah passes, the priests will move up the coronation."

"Probably. I have most of the required runes in my personal stash, so I'd only have to make one or two others. But I have to admit . . . I left something out when we were discussing it, Marcus." A flash of his fear brushes my skin, strange and brief. "Because I had to be sure this was worth the risk. There's one more piece I need to complete the binding."

I straighten. "Anything."

"I need the Shifter's blood."

Apos. I grit my teeth, cursing that I thought this would be the end.

"Conlee," Marcus growls. "That's a very critical detail to have left out. We may only have a *day*—"

"I know, my friend, I'm sorry. I thought I was being careful. I didn't know we'd be so crunched for time."

I sigh. "How much do you need?"

"Not much. Enough to smear across six stones." He digs a couple from his apron pocket and holds them out. Each is as wide and tall as the knuckle of a finger. "My mother once made one from a floor stain. A Shifter cut himself breaking into a house, and it was enough. If that's helpful."

I nod, though my head already aches from imagining all the ways this could go wrong. This means getting very close to Kasta again. Possibly with a weapon, considering what we need. Which I don't see going well at all.

"Then we'll get it," Marcus says. "Thank you for your help."

The Runemaster bows. "I'll be here. But do you mind if I hold on to these pelts, *dōmmel*? I will keep the Shifter's identity secret, but if anyone catches me making this, I can assure them with these that the necklace is legal. I'll keep them safe in case you need them again, I promise."

He reaches for the bag, but I step back. It never occurred to me I might have to leave the evidence, and I'm suddenly paranoid that he wonders if they're fake. But that would be ridiculous. That would mean someone Marcus trusts is lying to me, and push me even closer to becoming Kasta, who wouldn't trust anyone with anything at all.

Gods, I'll be so glad when this is over.

Marcus raises a brow, and I thrust the sack forward. "Of course. Not a problem."

The Runemaster takes it. We step back into the armory, and I shake off my nerves, determined to see this through. Just one piece left. One more before I make Kasta confess how he survived . . . and he discovers exactly how far I went to stop him.

The death horns sound just as Marcus and I emerge from the armory.

The High Priests' guards find me before we've even left the military wing. I'm taken to a private room, where I sit behind a wooden scholar's table and one of the Mestrah's somber-faced advisors lays out my future like a terrible hand of cards.

The Mestrah is dead.

Kasta and I are unofficially Orkena's rulers.

And our coronation has been rescheduled for *tomorrow night*.

This is a show of force, he says. To show our enemies that Kasta and I are so unfazed by the last attack and the king's loss that we can step up to our duties at the drop of a hat. Just as we will step up, very soon, to handle Wyrim.

He tells me these things as if I said them myself.

And what else can I do but agree?

I leave in silence. A handmaiden brings me a gray mourning cloak, and I slip it on without seeing her. I have less than a day to get Kasta's blood. Less than a day before I become locked into a future from which I will never escape, before I fail Maia, before I'm forced to face a war with a boy who literally thirsts for death.

I already have the start of a plan. It involves swords and a great deal of risk, and I will not be telling Jet about it. Even Marcus agreed to wait until morning to fill Jet in on what we did tonight. He has more than enough to deal with already.

But even in my urgency, I know Kasta has enough to deal with right now, too. And so I will give him the night to mourn.

And tomorrow, this ends.

XVIII

IN the morning, after the Royal Materialist has stopped in to take my measurements for a coronation gown, and a commander has briefed me on security measures for the ceremony, and approximately a thousand servants have streamed into my room to set incense around and ask my preferences for food and colors and décor, I stand before Kasta's door.

I have three hours until I'm supposed to be back to get dressed. Three hours to finish this.

I knock.

No answer. No rustle of movement. I wait, and knock again. The guards at either side of the doors watch me, and just as I'm about to ask if he's in, the shorter guard tips his staff.

"He's only let two people in all morning, *dōmmel*," he says. "Though I imagine you'd be the third, if you announced yourself."

"Thanks," I say, heat prickling my skin. That I've fooled even them into thinking everything's fine between Kasta and me sits like oil in my stomach.

I turn back to the doors. "Kasta?"

More silence. This is not going to work if he won't even see me.

"Kasta. It's not about the coronation."

More silence. I tip my head back, frustrated, fretting that now I'll need yet *another* plan, when the door clicks open.

Kasta looks out at me, entirely unkempt.

His hair falls into his eyes, unruly and tangled. He's dressed in the same white tunic and belt as yesterday, and old makeup smudges around his eyes, less sharp lines and more like bruises. He's still wearing sandals. It doesn't look like he slept.

"Gods," I say. "You look terrible."

All things considered, this is not a very sensitive thing to say, even if I am hoping he's in prison by this evening. But Kasta gives me a small smile.

"Come in," he says.

"Actually," I say, alarmed by the invitation, "I think what we need is some time at the training grounds." He raises a brow, and I twist my hands together. "You just lost your father, and it's clear to me now that I really need to know how to defend myself without magic. I'm worried there will be another attack today. I meant to look into this soon anyway, but then the Mestrah . . ."

Kasta winces, and I rush on.

"Will you teach me to use a sword?"

His hand drops from the door. Whatever he was expecting, this wasn't it. "Right now?"

"I want to carry one for the coronation. And actually be able to use it, if needed."

His eyes narrow. "Does Jet know you're asking me?"

"Jet and I . . . disagree on this," I say, which I'm very sure would be the truth, if Jet knew what I was doing. "And I—" My heart ticks up. Please, gods, just say yes. "I want to learn from you."

Hook, line, sinker. Kasta's shoulders drop, and he searches my eyes with something like disbelief, maybe relieved that he's won, that he's finally turned me to him. It's everything I have to hold his gaze. To convince him that I've yielded and am thinking only of our cooperative future.

He pushes a hand over his hair. "Fine."

He doesn't even bother to change, just closes the door and joins my side. At which point I'm certain I've now gone way past the line. Anyone who can add *lured a boy who just lost his father out to cut him during a fake sword practice* to the list of things they've done is not a hero, and then I have to tell my brain to shut up, because I need to focus. Boy who just lost his father or not, he's still dangerous. And I still have to stop him.

The training arena waits on the northern side of the palace, a wide, sand-filled stretch settled at the corner of the eastern wall. As we step onto the flagstone path, stone sheds come into view, all freshly built and filled with gleaming weapons that look as new and out of place as scabs. An iron fence circles the arena in curled gods' symbols, and I imagine on a regular day soldiers would pack the space, but with the coronation and the Mestrah to grieve, it's empty.

Kasta approaches the nearest shed and pulls two blades from the rack. The sun flashes from their curved, jagged edges, and unlike most weapons that come alive with flame or ice when touched, these stay unchanged. I take the one he offers me—and nearly drop it.

"*Apos.*" I heft the tip up. "Are they all this heavy?"

Kasta, who jerked back to avoid me slicing his face in half, gives me a look. "If they're not imbued with magic, yes. And watch where you're swinging that."

"Sorry." I wrestle back a stressed smile. I didn't mean to do that, but I think it's set the stage nicely for what's to come.

Kasta moves for the arena. "If we were doing this the right

way, I would start you off on targets and wooden swords for at least a week. But seeing as we have a few hours, I'm going to try something else."

I follow him through the arena gate. Kasta points with the sword where he wants me to stand, and I step to it, awkwardly turning the hilt in my hands.

"Keep your grip firm but not clenched." He shows me with his own hands. "If you hold too tight, you'll be stiff when a blow lands, and it could strain your wrist. Tighten when you're attacking, and relax again when you pull back. You should be constantly shifting your grip."

"That doesn't sound complicated at all," I mutter, frowning at my hands. I turn the hilt until it feels comfortable and hold the sword out. "Is this right?"

He shrugs. "Let's see."

He twists and slams his blade against mine, sending mine flipping over my head and into the sand. My hands sting from the vibration. I blink, incensed.

Kasta smirks. "No. That wasn't good at all."

"That was foul." I turn angrily for the blade. "This is the first time I've held a sword. You have to tell me what you're doing."

"Your attackers won't. You should expect them to fight dirty."

"But you're my teacher. Don't I at least get to learn some basics before you humiliate me?"

I swear I hear distant snickering, and my gut twists when I notice the many windows that surround the space . . . and the people steadily filling them. No one is brave enough to step outside and openly watch, but I can only imagine how fast news of us sparring will spread. At least I'll have plenty of witnesses should this start going poorly.

Including Jet, who I can only pray will forgive me later.

I bite my lip and yank the sword free.

"I'm trying to keep you alive," Kasta says. "If you want to be pampered, you'll have to appeal to Jet."

Right. Or rather, he's trying to show all his soldiers why they should turn to *him* when it comes to the war. I huff and raise the blade. Kasta waits, sword down, long enough that I wonder if he's expecting *me* to attack—until he darts forward. I clench the hilt. The blow sings off the blade but I hold on to it, and just as I'm exclaiming that I've done it, his second strike comes for my neck.

And stops centimeters away, the wind from it feathering my hair.

My breath catches. Kasta's face is unreadable, neither angry nor smug, and slowly, he lowers the sword.

"Assume they'll strike again." He steps back. "Assume the first attack is meant to open you up for another. Keep your blade in my way and widen your stance."

I look down at my hands, already aching from holding the weapon. Kasta moves to show me how to stand, nods when I mimic him, then turns his grip so I can see how his hands are positioned. Which he would not do at all if this were truly about humiliation.

I raise the sword—and lower it.

"You're taking this seriously," I say, shaking my head. "You're actually trying to help me."

He straightens. "Shouldn't I?"

"No," I say, the frustration of these weeks boiling to the surface.

"You hate me. I've been in your way since the beginning. I stopped you from being crowned weeks ago, and from ever ruling on your own, *ever*. You think I tried to kill you. You disagree with my approach to pretty much everything . . . you should be giving me bad tips. Something that will get me hurt, so you come out as the savior again."

Kasta lowers the blade. "That's what you think of me?"

"What else am I supposed to think? The last time I hoped for you, you chose magic instead. So yes, that's what I think." Which is already more than I wanted to say. I should have just said yes. I should not be mentioning hope, like I had nearly been there again before yesterday.

He sighs. "You think I'd do it again."

"Obviously. What's that saying? *Fool me once, shame on you. Fool me twice . . .*"

"I told you, I'm done with that." His blue eyes flash, and the blade glints. "I was desperate then . . . I thought you'd do worse to me. But now I understand what the gods meant me to see. I want to start over. We can help each other."

"Stop it!" I lift my blade and start for him. This is not the smartest idea I've ever had, but I can't waste any more time. "Quit messing with my head. I know what you'll do the next time you feel threatened. I can prove you wrong right now."

He eyes the sword but doesn't move. "You don't even know what you're doing."

I jab forward, and he easily deflects. No, I have no idea what I'm doing, but if I strike at him enough, I should be able to hit him once.

"You're leaning too far," he says, stepping out of reach. "Don't stab forward. That's your natural instinct, but it leaves you open. Slice at me instead."

I seethe. "Stop. Helping. Me!"

I whirl and slice, and again he parries, deflecting to the side. I strike for his leg, and he shoves the attack up, eyeing my ribs as if he might kick me. He doesn't. He shoves back on our crossed hilts, and I stumble to catch my balance.

"Too predictable," he says, twirling the blade. "Trick me. Do something unexpected."

In answer, I charge for him—and at the last second, when he twists his blade to deflect mine, I jerk sideways and circle the sword down. The blade slices the bottom of his forearm. Kasta swears, and my heart leaps at the line of crimson—

Kasta slams into me, hooks his arm around mine, and yanks the hilt out of my grip. The swords go flying to the side. I grunt as we fall, and in a blink Kasta rolls, straddling my torso, pinning my wrists against the sand.

For a moment we stare at each other, chests heaving, his face shadowed and that strange, quiet emptiness sinking into my veins.

"Zahru," he growls, flexing his grip. "Why does it seem like you're more interested in hurting me than in the actual lesson?"

I laugh and squirm; he's far, far too close. "I'm not. I'm just . . . angry."

That much he should understand. The blood from his forearm slides earthward, bright red against his sand-dusted skin. In a moment it will drip onto my sleeve, and I go still.

Something changes in Kasta, too. His grip softens, but he's not looking at the blood.

He's looking at me, and the way I am beneath him.

"You believed in me, once," he says softly. "Have I not done everything you asked?"

I shift beneath him. The longer he holds my wrists, the more I drop into that quiet, and where before it felt like shallow water, now it's starting to feel like the deep.

"You have," I acknowledge.

"What else can I do to convince you? How much more can I yield? I can be everything you wished I could be." His eyes are bright; agonized. "I know what I did. I know I can't undo it. But I swear I will do everything in my power to make it up to you anyway."

My blood lurches. "Kasta—"

"You were angry, in the desert." He swallows. "When I couldn't answer whether I'd spare you. Because even though I wanted to, I didn't want to lie. Which is how you know I'm telling the truth when I say I will *never* do anything like that again."

His blood trickles onto my sleeve. My heart pulls between anguish and disbelief, splintered between the stubborn conviction that he *could* do again what he's done once . . . and the true pain on his face. The heaviness in his words. The teacherous part of me I've tried so desperately to bury that wants to believe, even after everything—or maybe especially because of it—that he means what he says, that I am worth the change.

"Rule with me," he says, and my stomach drops. "Fight *beside* me, and we will be unstoppable. I will do everything you ask.

Let's start over, and become what we're made for."

I close my eyes, fighting the drug-like emptiness in my bones. The traitorous ache in my chest. How aware I am of everywhere we touch, that even now feels like the edges of lightning. This is what I wanted him to tell me in the Crossing before everything went so wrong. This is what he's telling me is now possible, if I want it to be.

Maia, I think. *Remember Maia.*

"You won't harm me," I say, flexing my hands. "What about everyone else?"

"I can't promise it for our enemies. Not if Orkena is to survive. But for you, and everyone you care about . . ." He lets go of my wrists. "Never again."

My throat pinches. Doubt is creeping in again, slick as rain. Maybe he actually did say the name of the antidote aloud and I'm just not remembering right. Maybe the quiet bird Jade thought she saw was just that, a bird that wasn't thinking, and I'd freaked Jade out telling her to watch for Shifters. Maybe Kasta is that much stronger when he fights now, because he's no longer afraid.

Maybe I've only seen what I wanted to because I'm so terrified of being wrong again.

He's been calm these past weeks. Thoughtful. He's focused on Orkena, and even with his Influence not working as he wants it to, he's deferred to what *would* work instead. To me.

All of this, for me.

He starts to rise, but I catch his wrist. I have to know. It's risky to ask, but if the answer is not what I've been assuming . . . I don't know what I'll do.

I don't know what I'm doing.

I'm already touching him. I don't need to be closer to try and push my Whispering abilities past whatever wall blocks me from his thoughts, but I sit up anyway and reach for his face. Aware that everyone's watching. Aware of the way he goes still, but doesn't move away. I slide my hand over his cheek, tuck my fingers around his rough jaw, searching for secrets. He closes his eyes, but hard as I try to reach, I get nothing. No thoughts, no emotion.

Except for the pounding of my own heart.

"Kasta?" I whisper. He opens his eyes, that silver-blue that has ruined me. But the question about Maia lodges in my throat. Something glows on the back of my hand, a tiny circle like the reflection of sunlight off a coin. His clothes don't seem to have any metal. It must be coming from under his collar. I prop myself higher and slip my hand down his neck, fervently ignoring the way he shivers, the way he inhales.

"Zahru—"

I hook the leather necklace and pull it up.

Six frigid, heavy *forsvine* beads glint across my fingers. Enough metal to neutralize his Shifter magic . . . and the magic of anyone standing close to him.

Of course. *This* is why his touch feels so empty. Why the Mestrah couldn't read his mind and he hasn't advanced in Influence; why I could read his thoughts during the assassin attack, the only time he took the necklace off to ensure I could use my magic. Because he doesn't have Influence at all. He *would* have had it, if he'd waited, if he'd left those caves without hurting anyone else. The knife had marked him. His Influence would soon follow, as mine did.

But even divine power is no exception to the rule of the Shifter's curse: that if he kills for the magic, it erases anything else he had.

I close my fist around the necklace. "Where's Maia?"

He grabs my wrist. "It's not what you think."

"It's not?" I try to rip it free, but his hold is iron. "Then take it off. Take it off, and we'll see what the truth is."

"I was going to tell you. After the coronation, I was going to confess—"

"That you killed her?"

"Never," he snaps, prying at my fingers. "I didn't want this. I would *never*—" His voice cracks. "Maia did this to *me*."

I tighten my grip. "Odd way to put it, since you're the one alive."

His fingers dig into my arm. He glances at the windows, and I'm suddenly grateful for our audience. He can't do anything to me without them knowing about it.

"She forced me," he growls. "You didn't know her. To her, this curse was worse than death."

"I don't believe you."

His eyes burn, and he tips closer to ease the pressure I'm putting on his neck. "Let go of me, Zahru."

His voice is quiet, deadly. But I know now which of us is more dangerous. I could make him confess. I could make it his idea. And he knows it.

I feel the necklace loosening, and I smirk. "Or what?"

He reaches behind my head and pulls my mouth to his. I gasp in surprise—except his lips move with mine, and he *kisses* me, and heat jolts through me, wild and wrong and tangled with memories, and he pulls back just as fast, except he's still too close, he's looking at me like he's waiting for me to wake up—

"I didn't!" he says, shaking me a little, and I feel like I should slap him, I feel like I should *want* to slap him, but I don't, and he notices, and the fire shifts in his eyes and then—

Oh gods, then—

"I didn't," he murmurs on my lips. He kisses me again, softer this time, slower, and I groan in protest . . . but I don't move away. "I didn't."

Another kiss. Longer, heavier, because I'm starting to move but it's all wrong, it's my lips, it's my mouth opening with his, but I tell myself it's nothing, that I'm only letting him because this is how I'll figure out if he's telling the truth—but his fingers shift through my hair like the wind drawing me toward the edge of a cliff, reminding me of what we were, of what we could be if *I* would just trust him, like this strange reversal of the Crossing where I'm the one in the shadows and he has the light and I feel myself slipping, fire splitting through me as he kisses me harder; I need to pull back, I need to *think*, but he presses my palm to his chest, and slides it down his thin tunic, and guides it *down his stomach*, and it's when a new kind of hunger twists through me that I finally snap awake, I remember where we are—

And I panic at what I'm doing and shove him—

And Kasta jerks to his feet with ease, smiling as he adjusts the necklace and turns for the iron gate.

For a moment, I can only stare at my open hand.

Funny how I compared that to getting free of him in the

Crossing, because *that's exactly the kind of distraction he intended it to be*.

With everyone watching.

My blood boils; I would tackle him if I thought I had even the smallest chance of not humiliating myself in front of the palace more than I already have. I suppose he enjoyed that, dragging that reckless part out of me, making me show him how far back he's pulled me—

But I focus my rage. I have what I came for, and it won't matter much longer.

I shove to my feet and whirl for the southern exit.

"Zahru," he says. I don't look back. "Don't do anything rash. I meant what I said. Think it through." The swords slide free of the sand with a metallic hum. "Don't make me your enemy again."

I shake my head to block him out. I won't listen, I *can't*, and I slip through the arena fence, my blood on fire.

When I reach the eastern wing's stone archway, I break into a run.

I don't see anything but a blur of faces as I enter the palace. They part for me like gazelles for a lion, and I imagine I don't look too far off from that, with sand in my hair and blood on my *jole* and every muscle in me coiled to spring. Whispers follow me like flies. Murmurs thread Kasta's and my name together. Kasta's own words work at me like broken glass, cutting, churning.

Have I not done everything you asked? Let's start over.

I didn't want this.

Rule with me.

His kiss burns on my lips. I slow my pace, trying to get him out of my head, but I'm not paying attention to where I'm going, and when I round a gilded corner into the main foyer, I collide hard with Jet.

"Gods," I say, gripping his armor for balance. Jet grabs my shoulders to steady us—and steps away just as fast.

"Jet!" I say this as brightly as I can, like I wasn't just thinking about Kasta, like guilt isn't still eating me alive for what I did to Jet last night.

And for what he must have just seen outside.

"Sorry," he says, his tone guarded. "Marcus said you and Kasta were sparring . . . I got here in time for the end. Are you all right?"

"Yes. Thanks." I glance out the nearest window, but Kasta has already disappeared, and even though there are a thousand questions in Jet's silence, I motion for him to follow me into the foyer. "Sorry. I would have told you, but I didn't want to bother you after last night. But I got what we needed. Did Marcus tell you?"

I lift my bloodied sleeve, and Jet exhales in relief. "Oh. That's all you were doing?"

I blink. "The coronation is in two hours. What else would I be doing?"

"I don't know. It's hard to guess anything you're up to anymore."

There's a barb in his voice that I don't like, but I choose to take this as a compliment, and not as an implication that my motives are becoming questionable. Also, I'm in no mood to argue with a boy whose eyes are still red and puffy from grieving, so I let it go.

"I'm sorry if I worried you," I say. "I didn't really have time to tell you."

"It's . . . fine. Do you think he suspects anything?"

I laugh. I can't help it; this is the greatest and worst joke of the day. "I almost pulled the *forsvine* he's been wearing to hide his Shifter abilities off of his neck. Which is also why he kissed me . . . which I really don't want to talk about. So, I doubt he knows we're so far along in our plan, but he definitely knows I'm onto him."

"Ah." There is an understandably awkward pause, during which I pray there are no follow-up questions. "We'd better move fast, then. Kasta can do a lot with two hours."

So he can.

But there's a problem as we move through the main foyer. A cloud that starts in the back of my mind, growing, darkening as we move between clusters of staring nobles and past a statue of Apos, god of deceit, with the stars spinning between his hands. Because the more I try to convince myself Kasta is lying about how Maia died, the more I realize it couldn't have happened any other way. Maia had been furious with him at the end. She was so strong; she knew Kasta's tricks better than any of us. Kasta was weak, bleeding out. By the same logic I determined he couldn't have survived the race without Healing, there's also no way he could have survived Maia in the same state.

And then there was the shocked cry I heard from him as we left the caves. Which I'd thought was irrelevant after I learned he was alive, but now that I think of it from this angle, it was definitely not a sound made by someone who was in control.

Leave the monsters to monsters, Maia said.

Gods, this is what she meant by it.

Kasta is telling the truth. And everything he's done these past weeks . . . has been real.

Odelig. Helping me with Influence, a power he will never master. Breathing life back into me . . . his relief drenching my skin. *His*, not Jet's, raw and involuntary and pure, now that I know he wasn't wearing *forsvine* when he saved me.

I sway, clutching my aching head.

Jet catches my arm. "Are you all right?"

"No, I'm really not." I scrub my face. "Jet, I don't think I can do this."

"What?" He tugs me to the side of the foyer, out of the way of the crowd. Silence closes around us as he raises his bubble. "Do you have heatstroke? You could turn him in before without proof, but you can't do it *with* it?"

"I don't know, I—" I bite my cheek. "I just figured out he didn't kill Maia."

"Then he hunted another Shifter. I don't understand why this changes anything."

"No, I mean—he did kill her, kind of, but only because she *forced* him to. She was angry with him for what he'd done. So she sentenced him to a fate worse than death."

Jet feels my forehead. "You do feel a little hot."

I jerk back. "I'm fine! I'm not sick. I'm just thinking . . . he's so different now. He's been patient, he's worked with me; gods, he agreed to train me in swords today, after you both just lost your father! He's focused on Orkena . . . He could help us."

Jet shakes his head slowly, like I'm suggesting we burn down the palace. "You want to leave him in power?"

"I . . . Yes? No! I don't know. The gods still marked him, didn't they? And even your father said we were meant to be a partnership. Maybe we could talk to him, get him to abdicate. I feel like *Hey, do you want to be an advisor or in chains the rest of your life?* is a pretty clear-cut decision for anyone."

"You think that conversation will go smoothly? You think he'll give up godhood, and thus being pardoned of his curse, that easily?"

"I'll be Mestrah soon. *I'll* pardon him."

"And you believe he'd trust you with that?" He glances at my lips, and horror simmers up his face. "Gods, you do. What has he done to you?"

"What? He hasn't *done* anything to me. I'm about to inherit a kingdom. I have to be thinking about our future, not just this moment."

"But you know this is what he does. He's putting on a front to get what he wants. What about after he's pardoned? Did you find out why he stopped the research on *forsvine*?"

I push off the pearl-flecked wall. "I don't care. I've been assuming the worst of him this whole time, and I just found out I was completely wrong. I'm going to ask him. I'm going to give him a chance."

I make to leave, but Jet steps in my way. His hands raised, still not touching me. "Zahru," he says, his voice tight. "That you always want to see the best in people is something I very much admire about you. But this is not that. He is *dangerous*, and he's playing you as he would an enemy in a war. He will do whatever he must to save himself right now. You of all people should know this."

His fear prickles the air, but I only smile. "I'm dangerous now, too. He'll listen. You'll see."

I move around him, Jet scrubs his hand over his shaved hair, and I start out of the foyer alone. Planning what I'll say. Feeling grateful Maia wasn't a victim but a key in our plan, a way to keep Kasta in check.

Except now this story can have a much better ending. Maia would have liked to see Kasta come back like this, to see him prove himself as he has. I know it's only been a few weeks. I know I still need to be careful, and ask Kasta about the stopped research on *forsvine* just in case. But what I'm not telling Jet is, depending on the answer and how this goes—and especially now that I know I could Influence Kasta if I needed to, which is really not what I should be thinking about, but there it is—

I may just let him keep his crown.

I've reached the base of the stairs when footsteps sound behind me. Jet slows when I turn, his brow pinched.

"All right," he says, dropping a hand on the marble banister. "All right. If this is what you want, if you believe him . . . then I trust you. To be clear, I still don't trust *him*, but I trust you. How can I help?"

I take him in, his worried eyes, his tight shoulders, his hand on the hilt of his sword, and an unexpected surge of relief pushes through me. Whatever's cracking between us, at least I haven't lost him completely.

I smile. "Come with me?"

He nods, and we start for Kasta's room. I'm not actually sure if Kasta will be in, or if that's even where I want to confront him, but we can speak to his guards, and Kasta will know what I want. We'll figure this out, and by tonight this will all be sorted, and I can finally, finally check off one of the biggest stress items on my list.

We're just passing my doors when a crash sounds from inside them.

My stomach dives. My immediate assumption is more assassins, and my guards shove the doors open by their crescent moon handles, lightning and fire between their fingers—and another *SMASH* sounds as Jade launches herself off a standing vase on the far side of the room, tearing after something small that runs on the ground. One of my guards brings her arm back, ready to throw her ball of fire—

"Wait!" I say, catching her shoulder. "You could hit Jade!"

Chase! Jade's thinking. *Rat! Eat!*

A brown streak shoots under the couch, its thoughts a spike of fear. My first bizarre thought is that Kasta got into my room somehow, *as a rat*, either to talk or set some kind of trap for me—followed by the jolting realization that I know exactly what's happening.

"Jade!" I yell, pushing past the guards. "Stop! Don't eat my spy rat!"

"*Dōmmel!*" cries one of the guards.

"Stand down," I say. "She's just after a rat. Jade!"

CRASH. A display of decorative glass balls tips off an end table as Jade bumps it, but she's too big to fit under the couch, and her shoulders slam into its low edge. She twists on her side and reaches under, batting and clawing.

Mine, she thinks. *Get!*

"Jade, I told you to stop!" I heave her up, struggling to keep her as she wiggles. "Friend! This rat is a friend, and he could have a message for me! Don't hurt him!"

Jade stops squirming and turns to me with betrayed eyes. *No chase?*

"No, I told you to leave the rats alone! Are you going to behave if I put you down, or do I need to lock you on the balcony?"

One of my guards shifts behind us. "Er, we'll just . . . be right outside if you need us?"

I consider this is a rather unusual scene for people who can't hear the other side of this conversation, and I straighten, adjusting Jade in my arms with as much queenly elegance as I can muster. "Yes. Thank you."

They shut the doors. I share an exasperated look with Jet, as

335

though he well knows the struggles of employing spy rats with an active leopard in the house, but before I can ask Jade again whether she'll contain herself, the rat zips across the rugs, over a shattered statue of Tyda, and through the smallest crack between the balcony doors.

Outside, never to return again.

"Oh well." I sigh and set Jade down, who immediately streaks over to the balcony and sniffs at the doors. "Not like anything it found would have helped us now."

Jet snorts, impressed. "You had a rat spying for you?"

"Yes, since I wasn't finding anything in Kasta's room. I thought maybe he had a hiding place we couldn't reach. You know, like he could turn into a mouse or something and put the pelts far out of sight."

"That was a good thought." Jet leans against the couch, still watching me in that guarded way. "So how are we going to do this next part?"

"Well, I—"

Message, Jade thinks, trotting over with her tail high. She jumps up to put her forepaws on my legs, a small, crumpled scroll between her teeth.

"What's this?" I ask.

Spy, she thinks. *Message*.

My chest tightens. This is something the rat dropped . . . something it found in Kasta's room. Though even as I unfurl it, I'm sure it will only be more of the same: another letter about the Forsaken, maybe the reason Kasta stopped researching *forsvine*. It will be nothing. Jet joins my side, and my breath hitches as I take the drawing in.

A serpentine blade. A balancing scale hilt. Equations cluster the margins in Kasta's tight scrawl.

It's a schematic of the sacrificial knife.

I'm not sure what it means that my first reaction is that it can't be real.

"This rat is a *liar*," I say.

At which point Jet actually grabs my shoulder, his concern flaring through me. "I need you to snap out of it, please. Are you sure he didn't drug you?"

"He didn't! I just . . . this makes no sense. He said he was done with this. He *promised* me. Maybe it's old, from before the Crossing? What are these equations?"

I have worried Jet to a level I've never seen before. He lowers his hands to the schematic, each movement slow and careful, as if I'm an animal that might bolt.

"I don't actually know," he says, slipping the parchment from my fingers and hurriedly rolling it. "Yes. Maybe it's old. Why don't we have Melia take a look? She'll know what these equations are."

"All right," I say, though I suspect he's only agreeing to placate me, especially after he strides for the door without a glance. I follow, twisting the shoulder of my *jole*. I don't want this to be what it looks like. Like instead of focusing on *forsvine*, Kasta is still researching the knife; like he still hopes to get Influence, one way or the other.

Like I am wrong, again.

Nausea curls my stomach as we make our quick way out of the royal wing, skirt the indoor pool outside the gardens, and slip into the residency halls. Water cascades down the center of the hall in a silvery sheet, and Melia's door lies a few meters in, droplets flecking our backs as Jet knocks.

She answers, and we step inside.

I'm no longer surprised to see Hen already here in a green *jole*, lying on her stomach on Melia's bed, her fingers working over a swatch of blue satin. An abandoned game board sits on a low table alongside empty chalices. Hen bounces up to join us, and I have time to regret that, in another life, *this* could have been the way I spent my morning, when Melia crosses her arms.

"Marcus told us you found proof yesterday," she says. "Did you get Kasta's blood?"

I nod and raise my sleeve, adamantly not speaking to the *proof* part.

"Good," she says. "Then what are you doing here?"

Jet hands her the rolled parchment. "Zahru is . . . considering changing the plan." He's speaking in that slow, careful way again. "This should help make up our minds. One of her spy rats smuggled it from Kasta's room."

"Spy rats?" she echoes, unfurling the paper.

Hen squeezes between Melia and me. "Brilliant. Also, I have a lot of questions about what just happened in the arena."

"Later, please," Jet says, cutting her a meaningful glance. He points to the markings and turns back to Melia. "Can you translate these equations? They're far above what my tutors ever covered. Maybe you studied these in your Healing courses?"

Melia inhales—she recognizes the blade. She moves to the purple couch, brushing aside the gemstones from the game board to lay the scroll over it. We crowd around her, shoulder to shoulder.

"These are formulas." She traces the numbers drawn around the hilt. "Give me a moment to work them out. They look like energy equations, but no one still alive knows how this knife works." She grabs a scrap of parchment and a quill from the game and turns the paper over.

Hen, all business now, taps a list with a red box around it. "This is a materials list. Firestone, holy water, leather, gold."

I work one of the game's sapphires between my fingers. "Can we tell how old it is? If it's something he drafted before the Crossing?"

"Yup," Hen says. "But it's new. Right here it says *Zahru lived. Blood sacrifice must die, to prevent repeat*—and then an arrow to one of the formulas Melia is working on."

"What?" My blood spikes. Both at the realization that Jet should definitely have been able to tell this wasn't old when I first asked—and didn't trust me to believe him—and the more horrifying implication of that statement.

This is not the research of a boy who has changed.

"He's going to try and get Influence again?" I say, my ears going hollow. "The same way he got it before?"

"No. It's worse." Melia stops mid-stroke. "The sacrificial knife *can't* be activated without the power of the three High Priests. Otherwise any royal heir could use it at their leisure, if they disapproved of the Crossing's results. Kasta is not trying to find a way to use the knife again." She shows her work to Jet. "He's creating a new knife, one that will bestow a different type of magic with every kill."

"Gods." Jet takes the paper, nearly crushing the edges. "If this works, he could possess every power imaginable."

Melia nods. "This is a weapon for war. Every soldier he fells will make him stronger."

All the power he could ever want. This is my answer for why he's not working on *forsvine*. He doesn't *want* a solution, because a war is the perfect place to test this weapon on unlimited bodies.

A fire ignites inside of me, dark and searing.

"Oh." Hen looks up. "I wonder if that's what you cut your foot on in the closet? One of his prototypes?"

But I'm hardly here. I'm back in the hunting meadow weeks ago, when I reminded myself not to believe anything Kasta was doing, because it would only last as long as things went well for him. And this is why. Everything is going his way down to the smallest detail, so of course he claims he'll do anything for me now—he's already halfway to having all the magic he can dream of.

Jet shifts, and even though he doesn't say it, I can practically read the *Do you believe me now?* in his eyes.

"You've been concerningly quiet," he says. "What are you thinking?"

That fire snakes through my core. "That I've already wasted way too much time. Hen, Melia, take this to the priests. Jet, let's get this done."

HEN rolls the scroll with a flourish, and she and Melia start for the temple while Jet and I turn for the armory. My mind buzzes like a hive. I'm furious I let Kasta get to me. That I let him play me like one of the kingdom leaders, as he knew exactly what I'd soften to, exactly what I'd want to hear. How foolish I would have felt if I'd let him keep his crown, thinking he was an entirely new person, only for him to manipulate me into fighting at least one battle so he could use his new knife.

And after that, the war would explode.

This is possibly the wrong lesson to be taking away from this, but I'm so glad I went ahead with framing him.

Jet and I move quickly, silently, glancing over our shoulders for Kasta, slipping between servants carrying armfuls of ribbons and flowers for the coronation and around groups of tipsy nobles. A few of them call to me—Jet silences every one. The armory doors come into view, cracking open in the middle when we approach, and we step into the heat.

With everyone off of work for the coronation, the tables sit empty. An eerie quiet swirls the space instead, the melting vat hissing as we move deeper inside.

Jet points to the supply closet, the same one where Marcus and I showed the Runemaster the pelts. "Marcus told Conlee to wait in hiding, in case Kasta stopped by and questioned why he's here. He should unlock it if we knock six times."

We pause outside the door, and I knock as Jet said. The melting vat bubbles, the hum of finished runes prickles my skin, but finally metal slides as a key turns in the lock. The Runemaster peers out, his messy hair a shock of red against the shadows.

"*Dōmmel*," he says, touching his forehead before nodding at Jet. "*Aera*. Here, I have everything ready." He moves to his workbench, and Jet and I stop on the other side.

"Thanks again for your help." I lift my sleeve. "I have what you need."

The Runemaster nods. "Of course. I'm happy to stop corruption wherever it may lie."

"How long will this take?" Jet asks.

"Not long. A few minutes." The Runemaster pulls a familiar leather string lined with square-cut runes from his pocket and sets it on the table. From his other pocket he pulls a silver band that looks much like an advisor's armband, the inside marked with black symbols. "Controlling necklaces work in two parts. You wear the necklace, and the Shifter wears this to complete the bind." He taps the cuff. "Ultimately this spell will be imbued into the Shifter's armor so it can't be broken off, but this will work until an Enchanter can fit him for that."

"Good," Jet says, inspecting the cuff. "We'll have the priests put this on him in the temple."

"Just give me a moment to finish the rest. May I have the sample, *dōmmel*?"

"Of course." I come around to his side and offer my sleeve, and the Runemaster picks up a shining pair of scissors to cut it free. My nerves flash. I should have come here first; I don't know what Kasta will do if he realizes I'm past negotiation. I want to say

342

there's nothing he *can* do once I bring the pelts and the binding necklace to the priests, but that's the problem. I still have to get there.

The Runemaster is just starting to make the first slice when something hits the armory doors.

My blood stops. The Runemaster freezes, and we wait, all of us on thorns, but no one comes in. The doors shudder and creak. Silence follows, then a muffled cry—and the *CRASH* of something breaking.

"Jet!" comes Marcus's muffled voice. "Someone followed you—"

Another crash. Jet shoves the binding cuff into my hand and draws his sword. "Get this done. Don't come out until I say it's clear."

He takes off for the door. Something else smashes farther down the hall, and I bounce on my heels, remembering too late that Jet warned me, way back before the Crossing even happened, that Kasta had half the palace servants employed as spies. I'm reassured that I've been paranoid enough to keep all our important conversations behind closed doors, but if Kasta is looking for me, I'm pretty sure he'll soon know where I am.

I turn back to the Runemaster. "Just a few minutes, right?"

He's nearly cut the blood sample free. "Yes, *dōmmel*. I'll do this as quickly as I can."

I shift, anxiously watching the closed door, but nothing else sounds from the hall. I'm grateful Marcus, at least, had the foresight to play lookout. Melia must have told him Jet and I were making our move. I'm just starting to praise myself for my excellent choice in advisors when the Runemaster turns my hand, shoves my wrist into a metal shackle, and clamps it shut.

My magic leaves me in a sickening lurch. I jump back, dropping the binding cuff in surprise—and a chain rattles, locking me in place. What I'm looking at doesn't even make sense. A shackle, clearly made of *forsvine*, attaches me to the side of the table by a short chain . . . one that I realize now was hidden beneath the Runemaster's burlap satchel. The Runemaster himself moves quickly, tucking the cut sleeve and the rune necklace into his pocket, snatching the binding cuff from where it rolled on the floor.

He hesitates a moment, as if he's forgotten something, then turns on his heel.

He's leaving. He attached me to a table, and he's leaving.

"You—" I tug on the chain. *"What are you doing?"*

The Runemaster grabs a few tools from the next table over. He's already slid the scissors into his bag. "I'm sorry, *dōmmel*. But I could not sit by and let you enslave Prince Kasta. I know the pelts are fake. I had them tested. I would have been happy to help you catch a Shifter, but it's clear that's not your motive."

I gape at him. "What? Kasta *is* a Shifter! He's been wearing *forsvine* this whole time . . . I'm just about to prove it!"

"As I told you, I'm dedicated to stopping corruption wherever it may lie." He backs away, holding the satchel close. Like he's planning to leave the armory for good. "Prince Kasta warned all us Runemasters weeks ago that you were understandably angry with him, but that it had twisted you, and he'd overheard a plot to ensure you rose to power alone. That we should tell him if you approached one of us."

Oh gods. *The Runemaster* is one of the servants Kasta has in his employ . . . and the bird that freaked Jade out was definitely Kasta, spying on me. "He said it had *twisted me?*"

"I wasn't sure I believed him, especially when it was Marcus who came on your behalf, because I know Marcus's heart is good. So I decided I'd help and determine for myself who was right. After you brought me the false pelts, the truth became clear."

"Oh, no no no." I pry at the shackle, digging my nails under the metal. "I'm not the bad guy here. You can't turn me in; I have to stop Kasta! And fine, yes, I faked the pelts, but that's only because Kasta is very, very careful, and I couldn't get anything on him that wasn't circumstantial. I had no choice! But I know I'm right, and if you would just trust me for *ten minutes*, I can prove it!"

Was that a villain monologue? Oh my gods, what is happening?

"Yes," the Runemaster muses, more to himself. "He said you'd be very convincing, but I'm afraid I won't fall for it. But lucky for you, Kasta is more merciful than you paint him to be. He isn't getting the priests involved, yet. He wants to talk this through."

"Talk!" I laugh, and jerk hard at the chain. "I guarantee you he is beyond talking right now. You can't leave me here wearing *forsvine*. No one will ever see me again."

But the Runemaster only turns and quickens his pace. He's not listening. In his eyes I'm the bad guy, and no one wise ever listens to the bad guys.

Which I really should have remembered before all of this.

Jet is still out there, I remind myself, not like that does me any good. He'll be no match for a Shifter if Kasta arrives, safe to use his power now that I can't use mine. I huff and hang on the chain, but the end of it is embedded inside the stone. The table only shifts, a slab of solid ironstone too heavy to even tip with all my weight.

I attack the shackle instead. A slit marks the place where the two sides connect, but whatever locks it, I can barely pry it farther apart than a hair. I need a tool. The Runemaster took everything off this table, but a hammer lies on one nearby. I lurch for it—my table doesn't budge. It's still half a meter out of reach.

The far door clicks open.

"Jet!" I yell. "Jet, I'm chained to a table—"

The Runemaster bows low, his fingertips to his forehead.

And Kasta steps in.

The torchlight ripples across his pearlescent tunic. He's cleared the smudges from his face and darkened his eyes in fresh kohl, ready for the coronation. I wish I could take the unreadable set of his face as a good sign, that maybe he does only want to talk, but I know this calm. I know the shadows slipping under his skin.

And it's a very bad sign that Jet isn't answering.

"Mestrah," the Runemaster says. Like Kasta is already crowned. He hands Kasta the binding necklace, the swatch with the blood, and the silver cuff. Kasta thanks him—*thanks him*, like this was a civilized transaction—and the Runemaster strides out like he's just saved the world.

The door drifts shut.

His eyes on me, Kasta shoves down the heavy metal bar that locks it.

XXXI

THIS is not the way heroes are supposed to die, chained to tables by law-abiding Runemasters while their nemeses sift through different recipes in their minds. I will be a steak; I will be mashed into tiny pieces and stuffed into meat pie. Of course I don't know exactly what Kasta's thinking, but I imagine it's something along those lines. And I only have myself to blame.

This is what I get for lying. For dropping to Kasta's level and thinking I could win.

"I see you've made your decision," Kasta says, in that cold, quiet tone.

"Where's Jet?" I ask.

"In a cell, where he belongs. I had your entire advisor posse arrested as soon as they came to the priests with military plans stolen from my room. It turns out magical research is not actually illegal, but spying on a crown prince definitely is." His mouth twitches. "Then I just had to lure Jet out to join them." His voice shifts—to Marcus's deep tone. "Which was very easy."

My stomach twists. Gods, Jet and I even knew better, that we should never trust anyone we couldn't see face-to-face, but we were so close to winning, neither of us stopped to think—

"I'm afraid the priests want to speak with you, too," Kasta says, starting slowly forward. "I told them I'd take care of it."

My nightmare flashes behind my eyes. I lurch again for the hammer and the table slides, just a little. Not enough.

I hiss and grab the chain, leaning all my weight on it.

"I'll admit I'm impressed," he says, strolling to the melting vat. "You made a few amateur mistakes: not checking the windows before you first discussed your strategy with your team, leaving your blood behind in my closet. But the pelts . . ." He tsks and drops the fabric with his blood on it into the vat, where it vanishes in a burst of fire. "Very clever. If I hadn't gotten to the Runemaster before you did, he would never have thought to verify them. And our positions would be switched."

I inhale and heave; the table slides, almost enough. I'm fingertips away.

"If I didn't know better," he says, moving again, "I would say you've learned some things from me. It's making you unpredictable. It's making you *formidable*."

The approval in his tone, especially in contrast to how Jet now sees me, sends a shiver down my spine. I pant and lurch again— knocking the hammer, which slips off and falls to the floor. Out of reach.

Oh gods.

"So now what?" I say, my laugh bitter. "You kill me, eat my remains, and take the throne? You don't think the priests will find that convenient?"

He winces. "I suppose I deserve that. I wouldn't trust me so fast, either, after everything. But we'll have plenty of time to fix it. You see, I've learned some things from you, too." He ties the binding necklace around his throat, the runes gleaming red as he hides it, carefully, beneath the collar of his tunic. And a hollow opens in my stomach. "This is where it gets interesting. Will you condemn me for doing exactly the same thing to you as you planned to do to me?"

He cracks the binding cuff open along the seam, his eyes dark as shadow. And realization jolts through me for why the blood pool I left in his closet was so small. "You had him make a binding necklace for *me*?"

"I told him you were in league with another Shifter to complete the charade." His gaze slips to the gods' mark on my chest; to the power of Influence, that will soon be his through *me*. "The pelts I brought him were real. He was so upset with you at that point, he didn't even ask who your Shifter *was*." His smile curves. He's almost here. "I didn't want it to come to this. I truly hoped you'd wake up and trust me, and we could do this together, but you forced my hand. Orkena needs us both, and I'm not letting you throw that away. So here's what we're going to do." He's one table away. "You're going to change your advisors' minds about me"—he steps closer—"you're going to place a crown on my head"—he's within reach—"and very soon, you and I are going to bring the world to its knees."

He lunges for my arm. I make one last grab for the hammer, but Kasta catches the chain and heaves me back—it nearly snaps from his strength. My heart jerks. He grabs for my free hand, and I remember what he said during our sparring match—to do something unexpected—and just as he moves to latch the cuff, I shove *into* him, slamming his wrist with my elbow.

The cuff flies, flashing, toward the storage closet. Kasta swears and starts after it, but I twist the chain around his wrist and he doesn't even think about it, he pulls to free himself—

The chain snaps.

His eyes widen. He grabs for me, but I roll under the table and bolt for the door, my pulse thundering in my ears. I weave between workbenches, and I'm six tables away, then four—

A cheetah streaks past me, bumping my arm as it leaps off of a table and lands awkwardly in front of the door. I skid to a stop so fast that I fall backward, and the cheetah twitches and grunts, fur rippling as Kasta transforms back to human in a blink. He gags at the end, as if he hadn't meant to do it so fast, and eyes the *forsvine* shackle still attached to my wrist. It neutralizes his magic if he touches me, too.

"Hmm," he says. "You seem suddenly opposed to this plan, when you're on the other side of it."

He starts forward, and I shove to my feet, backing toward the melting pool. "This is absolutely not the same. I almost gave you the benefit of the doubt . . . I *wanted* to." My voice cracks. "I was on my way to find you, to talk this through, when we found your plans for the new knife. You say you've changed, but your mind is still on power. On who you can kill to get it!"

He shakes his head. "You're making assumptions again. Just like you did when you assumed I'd killed Maia."

"Oh, really?" I round the melting vat; heat rises from its yellow surface in a deadly steam. I grab a freshly made dagger from its edge. "Is that why you were hiding it away? You were afraid someone would find it and think, *This* murder weapon *will be entirely misunderstood, since all of these equations point to death!*"

"It's not for me!" He rounds the pool, passing finished swords and spears. Not threatened by me in the least. "That's a prototype for a weapon to protect us in the war. I'm going to make them for the Forsaken."

"The—" My heart jolts, remembering the first letter Hen and I found. "You're going to send *them* to fight the war?"

"I'm going to send them to gain the magic they are owed. Every enemy they slay will make them more powerful, and after we cut Wyrim down, the Forsaken will return as heroes."

I gape. "And thousands will have died for it. The *Forsaken* may die—"

"And what else would you have for them? Without magic, no amount of wealth will make them equal here. The elite will still exclude them. They'll still be doomed by the gods to wander the afterlife for eternity." Kasta shakes his head. "I don't understand you. Everything I've done, I've done for *you*. You wanted me to seek counsel. To use my power to help!"

"But not to harm! You're talking about fueling a war, letting untold numbers of people die—"

"Those untold numbers *want us dead*," Kasta says, stopping. "We're out of time to do this any other way. Wyrim is beyond negotiation. *This* is how we'll end the unrest quickly, with the casualties on *their* side, and once we're safe, we can start talking about alternatives. Anything less and you are sentencing Orkena to death."

I laugh in disbelief. "That's if our allies don't turn on us, terrified of what we're becoming. You have *no way* of knowing how long this war will go—"

"Which is why I have you." His fingers twitch, and my stomach pulls, waiting for him to lunge. "You think they're afraid of you now. Wait until we show them what you can really do."

"And we're back to magic." I flex my grip on the dagger. "Gods,

Kasta, if you would focus that brilliant mind of yours for *one second* on anything else—"

He scoffs. "And you're so immune? They never looked twice at you when you were a Whisperer. Now they bow. Tell me there's no difference." His eyes flash. "Tell me you would give your power back."

I grit my teeth. "I agree that the system is broken. But more magic won't fix it, and neither can this war!" I step back, eyeing the tables. "I will make you regret doing this. I will fight you every step of the way."

His lips quirk. "I'd hope for nothing less."

And he *sprints*. I bolt in the other direction, but he's already rounding my side, and before I've even reached the nearest table, his hand locks around my arm. The world lurches to a stop. I whirl to stab him, but he catches my wrist, the blade trembling a whisper above his heart.

"Careful," he says, a hint of disbelief in his voice. "Remember what happens if you kill me."

I startle, realizing how careless a move that was—and that I *would* have killed him if he hadn't stopped me. Is murder that easy for me now? Am I willing to kill him to save myself?

Have I become him?

Kasta presses my palm until I gasp and let go of the knife. Then he spins me, pinning my back to his chest, and drags me toward the storage closet. Toward the binding cuff. I go limp. I drag my feet. I claw his arm and try to twist away, but his grip is a vise, even without his magic. Panic flushes through me. I could choke on it, on the thought of being his pet until the bitter end, of the things he'll make me do—to the Wyri, to anyone else who would oppose us. Of what *he'll* do to them, without anyone to stop him.

And then an emotion brushes the back of my mind, light as a feather: anticipation.

I freeze. It's most certainly not mine. For a moment I wonder if I imagined it, but it comes again, a little stronger. And a little stronger still, like a flame working on wet tinder. A flare of Kasta's own magic trembles through me, just as faint. The shackle warms on my arm, and a hairline crack works over the surface, slow as a water drop.

Our power must be overwhelming it. Whatever energy this amount of *forsvine* is made to absorb, the both of us are too much for it.

I focus on that tiny thread, and *shove*.

My magic surges. The shackle burns my wrist, glowing red, and Kasta hisses as it sears his arm, but I push harder, and he drops me. I jerk the burning metal off, yelping at the heat, and then it's in two pieces, melting into the floor.

My power returns like the flow of fresh blood. Kasta gapes at the ruined shackle, and his gaze slides slowly, disbelieving, back to me.

Rie, he thinks, his voice strong in my head. And I can't help but smile.

He bolts for the binding cuff, but his urgency, his panic is so strong it's like catching a rope that's already sliding through my hands. And unlike when I did this with strangers, I know the very fibers of this rope. All of Kasta's hopes, his desires.

His fears.

I pluck that single strand free, and *pull*.

Leave it, I command him. *You don't want the cuff anymore.*
Leave it.

The invisible bridge between us surges. Centimeters away
from the cuff, Kasta snatches his fingers back. And turns wide
eyes on me.

I stand, shaking, power humming through me like wine.
Holding his fear at this level is intoxicating. I reach for other
threads: worry, anticipation. I imagine him bowing, apologizing;
begging for my mercy as I once begged it from him. I wish he
could feel even half of my frustration with him. For every time
he's pulled me in, every time I hoped for him, only to find he still
hasn't let go of *this*—

Kasta turns on his knee, his head low. "Please forgive me, Zahru.
I—"

My focus slips. I'd expected those exact words, strange as it is to
hear him say them, but I don't understand how he's also kneeling
in the way I'd pictured. As if I have control of so much more than
his words. Kasta shakes his head. The binding cuff glints several
paces away. He jumps for it, overriding the command I'd given
him—and with a jolt I picture him stopping in place.

He does.

His fear spikes. On its own this time, not from me. My power
sings; I am a goddess, I am a monster. I want him to rise to his feet,
so he does. I want him to pick up the hammer. I want him to crush
the binding cuff beneath it until it's flat.

With his teeth gritted, he complies with my wishes. Every
one of them. Anger simmers now beneath his fear, as does a

sharp dread that makes something terrible smile inside of me. My Influence must work differently on him, with his mind half-animal. But that only means he knows what I'm doing, not that he can resist it.

And now I have control of him.

Is this what it feels like, to be him? Even before he was a Shifter, to know his strength was enough to command me, to pass by weapons and know he wouldn't need them? I do the same now. I stop across the workbench from him, where he glares down at me, the cuff smashed beneath the hammer.

My smile curves. "Does it make you feel better, to know you created me?"

"You can't hold me," he growls. "You'll tire before we reach the priests."

"And what will you do then? Kill the guards? Hold me for ransom?" My scar burns, and my anger with it. "Maybe I shouldn't give you the chance."

A terrible new scene flashes through my mind, unbidden: Kasta walking toward the melting vat . . . Kasta pulling himself in.

"Zahru," he says.

"It would be easy," my magic whispers, though the words come out of my mouth. Kasta must be able to sense what I'm imagining, or maybe see it in his mind as I can. My power thrums; it plucks at my anger like a puppeteer lifting strings. "I wouldn't have to take your curse. I wouldn't have to worry every day how you'd get back at me, or who you'd hurt next."

His fear flickers. "You wouldn't. You'd never—"

"Kill someone?" My stomach tightens, part of me screaming to stop, the other wondering what choice I truly have. He turns . . . and starts walking. "But that's what you've taught me, isn't it? That sometimes, for the greater good, others have to die."

My blood is made of lightning. A brighter, deeper fear blossoms in Kasta, heavy and chilling.

"You don't want to do this." Kasta shoves back on my commands, but my hold is too strong. "This is your magic pushing you . . . it has to be. I know you're still in there."

"Because you don't think I'd hurt you?" Something is wrong; the words feel distant. "I thought that way in the caves, too. I thought I could still reach you. But now I'm starting to understand: it's not really about that at all."

"I was still *wrong*." He presses against my will. I walk at his side, unafraid. "The lives this war will take are inevitable. It's not the same as *this*. And I've listened to you . . . I've been doing *better*. But the gods won't recognize that if you do this. If I'm not crowned, if I'm not made a god . . ." He pushes again, and his voice cracks. "You can't truly want this. I am *so close* to living a life that I don't have to fear. Don't send me somewhere worse."

We stop an arm's length from the vat. He's referring to a Shifter's afterlife, of course, because even the Forsaken, fated to eternally wander the sands outside the holy city of Paradise, wouldn't envy the Burning Fields: the place for the soulless, a prison of eternal fire. If he's crowned, he'll earn a place among the gods, Shifter or not. And though he's made it clear he's not afraid of the gods in *this* life, given how far he's been willing to go—he clearly doesn't share that confidence for what they'll do to him in the next.

And no, even with my magic pulling at me, of course I don't

want to kill him. Not for spite. Not at all. But this must have been what he was thinking on that altar, when he held the knife to my chest. That he didn't want to, that he wished there was any other way, but that there were more important things at stake: his own future; Orkena's. And now it's the same for me.

I flex my hands, shivering.

Because I'm recognizing that I've indeed become the worst parts of him. I've gone to extremes to get what I want, and justified it with my pain. I've let fear drive me, and allowed it overshadow everything I do, no matter the expense.

I close my eyes. Maybe I'm more like him than I want to admit. Maybe I'm not the same sweet, starry-eyed girl from Atera that everyone expects me to be. But that only means I know that I have to do better, too.

"Then let it go," I say.

Kasta falters. He accidentally takes a step closer to the vat—and jerks to a stop. "Let what go?"

"All this fear. This obsession with believing *what* you are, not who, is all that matters."

He clenches his jaw. "Because it is. If you only knew—"

"What it's like to feel utterly and completely powerless?" I turn on him, and he flinches. "I know that well. But you have *got* to stop letting it control you like this. You are so much more, and if this is what it takes to finally get through to you, so be it."

I reach out with my power and find those tangled strings of fear. They recoil from me, as Kasta would too, I imagine, if I let him. But he can only stand before me, wincing, his arms trembling with the effort of trying to resist.

"What are you doing?" he says.

"You're letting go." Static builds at my fingertips, razor-edged. "You're not going to care about magic ever again."

"You can't," he says. "*I* can't—"

"You will."

I bring my fingers to his temples, and Kasta cries out and falls to his knees, his hands gripping my wrists. Power surges between us. I am fury. I am vengeance. I am the pain Kasta's inflicted and the pain he's endured. I command him to give me the fear that's driven him, warning that I will pull it from him if he doesn't, and suddenly I'm before the Mestrah, learning that if I'm Forsaken, I'll walk the streets; I'm drinking tonics that make me heave, desperate to make my magic surface; I'm in Kasta's laboratory, trashing the tables, shredding equations, chucking that beaker at Jet's head when he comes in—

Something shatters in the connection between us, and my strength leaves me in a gasp. Kasta wrenches free, and I collapse onto my hands and knees, every muscle screaming like I've been drained of blood.

Kasta drags himself backward, until he stops a few paces away, his chest heaving.

I can only watch him, his memories swirling at the edges of my vision, flickering in and out like shadows.

"You . . ." He pushes up to his elbow, wincing. "What have you done?"

"What you couldn't," I whisper, a relieved smile pulling my lips. I feel terrible. I can't move without my bones shrieking, but the pain feels cleansing, like draining the infection from a wound.

"And what am I now?" Kasta looks at his trembling hands. "What's left of me?"

"You tell me." I slowly sit up. My magic slips from my reach when I ask for it, and I swallow a surge of nausea. "What could you have ever wanted more than magic?"

Kasta doesn't answer. But I hear the catch in his breath. I see the shift in the way he looks at me, and my heart jerks.

Someone bangs on the door, startling us both. "Zahru!" comes a muffled voice. "We're coming in; hold on!"

Jet? The General must have appealed to the priests—or otherwise convinced them to check on us. I lean upright against a table leg, pain still throbbing through me.

"Wait," Kasta says. He tries to gain his feet, but whatever I did has drained us both. "Tell him to wait. It's done now, right? You've broken me. You win. I'll yield the throne . . . I'll go as far from here as you command. But please don't—" He grimaces and rips the binding runes from his neck. "Please don't make me serve."

He tosses the necklace into the vat. The stones float for a moment, gleaming red, then they sink and spread, little pools of ink on the molten surface. If I turn him in, he'll be more than punished for what he did during the Crossing. He'll be bound and shackled in Shifters' armor; sentenced to serve the army as a weapon for the rest of his days.

I could let him go. The horror of what I almost just did is sinking in, wrapping cold hands around my ribs, making me shake. That was definitely enough for me. I have nothing more to gain from imprisoning him, too. And his plan with the knives was still just a plan—I might yet have convinced him not to do it. Even his plans for me might never have formed if I hadn't gone after him first.

That's how the heroes would do it, in the stories. Strike a truce, let him leave.

But all I can think about is the complex equations he came up with for the knives. The kingdom leaders yielding to his silver tongue. How much better he's truly been doing with the right focus. We *do* work well together, and it would be foolish of me to let that go to waste.

I tell myself those are the only reasons I don't want to lose him.

Maybe this is a cruel mercy, to spare him from servitude only to chain him to me instead. But then, this is almost exactly what he planned for us, isn't it?

I really have learned too much from him.

"All right, Kasta," I say, holding my aching head. "Here's what we're going to do."

XXXII

NO ONE questions me, of course.

After Jet literally breaks into the armory with the help of his mother and an Earthmover, they find Kasta and me standing together, having calmly talked through our issues without the use of shackles or melting vats, wherein Kasta definitely decided to cease his research on the knives, and—benevolent future queen that I am—I forgave him graciously, but also determined he should probably abdicate to be my advisor. To which he responsibly agreed. This explanation earns more than a few raised eyebrows from Jet and the priests, especially since Kasta does not do well with looking agreeable while he's wincing and holding his head. But if he doesn't play his part, I have the option to either make him say what I want or reveal him as a Shifter, and he wants that even less.

Jet glances between us like he knows exactly what I've done. But Kasta is not getting his crown, and so he says nothing.

It almost looks like he approves.

And that is how I come to stand at the top of the palace stairs again, not in the foyer, but the ones that lead outside, where the Stormshrikes and Wraiths can better watch the crowd.

In the exact same place I stood at the start of the Crossing in a sacrificial gown.

Now I'm in a golden *jole* embroidered in crimson scorpions, my arms painted with Cybil's crossed swords, my hair pinned to hold the weight of the upcoming crown. The High Priests, with a concerning amount of intensity, refused to postpone the coronation even an hour more, so here I am, barely ready for what's about to happen. I'm still exhausted, even though Melia did her best to restore my energy. She's the only one who knows just how much magic I used to overcome Kasta.

What did you do? she whispered when she sensed the extent of the damage in my body.

I couldn't answer. I'm still not entirely sure.

"Ready?" Jet says from behind me.

Twisting silver leaves crown his black hair, and a tunic of royal blue sets off the flecks of green in his eyes. The rest of my friends, and my family, wait nearer to the raised platform at the center of the stairs, where I can just see Hen leaning into the aisle, waving with Melia. I wonder if Kasta can hear the horns from his new room, where he is to stay until this is finished. The grumpy High Priest makes the last of his announcements: that Kasta has abdicated under new direction from the gods, that our allies are eager for my ascent.

I thought I would be nervous when this time came. Thinking of myself becoming an actual goddess is still overwhelming on so many levels. But I have fought, bled, and nearly died to be here. I have my friends, I have my family, and as much as I feared changing . . . I'm still me.

And as long as I have that, I'll be fine.

"I'm ready," I tell Jet.

He takes me in, that strange mix of pride and sadness in his eyes.

That new distance still swirls between us, and I have yet to ask what he's afraid I'll feel from him if we touch. But I think I know. I think he's just realizing, like I am, that maybe this is all we were ever meant to be, and that I'll feel that hollow in him where there used to be warmth. I still can't imagine doing this without him.

But when we smile now, all that stirs in my chest is gratitude.

"We'll get through this," he says. "I promise. The war, everything. Just as you stopped Kasta, I know you'll stop this peacefully, too."

I think of the awful truth behind that statement . . . of the magic I used on Jet that I still haven't admitted to. And I force a smile. "Thanks. I have good help."

He chuckles. "Not that you need it. You know, you're actually slightly terrifying now."

My blood jerks. "You mean that as a joke, right? As in, *Hey, I know you knocked out an entire room full of assassins and intimidated a Shifter into abdicating, but I also know you'd never use it to do anything shady?*"

"Zahru." Jet snorts. "If you're still worrying about using Influence at the party, stop. It was one time. And anyway, you could have done far worse to Kasta, and we found you two just . . . standing around together, talking."

"Right." My laugh is nervous. "Completely voluntary on all counts."

His lip quirks. "I know it was more than that. But I said I trust you, and if this is where you feel Kasta is best, I won't question it. And with you checking in on him, I might just get my brother back yet." He straightens the shoulders of my cape. "Don't worry about it. You're almost up."

Anticipation flashes through me as the grumpy High Priest raises his arms and the crowd erupts like a storm. People cheer from the stands, from the streets, from the bridge arcing over the river; from the market square beyond. The noise vibrates through my body like power. My gods' mark thrums on my chest. As tired as I am, I assumed it would take days for my Influence to fully recover. But I already feel it again at the edges of my mind, as sharp and ready as an arrow.

Tell me there's no difference, echoes Kasta's voice in my head.

I take one step down, remembering the silence from before, when this same crowd bowed their heads, so easily accepting I was meant to die. But I grit my teeth. I will prove to Orkena that there are things more powerful than magic. I will prove to Kasta it can be done without reinforcing the current system.

Tell me you would give it back.

I hadn't answered. But just as I'm thinking that of course I would give Influence back, that I don't need it . . . something new presses into my mind. Something foreign and unwelcome, a shadow made of teeth.

For without this power, would I even be here at all?

And the answer shifts.

"No," I whisper, feeling strangely like I've just woken up. "I couldn't."

EPILOGUE

—Kasta—

MY new room overlooks the sparring arena.

I suppose so I can remember, every day, just how close I was to having everything.

It's a much smaller space than I'm used to. The military wing houses hundreds, and so its plain marble walls barely fit my desks and a bed, with a simple en suite bath comprising a basin, toilet, and tub. No balcony. The windows of other rooms open, but not mine. That was the first enchantment Zahru commissioned for the room, along with the second, that seals even the smallest cracks and holes in the walls, lest I'm tempted to slip through them in another form.

And always there are convenient guards wandering outside my door, trailing me if I leave, undoubtedly reporting my every move back to her. I don't know where she thinks I'll go. But I find I like it more than I should, that she's so afraid of losing me.

I sigh and push away from the window, pacing again, restless from two weeks without seeing her. Her other advisors don't trust me, and especially not the two of us together, and so Zahru sends my orders on parchment, and *trielle* officers use Obedience spells every evening to ensure I'm not leaving anything out of my daily reports. I work in the murmuring noise of my new room, trying to break *forsvine* as Zahru and I did in the armory. I'll admit I'm motivated to succeed less for the good of Orkena and more so Zahru will come to me. So she'll let me out of this half imprisonment and let me prove I was almost there, that I can be what she needs.

Why I didn't do this before, I can't remember. Maybe something was holding me back. Maybe that's what she took from me in the armory, an absence that gnaws at me now like a constant hunger.

I intend to get the answer to that, too. But first I need her to remember what we achieved together; the real reason why she couldn't put me in chains.

I'll make it up to her.

She'll come.

I settle into my desk chair, pressing my hands through my hair, glowering down at pages of failed formulas. I'm lifting the quill to start over yet again when a knock sounds at the door.

It opens, the bubbling conversations of a dozen passing soldiers breaking through the silence, along with a bright slice of sunlit hallway and—*finally*—the sharp bronze feathers of a crown, a doll's curve of a jaw, and the guarded amber eyes of the girl who ruined me.

She's alone. I wonder if her advisors know where she is.

I almost smile.

Zahru clears her throat, glancing around the room, her focus hitching on the glass instruments of my laboratory, the mountain of crumpled parchment in the waste bin. I might be fooled into thinking she was simply curious if her magic wasn't already slipping into my head, searching for how I feel. Something about my Shifter power interferes with her Influence. I should not know she's using it on me; I should not remember how she controlled me in the armory. And yet I do. I'm careful to keep any clear thoughts from surfacing for her Whisperer's magic, either. If it's not enough that she can physically move me, she can also read my mind.

Which is fascinating on a scientific level, and extremely frustrating on a personal one.

"Mestrah," I say, the word snapping her attention back to me. "To what do I owe this pleasure?"

The phantom fingers of her Influence retreat, and she bristles. "Stop it. We're way past formalities. And how are you not angry with me at all?"

I shrug. "Do you really think there's anything I wouldn't forgive you for?"

She closes her eyes, and I would point out that she seems excessively stressed for someone who got everything she wanted, but I'm finding I don't want to provoke anything near a repeat of what she almost did to me two weeks ago.

She groans. "I can still hear you thinking. And can we both agree things got way out of hand? I'm still really mad at you for the knives, but—I'm so sorry I almost melted you." She leans her head on the doorframe. "Are you at a stopping point? I have something to show you."

I nod, and her gaze flits down my black tunic—I couldn't stand white anymore when they asked what I would keep from my wardrobe—before she turns to go. I follow, the clamor of the military wing rising around us. Soldiers touch their foreheads as Zahru moves, parting for us like fish before a boat, their eyes catching on me with the smallest twist of their lips. Some rumors say I got better than I deserved. Others warn I was the only one who could keep Zahru's power in check, and look where I am now.

How amused they would be to know both are true.

"Has Wyrim finally surrendered, then?" I ask, guessing at what she'd show me.

She doesn't look over. "No, we're—" She turns, taking us toward the archway to the outdoor arena. "It's complicated. I've confirmed all three of the alliances we set up, and their armies are on standby to defend us. Even the Pe are uncertain about aiding Wyrim, since we didn't retaliate after their attack. But the Wyri queen still won't talk to me. All we can hope at this point is that the war will be fast."

I scoff. Always hope with her, even still. "Then what do you need me for?"

"You'll see."

An irritating answer, but I don't press her. I follow her outside into the afternoon heat; past the training arena, where Zahru stares pointedly in any direction that is not at me or it; up the stone stairs that climb the north wall of the palace. The guards straighten as we top the wall, stepping back when we pass, their grips tight on staffs and spears. We're overlooking the civilian docks now, not the royal ones connected to the palace but a section of wide shore at the corner of the city where the largest of the trading ships stop. Three of them currently line the river, Orkena's white-and-gold banners hanging from their railings. Children dart along the glass decks, shouting and waving to the people on land.

Of which there are hundreds, holding one another and pacing.

Zahru leans on the stone balcony, her wavy hair trailing over her shoulder as she looks to me. I don't understand what she wants. Are these allies? Refugees she doesn't know how to handle?

"I sent your letter off for the Forsaken," she says as wooden planks lower from the boats to the shore. "But I thought it would be best to return the youngest to their families."

A lance hits my chest. I didn't think she could break me any more than she already had, but something new cracks inside me, and I clutch the rail for support. Children pour down the planks, a tide of longing, and I watch what both was and never was my life as they run into open arms. Fathers weep. Mothers laugh. Families welcome the Forsaken as if they were missed, as if they are loved.

I see my father's cold eyes all those years ago, when I asked what would happen if my magic didn't surface.

Zahru's hand slides over mine, warm and steady. I can't move. She has a war to prepare for. She didn't have to show me this . . . she didn't have to do this at all.

"No one will ever go through what you did again," she says. "And I imagine the same thing is happening in the afterlife, too. I asked the gods to allow all the Forsaken into Paradise. And I'm going to open schools and create jobs for them, some as high in honor as our Wraiths. I'm thinking of calling them Scholars."

A new name. A new eternity. It's no longer mine, but that doesn't mean I'll overlook what she's done. That even after everything, she continues to find the good in me and bring it to light.

Her hand slides from mine, but I grab it again, not wanting her to go. Zahru goes still, her Influence already flexing through my head, but whatever she finds there, her magic vanishes again just as fast.

And she does not let go.

If only she knew the kind of power she holds over me, even without magic.

"Thank you," I say.

My grip relaxes. Zahru stares at our hands, the long shadow of an Orkenian flag sweeping over her.

"Could you really have done it?" she asks. "Made me hurt the Wyri, if you'd gotten your way?"

A familiar anger curls in my chest, pressing against my lips, ready to ask how she could not *want* to hurt them, especially now—but I think of her in the armory, how I'd watched my own ruthlessness come alive in her, and I think of the devastation on her face when she looked over the unconscious Pe assassins, as if she'd lost a part of her she could never get back. I imagine standing with her before an army and making her do it again.

And the answer shifts. "No. I couldn't."

Her fingers tighten, her brow pinching, like I've said something strange. But she can feel the truth of it in my veins. Perhaps it took this long to work, that kindness she poisoned me with so long ago, when I told her I was nothing and she saw so much more.

She laughs bitterly, her hand dropping from mine. "But, see, I think you were actually right. Their queen is vicious, just like you warned me. We've thrown every peaceful solution we can think of at them. They don't care about new trade agreements, or apologies, or reparations. Nothing I'm doing is working, and"—she leans against the half wall, fingers pinching between her eyes—"they sent my last messenger's head back in a box."

Her amber eyes glitter, the pain in them like looking into a mirror, and I'm moving before I can think better of it, slowly, giving her time to stop me, but she doesn't, and when I bring my arms around her, she exhales and relaxes her head against my chest. It's the first time I breathe right in weeks. Her hands slide around my back, trembling, and I try to remember what she's taught me about mercy—I *try*—but feeling how much Wyrim has broken her cuts against me like teeth.

"Will you help me fix it?" she whispers.

I know what she's asking. She wants me to hurt them, to break them, and I'm very sure now that her advisors don't know she's come to me. Or at least they don't know she's asking about *this*. But I tighten my arms and look out at the Forsaken, and decide that if I'm going to do this right, I can't let her give up as I once did. If she wants peace, I can't let her forget it. And if that means my only purpose from here forward is to sew her back together as she did for me, to remind her that good can come from even the most lost of causes . . . then I must do it.

And maybe then, when nothing else in my life ever has been, it will be enough.

"I am yours," I say, resting my chin on her hair. "Tell me what you've tried."

GLOSSARY

Adel: Esteemed One; formal address for a member of the nobility

Aera: Your Highness; formal address for a prince or princess

Dōmmel: Divine One; formal address for the crown heir

Fara: Papa; endearing term for father

Forsvine: A magic-neutralizing metal invented by the Wyri. Translates to "to vanish."

Gudina: Holy One; formal address for a god/goddess

Jener: A gender-neutral address similar to sir/madam

Jole: An elaborate wrap dress favored by the nobility, often embellished with gemstones or decorative threading

Kar-a: My heart; term of endearment

Mestrah: Your Majesty; formal address for the ruler

Mestrah, the: The supreme religious and political ruler of Orkena, believed to be divine (translates to "Master")

Mora: Mama; endearing term for mother

Stefar/Mamor (Stef/Mam): Grandpa/Grandma (Pa/Ma)

Tergus: A formal kilt tied with a colorful sash

Trielle: Superior magicians capable of manipulating many types of magic through written spells

Valeed/Vala: Formal word for father/mother

ACKNOWLEDGMENTS

THIS is the first sequel I've ever written, and also the first book I've ever completely rewritten at a late draft stage during a pandemic on a seven-week deadline. Needless to say, after having years to write *The Kinder Poison* with the luxury of no deadline at all, *The Cruelest Mercy* was an Experience. How grateful I am to have such a phenomenal support system who not only helped me survive it, but made this into a story I love just as much as the first.

For God, always, who keeps me hopeful and grounded, and continues to connect me with the most amazing, generous people.

For my husband, who keeps the house afloat when I need to work nights and weekends, and knows exactly when to bring me a gigantic box of chocolates.

For my daughter, who possesses more energy than should be legal, and constantly inspires me with her creativity, joy, and the kinds of hilarious life observations that only four-year-olds can make.

For my parents, who taught me to love stories and always bolstered my creativity. For my second parents, Rob and Kathy, who are always there when we need them. To my siblings, Brent, Ty, Gentry, and Bailey, who make everything more fun.

For Lori Goldstein, who is not only an incredible friend but also has a wicked eye for editing and helped me find the heart of this story in more ways than one. For my *Kinder Poison* blurbers: Brenda

Drake, Lori Goldstein, Colleen Oakes, and Chelsea Bobulski, who made time for me in their very busy schedules to read on a tight deadline, and constantly inspire me with their generosity and kindness. I'm so grateful for you.

For Marisa Hopkins, literal angel who read all 416 pages of *The Kinder Poison* **on her phone** so that she could design the epic maps you see every time you open these books. You have a gift, my friend, and I can't wait to see your artwork take over the world.

For my agents Bri Johnson and the rest of the Writers House team: Allie Levick, Cecilia de la Campa, and Alessandra Birch, who are my support pillars and continue to champion these books like their own. Thank you for all you tirelessly do.

For my editor Chris Hernandez, whose brilliant notes always bring my work to the next level. Thank you for answering a million questions and helping me shape stories I'm proud of. Many thanks also to Gretchen Durning, Krista Ahlberg, and Kat Keating for the valuable final touches you helped apply, and for ensuring both that I'm writing in actual sentences and that characters are properly dressed before they go outside.

For my publicist Tessa Meischeid, actual rock star who shouted so much about *The Kinder Poison* that it made its way into *People* magazine, amongst many other outlets I could only imagine in my wildest dreams. I am so, so grateful for how hard you work to get my books out there.

For Shannon Spann, who I would like to hug, for the incredible marketing content and excitement you created around this series and for being a stellar human in general. Thank you for yelling about these books and riling up #TeamKasta. For Felicity Vallence and the rest of the PenguinTeen marketing team, a million thanks for being delightful and getting my work in front of readers.

For Theresa Evangelista, who blew my mind again with this incredible cover and interior design—your work is magic.

For Jesse Vilinsky, who brought Zahru and the rest of the cast to life as only an audio goddess can. Thank you for making these characters real. And for the rest of my audiobook team, especially Joe Grimm, Emily Parliman, Rebecca Waugh, Brieana Garcia, and Molly Lo Re, thank you for your excitement for these books and for everything you do.

For the rest of the team at Penguin Random House and Razorbill who have worked with me or helped my books reach readers— thank you, thank you, thank you.

And last but certainly not least, my infinite gratitude to my readers—to every bookseller, librarian, reviewer and fan who has passed these books on, especially my *Kinder Poison* army and my *Kinder Poison* cult. You are the lifeblood of this series, and it is an honor to write for you.